LOST
and
FOUND

OTHER BOOKS AND BOOKS ON CASSETTE
BY CLAIR M. POULSON:

I'll Find You

Relentless

LOST
and
FOUND

a novel

CLAIR POULSON

Covenant Communications, Inc.

Published by Covenant Communications, Inc.
American Fork, Utah

Printed in Canada
First Printing: September 2002

09 08 07 06 05 04 03 02   10 9 8 7 6 5 4 3 2 1

ISBN 1-59156-092-6

To my sons Alan and Wade Poulson, and my sons-in-law Wade Hatch and Ben Semadeni—for the fine men that they are, and for the memories we created together on the Fall Creek trail in the High Uintah wilderness area. That trip provided part of the inspiration for this book.

Acknowledgment

I want to express my heartfelt gratitude to the outstanding people who make up the staff of Covenant Communications. My special thanks to Lou and Marilyn Kofford for giving me the chance to share my stories with so many others and for helping make my books successful. And I can't say enough about the editors. Angela Colvin has been such a tremendous help to me in completing this work as well as *Relentless*. I also owe much to Shauna Nelson for her work on *I'll Find You* and her constant support in all my efforts. And to all those who went before on previous books, I can only say thanks.

PROLOGUE

Leaning low over her horse's back, her long hair streaming behind her like a golden flag, the young woman coaxed more speed from the frothing animal. She felt it respond between her knees, and glanced behind her. The four-wheeler was gaining ground on her. She turned back and surveyed the lay of the land around her. It was risky, but she decided a horse could better maneuver the rough terrain to her left than the man angrily closing in on her with his four-wheeler.

The big gelding immediately responded to the light pressure of the rein on his neck. Turning, the animal entered an area strewn with rocks. It had to cut back and forth as it ran, but it never once stumbled. A moment later they reached a small but deep gully. Without losing speed, her mount leaped across, and the young woman stuck to its saddle like she was part of it. A short hill rose steeply before them, and the horse went up it in huge bounds. A less experienced rider might well have been thrown from the horse, but not her.

Reaching the top of the hill, she looked back again. As she'd hoped, the four-wheeler had lost speed, but it was still coming. She directed her mount along the ridge, then rode down the far side at a dangerous and reckless pace; but she knew that nothing was more dangerous than to let her pursuer catch up. Her horse nearly lost its footing at the bottom of the hill, going to its knees for a moment, but it recovered quickly and the slender rider again pressed her knees firmly into its side and directed the animal south, up a gully.

When they approached still another but steeper hillside she again tapped the gelding lightly with her spurs and it gamely attacked the slope. By the time it reached the top, the horse was wheezing for breath, and she wisely pulled it to a stop so it could get its wind back. As it was taking great gulps of air, she turned and scanned the area they had covered.

As she watched, the four-wheeler pulled to a stop at the top of the first hill and the driver climbed off. Puzzled, she continued to watch as her horse regained its strength. A moment later the man was on his knees, pointing with both hands in her direction. Something glinted in his hand, and she desperately dug her spurs into the gelding's side. A bullet whined past as she dropped off the far side of the hill, out of the gunman's sight.

Her horse responded gallantly to her panicked coaxing, racing toward a road in the distance. There would be traffic there, and safety. The man who was after her wanted her dead, but he wouldn't want witnesses. Had a tire not blown out on her truck, she'd still be driving instead of desperately riding her horse in this unfamiliar countryside.

Two minutes passed and her mount was slowing before she again saw the four-wheeler. The driver was taking the hills and gullies in reckless disregard for his own safety, knowing that what she knew was far more perilous to him than his speeding vehicle or the rugged terrain.

How she regretted her angry outburst, threatening to share what he'd done with the authorities. It had been foolish and stupid, but then a lot of what she'd done these past couple of years was both foolish and stupid. And now her choice of company and her other mistakes were catching up with her.

She tried again to coax more speed from her horse, but it was running out of steam. Another half mile passed and she was almost to the road. She looked back again. Her enemy was very close now. She could see the pistol clutched in one hand as he steered his four-wheeler after her.

"Please, Roscoe," she begged the horse, "you've got to run faster." She dug her spurs into its side again, and miraculously the gelding found the courage and the strength to surge forward with greater speed.

Suddenly, a narrow highway loomed just ahead. She approached it directly, hoping to flag down a car or truck, catch a ride, and leave her poor horse behind as she'd already been forced to do with her truck and trailer. Seeing no cars, she simply turned up the shoulder of the road and hoped someone would appear from around the bend that lay just ahead.

Someone did, and he laid on the horn of his semi. Startled, the bay gelding jumped sideways, lost its footing at the end of a culvert, and fell on its side. The slender rider had managed to pull her right foot from the stirrup as the horse went down, but as she tried to jump free of its flailing legs, her other foot caught tighter in the stirrup. She struggled to escape, but failed before the horse succeeded in gathering its legs beneath it and leaping to its feet. Panicked, it began to run, dragging its terrified rider along the roadway.

The last thought she had before losing consciousness was that she was going to die.

Two men approaching in a truck had a different idea. The driver slammed on the brakes and was not even to a complete stop before his partner jumped from the truck and ran into the path of the frightened but exhausted horse. An experienced horseman, he succeeded in grabbing the reins and pulled the horse to a stop. His friend was there within seconds and freed the young woman's foot from the stirrup.

Amazingly, other than being unconscious and bleeding from numerous minor cuts, she seemed to be all right. As one of the men returned to their truck for a cell phone, the four-wheeler came onto the roadway. At the same time, another pickup and two cars stopped beside the cowboys and the injured woman. Few noticed the four-wheeler as it spun around and roared back the way it had come.

Two days later her consciousness returned. Lying in a hospital, with two young but concerned cowboys standing beside her bed, the blonde forced her eyes to open. It was ten minutes before things came into focus. One of the young men grinned and said, "Sure glad you could make it to the party."

Her face was blank. "Don't joke, Joe," the second young man said. "She's probably not in a very humorous mood."

Looking sheepish, Joe leaned closer. "I'm Joe, and this here's Rick. We're sure glad to see you wake up. You gave us an awful scare back there when your horse was dragging you. But the doctor told us you'd be fine when you regained consciousness."

Rick touched her hand where it lay motionless at her side. "Not a single broken bone," he told her.

Her face was still blank, but her eyes darted around the room.

"So what's your name?" Joe asked. "You didn't have one bit of identification on you."

She didn't say a word and the two looked at each other, puzzled. "Hey, really, you'll be all right now," Rick said, trying to be positive. "We took your horse out to the ranch. Looked like you'd ridden him awful hard, but he's going to be all right too."

The young woman, fully conscious now, was confused. She didn't remember a horse, much less being dragged by one. She tried to explain as much, but got choked on the words as she realized in fear that she didn't even know the young man.

"I'll get a doctor in here," Joe suggested as he turned and left the room.

"So what's your name?" Rick insisted after Joe had gone. "You can talk, can't you?"

"Y . . . yes," she stammered.

"Your name?" he urged. "I'm Rick."

But she didn't say anything else. With a sense of panic she realized she had no idea what her name was. In fact, she had no idea who she was or what she was doing there. Her memory and whatever it had held were gone. She looked hopelessly at the young man who called himself Rick. And her eyes began to mist as she squeezed them shut.

CHAPTER 1

The horse trailer rocked as the horses stamped impatiently. Luke Osborne looked up and said under his breath, "I know it's hot in there. It's not exactly cool out here."

He coaxed a little more gasoline into the tank of his black Dodge Ram before pulling the nozzle free and hanging it up. It was one of his days off from the sheriff's department where he'd worked as a deputy for the past five years. A detective now, his days off varied depending on what he was working on. But most of his Sundays were free, and he liked that.

He pulled his black cowboy hat from his head and wiped his hand across his brow, then through his relatively short but tangled mop of dark brown hair. A Greyhound bus pulled up, so he hurried into the store, not wanting to get caught in a line when he paid for his gas. As he stepped out a minute later, the passengers were getting off and heading for the store. Luke nodded to an old fellow as he passed, and then peeked in the horse trailer at the pair of two-year-old colts he was breaking, a filly and a horse colt. Bringing them to town provided a much-needed break from his other responsibilities at the ranch.

He'd finished hauling the first crop of hay that morning on the ranch his father had more or less handed to him a year ago. He'd helped the senior Osborne for years, but when a heart attack slowed his father down, Luke had to take over most of the work. They'd also hired some help for when even Luke couldn't get to it. With this afternoon free, Luke decided to take the colts to town and work them in the rodeo arena at the fairgrounds.

Luke spent as much time as he could riding. He had far more horses than he needed, but they were all from good American quarter horse bloodlines, and he made decent money selling the young ones he'd trained to ranchers from miles around. He was anxious to ride the two colts this afternoon; they were both coming along nicely.

He'd left his five-year-old son at his folk's house here in town for the two or three hours he planned to work the horses. As usual, Monty had protested as only a five-year-old could and Luke had promised him a ride when they returned to the ranch that evening. As a single parent, Luke spent all the time he could with his son; he and Monty were almost inseparable when he wasn't working with the sheriff's department.

"Nice horses."

Luke hadn't heard anyone approach and was surprised to hear a soft feminine voice behind him. He turned and was struck by the soft gaze of a pair of dark brown eyes. The young woman standing behind him smiled and asked, "What are they?"

"Quarter horses," he said, unable to pull his eyes from the delicate face.

"May I have a closer look?" she asked.

"Uh . . . sure. Of course," he stammered.

The young lady stepped past him and peeked into the trailer. "Here, I'll open this side door and you can get a better look," Luke said, finding his manners. With her beside him, Luke was pleasantly surprised at her height. Her slender build had made her appear to be almost as tall as he was, but up close, he could tell that she was a good three or four inches shorter than him. At just under six feet, Luke felt a little stocky, but he stayed in good shape and knew he didn't look as old as he was. Not that twenty-nine was old, but sometimes being a single father made him feel old.

She smiled at him. "Why, thank you." Her smile nicely accented her narrow face, shining brown eyes, and long blonde hair.

"I take it you like horses," he said as he opened the door and stepped back while she looked at the colts who were stamping impatiently inside the trailer.

"They're hot," she observed.

"So am I," he agreed. "But I'm just taking them down to the rodeo arena to work with them for a couple of hours. They'll be out of the trailer in five minutes."

She smiled again.

Wow! He hadn't seen a smile like that since Jamie's. The memory of his wife's smile brought back the morning she'd left for Roosevelt that last time. Thinking of her caused a twist in his stomach as it did every time he thought of the terrible tragedy that had stolen her from him and Monty nearly four years ago.

Remembering Jamie also made him step back from the young lady who was admiring his horses. Even after several years, Luke still found it difficult to spend much time with other women. He'd loved Jamie deeply, and though time had softened the loss, his heart still ached and her memory still burned brightly.

As did the memory of the man who'd taken her life. She'd died when her car was struck head on by a man who was high on methamphetamine. He survived, did a few months in jail, and then walked out a free man. That man, Victor Hampton, was one of the reasons Luke didn't give up his job in favor of ranching full-time. Victor was still in the area and was still suspected of dealing drugs, perhaps even manufacturing meth, but he was as slippery as he was treacherous. Luke hoped to nail him someday and put him away for a long time.

The woman stared at Luke for several moments. Her smile faded. "I'm sorry, did I say something wrong?" she asked.

Luke shook his head. "No, of course not," he answered lamely.

She extended a hand. "I'm Coleen Whitman," she offered.

"Luke Osborne."

"Beautiful horses."

"Yeah, thanks."

"Are you breaking them?" she asked.

He nodded. "They're coming along well."

She grew silent, and he studied her face after closing the door to the trailer. He was surprised at the faraway, even sad look in her eyes.

"When were you on a horse last?" he asked for the sake of conversation.

"It's been awhile," she answered. "I think."

What a strange answer. Surely she knows, Luke thought.

"Do you have horses?" he asked, noting for the first time that she was dressed in a pair of nicely fitting blue jeans, a western-cut blouse, and cowboy boots. She looked like a real cowgirl, and the look fit her well.

"No, I don't think so," she answered evasively, and as she spoke she started to back away. She seemed confused for a moment. "I . . . I sold one," she stammered very quietly, looking away from Luke. "I better go. Bus'll be leaving in a minute."

Luke was intrigued by the young woman.

"Where you from?" he heard himself ask.

"I just came in from Colorado," she answered hesitantly.

"So that's where you're from? What part?"

"I'm not sure," she stammered, clearly uncomfortable for some reason.

How can she not be sure? Luke thought as he heard the bus engine fire up. He wondered briefly if she was on something, but her eyes were so clear that it seemed unlikely. He could recognize when people were on drugs. And despite her strange behavior, she didn't fit the mold. But something was wrong with her; she wasn't acting at all normal. Then of course, all sorts of suspicions regularly entered his detective's mind.

"Good to meet you," she said. There was no longer a smile. "I better go."

"Where you headed?" he asked, wondering what kind of answer that simple question might bring.

"Salt Lake," she said directly.

"What are you going to be doing there?" he asked, realizing he was acting very much like a cop, but unable to curb his curiosity.

"I don't know. Get a job, I guess."

"If you had time, I'd let you ride one of these horses," he volunteered, surprising himself as much as he surprised her.

"Oh, I'd love to," she said, but there was uncertainty in her voice and Luke found himself wondering if she'd ever really been on a horse. Maybe the clothes were part of a fantasy. "But I don't have time," she added.

Just then the bus pulled past and roared onto Main Street. "Hey, my bus!" she cried. Luke felt like a total fool. He hadn't meant to distract her to the point where the bus would leave her stranded. He didn't know what to say.

Coleen looked at him, her eyes misting. She was obviously under a lot of stress for some reason. "Now what'll I do?" she asked.

He had to say something. "What time did you have to be there?" Luke asked. "Was someone meeting you?"

"No," she said blankly.

"Did you have an appointment you had to be there for? A job interview or something?"

"No," she said again.

Feeling very responsible for her predicament, Luke decided he owed her a favor. "Hey, there won't be another bus through until tomorrow, but there are motels in town. I'll help you find a room."

"Thanks." She sounded somewhat relieved when she added, "That would be nice."

"And meantime maybe you could come on down to the fairgrounds with me. You could have a ride."

Coleen brightened. "Really?" she asked hopefully.

"Sure, why not? These two colts are great. I'd be glad to let you ride."

"Okay, Luke. Thanks," she said. "I think I'd like that." Her pretty smile returned, and Luke found himself relaxing a little.

He opened the door and she climbed into the truck. He got in and a couple of minutes later they were at the fairgrounds. She seemed a little unsure when he led the first colt from the trailer and handed her the lead rope, but as he exited with his favorite colt, a tall, graceful chestnut gelding, she was stroking the bay filly's neck and chest. "She's so beautiful," Coleen said without looking toward Luke.

"Good temperament, too," he added as he quickly tied the chestnut to the trailer. "I'll get the gear."

Luke hesitated as he began to remove Jamie's saddle from the tack room in the front of his horse trailer. He still hauled it around with him after all these years, but no one had used it since her death. It held such tender and tragic memories. But it was a good saddle and the only spare he kept in the trailer, so with a twist of pain in his chest, he pulled it free and stepped out, the saddle in one hand and a saddle blanket in the other.

He flipped the blanket onto the bay's back and then followed with the saddle. "I'll get it from here," Coleen said. He stepped back and watched as she tied the colt to the trailer and began to cinch up the saddle.

When he came out with the blanket and saddle for the chestnut colt, Coleen had already fastened the back cinch and was working on the breast band. She obviously knew what she was doing. As she worked, he watched her from the corner of his eye as she untied the colt and led her around for a moment, then tightened the cinch. When he'd finished saddling his own horse, he got the bridles from the trailer and they put them on over the halters.

"There, all ready," he said, satisfied that everything was in place and secure.

Luke smiled when he noticed that Coleen's eyes were shining.

Coleen knew that *this* was a part of her. It felt like her. But she felt her stomach churning even as she anticipated the ride. So much fear . . . Despite the things the two cowboys in Colorado had told her, she didn't exactly recall ever having saddled or ridden a horse before, and yet every movement came naturally; every piece of tack seemed familiar. She'd surely be able to ride all right . . . wouldn't she?

"She's easy to mount," Luke assured, sensing her hesitation. "She'll stand right there while you get on."

Coleen seemed nervous again, but Luke tried not to let her know he noticed. Instead he stuck his left boot in the stirrup and swung easily aboard the chestnut colt. Coleen followed, mounting as easily and gracefully as he had. Relief flooded over him. He'd sure hate to get this total stranger hurt, but she seemed to know what she was doing.

"Stirrups okay?" he asked.

"Perfect length," she answered.

Luke wasn't surprised. Coleen was about the same height Jamie had been.

"Whose saddle is this?" she asked as they turned the horses in unison toward the arena.

Luke choked up. He had hoped she wouldn't ask. "My . . . my wife's," he finally managed to say.

"Oh," Coleen said brightly. "So is this her horse too?"

"No."

"Why isn't she here?" Coleen asked. "She must like to ride."

Luke found his voice faltering badly as he said, "She doesn't ride anymore."

"Oh, I'm sorry. I'm being nosy. No more questions," she promised. But after a moment, as they entered the arena side by side, she said, "Well, maybe one more question, Luke. Would your wife rather I not be here? I really don't mean to intrude or anything."

Luke had experienced many awkward moments with women since Jamie's death. Some of the worst moments were with one of the secretaries in the office who was always trying to corner him. Although she was very attractive and really quite nice, it always made him uncomfortable. But never had he felt more awkward than right now with this pretty stranger.

"It's all right," he threw Coleen the short answer as he spurred the colt into an easy lope.

Luke had intended to spend an hour with each horse, but everything he did with the chestnut colt, Coleen did with the bay. She was an experienced, excellent horsewoman. And he could see that her experience was not just in riding; she was too good not to have trained horses.

Coleen was also amazed at herself. She had no idea she could do these things on a horse, especially a young, green-broke horse. She hadn't been this happy or relaxed since . . . well, she couldn't remember ever feeling like this. But she must have been sometime, sometime in that dark and mysterious past that she couldn't recall. She brushed aside the frustration of not knowing who she'd been, excited to have found at least some part of herself.

They rode for another hour, both in the arena and on the streets of town near the fairgrounds. Finally Luke said, "Guess we better quit. They've had enough for one day."

"Weren't you going to work with this one too?" Coleen asked as Luke dismounted beside the horse trailer.

"Yes, but there's no need. You got her to do every move I would have worked her on. Why didn't you tell me you'd trained horses?"

"I . . . I . . . didn't know . . ." She didn't complete that thought, but instead answered, "But thanks for letting me ride her."

Again Luke was struck with Coleen's strange behavior, but he said nothing. It was no concern of his. Just then, however, a thought occurred to him that did raise his concern. Her bags had gone with the bus. She had nothing to wear but what she had on now. Once again he felt terribly awkward but equally responsible, so he said, "I'm sorry I made you miss your bus. I just realized your bags must be on it."

Coleen laughed, something she had done very little for the only three months of her life that she could remember. She'd thought about her bag, the one that contained everything she had accumulated these past few weeks, and there wasn't much of worth in it. She had a little money in her pocket, and that was all she really needed. She'd been a drifter since leaving the hospital. She'd worked odd jobs waiting tables and cleaning hotel rooms, and she never stayed at any of the jobs for more than two or three days because they would always insist on a social security number, and she didn't have one. She would stall for as long as she could each time, but it always ended the same: she was fired, given a small wage in cash, and sent on her way. She'd drift from town to town and state to state, surviving on the meager wages and some generous tips, hoping that somehow her memory would return and she could get on with her life, whatever that had been. In the meantime, she'd been careful with every dollar she earned. And she still carried most of the fifteen hundred dollars Joe and Rick had given her for the big gelding they said she'd been riding when she was hurt. She always kept it on her.

"I can buy some things," she said, feeling bad that Luke was so obviously worried about her and felt responsible. He didn't need to do that. The same problem cropped up for her everywhere she went— strangers worrying about her. Only this time, with Luke, it was different. He was a married man. No, she couldn't even think about accepting his help, or his company. She'd had a fun afternoon, but she needed to get away from him before she caused him problems.

"Are you sure?" Luke asked.

Coleen flashed him one of her disarming smiles and said, "Of course I'm sure. If you'll just show me a motel and a store, I'll take it from there. And thanks for letting me ride one of your horses. You have no idea how much this has done for me."

No, he certainly didn't. He was curious, but he was also a gentleman, so he suppressed the questions his detective's mind kept wanting to ask and began unsaddling his horse.

CHAPTER 2

A call that evening to the Greyhound depot in Salt Lake City left Coleen a little unsettled. They didn't seem to know anything about her bag. "Someone must have taken it," she was told. So now she had nothing but what she'd bought at Kohl's an hour earlier and the clothing she was wearing. She was assured that her ticket would still be honored if she wanted to continue on to Salt Lake the next day, but she didn't know what she wanted to do. It was so depressing not knowing who you were or where you belonged. Not having a friend in the world to turn to, talk with, or share your problems with.

Duchesne seemed like a nice place. Maybe she could work here for a few days before going on. When she went to Cowan's Café for dinner an hour later, there was a sign in the window saying that they needed a waitress. The next morning she returned and was hired on the spot. She began that next evening.

It was all so familiar now—a new job, one she knew wouldn't last, but one she could easily handle. And she enjoyed the people who came in, most of them asking her name and where she was from. She still didn't know where she was from, but that cowboy, Luke Osborne, had assumed she was from Colorado, so that's what she said. No one pressed her further, and she felt comfortable, or as comfortable as she could feel without a past.

* * *

Of course everyone has a past, and Gil Stedman was at that very moment worrying about the past of a young lady he'd been determined to take care of—permanently. And what she knew about his past could affect his future.

"I thought you said she'd been killed?" his boss, a man he both hated and feared asked, a fat finger pointing straight at Gil's nose.

"I thought she had. That horse dragged her for a quarter mile," he exaggerated. "No one could have survived something like that." he shifted uncomfortably, his new shoes slightly scuffing the polished floor.

"But she did," burly Judd Aspen reminded him. "Those two punk cowboys over in New Mexico bought the horse she was riding. And they bought it from Carly Crockett, your girlfriend!"

"So they say," Gil agreed. "But they said she couldn't remember anything and I took her truck and trailer and her purse was there. She has no ID now, so she's no longer a threat to us."

"Maybe they were lying," Judd said darkly. "And if they weren't, then maybe she was!"

Gil hadn't thought about that. But he knew it was only too possible.

"She's a threat to you, Gil," he was reminded in a tone of voice that indicated she was not the only threat.

"I know, sir," Gil muttered.

"And that makes her a threat to me," Judd continued.

"I know, sir."

"I don't like threats," Judd reminded his employee.

Gil certainly knew that.

"So find her. And I don't ever want to see her again. All I want is proof that she's no longer a threat."

"Yes, sir," Gil said. "But I don't know where to begin. It's been three months."

"Yes it has. Three months in which you lied to me. You figure out how to find her, Gil. Now get out of here. I don't want to see you again until the job's finished."

Gil turned, anxious to leave. But as he opened the door, Judd added, "If you fail, you know what will happen to you."

Gil knew, and he shuddered at the thought even as his indignation rose. He despised being treated like a dispensable lackey. He'd find Carly, he thought as he slipped on an expensive leather jacket, and she'd wish she'd never put him in this position.

* * *

Burglary cases out in the Pinon Ridge area west of Duchesne were almost impossible to solve; the area wasn't heavily populated and owners often didn't check their property for months at a time. But this had been a particularly lucrative one for the burglar, and the sheriff had pressed Luke to give it everything he had. For a month now, Luke had spent several hours a week working on the case, and then he'd gotten a lucky break. A gun that had been taken from the cabin showed up in a pawn shop in Salt Lake. A quick trip there on Wednesday had paid off, and the next day Luke had made an arrest.

Now, exhausted but glad to have the case well in hand, he told little Monty, "We've earned dinner in town tonight."

"Oh, goody," Monty said happily. His dad's cooking wasn't always the best.

"Don't seem so happy," Luke chided his son playfully, but he gave him an affectionate hug before herding him out the door and to the truck.

"How did we earn dinner?" Monty asked, cracking a smile that spread his freckles across his cheerful little face.

"You were really good to help Grandma today, and I arrested a bad man," Luke explained to his son as he tousled the boy's messy blond curls. He'd have to cut the kid's hair before Monty started looking like a girl, Luke thought.

Neither of those two things were news to Monty, but he was happy for whatever excuse his dad had to go into town for dinner. "Where we gonna eat, Dad?" Monty asked as they drove down the Utahn Road from their little ranch in Utahn, the beautiful, several-mile-long valley between Tabiona and Duchesne.

"Well let's see, we could go to Al's Foodtown and get a pizza," he suggested with a twinkle in his eye.

"Daaad!" Monty threw the name out in frustration. "We have one of them in the freezer already. And you have to cook it!" He hit his dad in the arm with his little cowboy hat that had been laying on the seat, then put it on his head, mustering up a tough defiant look.

"Oh, that's right. Well, let's see then, how about Cowan's Café?"

"Okay," Monty agreed. "If I get ice cream after I eat my hamburger."

"Sounds good to me," Luke said. "So it's settled." Then he playfully smashed Monty's cowboy hat down over his son's eye's.

When they entered the café a little while later, it was late and most of the dinner crowd was gone. Luke selected a booth on the west side of the room and sat down across from his little son. Luke looked up in surprise when a familiar voice said, "Would you two like a menu?"

"Coleen, I thought you were going to Salt Lake," Luke said, surprised at how excited he suddenly felt to see her again.

She was as surprised as Luke was. She hadn't recognized him from the back with a baseball cap on his head. She'd only seen him with the large Stetson that had drooped over both his collar and his forehead. She'd liked the way he looked in that hat. But she also liked the way he looked now. "I was, but they needed help here," she said, hoping he wouldn't press her further. She knew he'd feel bad if he learned that her bag had been stolen at the bus depot.

"Well that's great," he said with a genuine smile. "This here's Monty, the five-year-old cowboy," he said, pointing across the table at his grinning son.

"Good to meet you, cowboy," Coleen said with a chuckle. "My name's Coleen. So what brings you guys to town?"

She seemed to be addressing the question to Monty, so Luke let him answer. "Dad didn't want to cook tonight," he said.

"Hey, that's not right," Luke cut in with a laugh. "I told you it was because we'd earned a reward."

"You always say that, Dad. But you just get tired of cooking," Monty said, defending his position expertly.

Coleen laughed. But as she laughed she wondered about Luke's wife. Apparently there was something she didn't know. But she sure liked these two. "Well, how about it, do you want a menu?" she asked as she started to put one in front of Monty.

"Nope," the little fellow said. "I just want a hamburger and fries and ice cream."

"How about you?" she asked, turning to Luke. "Or do you know exactly what you want too?"

"We earn rewards a lot," he said to her with a smile. "We pretty well know everything on the menus both here and at the Country

Kitchen. I'll have the chicken-fried steak. And blue-cheese dressing on my salad."

"Sure thing. Anything to drink, Monty?" she asked.

"Milk," he said.

"And coffee for Dad?" she asked.

"No, don't drink the stuff. Better make it a large buttermilk," Luke said.

"How can you drink that?" she asked with a grin.

"Goes down smooth. It's coffee I wonder about," he countered.

"I'll be back in a moment with a glass of water for both of you," she said as she realized that Luke must be a Mormon. It made sense as she'd learned she was in the Mormon state. She'd heard about the religion a few days ago over in Colorado, and she'd been told they didn't smoke, or drink coffee, tea, or alcohol.

Coleen had no sooner disappeared into the back than the front door opened and the sheriff's secretary and her roommate, Liz Browning, spotted Luke and Monty and headed in their direction.

"Hey, guys," Bianca said, looking fondly at Luke, "What brings you two to town?"

Before either answered, she said, "I know, you're tired of your own cooking."

After chatting for a few moments, the two young women sat at the table nearest to Luke's booth. Bianca always maneuvered herself close to Luke. She was well aware of how uncomfortable he was around women, but she was convinced that sooner or later that would change, and she wanted to be close by when it did. She really liked Luke Osborne.

And Luke liked Bianca, but not in a romantic way. Besides, he just wasn't ready to date yet. He wasn't sure he ever would be. And even though he resented her pushiness a little, he didn't let it bother him too much. Her company wasn't offensive, as she was very attractive with a dark complexion, almost jet-black hair, and very dark eyes. She was almost as tall as Luke, but didn't seem like it as he always wore boots and she never wore anything that made her look taller than she was. Luke realized that a lot of the people in town figured that sooner or later they'd end up together. That didn't bother him either, because talk didn't change anything, and he had no such plans.

Monty was especially fond of Bianca. She was always giving him treats or other little presents. He looked at her expectantly now, and sure enough, she opened her purse, found a mint, and handed it across to him, winking as she did so. Monty thanked her and laid it on the table. He knew his dad would tell him to wait until he'd eaten if he began to unwrap it now.

Coleen hadn't heard anyone come in and was surprised to see the table next to Luke and Monty occupied. She gave them the two waters and turned to the women. They wanted menus, and so she left, returning a moment later with a glass of water and a menu for each of them. As she placed them in front of the two young ladies, the darker-complexioned one spoke to Luke. "The sheriff's sure happy that you caught that guy today. Tom Evans has been calling him almost every day. That's why he's pressed you so much to solve the case."

"I knew that," Luke said as Coleen turned away. "But I don't blame him, Bianca. Tom suffered a big loss."

"Well, you did a good job," Bianca said. "I heard the sheriff say to Lt. Peterson today that you're the best detective he's ever had work for him."

Coleen's mind was swirling as she stepped out of earshot. Luke Osborne was a cop! For some unexplainable reason, that seemed unsettling to her. She'd thought he was a cowboy. In the two hours they'd spent together, he hadn't said a word about law enforcement. There was sure a lot she didn't know about Luke; not that she should, as there was still that mystery surrounding his wife. For a married man with a son, he sure seemed to attract women's attention. At least, the woman he called Bianca clearly had a thing for him.

Coleen carried Luke's salad in to him a moment later. Bianca was still talking rapid-fire to Luke. "Lt. Peterson said he saw Victor Hampton at Killian's Service Station today," she said. "The lieutenant told me Victor sort of sauntered over when he pulled in. He even leaned against the lieutenant's car, and you know how mad that makes him."

A shadow seemed to cross Luke's face, and his eyes narrowed. There was a side of Luke Osborne that could be dangerous, Coleen realized with a jolt. The shadow darkened when Bianca went on, "Victor asked Lt. Peterson how you were doing."

Luke pressed his fingers over his closed eyes for a moment, like he had a headache or some other kind of pain, then he said, "It's just a matter of time. I'll get him."

Coleen shuddered as she again headed for the kitchen. Whoever this Victor guy was, she'd hate to be in his shoes. Luke had sounded almost deadly just then, and it was clear that Victor was someone he thoroughly despised.

Luke struggled to control his shaking hands. He was being goaded. Victor had meant for him to hear what he'd said. And it wasn't Bianca's fault, she didn't know that. All Luke needed was a little patience. Revenge was beneath him, but good police work was not. He'd get a break someday, and when he did, Victor Hampton would land behind bars again, right where he and his kind belonged.

After Luke left, Coleen was ill at ease the rest of the night. She knew she shouldn't be, but she'd been attracted to Luke from the moment she'd first seen him, and he'd seemed like such a kind and caring man. Now she saw that there was another side to him, and she wasn't sure she liked it. She waited until the café closed an hour later to ask questions of the other waitress, a girl named Sadie King.

"That guy and the little boy who were in here tonight—" she began.

Sadie grinned. "Detective Luke Osborne. The most eligible man in Duchesne."

"Eligible?" Coleen asked in surprise. "But what about his wife?"

Sadie's face became serious. "Jamie? She was killed in a car wreck four years ago. Some say Luke'll never get over her, but Bianca Turner has other ideas. Time will tell I guess."

"Oh, that's terrible. He seems like such a nice guy."

"He is a great guy. Everybody loves him. They say he'll be sheriff here someday. He'd be a good one. But they also say he's obsessed with the guy who was driving the car that killed his wife. The guy was high on meth at the time but only served a few months in jail. Now he throws it in Luke's face."

Coleen shuddered. "Victor Hampton?" she asked.

"Yeah, how'd you know?"

"Bianca mentioned him when I was serving them tonight. And the look on Luke's face was scary."

"Yeah, it would be. Victor's bad, and Luke knows it."

"Does he live here in Duchesne?" Coleen asked.

"Victor? No, he's from over by Roosevelt somewhere. But he does live in Duchesne County. That's what gets to Luke, I think. He'd like to put him away for life. And I hope someday he does. Jamie was one of the nicest people I ever knew. She didn't deserve what happened to her. Neither did Luke or Monty."

* * *

Luke couldn't sleep that night. First he would be thinking of Victor Hampton and fighting the hatred that threatened to canker his soul. Then he would see the dark brown eyes, long blonde hair, and bright smile of Coleen Whitman, and he would begin to feel better again. He found himself wanting to talk to her again, to be with her. What was it about her? He was sure she wasn't LDS. Why was she so attractive to him? She wasn't much prettier than Bianca, but there was something about her that got to him. Maybe it was the air of mystery that surrounded her.

The mystery deepened when he was referred to the management at Cowan's Café the next morning. It seemed they wanted to learn more about Coleen too. He dropped in, almost hoping she would be there, but he was told that she wouldn't be on duty until later in the day. "What's the problem?" he asked.

"She's great," he was told. "Customers love her. But it seems that she has no kind of ID. She can't even give us a social security number. And we can't put her on the payroll without one."

Luke felt a shiver run up his spine. Coleen Whitman must not be who she was claiming to be. He told them he'd check it out and left. He found her at the motel across from the grocery store ten minutes later. He almost couldn't stand it when she greeted him with that wonderful smile of hers and welcomed him in.

"Why do I have the honor of the presence of Detective Luke Osborne?" she asked mischievously. "I hope you're not on duty." She was trying to be lighthearted, but inwardly she was in turmoil. She expected the worst the moment she saw him there, and from the look on his face now, she knew she was right. Her smile faded and fear filled her heart.

"I just need to ask you a few questions," he said calmly. "And please, Coleen, don't look at me like that. I'm not such a bad guy."

"I know that. In fact, you're the nicest guy I know," she said, wondering if he was the nicest guy she'd ever known. She couldn't remember anyone from before that morning when she woke up in a hospital in New Mexico, her past wiped clean.

The look of dejection and fear on Coleen's face made Luke want to reach out and take her in his arms—a most unprofessional feeling. He tried to shake it off as he said, "Listen, could we sit down and talk for a minute?"

"Only if you promise you won't arrest me," she said, trying her best to smile, but failing miserably.

"I can't imagine why I'd want to," he said, wondering if there was some terrible dark secret in her past that might force him to do just that.

They sat across a small table from one another. Her pretty face was drained of color, and those bewitching, very dark brown eyes were sad and hollow. "Who are you?" he asked after a moment. "Who are you really?"

* * *

Gil Stedman leaned across the counter in a bus terminal in Dodge City, Kansas. It was the third time today he'd been in such a place. He held a picture of a smiling, blonde-haired young lady in one hand and a fake FBI identification in the other. He shoved the ID in front of the attendant there and said, "Roger Smith, FBI." Then he put the ID away, taking his time so that the significance of who he purported to be would be impressed upon the mind of the man across the counter.

Then Gil showed him the picture and asked, "Ever seen this girl?"

"No, I don't think so," the man said quickly.

"Don't lie to me, man. She's dangerous. She's wanted for kidnapping by the FBI, and anyone who tries to cover for her will be arrested as an accessory."

The man was duly impressed and looked closer at the picture. The young lady smiling back at him was very pretty, and she was familiar. She hadn't looked at all like a kidnapper in her cowboy boots, blue jeans, and western-cut blouse. But, yes, he'd seen her. He'd sold her a ticket.

"You remember her, don't you?" Gil said in an ugly, very un-FBI voice, a voice that didn't match the professional, expensive attire he wore.

It made the ticket vendor nervous, but he answered nonetheless "Yes, now that I look closer, I think I do."

"When was she in here?"

"Oh, maybe five, six weeks ago."

"Sell her a ticket?"

"Seems like I did."

"Not an easy girl to forget, is she?" Gil asked knowingly. "You don't see many girls like her buying tickets for the bus, do you?"

"Not many," the ticket agent agreed.

"She's not at all like she looks," Gil said darkly. "Where did she buy a ticket to?"

The man was thinking hard. Then he remembered. "Denver, Colorado."

Gil turned without so much as a thank-you. Finally, he was on Carly's trail. Luck was turning his way. He'd track her down and bury her knowledge with her.

CHAPTER 3

At first Coleen didn't know what to say, but the face of the officer across the table softened, and she figured Luke was as good a person to trust as any. She said, "I wish I knew who I am, Luke. I really wish I knew."

Luke was taken aback. That was not at all the answer he'd expected. "What do you mean, Coleen?" he asked. "Are you telling me you don't know your own name?"

"The only name I know is Coleen Whitman," she began, hesitantly. Then, committing herself to sharing her secret, she plunged on. "I lost my memory. I can't remember anything about my past. Not my name, not my age, not where I'm from. Nothing. Last March I woke up in a hospital in New Mexico and didn't know the two guys who were standing beside my bed. They were both cowboys, and they seemed concerned about me, but it didn't make any sense. They asked me my name and I couldn't tell them. I couldn't remember. I still can't. It's so frightening."

She finally paused, and Luke did what he was an expert at. He began to question her, to try to fill the holes that always existed in anyone's story—suspects, victims, and witnesses alike. "These two men, why were they there?" he asked.

"You believe me?" Coleen asked. "I quit telling people because they never believed me. I've had so many jobs, but none for more than a week. At first I tried telling people I didn't have a social security number because I had amnesia." She grimaced. "I hate that word."

"And the people you told didn't believe you?" Luke asked, knowing it was true, for he was struggling just a little with the concept himself. But he was determined not to show it.

"That's right. So they usually pay me in cash and send me out the door."

"That's terrible, Coleen, but it's also understandable, don't you think? Employers are bound by laws, things like withholding taxes."

"I know that," she said, "and that's part of what's so weird about this amnesia thing. I can remember some things, like what the laws are, how to live my life, how to talk and read and all those kinds of things. I even knew what kind of clothes I liked. That's why I'm dressed like I am. I was even pretty sure I knew how to ride; it seemed like the most natural thing in the world. But other than riding with you the other day, I don't remember ever being on a horse. But I remember the feel and the smell and even the love I have for horses. It's like I'm this crazy woman, Luke. You can't imagine what it's like not to know yourself."

Luke expected tears at any moment, but Coleen was apparently strong; or maybe she'd already cried so much that she couldn't anymore. He found that he was believing her and that surprised him. He hoped it wasn't because she was so attractive. "About those two cowboys," he reminded her.

"Yes, Joe and Rick. They saved my life, I guess. At least that's what they claimed. They said that I was on a runaway horse, a big bay gelding, and that I was being dragged by one foot that was caught in the stirrup. They stopped him and got me to a hospital. They said the horse wasn't really running all that fast, even though he appeared to be spooked. He was exhausted to the point of nearly collapsing. In fact, they said he had fallen up the road a short distance and I'd been thrown or tried to jump or something, and that my foot must've got caught in the stirrup when he got up."

"How did they know all this?"

"Apparently they helped the police retrace the path my horse had taken. I guess I'd run him for several miles," she said.

"Did they have any clues as to why you would do that?" Luke asked. "You don't seem like the kind of person who would do anything to hurt a horse."

"Thank you, Luke. I don't think I am either. But yes, they said there were four-wheeler tracks that followed me to where I rode onto the highway. Then they turned back. The police retraced them, but the tracks ran out on a paved road several miles away. They couldn't find anything else."

"Okay, so the police were involved. Did they fingerprint you or do anything to try to help you discover your identity?" he asked.

"Oh, yeah. They took my prints but told me they weren't on file anywhere. They circulated my picture in the area and came up with nothing. Then," she said sadly, "they began to question me in a way that I could tell they thought I was making it all up. Even the doctors seemed like they weren't sure I wasn't lying. Why would I lie? I wish I knew who I was." Now an errant tear appeared, but she brushed it away quickly and regained her composure. "When they let me out of the hospital, I simply began to drift."

Luke continued to ask questions and Coleen continued to answer them. He felt terrible about the way she'd been forced to wander, working a few days in one town and then a few in another so that she'd have something to live on. She carefully hoarded the money Rick and Joe had given her for the horse she'd been riding. And he didn't blame her. How terrible it would be for her to be homeless and broke.

Finally, after an hour of questions and answers, Luke smiled at her and said, "Coleen Whitman. That's a very pretty name. Care to tell me where it came from?"

Coleen smiled, her normal, beautiful, bright smile, and it struck deep in Luke's lonely heart. He realized with a jolt that he was really beginning to feel something for this woman. And that was dangerous. He was LDS, and had a son who watched and learned from everything he did. And he was active in the Church. The likelihood that she was also a member of the Church was pretty slim, and without knowing her real name, it would be impossible to find out.

And, of course, there was the memory of his sweetheart, Jamie. He never wanted to do anything that would even appear as if his love for her were fading. That could never happen.

Coleen broke into his troubled thoughts. "At first I went without a name, but let me tell you, that's hard, Luke. I spent some time in a library just after they let me go from the hospital. I was trying to learn about amnesia. Oh, I really do hate that word!" she said with a grimace. "But I did learn a little, although it wasn't very encouraging."

"Like what?" he prompted.

"Like the fact that it's extremely rare for a person who gets this . . . this condition from head trauma to ever regain their memory. Other forms of memory loss, such as from psychological causes or disease, are more likely to allow either partial or full recovery of memory. Pretty discouraging, since mine came from a head injury."

Luke nodded, and Coleen went on. "So anyway, while I was in the library, after I'd read that stuff, I thought that if I might never regain my memory, then it might be best if I figured a name out for myself. I found a book of names with definitions for each name." She paused and chuckled. "This is kind of silly, but I chose both of my names based on their definitions more than how they sounded or how they might fit me otherwise."

"Sounds kind of sensible to me," Luke assured her. "So what does Coleen mean? It really is a pretty name and it fits you perfectly."

"It does?" she asked. "It feels awkward to me."

"No, it's great, but you've really got me curious. What does it mean?"

"Coleen is an Irish word and it means *girl*. I know it's simple, but since I am female, it seemed as good as anything." She smiled and this time Luke chuckled.

"Interesting," he said. "So Whitman, what does that mean? Is that Irish too?"

"No, it's Old English," she told him. "And it means *fair-haired*." She fingered a strand of her long blonde hair as she spoke, then waved it jokingly toward Luke.

Luke laughed. "So your name simply means *'fair-haired girl.'*"

"I told you it was silly," Coleen said. "But that's how I came by the name. It's nothing more than a brief description of what I am. I lost everything else."

"You're very creative and I love the name. Even if we find out who you really are," Luke told her, "I'd have a hard time calling you anything else."

Coleen's face brightened. "You mean you'll help me try to find out who I am?"

"Of course I'll help you," he said. He grinned at her. "But if we're successful, you have to promise that I can still call you Coleen."

"Deal," she said.

"That's great," he said with a smile. Luke was thoughtful for a moment, then his face grew serious as he said, "But if we can't find out who you are, I know several good attorneys, and I'm sure one of them will help us get your name legalized so you can get a social security number, driver's license, and all that."

As strange as it seemed, Luke's statement brought the flow of tears she'd so bravely repressed through the entire interview. "Thank you, Luke," she said. "Thank you so much."

* * *

"I don't believe her for one minute," Bianca told her roommate that night. "Can't remember who she is," she scoffed. "But she sure has Luke convinced. Besides that she's too young for him. She can't be more than twenty-four years old."

Liz grinned. "Competition, huh? She is rather pretty you know. And you're not much over twenty-five yourself," she teased.

Bianca did not grin. "Yeah, I did notice that Liz. Thanks," she said sarcastically. "She was with him the entire day, at least until she had to go to work. But her job won't last long. There's no way she can work if she doesn't tell her boss her real name and her social security number."

"I hadn't thought about that," Liz said. "That could be a problem all right."

"So why doesn't she want to say?" Bianca asked shrewdly, more to herself than to her roommate. "Unless she's got a questionable—even criminal—past. She's probably wanted someplace for stealing or murder or something."

Liz had to draw the line there. "She really doesn't look like a murderer," she interrupted, shaking her head. "In fact, she seems really nice to me."

"Oh, yes," Bianca agreed. "She seems really nice all right. Part of her act, I'm sure. Anyway, Liz, tell me, what does a murderer look like?"

"Well, uh, let's see. Dark, sinister . . ." she began, then stopped.

"See, you can't describe one. Nobody can, because they come in all shapes and sizes and colors. You've heard about mothers who murder their own kids and then go sobbing to the cops about how they were kidnapped and would the cops please help find them," she said smugly.

"You don't really think Coleen did something like that, do you?" Liz asked in alarm.

"I don't know what I believe. I just don't believe she can't remember who she is."

"Boy, you're really jealous." Liz grinned.

"She's after him, Liz," Bianca agreed. "And I can't just stand around and let her take him. And she's already got her claws in him. Even after she went to work, he spent the rest of the day trying to find out who she was. And get this, he even talked to the county attorney about how she might be able to get her name, her *Coleen Whitman,* made legal. The whole thing really stinks. Nobody just drops into town like that and immediately goes after the best-looking and most eligible bachelor. It just doesn't happen."

Liz wasn't convinced. "How did they meet, anyway. Did Luke say?"

"He sure did. I heard him talking to a deputy. She came in on the bus as he was gassing up his truck. And she got so interested in his horses and trailer that the bus left her stranded. And so what did she do? She got Luke to take her riding with him! It makes me so mad."

"But all that could have really happened," Liz countered.

"It did happen, I'm not questioning that. But it was no accident. She had it planned. She's after him. It's that simple," Bianca growled. "*He let her ride his horses.* He's never let me ride one of them."

"Have you ever asked?" Liz queried.

"No, but he knows I'd like to."

"Maybe, but I bet if you asked he'd take you riding," Liz suggested.

"Hey, great idea, Liz. I'll do that," Bianca said with a glint in her eye. "I won't let that strange woman come into town and just walk off with him. She's got a fight on her hands, and I intend to win. It's time Luke Osborne got married again, and I intend to be the bride."

"What if I wanted him?" Liz asked with a chuckle.

"Don't even think it, girl," Bianca said. "That guy is mine. He just doesn't know it yet. But I think Monty's getting the idea. He likes me a lot, and I really adore that little guy. I'd make him a great mom, don't you think?" She brushed a stray lock of dark hair from her face and grinned. "Bianca Osborne. Has kind of a ring to it, doesn't it?"

* * *

The phone woke Luke from a deep sleep. He groaned and looked at the clock beside his bed. It was just a little before two. That meant he had work to do; the phone never rang this time of the night unless he was being called out on a case. He was tempted to ignore the ringing, but he was too good an officer to do that. So he reached for the phone.

"Detective Osborne?" It was a voice that Luke didn't recognize.

"Yes, this is Detective Osborne, and who are you?" he asked, searching his memory for a clue to the deep voice on the line. It definitely wasn't a dispatcher or an officer from the department. He knew all their voices too well to mistake them.

"It doesn't matter who I am," he was told. "But I have some information I think you want." Luke was checking his caller ID. The number the caller had dialed from was not identified. After a brief pause the caller said, "Victor Hampton. He's got a meth lab going over in Hancock Cove."

Luke was immediately interested. "Is he there now?"

"That's why I'm calling."

"Tell me how to find this place."

"Well, I would, but it's kind of hard to explain. Why don't you meet me, and I'll show you. Then you can get some other officers and bust him. Believe me, he's making the stuff and he needs to be stopped," the caller said.

"Try giving me a description of his location first," Luke said, feeling uncomfortable. "I know the Hancock Cove area pretty well."

"No, we've got to do it my way. I can't afford to let you make a mistake. If you don't get him now, he'll figure out who turned him in and I'll be as dead as Jamie."

Luke bristled at the mention of his wife's name. Something didn't seem quite right here, but he would sure love to nail Victor with a meth lab. That man would do some serious time, and Luke wanted nothing more.

"And Detective Osborne, come alone. I don't want nobody but you knowing who I am. Like I say, Vic would gun me down in a heartbeat if he knew I was turning him in."

Luke didn't feel very good about it at all now, but he wanted Victor so badly that he wasn't about to pass up an opportunity like this. "Tell me where and I'll get there as quick as I can."

"Good," the caller said, and he gave Luke a location.

"I'm on my way," Luke told him. "Give me forty-five minutes. It'll take that long to get there."

"Don't bring your police car. It might be recognized. Come alone," Luke was reminded, "and I'll give you Victor Hampton on a platter."

As soon as the line was clear, Luke punched in his parents' number in town. There was no answer, and then Luke remembered his father had a doctor's appointment that morning in Provo, and his father and mother had planned to drive that way yesterday afternoon and stay with Luke's sister and her family in Orem.

So what could he do? He couldn't take Monty with him, but he also couldn't leave him with just anyone. He thought of Bianca. Monty really liked her, and she would take good care of him. He dialed her number.

"I'm sorry to call at such a terrible hour," he said after identifying himself. "But my folks are out of town and I need a place to leave Monty for a few hours. If I'm not back by the time you need to go to work, leave him at daycare, if you would. I have a call I need to respond to."

"Bring him over," Bianca said quickly, thinking that she'd found her in. "What kind of call do you have?" she asked.

"I can't say," he told her. "But I need to go right now."

Bianca felt a twist in her gut. "Who's going with you?" she asked.

"No one," he said.

"Luke, this sounds dangerous," she told him, the concern in her voice genuine.

"Goes with the job," he told her sharply. "You of all people should know that."

"I know, I'm sorry, Luke. Bring Monty over."

"Fifteen minutes tops," he said.

"I'll be waiting," she said as a thought came into her head. "Oh, and it'll cost you," she added with a laugh.

"Whatever you say, I'll pay," he responded.

"A ride on one of your horses," she said.

"Deal," he agreed, his mind more on Victor Hampton than on the fact that he'd just been conned into a date with Bianca Turner.

As he handed the sleepy boy over a few minutes later, Bianca said, "Be careful, and remember, you owe me a ride."

"Got it," he said and, bending down, he kissed his son on the forehead and then quickly trotted back to his truck.

Bianca began to tremble as she stood holding Luke's son and watching Luke drive off, his tires squealing in the still night air. For some strange reason, she was suddenly afraid. Luke was headed into danger, she could feel it in her heart, and she hugged his little boy to her chest, trying to calm the unrest that had so chillingly settled over her.

Her fear prompted action, and in a couple of minutes she had the sheriff on the phone. She quickly told him about Luke's call and the secretive way he was handling it. The sheriff was as concerned as she was.

"I'll get hold of him," he promised.

"Oh, and there's something else, Sheriff," she said, unable to keep the trembling from her voice, "he was in his own truck."

"Maybe he took a handheld radio," the sheriff said. "I'll get right on it."

Luke had a handheld, all right, but it was turned off. He didn't want anyone who might be listening in to hear his voice on a scanner, just in case Bianca tried to have someone call him. It did occur to him that she might try, and there was no way he could take the chance of answering anyone on the radio. He took it only in the event that he needed it later to coordinate a search.

Or if this whole thing went south on him, which he prayed it wouldn't.

He also had his cell phone, but it too was turned off for now. He knew that what he was doing was risky, but he owed it to Jamie's memory to do whatever was required of him to put Victor Hampton away.

CHAPTER 4

The closer Luke got to the spot he'd arranged to meet his informant, the more his stomach churned. He just couldn't get it out of his mind that someone handing him Victor Hampton *on a platter* was just too good to be true. Nervous, he slowed down, peering intently into the darkness beyond the area lit by his headlights. He reached over and turned on his handheld radio. There was nothing but an occasional bit of static. He also turned on his cellular phone. He felt less alone now and picked up his speed ever so slightly, but rolled down the windows of the truck to listen better.

Still nearly a quarter mile from his rendezvous point, every one of his senses was alert. Luke slowed down again and shut off his lights. He hadn't gone more than another couple of hundred yards when his eyes caught the flash of a muzzle blast to his right in a small stand of cedar trees, and his foot jammed on the brake. He felt more than heard the sound of the bullet as it passed through both open windows, narrowly missing his face. A second shot, only a fraction of a second behind the first, ricocheted off the hood of his truck. He ducked low as the truck continued to slide to a stop.

Another bullet missed altogether as Luke jammed the gear lever into Park. Grabbing his radio and his pistol, Luke shoved open his door and rolled out as two more shots hit the body of his truck somewhere on the far side. Within seconds he was off the road and had melted into the blackness of the night.

He'd expected to hear more shots, but there were none. He crawled silently into the brush and waited. For what seemed like an hour, but was probably only two or three minutes, there wasn't a sound in the darkness about him. Then a familiar deep voice, spoken low but carrying clearly in the night, said, "Think we got him?" It was without a doubt the voice from the phone less than an hour ago.

"Probably," came another voice that Luke immediately recognized as that of Victor Hampton.

"Let's have a look," the first man said.

"You go, I'll cover you," the second replied.

Luke silently fastened his radio to his belt, then slowly pushed his gun out ahead of him, steadying his right hand with his left. A moment later, a shadowy figure emerged from across the road and several yards to the rear of Luke's truck. It moved slowly, and not until it was beside the truck did a small flashlight come on. That was all Luke needed. He held his breath and slowly squeezed the trigger. A bright flash of light from his muzzle accompanied the loud blast that filled the night. Luke was already scrambling to his right as the light fell to the ground and the shadowy figure began to slump.

Another gun fired, a rifle, and the bullet struck right where Luke had fired from. He continued to move deeper into the brush at the side of the road. The deep voice that had disturbed his sleep earlier screamed, "I'm hit . . . help me!"

And as the injured man continued to wail, Luke grabbed for his radio. Speaking softly he called into it, telling the dispatcher in Vernal his location and informing her that he was under fire. He'd no sooner finished his transmission than the sheriff came on and said, "All cars proceed to that area at once." Then directing himself to Luke, he said, "Mike Ten, we're on our way. How many shooters are there?"

"Two," he answered quickly, "but one's down."

"We'll be there soon." Then there was silence and once more Luke began to crawl. Again another rifle bullet struck very near where he'd just been. But he saw the muzzle blast this time and fired a shot himself before swiftly moving back the way he'd just come. A wise move, as the rifleman fired where Luke would have been had he rolled to his right again. He expected to hear another shot at any moment and he kept moving for several seconds. When he stopped and lay still he could hear only the moaning of the man near his truck. Then the one he was positive was Victor called out, "Either get over here on your own power or I'm leaving you."

"I'll try," came a plaintive reply. And Luke could hear the man dragging himself away from the Dodge Ram. He knew they were going to try to leave, but he also knew that any attempt to stop them had to be made from right where he was at. If he stood and tried to get closer, he could well draw more fire from Vic. So he stayed put until he heard a car door slam and an engine roar. He came to his knees and a moment later a pickup careened onto the road and accelerated north, the direction Luke's truck was facing. Luke fired a shot and felt a little satisfaction as he heard it hit metal. But then the truck was too far away, and he held his fire.

"Mike One," he said into the radio, "they just left northbound in a pickup. There'll be a bullet hole in the vehicle somewhere."

"Stay put, Mike Ten," the sheriff responded. "I'm only about ten minutes out."

When the sheriff arrived almost fifteen minutes later, Luke was leaning against his truck. The first thing the sheriff said was, "Not the smartest thing you ever did, Osborne."

"I know," Luke admitted, bracing himself for more.

"Good try though. I'd have done the same thing, I suspect. But next time call for help."

"Sorry, Sheriff," he said.

"Two men?" Sheriff Gavin Robinson asked.

"That's all I heard."

"Any idea who they were?"

"Victor Hampton was one of them. The one I hit was the guy that called me at home an hour or so ago. Deep voice. Have no idea who he was."

"But you're sure of Hampton?" Gavin asked, clearly surprised. He knew how badly Luke wanted Hampton back in prison, but he had no idea that Victor would want Luke dead.

"I'm positive it was Hampton," Luke answered.

"See him?"

"Nope, just heard his voice. I'd know it anywhere," Luke responded.

As they talked, the sheriff was slowly walking around Luke's truck, assessing the damage. "Could have been worse," he said. "Looks like you can still drive it."

Luke had already looked it over. None of the bullets had hit a vital part of the truck, and all the glass was intact. He was really quite grateful. "It'll be fine," he said.

"May still get them tonight," the sheriff commented a moment later. "Men are out looking. Trouble is, we had no idea where you might have gone, so none of us were as close as we might have been."

Neither Victor nor his accomplice were found. Their truck, found with a bullet hole in the back of the cab that went clear through to the dash, was abandoned in Cedar View. It was clean of prints and had been reported stolen two days before in Provo. The passenger side of the cab was smeared with blood, but both men had somehow gotten away. The sheriff ordered that an intensive search of the area be conducted, but neither Luke nor the sheriff held much hope of finding them.

It was nearly seven when Luke tapped on Bianca's apartment door and retrieved his son. She didn't know what had happened, although Luke knew she soon would. The first thing she said when he answered the door was, "Are you all right?"

"I'm just fine. Why wouldn't I be?" He answered with a tired smile.

"I don't know, Luke. I just had these awful feelings when you drove off this morning."

Luke grinned. "You were just afraid Monty would keep you up the rest of the night."

"Oh, no," she said quickly. "I just love that little guy. He's so good. He never even woke up all night."

But Monty did wake up when Bianca picked him up from the sofa where he'd been sleeping. "Hi Dad," he said, wiping the sleep from his eyes. He looked around and then asked, "Where are we?"

"Bianca's been watching you for me, son. I had to go do a little work during the night," Luke explained.

"Did you arrest a bad guy?" Monty asked.

"Nope, not this time. Tell Bianca thanks."

Monty did, and then Bianca handed him over to Luke. "So when do I get my ride?" she asked.

Luke had forgotten all about that. He was trapped and figured he'd just as well get it over with. "How about tonight, around seven? You can meet us at the ranch. Monty'll be coming along too."

"That's great, Luke. I'll be there," she said, her eyes shining.

At about ten that morning, Luke and the sheriff met with the county attorney, the prosecutor for Duchesne County. After explaining all that had happened that morning, Sheriff Robinson said, "So what do you think? Is it enough for a warrant?"

The tall, graying man slowly shook his head. "I'm sorry, but it just isn't. If the other fellow had even said his name, I might have been able to make a case. Or if you'd seen him, it would have done it for sure. Now the only hope of ever getting a conviction is either for you to find the weapons and be able to tie them to both Vic and your truck, or else find the guy that called you and get a confession out of him and get him to turn on Vic. Even when Vic turns up, we all know he'll deny everything."

Luke was disappointed but not surprised. He was positive that the voice he heard had been that of Victor Hampton, but he also knew that any good defense attorney could create reasonable doubt in the minds of a jury. Luke could only wait and hope for another chance. In the meantime, he knew that he'd have to be careful. Victor might try again.

* * *

"Luke Osborne, you could have been killed," Bianca fumed when Luke and the sheriff came into the office after meeting with the county attorney. "You didn't tell me you'd been in a gun battle."

"You didn't ask," he said with a grin, "and I couldn't see any reason for getting anybody all worked up, especially with Monty right there. I'd really rather he didn't know."

Bianca calmed down. "I'm sorry, but I can't believe what a close call you had. What would that precious little boy do if something happened to you?" she asked.

Luke looked her directly in the eye. "In this profession, you try not to think about such things. But thanks again for helping me with him."

"You know I'll take him anytime," she said. And she'd take Luke anytime too, she thought, but that was going to take some work. Maybe she ought to dress a little nicer for work, do a little something to make him notice her more often, she thought. She was committed. "You said seven tonight, right?" she reminded Luke.

"Seven. And bring your spurs," he said, trying to sound light-hearted, even though he was not particularly looking forward to the evening.

Then he thought, *maybe I'm being too stubborn. Bianca really is a good woman, and she does care about Monty. And I don't have to make any commitments.*

But there was still Jamie.

* * *

Coleen was humming to herself. It was a tune that was familiar, although she had no recollection of having ever heard it. It was so weird. Her whole life was weird. But she was happy this morning. Luke had promised to help her get an apartment today so she wouldn't have to keep paying the high cost of a motel room. The money she'd received from Joe and Rick wouldn't last forever. And neither would her job unless something happened quickly. Luke had spoken to her boss and he'd agreed to give her another week, but he didn't dare go beyond that.

She was to meet Luke at eleven and it was almost that now. She found herself girlishly anxious to see him. When he didn't arrive right at eleven, she felt uneasy. When he still hadn't come thirty minutes later, she was bitterly disappointed. But when he finally showed up at noon, she was ready to forget he was late, it was that good to see him.

"Sorry I'm late," he told her. "I've had kind of a busy morning and I had some reports to write. But I did call the owner of the Twin Rivers Apartments, and you're lucky. They have a vacancy, and when I explained your circumstances, he said you'd qualify for really low rent. But we need to get over there right away so you have time to fill out some forms before you're due at work."

"Thanks, Luke, that's wonderful," she said. "When can I move in?"

"Get your things together now," he said. "He'll let you in today. It's a furnished apartment, so you'll be fine."

It didn't take Coleen long to pack. She had only a handful of clothes and very little else. She'd called Greyhound again, but her bag had never shown up. It seemed unlikely it ever would. But she found that she really didn't care. As long as Luke Osborne was around, the world didn't seem nearly as bad as it had.

He helped her into his patrol car and delivered her to the apartments. "The only bad thing about this place is that it's a pretty good hike to your work from here. Not like being at the motel," he said.

"I don't mind," she responded. "I'm just grateful for a place to stay."

"Listen," Luke said after introducing her to the manager of the apartments, "I hate to do this, but I'll have to let you work things out from here. I've got to get back to the office. I'll get in touch with you tomorrow about how things are coming. So far, I'm not doing any better than those cops in New Mexico. But I have sent a bulletin out that will go to police departments all across the country. Who knows, something might turn up. In the meantime, the county attorney promised that he'd find out what has to be done to get you a legal name and ID."

"Thanks, Luke," she said, disappointed that he had to leave so soon, but grateful for all he was doing to help her.

She got settled into her apartment and then walked to work. Her shift started at two, so she didn't have much time. The café was slow until about five, then it became very busy. She found herself thinking often of Luke as she did her work, and realized she was getting far too emotionally involved. For all she knew, she might have a husband and children somewhere. That thought depressed her, and she was feeling quite low when she heard a customer mention Luke's name.

She couldn't help but listen closer and scrubbed the table she was at far more than it needed. The customer told his dinner partner, "I guess it was pretty close. He only had a pistol, and shot it out with two men with rifles."

"They get away?" the other man asked.

"So far. I heard Luke hit one of them. But they seem to have vanished. The truck they were driving was stolen. Crazy thing, it was. A genuine ambush. Just like outlaws used to do in the Old West. Luke's really lucky to be alive."

"Does the sheriff's department have any idea who they were?"

"Not that I know of. If they do, they aren't saying."

A customer called her away from her sorely scrubbed table, so she didn't hear any more of the conversation. But she listened carefully to whatever was being said in the restaurant as the night went on. She caught fragments of the same story several times, but she didn't learn any more about Luke's shoot-out. His brush with death was the talk of the town. She found herself trembling whenever his name was mentioned.

And it was mentioned often, although the conversation at one table drew her attention sharply. There, a young man she'd never seen before, sat down at about six-thirty with the girl Coleen recognized as one of the two young ladies who'd been so friendly with Luke and Monty a couple of nights ago. She remembered the other girl's name, the dark pretty one, as soon as it was mentioned.

"Bianca has a date tonight with Luke," the girl the young man referred to as Liz said. "They're going riding together up at Luke's ranch."

"Bet that doesn't break her heart."

"I'll say not," Liz said. "She sort of . . ." she began, then she looked up and saw Coleen. She didn't say another word, but sent signals to the young man that this wasn't a good time to talk about this particular subject.

Coleen's depression deepened, and she began to entertain thoughts of catching the bus and moving on the next day. Then she reasoned with herself that it wasn't so strange that Luke might have women who were after him, or that he might have his eye on one of them. Bianca was very attractive, and she remembered now how much she'd seemed to like Monty. Again she thought how utterly stupid it was of her to even allow herself to be attracted to Luke, or any man for that matter, when she had no idea who might be in her past. She just needed to be patient and give Luke and the county attorney time to see if they could help her. Then, when she had a legal name, maybe she'd move on.

* * *

Of course, there was at least one man in Coleen's past. And that man was furious right now. He'd driven to Denver only to find nothing but dead ends. Nobody would admit to ever having seen the girl in the picture he showed at every bus stop, to every cabby, and to every ticket agent at the airport that would take time to look at it. But he was not about to give up. Carly had to be found and silenced. Surely someone, somewhere, would be able to lead him to her.

* * *

"When's Bianca going to get here?" Monty asked for the hundredth time. "I hope she comes soon."

Luke had to admit that even if he wasn't overly fond of Bianca, his son certainly was. Maybe he wasn't being fair. Maybe he really should give a relationship with her a chance. What would it hurt?

My memory of Jamie, that's what.

But what would Jamie want for Monty? Luke forced himself to think. Was he being selfish by denying his son the benefit of a mother in his life . . . or little brothers and sisters? For the first time ever, Luke found himself admitting that Jamie would probably want that for Monty, if not for Luke too.

He remembered his patriarchal blessing. He hadn't read it for a long time. But he felt the need to now. So he found it in the drawer where he kept it and sat down.

He'd remembered right, he realized with a jolt. It talked of children, not just *a* child. Luke broke out in a cold sweat, and a moment later he dropped to his knees. When he'd finished praying, he was certain that Monty should have the privilege of brothers and sisters. And that could never happen if he continued to refuse to date.

He felt foolish as he got up from his knees and began thinking about the single women he knew. Only two came to mind that he was at all attracted to. One was Coleen, and that just wouldn't work. The other, he admitted a bit sheepishly, was Bianca Turner. He made up his mind he'd show her a good time tonight. Maybe he'd even take Monty and her to dinner or dessert after their ride, if it wasn't too late at night. The more he thought about it, the better the idea sounded to him. When he suggested it to Monty, the little guy was ecstatic. And that really caused Luke to think.

"Come on, pal, let's get some horses rounded up," he said to Monty as he tousled his son's now-short blond hair.

Ginger, an older but well-trained sorrel mare was the one Luke selected for Bianca. Her registered name was long and cumbersome, but he'd always called her Ginger, an almost universal name for sorrel mares. She had a two-month-old bay colt at her side, and it was always fun to ride with a colt following along. Monty had his own horse, a small, very gentle paint mare called Fox. Luke couldn't for the life of him remember how she'd come to get that name. She was the only horse on the place that wasn't American quarter horse. For himself he caught Keno, the chestnut gelding colt he'd ridden when he'd taken Coleen to the fairgrounds.

He'd just tied Keno up at a hitching rail in the yard when Bianca drove up in her sporty little Mazda. He walked over, opened the door for her, and said, "You're just in time to help us saddle up." She stepped out, dressed in her best riding clothes, and Luke couldn't help but admire her for a moment.

When he said, "You look real nice, Bianca," she felt her heart turning somersaults. He'd never paid her a compliment before, either with his mouth or with his eyes.

Bianca didn't have the touch with horses that Coleen seemed to have, but she was an experienced rider. He almost wished he'd saddled Spider, named for the spider-looking white star on her forehead. She was the bay colt Coleen had ridden. But for some reason, he'd simply not wanted Bianca riding the same horse Coleen had. It was silly, but it had influenced him when he went out to catch the horses.

They rode up a draw and onto the bench where they could ride as far and long as they liked. Luke couldn't help but think how much like a family they were, riding side by side across the sagebrush flats. He thought often of Jamie. They used to ride up there at least once a week except when she was pregnant with Monty and for a few weeks following his birth. He felt a stab of pain as he remembered, but for the first time since her tragic death, he didn't feel guilty. It felt good being with a woman and his son.

It was almost nine before they reached the ranch yard again, but it was still plenty light. They unsaddled the horses, curried them, treated each to a handful of oats, and led them to the pasture. As they returned to the yard, Luke hoisted Monty onto his shoulders, and walked with his big black hat in one hand. "Thanks for letting me come up tonight," Bianca said as they neared her car. "You guys are so fun to be with."

"Dad, I'm hungry. Are we going to town to eat?" Monty asked after Luke had put him back on the ground.

Luke had been trying to work up the nerve all night to ask Bianca to dinner. All he'd needed was Monty's prodding. "Bianca, it's been fun having you up, and Monty and I were wondering if you'd like to have dinner with us tonight, in town."

Bianca couldn't think of anything she'd rather do. "I'd love to," she said, hoping she didn't sound as excited as she felt. Now that Luke was finally showing some interest in her, she didn't want to scare him away.

They went to the Country Kitchen on the west end of town, partly because Luke would have been most uncomfortable treating Bianca to dinner with Coleen as their waitress. The excuse he gave Bianca was that Cowan's closed earlier and it was getting rather late. The dinner was relaxing, and Luke enjoyed the company. Monty was his usual boisterous, cute self, and Bianca spent much of the time entertaining him. And Monty loved every minute of it.

That night Luke had a lot to think about. He hadn't had such a pleasant evening in four years. And somehow he'd finally come to feel that Jamie approved. Only one thing marred the evening for Luke. Despite his best efforts, he kept thinking of Coleen Whitman.

CHAPTER 5

Several days had passed and Luke had hit a dead end on finding the true identity of Coleen. But not at all discouraging was the progress made on getting her a court-ordered name so she could obtain a social security number, a driver's license, and other things she needed to live a normal life.

Coleen's employer, upon Luke's assurance of a social security number coming, allowed Coleen to keep working, but her money was held pending the court's order. In the meantime, what little money she had was dwindling away. She lived as frugally as she could, but even with very low rent and no car expenses or insurance, she was getting worried about what she'd do if she ran completely out of money.

Finally, three weeks after arriving in Duchesne, Coleen made an appearance in district court, and the order was signed that made her a real, identifiable person. It had taken the testimony of a doctor, notarized affidavits from Joe and Rick in New Mexico, and a lot of pro bono work by the county attorney. A couple of days later she had a social security number, and finally she was able to receive pay from her employer.

During those weeks, Coleen saw less and less of Luke, and she was aware that he'd gone out with Bianca two or three times. She knew that what he was doing was reasonable, even sensible, but she couldn't help how she felt about him. Once she had identification, she thought maybe it was time to move on.

When Luke and Bianca came together to the café for dinner one evening, she made up her mind. The next morning she packed her

few belongings and walked to Cowan's Café where she told them
something had come up and she felt it was best if she left Duchesne.
She told her boss that she'd send him an address where he could send
her final paycheck, called the manager of the apartments to tell him
she was leaving, and then walked uptown to meet the bus.

* * *

Luke couldn't help but see the hurt in Coleen's eyes when he and
Bianca had eaten dinner there the night before. And it kept him
awake much of the night. So when he rolled out of bed that Thursday
morning, he decided he'd go see her as soon as he got off work and
invite her to help him with his cattle on Saturday.

But when he stopped in at Cowan's for an early lunch, he was
surprised to learn that Coleen had been in earlier and told them she
was quitting and leaving town. "Please don't fill her job," he pled. "If
you'll give me a day, I'll see if I can get her to come back." He skipped
lunch and hurried to the bus stop where he learned that the bus had
left just a few minutes earlier.

He called the sheriff and told him he needed the rest of the day
off. Then he went home, leaped into his bullet-ridden black Dodge
Ram, and headed west on Highway 40.

The bus had already stopped in Heber before he got there, but it
appeared that Coleen hadn't gotten off there. He hurried on to Park
City where he just missed her. He passed the bus as he came down
Parley's Canyon just a few miles from Salt Lake City. He felt a smile
cross his face. He wondered what she'd say when she stepped off the
bus in the downtown depot and saw him waiting there.

* * *

Sitting on the bus, Coleen was experiencing that familiar churn in
her stomach that had accompanied her for the three months
following her accident, the three months before she stepped off the
bus in Duchesne and met Luke Osborne. She'd loved the little town,
but her feelings for Luke were not something she needed right now,
and they certainly weren't something he wanted. So as hard as it was,

she was headed to nowhere again. At least she had an identification now. It would be easier to find work again and a place to live.

She gazed out the window at the traffic. Normal people, people who knew who they were and where they were headed, crowded the busy freeway. She supposed that every one of them knew where they'd sleep that night. She had no idea where she would. They all knew what their destinations were, but she knew only that her ticket was good to Salt Lake.

But then, she could just get another one and keep going. If she went far enough, she could sleep on the bus. That would be one less worry for right now.

Coleen tried not to think of Luke, but when a black Ram that looked just like his passed the bus she could hardly stand it. She could picture him sitting behind the steering wheel, his black cowboy hat pulled low over his forehead, and she wanted to cry.

But she didn't. Coleen was strong, and she didn't need anyone else to help her make it in this world. She had needed Luke, but now that she had a legal name, she could make it on her own. She'd be just fine, she told herself. But for the rest of the ride to the bus depot in downtown Salt Lake, she couldn't get the black truck off her mind or the man from Duchesne who drove one just like it.

* * *

Luke watched as a smelly Greyhound pulled into the depot. He was sure this was the one Coleen was riding. He wondered what he'd say when Coleen stepped off. How could he convince her to come back to Duchesne with him without making her think that he was interested in her . . . in a romantic way? He was interested in her, but, well . . . why was he interested in her? What was he even doing here? He had no right to tell her what to do. He was interfering in her life. He'd even called Twin Rivers Apartments and asked them to hold her room, told them she might be coming back.

What was he thinking? Perhaps he better just turn on his heels right now and pretend he'd never come on this irrational trip. He did turn, and he was almost to the door when he turned back for just one little peek.

Coleen was staring at him, standing just a few feet from the door of the bus. Their eyes met. She smiled and his heart melted. He started back toward her. She took a few tentative steps in his direction, then suddenly bolted for the ticket counter.

He didn't run, but he hurried. When he stepped behind her, she was just telling the ticket agent that she would like a ticket to Los Angeles. Luke surprised himself when he said over her shoulder, "Never mind that, sir. She's changed her mind."

Coleen spun around. "What do you think you're doing?" she asked. He knew she was trying to sound angry, but the look in her eyes told him she wasn't, and he sighed in relief.

"I came to give you a ride back to Duchesne," he said. "You don't need to run anymore. Give yourself a chance and maybe you'll find that being Coleen Whitman isn't such a bad thing."

She felt like she had to argue. "Luke, I don't belong in that town of yours."

"Oh, so where do you belong?" he asked.

"That's not fair."

"I wasn't trying to be fair. I just think you didn't land there entirely by accident. Give it a chance," he urged.

"Luke, I owe you a lot. Thanks to you, I at least have a legal name. I can get a job. I can try to make a life for myself. And maybe someday, I might remember who I really am," she said.

As she said that she wondered now if she even wanted to remember. She almost wished she could quit worrying about who she used to be, and literally start fresh. But she knew she'd always wonder who she'd been, who she'd known, perhaps even who she'd loved . . . or who she hated or feared. Remembering what the New Mexico authorities had told her about the four-wheeler she was apparently fleeing, she wondered what she might have done to make someone want to hurt her? Perhaps some things were better off lost than found.

Luke was watching her intently, wondering what thoughts were running through her mind. He longed to take her in his arms. But what would Jamie think about that? Coleen almost certainly wasn't a member of the Church, and that was important to him. Bianca was, and she was nice, but . . .

"What would I do if I went back?" Coleen asked.

"What you were doing."

"What if I can't get my job back. I sort of left without giving much notice," she said.

Luke was hopeful. She was at least considering it. He grinned at her. "I told them they should save it for you," he admitted.

"Luke!" she scolded. But she had nothing else to say in protest.

"So, I guess you better come hop in my truck. You have a job waiting," he said.

She smiled briefly. "But I don't have a place to live. I . . . ."

Luke was grinning again. "You didn't," Coleen said, amazed and appalled.

"I did."

The smile she gave him now was the one he liked so much. She was so pretty when she smiled like that. "So let's get going," he suggested.

"I don't know," she said hesitantly as the smile faded.

"Hey, I'll be checking my cows next week. I could sure use some help. And Spider needs to be ridden."

"Spider?"

"Yeah, didn't I tell you her name?" Luke asked. "She was the bay you rode. Come on, I could use your help." *And your company,* he thought wistfully.

Coleen was out of arguments. A day on a horse, with Luke . . . that alone was worth returning to Duchesne. Anyway, she really wanted to go back, even though she knew that there would be pain— pain when she saw Luke and Bianca together.

She only had one little bag. Luke took it from her hand. Then, to make sure she was really coming, he took her by the hand. They walked to his truck where she stopped and stared. Her face went very pale. "Luke, are those bullet holes?" she asked.

He shrugged.

"Were you in this truck when it was shot at?" she asked, shocked. She'd heard about the shoot-out, but she hadn't realized he'd been in his own truck and that it had been hit several times. The thought made her tremble.

"I was in it part of the time," he said lightheartedly. "And I was tumbling out of the door when one or two hit. I'm really not sure, it all happened so fast."

"Oh, Luke, why would someone want to do this to you?" she asked. The fact that she'd been shot at herself was part of that past she didn't remember.

"He's a drug dealer. And he knows I'll get him someday and put him away." As he spoke, the anger he still felt seeped into his voice.

"There are lots of drug dealers. Why are you so keen on getting this one?" Coleen asked.

Luke opened the door for her. She climbed in, but instead of shutting the door, he said, "Do you really want to know?"

"Yes."

"I can't prove it was him, but I'd know Victor Hampton's voice anywhere. He's the man who killed Jamie—" He paused. "You've probably heard Jamie was my wife." At her solemn nod he continued, not wanting to discuss that just yet. "Anyway, he only served a few months for what he did. He needs to be behind bars," Luke said with a grimace. "Now, let's talk about happier things."

He shut her door, rounded the front of the truck, and climbed in beside her. "I missed lunch," he said. "Care to go somewhere and eat?"

Luke made a decision while they were having a late lunch. He would invite Coleen to go to church with him on Sunday. And she'd say she didn't have a dress. And he'd say he'd like to buy her one. And he'd do just that, and she'd go with him to church. He wanted to see more of her. He knew that, but he also knew that the Church had to be part of any relationship with any woman he might choose to date, now that he was finally at that point.

They were back in the truck when he said, "Coleen, I'd really like it if you'd go to church with me on Sunday, with Monty and me that is."

Coleen didn't even look over at him. She'd love to go with him anywhere he wanted her to, but she didn't have a dress. She didn't say anything.

So Luke said it for her. "You don't have a dress."

She nodded, looked over at him and smiled, then said, "And that really is a problem, Luke."

"Not one that can't be solved. Let's go shopping," he suggested.

She argued that she'd eventually be able to buy one for herself. Then she'd love to go to his church with him. But he was not content to wait. So he bought her a dress. And he bought her some shoes. And he bought her a few other things she needed to be a proper lady at church. And she promised herself she'd make it up to him someday—when she could.

* * *

When Luke didn't return to the office, Bianca wondered what had happened to him. She didn't want the sheriff to get the wrong idea, so she didn't ask him, although she knew Luke wouldn't take the day off without at least checking in with Sheriff Robinson. Instead, she drove up past Luke's ranch as soon as she got off work. His patrol car was there, but his black truck wasn't. She drove by his parents' house in town. Monty was playing in the yard, but Luke's truck was nowhere to be seen. She couldn't imagine where he could be.

When she walked into her apartment, Liz had news. "Hey, guess who left town today."

Bianca could not have cared less who left town today. She was worried about Luke and afraid he was off on his own trying to find Victor Hampton again.

"Coleen Whitman did," Liz said, anxious to see the look that bit of news would put on Bianca's face.

She was not disappointed. "Yes!" Bianca said, throwing her fist in the air. Then she tried to act more ladylike. "I hope she finds some-place where she can be happy."

"I was hoping you'd suggest that we go out to eat tonight as a sort of little celebration," Liz said slyly.

"Why not?" Bianca agreed. "Let's go to Cowan's. It'll be nice to be able to eat there without worrying about seeing *Miss Whitman*. I know this is awful, Liz, but I just know Luke likes her. He's been so much fun lately, but that girl has haunted me. I'm glad she's gone."

"Glad enough to buy tonight?" Liz joked.

"Sure, why not. Luke Osborne will be buying me dinner quite a bit now. So I can afford to buy for you tonight."

They were almost through eating when Bianca asked the waitress if she knew who would be taking Coleen's place now that she was gone.

"Oh, I don't think they're looking for anyone. Luke asked them to keep her job open. I guess he went after her," the young waitress revealed.

Bianca's world came crashing down around her. She lost her appetite and couldn't eat another bite. She felt betrayed and small. It was so embarrassing.

Liz tried to comfort her. "Hey, he probably just feels responsible for her," she suggested to Bianca.

"That's a big comfort," Bianca said morosely.

"Well, it might be true. You can't give up. After all, she's not even a member of the Church."

"As far as we know," Bianca amended.

"Hey, you know Luke," Liz said. "He'd never marry anyone who couldn't bring Monty up in the Church. It would never happen."

Bianca just shook her head. "Then why did he go chasing after her? Hey, will you hurry and finish? I want to get out of here."

By the time the two friends got back to their apartment, Bianca had worked up a head of steam. "Liz," she said, "if that woman thinks she's got even a chance with Luke, she's got a surprise coming. I intend to marry him and nobody is going to get in my way!"

"That's the spirit," Liz said. "I knew you wouldn't give up. You're much too determined to let a little setback like this get you down."

Liz was right. Bianca Turner was very determined. And if she had to, she could be a fighter.

Right now, with Luke Osborne's romantic future in the balance, she had to fight.

* * *

Bianca was not the only person concerned with Luke Osborne's future. Nor was she the only one willing to fight over it. Victor Hampton was disappointed when he learned that Luke had come out of the carefully planned ambush without a scratch. It would be more difficult than ever to try something like that again, but he had to take care of the detective. He knew that Luke was watching him, keeping track of his every move through informants and otherwise. And that was keeping Victor from making a huge profit making and selling his meth.

He knew that he could simply pick up stakes and move to another county, but he was sure that wouldn't make a lot of difference to Luke. The cop had a vendetta, and he'd find a way to haunt Vic wherever he went. Anyway, he really couldn't afford to move. Business wasn't good because too many of his former customers were afraid of Luke and had shifted their business elsewhere.

Victor would never admit it to anyone, but he was just a little intimidated by Luke. The man seemed to have good luck; if he didn't have, he would have been dead. But Victor had an idea, one that could make things rough on Luke and yet keep Victor from having to confront him directly. There was a way to hurt Luke, and if he was really careful and didn't rely on any but the most faithful of his small circle of friends, Victor could give Luke enough things to worry about that he'd forget Victor, allowing him to finally make a big score. Then he could afford to move far enough away that Luke wouldn't be a problem anymore.

He'd hurt Luke once and he hadn't even intended it. This time he would intend it. And Luke wouldn't have any idea it was Victor causing him all his problems, no idea at all.

CHAPTER 6

A fax had come through for Luke. Bianca, who checked all incoming faxes, read it quickly and couldn't suppress the gloating smile on her face. She immediately stepped down to Sheriff Robinson's office and said, "Do you know where Luke is today? A fax just came in that he needs to see right away."

The sheriff looked up from his desk. "Call dispatch," he said. "I haven't seen him this morning."

Bianca knew she should have asked the sheriff to read the fax, but then he'd tell Luke what it contained, and she wanted to be the one to hand it to Luke, to watch him read it, and to see his face when he got to the critical part. Luke wouldn't like it one bit; she knew that. But she also knew he'd do what had to be done. And that thought made her day.

* * *

Luke didn't like what he was seeing near the edge of the pasture belonging to a farmer in Altonah, an agricultural area in the northern part of the county. He'd gone out first thing that morning upon receiving a phone call at home from the agitated property owner.

"She was one of my best cows," Luke was told. "What in the world's going on here?"

Luke was on his knees beside the big Herford's mutilated carcass. "I don't have any idea, but whoever did this didn't want the meat," Luke observed. "I'm afraid this has the look of something that might have been done by a satanic cult." He rose to his feet. "I'd like to take a few pictures, and then I guess you can get rid of the carcass."

He'd heard of something like this happening quite a number of years ago, but it was new in Luke's personal experience. He hoped it was an isolated incident but feared that he might see more. He spent the next hour taking pictures and scanning the area for tire tracks and footprints. He found the tracks of a pair of tennis shoes of some sort, but did not find anything else. He shot pictures of the tracks and then gathered up his equipment and left the farmer to stew over his misfortune.

The sheriff was as concerned as Luke when filled in on the mutilated cow incident. He remembered well when a similar thing had occurred years before. Several places had been found in the county where a group had clearly been practicing some kind of satanic rituals. They were all in abandoned buildings, often in the basements of such places. No clear evidence had ever linked the mutilated cattle to the locations where the rituals had taken place, and no suspects had ever been found. He feared that the same thing was repeating itself now.

"We've got to give this a high priority," Sheriff Robinson told Luke. "Nothing gets under the skin of the farmers and ranchers in the area like this does. I hope we can find out who's doing it and end it quickly."

* * *

Bianca had no idea why Luke had been so agitated when he came in and walked past her office without so much as saying hello to her. Whatever it was, the sheriff and Luke were taking their time discussing it. And in the meantime the revealing fax for Luke was practically burning a hole in her desk. She couldn't wait to get it into Luke's hands. Whatever it was that had him and the sheriff tied up behind closed doors couldn't possibly be as important as the fax that had come in from a city police detective in Indiana.

She looked up when she heard the sheriff's door open, but instead of the sheriff and Luke coming out, it was the chief deputy going in. The door was shut again and another hour passed. When they did finally come out, Luke went straight into his little office. By the time she got there he was on the phone. She waved the fax at him and mouthed, "You'll want to see this right away."

He cupped his hand over the phone and said, "Thanks, Bianca. Just drop it right here. I'll get to it when I can. Something critical has come up and I'm working on it right away."

Afraid that she might not get to see his face when he read it, she dropped it right in front of him and said, "This is critical. It's very important that you read it right now."

Luke was annoyed at Bianca. He had a lot on his mind. "Yeah, thanks," he told her without even glancing down at the paper she'd dropped in front of him. "This is important too."

She suddenly wondered if he'd already learned what was on the fax. She didn't know how, but that must be it. He did seem awfully upset, as well he should be. She left, convinced that he was working on the case the fax referred to, and she began to hum.

* * *

Before the day was over, every deputy in the department had been notified to be on the lookout for satanic cult activities. If they found anything at all suspicious, they were to call either Luke or the sheriff directly. Luke also made several calls to other counties, but nothing like the mutilated cow incident had cropped up anywhere else. At least, not yet. He also did some research on the Internet about satanic cults and how they operated. It was a most distasteful subject, and he didn't enjoy having to deal with it. He only read what information he felt he needed to know, then wrote a report on the cow he'd seen and pushed himself back from the desk, ready to leave for the day.

The fax from Indiana was now buried beneath a pile of papers, and Luke never thought another thing about it. Most of the staff was gone by the time Luke left. He picked up Monty at his folks' place and headed home, tired and worried. He kept hoping that this strange new case would turn out to be an isolated incident, but he'd barely gotten to the house when the phone rang. The sheriff wanted him to head for Neola, in the far northeastern part of the county.

"Better get there before dark, Luke, so you can have a good look at the cow, but it sounds like a repeat of what we had this morning," Sheriff Robinson said.

So back Monty went to his grandparents, and Luke hurried to Neola, wondering what he was getting into. "Just found her a few hours ago," the elderly farmer told Luke. "Never seen nothing quite like it. She wasn't an old cow, wasn't even sick, but she's dead all right."

To Luke's dismay, the cow was mutilated in so much the same manner as the one from that morning that he groaned. Again he found footprints, but they led back to a well-traveled road. Although he couldn't identify any tire tracks, the footprints were like the ones in Altonah. He couldn't know for sure until he had a chance to get the pictures he'd taken at both scenes developed and compare them, but he was almost certain it was the work of the same twisted person.

The next morning when he entered the office, Bianca met him. "What did you find out?" she asked him urgently.

"Nothing much yet, but it's happened again," he said, thinking she was referring to the mutilation cases he was working on. He figured she'd probably seen his report already as it was her responsibility to proofread all the reports before they were finalized for signature. Bianca was efficient and kept things caught up very well. So he told her what happened. "The second cow looked just like the first one."

Bianca looked thoroughly confused. Luke chuckled. "I'm sorry, I guess you probably don't know that I went to Neola last night on another mutilated cow call."

That did nothing to clear the confusion from her face. She hadn't yet seen the first report, let alone heard of the second incident. Luke figured that out fairly quickly and said, "I'm sorry, Bianca. I thought you knew about the cow problem. I entered a report just before I left yesterday."

Bianca shook her head. "Who do you think I am, Wonder Woman? I've barely had time to open the mail this morning, let alone get to the reports from yesterday. I was referring to that alarming fax from Indiana. I can't believe you haven't done anything about that yet."

"What fax?" he asked, then he remembered. "Oh, yeah, that one. I'm sorry, I didn't ever get it read. This other thing—"

He didn't get to finish because Bianca cut him short. "Hey, you need to read it, Luke. It's critical."

"Okay, okay," he said, "I'll read it."

Bianca managed to smile. "Good. Let me know if I can help."

He couldn't imagine what she meant, but it piqued his curiosity. He left her standing at the door to her office and started down the hallway, determined to find and read the fax that had Bianca so worked up. But the sheriff saw him as he passed his open doorway and called out, "Luke, come on in. What did you find last night?"

Bianca watched with dismay as Luke entered Sheriff Robinson's office and shut the door. She was even more upset when the sheriff buzzed her a minute later and asked her to locate the chief deputy and have him join them as soon as possible. By the time she left for lunch, Luke still hadn't read the fax, and it was making her mad. She read Luke's report and concluded rightly enough that the mutilated cow case was nothing in comparison with the critical information contained in the fax. She was wishing now that she'd let the sheriff read it, but she hadn't; if she told him about it now, he'd be angry that she hadn't insisted he see it immediately. All she could do was hope Luke read it in the next few minutes. If he didn't, she'd see that he did as soon as she got back from lunch. She'd read it to him if she had to. It was that important to her.

She and Judy, one of the other girls in the office, had lunch together at Cowan's a little before one. It appeared that Coleen was now working an earlier shift since she was the one who waited on them. The very sight of the woman made Bianca bristle all over. *If only Luke would read that fax!*

* * *

Coleen wasn't angry at anyone, however, she wondered what had upset Bianca so badly. Had she heard that Luke invited her to help him gather cows on Monday? Bianca was jealous! That had to be it.

And that almost made Coleen laugh. Nobody knew how insecure she felt. It was such a nightmare not being able to remember anything about her past. And suddenly feeling like she was having to compete with the sheriff's secretary didn't exactly give her confidence. But on the other hand, the only bright spot in her life right now was Luke Osborne. And after he'd gone all the way to Salt Lake to bring her back, she wasn't about to spurn any attention he might decide to give her.

When she asked for Bianca's order, the lady glared at her, and for a moment Coleen wondered if she'd even permit her to take the order. But she finally spat it out, and Coleen hurried back to the kitchen. The more she thought about it, the more annoyed it made her. She hadn't gone chasing after Luke. And anyway, Bianca didn't have any ironclad claim on him. So why should she let the girl upset her? She made up her mind to simply ignore the looks she got from Bianca and try to be as positive and friendly as she could.

Her resolve didn't last long.

When she took the salads to Bianca's table a few minutes later, she smiled and asked, "Can I get either of you anything else?"

"Not hardly," Bianca hissed. "I know all about you, lady. I know who you really are!"

"You . . . you do?" Coleen stammered.

"Yes I do!" Bianca shot back, ignoring the questioning looks she was getting from the woman she was having lunch with. "And so does Detective Osborne."

A few moments and some harsh words later, as Coleen fled in tears to the kitchen, Judy said, "You really don't like her, do you?"

"No, I really don't," Bianca agreed. "And when you find out what Luke and I know, you won't either."

"So Luke really does know who she is?" the other lady pressed.

"He should by now," Bianca said, hoping that Luke had finally read the fax. "He got a fax from Indiana. I put it on his desk, but he was busy at the moment. If he's taken enough time from this stupid dead-cow business to read it, then he knows who she is," she said. "And he'll be as concerned as I am."

"And who is she?" the other woman asked, her curiosity getting the best of her.

Bianca told her and smiled to herself at the reaction she got.

* * *

Luke had to turn back from the door to answer his phone, his mind still half on the call he'd just received from the deputy in Fruitland.

Another upset farmer.

Another suspiciously dead cow.

He was about to ignore the call when he thought it might have something to do with these bizarre new cases he was working on. But he forgot all about them when he recognized the distressed voice of Coleen on the phone. He could tell that she was crying. She could barely talk. "Coleen, what's happened?" he asked her tenderly.

The distress sounded more like anger when Coleen managed to choke out, "Why didn't you tell me you knew?"

He couldn't imagine what she was talking about. "Know what, Coleen?" he asked.

Finally, anger seemed to help her find her voice. She said very clearly, "You told me you'd let me know the second you learned anything about my past. It seems you know exactly who I am and haven't even bothered to give me a call."

Luke was reeling. He had no idea what she was talking about. "Coleen, wait a minute. I don't know what you're talking about. I haven't learned anything . . ."

Coleen cut him off, her voice now as cold as the Arctic. "Well, Bianca knows and she says you do too," he was informed.

"Bianca knows who you are?" he asked, and then it dawned on him—the fax from Indiana that he had yet to read.

"Just a second, Coleen, and please, don't be angry. Bianca handed me a fax yesterday. I was working on a case and was on the phone, and it got buried before I had a chance to read it," he said urgently as he frantically dug through the papers on his desk.

He found it as Coleen said, her voice suddenly contrite, "I'm sorry, Luke. But she said you knew, and she made it sound bad."

He was reading now, and it was bad!

He had to follow up on this fax. But the rancher in Fruitland was waiting for him. And he had to get Coleen here, calm her down, and not let her run again before he had a chance to investigate the disturbing information he'd just read. He didn't want to lie to Coleen, but he also couldn't tell her what the fax revealed. She'd run for sure then, and he couldn't let that happen. So he did the only thing he could. He stalled.

"Coleen, I haven't got time to deal with the fax now. I buried it somewhere," he told her. "I'm working on a very difficult case right now and a rancher in Fruitland is waiting to meet me in just a few minutes. Please, calm down, and I'll find out what Bianca's blabbing about as soon as I get back to town. And I'll call you as soon as I find out more."

But could he afford to not talk to her right now? To ignore her could be dangerous. What if she decided that he hadn't been totally forthcoming with her? What if Bianca said something more to her? What if Coleen thought he really did know what was in that fax? And what if she suddenly recalled her past?

Or worse yet, had never really ever forgotten it, and decided to bolt right now?

He made up his mind. He had to get to her before he did anything else. The mutilated cows would have to wait. "Luke, please, you won't forget, will you?" Coleen pled.

No, he wouldn't forget. How could he? What he'd just read had put him in a tailspin. Luke was devastated.

"What time do you get off today?" he asked, trying to sound as calm as he could under the circumstances.

"In about fifteen minutes," she answered. "Are you sure you can't talk to me before you go to Fruitland?"

He was sure he could, but he didn't want to sound too eager. "Well, it's a pretty important case," he hedged.

"Please, Luke," Coleen begged. She sounded so sincere. What he knew of her and what he'd just read didn't fit, but the fax was so conclusive.

"Okay, Coleen. I'll come down now," he told her.

He hung up, in a cold sweat, then he dialed the number on the fax. The Indiana detective who'd sent it was out of his office. Luke left him a message and headed for his patrol car. He checked on to the radio as soon as he got in his vehicle. The dispatcher said, "Mike Ten, you need to call Mike Eight on his cell phone immediately."

What now? Luke wondered. He could only do one thing at a time. He picked up his cellular phone and punched in Deputy Samuelson's number. "That you, Luke?" John Samuelson asked after the first ring.

"Yeah, what's up, John?"

"You said to let you know if I found anything suspicious," John began.

Luke wanted to scream. *Not another cow!*

"What do you have?" he asked, suppressing all the bottled up anger and frustration.

"Well, I think I found a place where somebody's been doing some kind of satanic ritual. It's just out of Myton," he said. "It's an abandoned barn. The owner called a little while ago. He was pretty upset. Said somebody's been going in there and doing weird stuff from the looks of it."

Luke tried to focus on what he was being told. Myton was between Roosevelt and Duchesne. If this tied in with the mutilations, it would be just one more area of the county affected. This thing might be bigger than he or the sheriff had thought. And they'd imagined plenty.

"Have you been out there?" Luke asked.

"I'm headed that way now," John told him.

"Good, try to preserve the scene. Especially look for footprints. Take some pictures if you find anything the owner can't identify. And try to keep the owner from messing up any more evidence than he might already have," Luke instructed.

"Okay, but can you come over right away? You'll know more what we're looking for than I will."

"I'm on a matter right now that can't wait, John. But keep the place secure. I'll get back with you."

Deputy Samuelson didn't sound very satisfied with Luke's response, but what could Luke do? Everything was hitting him at once. He punched in the number of the deputy in Fruitland. "Stall the owner if you can," Luke told him a minute later. "I've got something here in town that simply can't wait. Take some pictures, look for footprints. I'll come when I can."

How in the world could he take care of all these things at once? Well, there was one thing he could do. He could take Coleen with him. Or he could put her in jail. But the fax, as serious as it was, wasn't enough to make an arrest on. He had to be sure first.

Coleen was waiting outside the café when he pulled up. His heart turned over in his chest. She was so remarkably attractive. Worse still, she looked completely innocent and harmless. In fact, she looked like she needed protection—his protection. How could that detective in Indiana possibly be right?

Coleen saw him and ran right to the patrol car. He double parked as she hurriedly opened the door and jumped in. Her eyes were red and swollen. And the smile that Luke liked was so far gone he wondered if he'd ever see it again. He drove off, still debating what to do. As he passed the highway that led north to the combined jail, sheriff's office, and courthouse, he guessed he knew what he was going to do.

"Where are we going?" she asked.

"To Fruitland," he responded.

"Why?" she asked. "I thought you were going to tell me who I am."

"When I know for sure, I will," he said, trying desperately to smile at her. "But in the meantime, I have an appointment with a dead cow."

Luke had hoped he could bring even a shadow of that wonderful smile to her face, but she saw no humor in the situation. Indeed she was right, it wasn't a laughing matter.

CHAPTER 7

For the first time that day, Luke felt relief. "This is the work of a mountain lion," he said after a short examination. He'd known the instant he saw the heifer that it wasn't the same as the others. It was a much younger, smaller animal, and it was partially eaten.

The animal's owner wasn't relieved, and Luke didn't blame him. Luke told him how to make contact with the state trapper. "He'll get the cougar," Luke assured him.

Coleen was horrified. At least, she certainly appeared that way, and after what Luke had read in the fax from Indiana, her reaction didn't make sense. Could she really be the kind of person who would have done those things? It just didn't seem like her at all. She was such a caring person. Wasn't she?

After leaving the rancher to talk with the other deputy, Luke said, "You can't imagine how relieved I am that it was a cougar."

Coleen stared at him, clearly baffled. "How can you be relieved?" she asked him. "How would you feel if it were one of your heifers?"

Luke was actually able to chuckle. "I'd hate it," he admitted, "but after what I've seen the past couple of days, this was nothing. Cougars will occasionally do something like this, that's according to nature's plan. For men to do what they did to those other cows is not."

"What did they do?" she asked. "And what's the difference between a mountain lion and a cougar?"

After explaining that they were two names for the same breed of wildcat, he briefly described for her what he'd seen at the site of the two cattle mutilations. She seemed to be absolutely horrified. *If she has her memory, and if she is who that detective in Indiana claims she is, this shouldn't be all that abhorrent to her,* Luke thought.

His next stop was the farm outside of Myton, close to an hour's drive from the place in Fruitland. Coleen seemed to be a little more relaxed, but when she tried to bring up what he'd learned, he put her off, and she got just a little angry with him. So most of the ride was in stony silence.

Once they were out of the car again, Coleen's mood lightened up a little. Luke's did not. There were quite a number of discernable footprints around the old barn. And one of them was, at least in Luke's opinion, the same as some he'd found near the other cows. There was at least one other set of prints. But he couldn't find where a car had been near the barn. Whoever was doing this didn't mind leaving footprints, but for some strange reason, they did mind leaving tire tracks, even though it required them to walk fairly long distances to avoid it. Inside, in a dark corner of the barn, a small area was decorated with graffiti—symbols of satanic worship. Partially burnt candles were in various places throughout the decorated area. But worst of all, a crude altar showed signs of very recent use.

Coleen, who Luke had felt he had to keep a close eye on, was allowed to come in with him. The color drained from her face when she stepped near the altar. She quickly stepped away, standing near the entrance to the barn. "Are you going to be all right?" he asked her a moment later as he was going to his car for equipment that could help him find fingerprints.

"I'm okay. This is just so awful," she said.

There are worse things, he thought to himself. And when he finished here, he planned to see if, in fact, she really did know about those *worse* things. Surely she didn't.

"And they come in here when it's dark?" she asked.

"I guess they do," he replied. And Coleen shuddered.

She followed him to the car, and he filled her hands with equipment, thinking maybe it was best to simply keep her busy. She seemed relieved to have something to do, and he found her quite helpful. John Samuelson also pitched in, and before long Luke was satisfied that the scene was processed as completely as he knew how to do so. But he was disappointed. There were no fingerprints anywhere, not even on the candles. And that bothered him. It just didn't seem reasonable that people who had so carelessly left footprints all over the place would be so careful not to leave fingerprints. He stored that concern away in his mind with the related question over tire tracks. Both could be explored later. There was always a reason for seemingly strange behavior, and once that reason was discovered, it usually wasn't so strange at all.

"Now can we get to the business of letting me know who I am?" Coleen asked him after they'd turned onto the highway and headed back to Duchesne.

"Shortly," he assured her. "First we will go right to the office where I can make some calls. I promise I'll let you know as soon as I actually *know* something."

"Thank you," she said.

"But don't get your hopes up. You may not learn anything," he added, wondering as soon as he'd said it why he had. His hopes were almost that they wouldn't learn anything.

* * *

Bianca was fuming. She'd just discovered that Luke was spending the afternoon working on his cattle cases and that he'd taken Coleen Whitman with him! She'd seen Luke pick her up in front of the café, and had been certain he was heading to the office with her. But when she got back from lunch, he'd never arrived. It wasn't until the deputy from Fruitland came in that she discovered where Luke had been.

She was outraged, and when the sheriff overheard her venting her anger on the deputy who'd brought the news to her, he called her into his office. "Bianca," Sheriff Robinson began, "what are you disturbing the work atmosphere over?"

Bianca started to act innocent and appalled, but the sheriff stopped her. "Now, I'm not the only one that's been noticing that Luke's personal life is taking its toll on *your* job. You may not think a bunch of old men can pick up on what's going on here, but ever since that Coleen girl has come into town you've been wearing dresses instead of jeans to work, and coming in late just so your hair and makeup are a little bit fancier. Now, jealousy doesn't suit a professional,

Bianca. I know that you've been dating Luke a little here lately, and I don't have a problem with that, but I also don't have a problem if he chooses to see anyone else. Please don't let your personal life interfere with your job."

He was right of course, and she should have taken her reprimand and said nothing. But Bianca was so incensed with the hold Coleen Whitman seemed to have on Luke that she just couldn't keep her mouth shut. "I'm sorry, Sheriff," she began, "but this isn't about Luke and me."

He raised an eyebrow. "It isn't?" he asked.

"No, it's about Luke and Coleen Whitman. She's a demon, and if Luke isn't careful he could get hurt."

"A demon," Sheriff Robinson said with a grin. "Now Bianca, if she's a demon and she's with Luke, and you care enough to be angry about it, it seems to me like this is still about you and Luke."

"But he's on duty," she said lamely.

"Yes, Luke's on duty. If Coleen's with him, which you seem to believe she is, then I guess I'll have to deal with him on that later. Now, I've said enough. I'll let you get back to work."

But Bianca wasn't through. "Sheriff, you don't understand. She's dangerous. She could hurt him."

The sheriff grew very serious. "That's a pretty heavy accusation you're making, Bianca. Would you care to explain?"

Bianca found herself backed into a corner, so she said, "There's a fax that came in about her. It's probably still on his desk. Read it and you'll know why I'm upset."

The sheriff rose to his feet and said, "Sounds like I better have a look."

When he didn't invite her to follow him to Luke's office, she slowly made her way back to her own. She hoped he'd find the fax. And she hoped he wouldn't notice when it had come. As she sat thinking about the whole situation, she found comfort in just one thing—Coleen was bad, as the sheriff was about to learn. And Luke would eventually wish he'd never taken the woman's word about her "amnesia." When it was all over, as Bianca was sure it would be, she'd be able to work on Luke again. She cared an awful lot for him, and felt she deserved his love more than a criminal Luke hardly knew.

The sheriff came in after only two or three minutes. He was carrying the fax in his hand. He looked like he'd aged in those few minutes. He sat down, rubbed his forehead like it was aching, and said, "I'm sorry, Bianca. You have a right to be upset. If this proves to be correct, Luke could in fact be in danger, and so could Monty."

Feeling vindicated should have made her feel better, but Bianca was instead feeling worse. Luke had allowed himself to get into a situation that could well bring harm to him and his son. She hated the very thought.

"Let's just hope it's not true," the sheriff continued after a moment of deep thought.

"Not true? What do you mean?" Bianca asked. "You read it. The man says it's got to be her. He says the picture is so close that he can't believe it could be anyone else. I just know . . ."

The sheriff raised a hand, cutting her off. "Bianca," he said patiently, "I know it looks almost irrefutable, but until it's proven don't be too sure. What if she was accused and then it turned out that she wasn't the woman that detective thinks she is? What if she not only isn't that person, but is someone who really does have amnesia? What would that do to Coleen?"

Bianca hadn't thought about that. But she still didn't think it likely that Coleen wasn't the terrible woman wanted for the abduction of two little children from a daycare center. But she conceded nonetheless. "It'd be awful. But I worry about Monty. What if—"

The sheriff cut her off and rose to his feet. "Yes, it would be awful, but let's not jump to conclusions. On the other hand, if it is her," he said, shaking the paper, "then I sure hope Luke's being careful."

After he'd left her office, Bianca sat at her desk staring at the wall. It hadn't even occurred to her that the detective who'd sent the fax might not be right. But it did occur to her now how angry Luke would be at her if the man wasn't.

She didn't worry long though. It was just too strange to be coincidence.

* * *

Coleen was sick with worry. She wanted so badly to know what Luke had learned. Did he really have an idea about her past? The way he was acting, she wasn't sure she wanted to know. What if she hadn't been a good person? She could hardly stand the suspense. When he pulled up outside the office, she dropped her head in her hands. Luke was such a decent guy, she hoped she was a decent girl.

Luke rounded the car and opened her door. "Come on, Coleen," he said as he watched her suspiciously. "Let's get this over with."

That sounded so ominous, but she did the only thing she could; she got out and walked with him into the large yellow building, dread hanging heavy on her heart.

He showed her to a room he called the squad room. "You wait here for a minute if you would," he said. "I've got some calls to make."

His voice was devoid of emotion or feelings of any kind. She had no way of knowing what he was thinking. She sat quietly, trying not to let herself worry too much. But it was so hard. The minutes seemed like hours and she kept glancing at her watch. She couldn't imagine what he was doing. She trusted him. She knew he wouldn't do something to hurt her . . . unless she deserved it. Oh, how she hoped she didn't.

Five minutes turned to ten. Ten turned to twenty. The woman who'd been with Bianca in the café when this latest nightmare had started kept walking past the door. *She is my guard*, Coleen decided. It was awful. She couldn't bear the suspense much longer. Gone were happy thoughts of riding out with Luke and Monty, working the cattle. Gone were happy thoughts of any kind. Why didn't he come back? She just wanted the torture to end.

* * *

Bianca was also tense. Luke hadn't spoken a word to her since his return to the office. When their eyes met he didn't glare or anything like that, he just seemed to look right through her. She'd been relieved when she heard he was here, but now she didn't know what to feel.

Judy was also nervous when she came in. The whole office seemed strained. "Where's she at?" Bianca asked, her dark eyes betraying her eagerness.

"Coleen?"

Bianca nodded.

"She's in the squad room. The sheriff asked me to look in on her occasionally."

"What's she doing?" Bianca wanted to know.

"Acting really nervous," Judy said. "But who wouldn't be?"

"Yeah, I guess you're right," Bianca said. "And what's Luke doing?"

"I don't know. He's been in his office most of the time. The sheriff's been in there with him for the past ten minutes," Judy said. Then, after watching Bianca's troubled face for a moment, she spoke again. "They both seem awfully serious. I think they know she's the one."

That made Bianca feel better. Or did it? She wasn't a cruel girl by nature, just a jealous one at the moment.

* * *

Luke considered the sheriff's question for a few seconds. It was the same thing he'd wondered about earlier and filed away for later consideration. He'd filled Sheriff Robinson in on the day's activities; both men were more worried than ever about the cult situation. The sheriff had asked Luke why he thought no attempt had been made to scuff the footprints. But both men also wondered about the culprit's seeming indifference to leaving footprints in the dirt around the crime scenes, and yet there was an absolute lack of fingerprints or tire tracks.

Luke finally said, "It's like they want us to find the shoes that left the tracks." As he talked, he pushed a picture around on his desk with his finger, refusing to look at it further.

Even as he said it, he knew it didn't make any sense. At least not in light of what they knew now. But of course, if and when they ever got the complete scenario, it would probably make perfect sense, at least from a criminal's perspective.

A call came in for Luke and he grabbed the phone. The mutilation cases were instantly filed away again as the voice of a Detective Howie Blume came on the line. Luke punched the speaker phone button so the sheriff could hear, but he still kept the receiver to his ear. "Sorry it took me so long to get back to you," the Indiana detective said. "Do you have her in custody?"

"We do," Luke answered, offended by the term *custody*. He still considered Coleen his friend. He wanted her to be his friend. But he was afraid that was simply not to be.

"Good. And did you get the picture I e-mailed you?"

Luke pushed the picture across the desk again, and then without looking down at it, said, "Yeah, I got it. Thanks."

"Think it's her?" Detective Blume asked.

Luke really didn't want to answer. He just couldn't imagine Coleen Whitman ever hurting a child, let alone kidnapping one. He couldn't answer the question directly, so he said evasively, "It bears a strong resemblance, but it's not all that clear either."

"I take it you're not sure," Howie said.

The sheriff was nodding his head, but Luke was shaking his. Of course, Howie couldn't see either one of them from his desk in Indiana.

"Wrong color hair," Luke said.

"She may have changed it," Howie reminded him. "Is your girl the approximate height and weight as the one we're after?"

"Yes," Luke agreed reluctantly. "We haven't checked her exactly, but . . ."

Howie broke in. "We didn't either. Remember, we've never had her in custody. That's why we don't have prints. And she left none at the scene. Our whole case, if we get her back here, will be based on eyewitnesses and some other evidence."

"I see," Luke said. "Are there any other identifying features? I'd sure hate to accuse her unless I'm pretty sure she's the woman you're after."

"I'm real sure," Howie said. "Like I told you earlier, one of the gals in the office misplaced that flyer you sent. But when I was down in Indianapolis, they had one posted on a bulletin board. I recognized her instantly."

"I understand that," Luke said, "but again, are there any other—"

Howie cut him off with an expletive followed by, "There is! Why didn't I think of this sooner? A witness described a tattoo on her left shoulder, I believe. Does she still wear sleeveless blouses?"

"No, she wears western clothes," Luke said as hope dawned, faint for sure, but it could clear her.

Or condemn her.

"What kind of tattoo?" Luke asked.

"A small rosebud," came the reply. "And it's on the back of her shoulder. You can't see it if she's facing you."

"Is there anything else?" Luke asked. "You know, birthmarks or something like that?"

"Well, I know it's a little difficult to see, but she does have a small mole beneath her right eye. About an inch down."

Luke was suddenly very hopeful. He knew Coleen didn't have any moles on her face at all. He had memorized her face. "Coleen has no moles," he said.

That didn't phase Howie. "Those are easily enough removed. You might check for a small scar or something."

"Can you hold the line?" Luke asked eagerly. The tattoo and the mole. Those could be checked out, and he had to know.

* * *

Coleen looked up as Luke stepped into the squad room. "Sorry it's taken so long," he apologized.

"Do you know who I am?" she asked. The tension in her voice was upsetting.

"Not for sure," he said. "But you can help me. Do you have a tattoo on the back of either of your shoulders?" He was studying her face intently as he spoke. As he recalled, there was no mole beneath her right eye.

Coleen hesitated for only a moment, but that moment was like a kick in the teeth to Luke. Surely she knew and could answer without having to think about such a thing. When she spoke it was with further hesitation. "No, I don't think so. I know I don't have any on me where I can see them."

The sheriff stepped up. "Do you remember ever having received a tattoo anywhere on your body?"

"I don't remember anything, Sheriff."

"I'm sorry," he said, but he really wasn't. It had been intended as a trick question. She answered the way he expected—hoped for Luke's sake—she would, but if she'd simply said no, he'd have had reason to believe the whole amnesia story was fake.

"Would you like to look for yourselves?" she asked.

"No, but one of the gals will look for us," Luke answered grimly.

"Not Bianca," Coleen said fiercely.

"All right," Luke agreed before the sheriff had a chance to say otherwise.

The sheriff left to find Judy. Luke waited awkwardly until Coleen caught his eye. "Luke, is it good or bad if I have the tattoo?"

He looked down, then up again into those pretty but pained eyes. "Bad," he said. "Very bad."

"Will I be arrested for something if I do?" she pressed.

"Yes."

"What?"

"Let's wait on that question," he said.

She kept looking at him, holding his eyes with hers. "And do you think it's there?" she asked.

Luke faltered for a moment. He so wanted for it not to be. The mole wasn't, and that gave him a lot of hope. Finally he said, "I'm still planning on taking you to church Sunday. And I'm also counting on you to help us check our cows Monday. So's Monty."

For the life of him, Luke couldn't imagine how she could do it, but that wonderful smile of hers made a brief appearance.

Then Judy walked in. Without another word, Luke simply smiled at Coleen and then walked out. Coleen didn't wait for instructions, she simply removed the western blouse she was wearing and turned her back to Judy.

Judy moaned, and Coleen thought the whole world would end.

Meanwhile, Luke could hardly stand the wait. Bianca had joined them, and she was as anxious as Luke. A minute passed. Then two. *What is taking so long?* Luke wondered.

Then, finally, the door opened and Judy came out. Her eyes caught Bianca's. A message passed between them that Luke simply couldn't read. Bianca turned away. Luke watched her for a moment, unable to interpret anything from the way she walked down the hall.

Then he turned back to Judy. "Well?" he asked.

"You're quite a guy, Luke," she said with an unreadably sober face. "She told me what you said. She's going riding with you and Monty on Saturday."

"Judy," the sheriff said sternly.

"No tattoo," Judy said. "And I looked close. There's never been one. Poor Bianca, she feels so terrible." She hated to admit it, but she was more concerned for Bianca than for Coleen. She had so expected, in a way even hoped, to see the tattoo in place.

Luke was relieved beyond words, and he frankly didn't care right now how Bianca felt. He turned to Sheriff Robinson. "Will you go talk to Detective Blume? I think Coleen needs some support right now. Oh, and in case he presses you, there's no mole and no scar."

CHAPTER 8

When Luke walked into the room, Coleen was sitting at the long table, her head in her hands. "Hey, it's going to be all right," Luke said as cheerfully as he could muster.

Coleen looked up, "So I guess we still don't know who I am."

Luke smiled. "I know who you are. You're Coleen Whitman."

Coleen stood and came around the table toward Luke. "Judy said there was no tattoo and never had been when she examined me. But I could tell from the way she groaned that she'd figured there would be, and even hoped it."

Luke nodded, "I'm sorry. She's Bianca's friend, and Bianca seems to have a problem with you and I being friends."

Coleen was very serious. "Luke, I have no right to interfere in your life. I probably should never have let you talk me into coming back."

He shook his head. "I'm glad you did."

"So it's settled then? Am I for sure not this wanted woman, whoever she was?"

"For sure," he said. "No tattoo. No black hair. No mole beneath your right eye."

"Mole!" she exclaimed. "So that's why you were looking so closely at my face."

"That and because it's such a lovely face to look at," he told her, and he meant every word. He stepped closer to her, reached up and touched her face about an inch below the right eye. "Right here is where the mole was supposed to be." He grinned at her. "No mole, no scar, no tattoo, but a remarkable resemblance. She's not as pretty though."

"Do you have a picture of this other woman?" Coleen asked.

Luke nodded.

"May I see it?"

"Sure," he said as he impulsively reached out, put his arms around her, and pulled her close.

For a moment she tightened up, resisted, then she melted against him with a sigh and slipped her arms around him. It felt so good to her to be held by someone. And it also felt good to Luke. He hadn't held a woman like this since the morning of Jamie's death. And somehow with this woman, it felt right again.

But was it?

He still didn't know who she was. All he knew was who she was not.

* * *

The ringing of the phone slammed his head like a brick. Gil Stedman clamped his hands over his ears. The hangover was intense. He'd drunk hard liquor and popped pills the night before until he'd passed out. He wasn't even sure how he'd gotten back to the hotel. One of his new friends must have brought him here.

The phone kept ringing. Surely it'd stop soon. He didn't want to talk to anybody right now. But it didn't stop. Finally, in desperation, Gil rolled over on the bed and reached for the phone. He fumbled with it, finally gained control and lifted it to his ear. "Don't want to talk right now," he said and hung it back up.

That should hold them for a while, whoever it was. He rolled onto his back and closed his aching eyes. The phone caused them to pop open again. It rang and rang until he was more than just annoyed, he was angry. He finally picked it up again and said, "I told you, I don't want to talk to anyone right now."

Before he could hang up again, the person on the other end got his attention. "Shut up Gil, and listen," Judd Aspen barked.

How did Judd find him? He hadn't checked in with the man for days.

"I'm running out of patience, Gil," Aspen growled. "I expected you to have that girl taken care of by now. You're not even trying."

"I've been searching all over," Gil said defensively.

"Not for a week you haven't."

Gil looked nervously about him like he expected to find someone watching him from a hiding spot somewhere in the plush hotel room.

"Get to work, Gil, or you'll be removed and I'll have one of the other men find her."

Gil knew a real threat when he heard one. Aspen was powerful. And he'd seen the man follow through on threats before. But Gil didn't know where to go from here, and he realized with a start that he needed to focus on what Aspen was saying.

It was like Aspen was reading his foggy brain; the man was uncanny. "Go back to Colorado, back to Denver. You know she was there. You keep looking until you find out where she went from there, and then you follow her trail. Her picture is showing up in police stations all across the country."

That was news to Gil, but then, he tried to avoid such places. "Okay, I'll get on it," he said evenly, feeling angry that Aspen had someone checking his work.

"Today. Now!" Aspen shouted at him. "You work twenty hours a day if you have to, but you find that woman. And lay off the booze and drugs until you do."

Before Gil could say anything more the line went dead. And dead was exactly what he'd be if he didn't find Carly.

And that was what she would be when he did.

* * *

Bianca poured her heart out to Liz that night. And her faithful roommate listened silently. When Bianca had finished, Liz asked, "They're absolutely sure Coleen isn't that kidnapper?"

"That's what the sheriff said, right after he reminded me not to jump to conclusions in the future."

"What if they're wrong?"

"Even the cop that sent the fax and e-mail is convinced it isn't her. I guess they must be right," Bianca said.

"You don't sound very convinced to me," Liz countered softly. "You said Judy showed the picture to you, the one that was e-mailed to Luke. What did you think?"

"It was her," Bianca said. "Either her or a twin."

"Twin!" Liz exclaimed. "That's got to be it. Coleen's got a twin. And if the twin's that bad, then Coleen certainly can't be much different."

Bianca hadn't thought of that. But that had to be the answer. The girl in the picture had to be Coleen's twin. The resemblance was just too strong. "But if she is a twin, that still doesn't solve my problem. Coleen is still here, and she has her claws into Luke."

"Hey girl, you sound like you're giving up."

Bianca looked sadly at her roommate. "Luke didn't say one word to me today. He'll never ask me out again."

"Then you do the asking," Liz suggested. "Don't let her beat you."

Bianca nodded her head. "I know you're right. And I'm not giving up. For Monty's sake, I can't give up. That girl is not what she pretends to be, I just know it."

* * *

Bianca was not the only one who was considering the twin theory. Detective Howie Blume was at that very moment preparing a new flyer on his computer to send out to as many police departments in Indiana and the surrounding states as he could. Side by side on the flyer were the picture of the woman in Utah who was calling herself Coleen Whitman and the picture of his suspect. Under the suspect's picture, he typed that she was wanted for kidnapping. But under the other one, he indicated that her identity was needed to see if she could help locate her wanted twin sister. The poster also mentioned a reward. Then Howie warned that both women should be considered armed and dangerous.

Howie was convinced that the Utah woman was not his suspect. But he was equally convinced that she knew his suspect and that she'd somehow duped the authorities in Utah into believing that she'd lost her memory. The purpose of his flyer was to obtain whatever information was out there, and then to sort through it. He would have to decide later what to do about the woman in Utah, if indeed he concluded that she could help him capture the real suspect, her twin sister.

After he'd completed his work Howie sat back and studied it. Satisfied, he printed a copy and then headed to the printer's shop that did all the work for his department. The next morning thousands of flyers were in the mail.

* * *

Luke's breath was almost taken away when Coleen opened the door to her apartment that Sunday morning. She was radiant. He'd never seen her in makeup and a dress, and he liked what he saw. She smiled at him and said, "Good morning, Luke." Then she looked down at Monty who was holding Luke's hand. "And good morning, Monty," she added.

"You sure look nice," Luke said, unable to tear his eyes from her face.

"Thank you, Luke. Well, I guess I'm ready," she said. "But you'll have to bear with me today. I don't know if I've ever been in a church before."

"You'll be fine," he told her. Luke's mother had offered to attend his ward to help Coleen feel a little less lost. He told her that wasn't necessary and that he'd arranged for one of the members of the ward Relief Society presidency to see that Coleen was comfortable in their meeting, since he'd be away from her for that entire hour. Other than that, he'd be her constant companion, and he looked forward to it.

Coleen felt out of place, even though Luke assured her a dozen times that she didn't look out of place. And she was so confused by the things she heard. Somehow, she felt that religion must not have played a role in her life before her accident. If it had, surely it would be like with Luke's horses; it would seem familiar and come naturally.

When she told Luke that as they left the church house, he just laughed. "It can become natural," he told her. "All you have to do is let it."

"I think I'd like that, Luke. Maybe I'll go again sometime," she said.

"Next week," he suggested.

She glanced at him. "I don't know . . ." she began.

"As my guest, of course," he added when she hesitated.

"Okay, if you insist," she agreed. "And if it's okay with Monty."

The boy looked up at her at the mention of his name. "Is it okay with you if I go to church with you and your daddy again?" she asked.

Monty said, "Sure, but then it'll be Bianca's turn again."

Luke felt his face redden. "That'll be up to your dad, don't you think?" Luke asked awkwardly.

"Yeah, but Bianca likes you a lot, Dad. And I like her."

"You like Coleen too, don't you?" Luke asked, casting a quick glance at Coleen's face. "I do."

Coleen was clearly feeling uncomfortable. But when Luke said that, she began to relax again. If only she could make Monty like her too. Monty then said, "I like Bianca and Coleen. Can't we be both their friends?"

Luke was ready to bring this conversation to an end. "We'll talk about it later," he said. "But right now Coleen has invited us to her house for dinner."

That was Monty's language. He was all for going with Coleen if she had food.

Coleen apologized when they got back to her apartment. "I don't think cooking is my thing. If it is, I've forgotten all I ever knew."

"Well," Luke said, "if you'd like some help Monty and I have had lots of practice."

Luke carried a pager on weekends, and it had this terrible habit of going off at the most inopportune times. It chose to go off right as the meal was cooking. He recognized the number. It was one of his best informants, a drug addict who was known as Rooster. Luke had long ago learned that you treated informants with kid gloves. They were touchy and could turn on a slothful detective at the first sign of a lack of interest or shortage of cash. Rooster was an important informant. He helped Luke keep track of Victor Hampton. And since the day of the ambush, not a word about Victor had surfaced. He had to return the call immediately.

"I'm sorry, Coleen," he said when she gave him a puzzled look as he studied the beeper. "This may be important. My cell phone's in my truck. I need to make a call."

"I have a phone now," she said, pointing to where hers hung on the wall. "Why don't you use it?"

"This call would be long distance," he said, really not wanting to talk to Rooster in front of Coleen and Monty.

"That's all right. Monty and I will be in the kitchen and we won't listen in, will we Monty? You just help yourself. Monty and I will start some cookies."

Monty looked at his dad who nodded. Then he grinned and said to Coleen, "Can we make chocolate chip ones?"

She patted Monty's head and said, "I think we can manage. If you'll help, that is."

"I'll help. I help Grandma make cookies all the time," Monty bragged as he hurried beside her into the kitchen.

"Maybe your dad can help us too when he gets off the phone," Luke heard her say as they disappeared through the doorway.

"Oh, Dad? He don't like to make cookies. We have to eat the kind that's already made, the store kind," Monty revealed.

"Then he can help us with dinner," she suggested. "I know he can do that."

Luke smiled and went to the phone. He'd have to talk softly; he didn't want to frighten either Coleen or Monty. But judging from the constant chatter that drifted from the kitchen, he didn't really think they'd hear a word he was saying.

He dialed, and Rooster picked up on the first ring. "Hi, Luke," he said in harsh, gravelly voice. "I need to see you."

"Can you give me a couple of hours?" Luke asked, knowing it was not a good policy, but also feeling terribly reluctant to leave Coleen this early in the afternoon.

"Can't do. This is important. Come now. I'll meet you at the usual place."

"Okay," Luke said, wondering how this would sit with Coleen. "It'll take me fifteen minutes," he said.

"Luke, come alone, and watch your backside. I don't need no tail following you. This is big. Could be your life, man." Rooster didn't wait for any further reply. He simply hung up. He liked to do most of his talking face to face. And he also enjoyed dramatics. But the way he said that last sentence sent chills up Luke's spine. The shoot-out with Victor was still very much on his mind. And though he never said a word to anyone about it, he was worried. He knew that Victor Hampton hadn't forgotten.

Luke tried not to let the nervousness that he was feeling show as he walked into the kitchen. But Coleen's face fell the moment she looked at him. "Do you have to leave?" she asked.

"I'm so sorry, Coleen, but it looks like I do. But if it's okay, we'll come back later and eat, even if it gets a little cold."

"Of course, Luke," she said, trying to mask her disappointment. "I have several questions I wanted to ask you about your church. I'll save them for when you're done."

"That's great. I'd love to tell you more about the Church. Monty, come on. I better take you to Grandma and Grandpa," Luke said, reaching for his son's hand.

"Daaad," Monty said, clearly frustrated, "me and Coleen are making cookies."

"Luke, if it would be okay with you, he could stay here with me," Coleen said, watching the detective's face closely.

She was relieved when he brightened. "Hey, are you sure you wouldn't mind?"

"I'd love to watch him. We can have a great time, can't we Monty?" she said, winking at Luke's son. "We could even keep dinner warm until your dad gets back. Of course, we may have to sneak a few bites of ice cream and some cookies to hold us over if he's very long, but we'll be fine, won't we?"

Monty was more than agreeable, and Luke was relieved.

Coleen was also relieved. Leaving his son with her was a huge indication of trust. She could almost cry it made her feel so good. But she held back the tears and took Monty's hand as Luke headed for the door.

"Be careful," she said, remembering only too vividly the bullet holes in the black truck he was about to climb into.

She didn't know who she was, but Coleen knew how she felt toward Luke Osborne. He was fast becoming far too important in her life. She was afraid for him and she was afraid of losing him.

* * *

Rooster was hiding in a small grove of young cottonwood trees when Luke drove up in his familiar black Dodge. He waited for two or three minutes before revealing himself, watching in the distance for any sign that Luke had been followed. When he was finally satisfied, he stepped into view and scooted to Luke's truck. He opened the door and jumped in. "What's up, man?" he said out of habit.

"You tell me, Rooster. You're the one that called," Luke said.

"This'll cost you double fee," Rooster said as he stretched his neck, an unusual nervous habit he had. It reminded Luke of a rooster that was about to crow. The long skinny neck and narrow head only added to the image that had been the reason for his name.

"Better be good information, Rooster," Luke said as he pulled two fifty-dollar bills out and held them in front of the informant's face.

Rooster snatched the bills and tucked them into a soiled shirt pocket. He craned his neck again, looking around outside the truck. Then he said, "Word's out that something big's coming down, Luke. Vic Hampton's not happy that his business is in a slump."

"Good," Luke said. "I'm glad his business is suffering."

"Ain't funny, man. He'd stiff me in a heartbeat if he knew I was talking to you."

"I'm not telling," Luke said with a grin.

"I'm telling you, he means business. You better quit grinning and start watching out for yourself." Rooster once again had a quick look about. Then, apparently satisfied that they weren't being watched, he said in a low voice. "It was Vic himself tried to waste you. Sharps Thomsen helped."

The man with the deep voice. Luke had never heard the name before.

"Sharps took one of your bullets, man. He ain't happy," Rooster added.

"Describe him," Luke pressed. He wanted to know, needed to know, more about this new friend of Victor's.

"Never seen him, man," Rooster said. "I gotta go. Keep your back to the wall, man. I don't know what those two are planning, but they aim to make things miserable for you."

Luke nodded. "Find out what they're planning, Rooster. And get me a description of this Sharps Thomsen. It'll be worth another hundred to me."

Rooster's eyes lit up. "I'll be in touch," he said, and then he was out of the truck and jogging for the trees.

Luke wondered what might lay in store for him. Victor Hampton had to be stopped. And Luke knew that he had better be more careful than he'd ever been. Especially when it came to Monty. If anything happened to that boy . . . Luke couldn't even bear to think about it.

Instead he drove swiftly back to town, anxious to see and hug his little son—and to try to relax over dinner with Coleen.

He made good time, parked his truck, and hurried to the door. He knocked, but there was no answer. The door was unlocked and it was with some concern that he peeked his head inside and called out. Then he went in. The table was set, dinner was still warm, and there was no one at home! Luke sank to the sofa, his head dropping into his hands. He was already worked up about Monty, and flying through his mind like pellets from a shotgun were the many possibilities of where his son—and the woman he had entrusted Monty to—might be. Slowly, he pulled himself from the sofa and dropped to his knees.

CHAPTER 9

All kinds of terrible thoughts raced through Luke's head as he finished his prayer, one in which he'd asked fervently that the Lord would protect his son. He thought of Victor and this fellow that Rooster had called Sharps Thomsen. He also wondered if there was anyone in Coleen's past who might have been looking for her with harmful intent. He remembered the four-wheeler tracks he'd been told about; maybe it had been ridden by someone who was pursuing her just before her accident and the loss of her memory.

Then Luke had a terrible thought, which he tried to dismiss before it really settled in. It was because of the woman who looked like her and was wanted for kidnapping children. But he trusted Coleen, and he was sure she would never do anything to hurt Monty.

And yet . . .

No! Coleen would never betray Luke's trust. Never! And she would never hurt a child.

He felt like a traitor himself as the thought kept intruding on his resolve, a thought that maybe she really was someone evil, someone who was a practiced actor and liar. But his heart simply wouldn't buy into that idea. Luke had begun to grow fond of Coleen, and in doing so had gotten to know her well. He felt an uncanny connection to her when they were together. He'd also spent a fair amount of time praying about her and a bit of time talking to her on the phone. He really felt he had accurately discerned what kind of spirit she had, and just knew she would never do anything to hurt him or Monty.

Still on his knees, Luke pressed his hands over his eyes, trying desperately to rub out the worry. But that wasn't easy to do, not after the warning Rooster had given him so very few minutes ago.

"Dad, what're you doing?"

Luke hadn't heard anyone enter, but the sound of his son's voice brought him to his feet in a single joyous leap. And he swept the little fellow up in his arms and held him tight. The relief was so great that he found it hard to hold back the tears. After a moment, he became aware of Coleen standing at the open door, her face in shock.

"Dad, what's the matter?" Monty pressed.

"Oh, nothing," Luke said as his eyes caught Coleen's.

He clearly read in her eyes what he least wanted to see there. Somehow she seemed to know that he'd doubted her, and the hurt he'd inflicted was deep. He placed Monty on the floor and stepped toward Coleen. Her face grew hard and Luke's knees trembled.

"What were you doing?" she asked. Then, before he could answer she said, "We just went for a walk to kill time while we were waiting for you. You thought I'd taken him, didn't you?"

"Oh, Coleen, don't be silly," Luke said.

But there was nothing silly going on here as far as she was concerned. "You don't trust me, do you?" she asked, her voice hard in a way Luke had never heard.

"I do," he protested. "I left him with you."

"Yes, you did," she agreed, "but when you came back and we weren't here, the first thing you thought was that I'd taken him, that I'd betrayed your trust."

"No, Coleen. That isn't true," Luke said. Now he was on more solid footing; that hadn't been his *first* thought exactly. And his doubt of her had been only fleeting when it did come, and he'd thrust it quickly aside.

But it had come.

"Then what were you thinking?" she asked, her face still hard and her pretty eyes full of pain.

"Coleen," he said looking with a concerned nod at Monty, "let's talk about this later. The past few minutes haven't been good ones for me."

Her face softened and her eyes cleared. "What were you doing when we came in?" she asked.

Luke looked long and hard at this young woman who'd begun to mean something to him. The best way to prove that he did trust her was honesty—open, complete honesty. "I had just completed a prayer and was thinking," he replied.

Coleen's eyes glistened. She didn't trust herself to speak; she wasn't sure what she was feeling. Luke sensed her feelings and said, pointing toward her kitchen, "Looks like a good meal in there. Let's not waste it."

The tension that had filled the atmosphere eased, and Luke took Monty and Coleen each by the hand and led them across the room. When he released Monty's hand, the boy darted into the kitchen, ready for dinner.

Luke gripped Coleen's hand, holding her back. He looked her straight in the eye and said, "For the briefest moment I did wonder if you'd taken him somewhere, but . . ."

The contours of her face grew tight, and she started to speak. But Luke put a finger to her lips and said, "Hear me out please." Coleen relaxed and he went on. "But it wasn't even a complete thought, because immediately I felt this surge of trust and . . ." he hesitated.

"And what?" she asked, her eyes glistening again.

"Affection," he blurted.

"Oh, Luke," was all that Coleen could say. But as she looked at him, her heart began to race.

Luke went on again. "But what I had thought about earlier was what I'd just received from the informant I went to meet." He stopped. *Complete honesty*, he reminded himself.

"He talked about the man who killed my wife."

"What about him?" she asked, fear darting across her face as Monty returned from the kitchen.

"Hey you guys, I thought we were going to eat," Monty said in as stern a voice as a five-year-old boy could muster.

Coleen's face was transformed as her smile returned, and Luke noticed how much she really seemed to like Monty. Luke tried not to think about where things could go from here if he wasn't careful and moved slowly. "Your father and I were talking about some very important grown-up stuff," Coleen told the little boy. "But we can talk about it later." She winked at Luke. "Right now you're right, we better eat."

* * *

"This is it," Sharps said as he slumped down in the seat of a light blue, old Ford pickup. He was still hurting from the bullet wound he'd received in his leg, and he sneered at the thought of the man they were currently trying to locate.

"You're sure?" Victor asked from the driver's seat.

"Yes, I'm sure," Sharps snapped.

"We'll drive down through there," Victor said as he pulled his cap low over his eyes.

They passed slowly between the two apartment buildings. Suddenly Victor laughed. "He's here all right. That's his truck right there, all full of bullet holes."

Sharps didn't laugh. "Should have been *him* them bullets was in."

Vic nodded as he passed on by and went down the street. "Luke ain't an easy man to kill. He must be making a visit to that girl he found, the one they say don't even know her own name." He drove in silence for a moment as Sharps brooded, still hunkered down in the seat. Then he added, "Well, we know where he's at. Let's get out of here before he spots us. We have some things need doin'."

The tone of Victor's voice brought Sharps out of his brooding mood. "Yeah, boss, let's make Luke's life miserable. Course, I think we ought to just do him right now."

Vic threw Sharps a dark glance. "We do this my way this time," he said, "and don't you even think of going off on your own and doin' nothing. We tried it your way last time, and we didn't even scratch him. No, we'll make Luke Osborne's life pure misery before we're through—he won't be a problem to me anymore."

Sharps frowned. "Quicker my way," he sulked. "If you wasn't scared of the man . . ."

Victor's right arm moved like a striking rattler, and the back of his hand bloodied Sharps's lip. "I ain't scared of no man alive," Victor said viciously. "And you better never say that again. He's just lucky, and I don't aim to let his luck get me hurt."

Sharps wiped his mouth, his hand coming away streaked with blood. He knew it was folly to cross Victor Hampton. But he also felt that Vic was intimidated by the cop he'd vowed to bring to his knees.

The ambush had been Sharps's idea, and when it failed, it only rein-forced Victor's notion that Luke was not someone you confronted in person. You did it behind his back, and far from his back. There were ways to hurt a cop, Victor often preached, without getting in harm's way.

* * *

The fresh smell of pines, the sharp bite of early morning air, and the animated mood of an awakening forest combined to give Coleen a sense of joy she never remembered feeling before. Monty squealed with delight as his dad lifted him from the truck, swung him around once in a big arc, and placed him on the dewy grass. Coleen sucked in a deep breath of the clean, fragrant air and smiled to herself. It was hard to believe she was in such a beautiful spot with a man she was beginning to think she could love, and his little boy that she some-times secretly wished could be hers, too.

The whole day, a bright and gorgeous one, lay ahead of her. She would be spending the entire day with these two guys who were fast becoming the most important elements in the short life she could recall. And they would all be on horseback, riding in this high forest rangeland, checking cows and calves. The horses were something she was at ease around. Now cows, they didn't bring that same ring of familiarity, but she could feel Luke's enthusiasm when he spoke of them, and she knew that she would also enjoy being around them.

Luke swung the rear door of the trailer open, and Coleen tossed off her daydreaming to begin what promised to be the most delightful day in her memory. Luke stepped into the trailer with the horses and backed out Monty's little mare, Fox. Coleen took the lead rope and led her around the side of the trailer and tied her up. As soon as Coleen got back to the rear, Luke was waiting with Spider. A shiver of excitement passed through her as she took the rope and led the young filly around and tied her a few feet from Fox.

By the time Luke had Keno unloaded, Coleen was already lugging the saddle she was to use from the trailer. She felt just a little awkward when Luke glanced at her, because she realized now the saddle had been Jamie's. In his eyes she recognized the unmistakable pain that would undoubtably haunt him at times like this for many years to come. She knew without him saying a word that he and Jamie had gone through this ritual many times. She was in another woman's place, and they both knew it.

But Luke smiled and said, "Cinch it down tight. We may get in some rough country before the day's over."

His smile helped ease the awkwardness, and Coleen happily set about her task. After all three horses were saddled, Luke brought out the saddlebags he'd packed with food for their lunch, along with a few tools and miscellaneous items he always carried. He tied them behind the saddles. Then they rolled their jackets and raincoats up and secured them over the bags. Finally, with canteens full of water, they were ready to ride. Luke lifted Monty onto his saddle and gave him the reins, tying them in a knot so if they slipped from his hands they couldn't fall to the ground. "Now you just stay with me, Monty," Luke told him. "Don't let old Fox drift away and you'll be just fine." Monty beamed at his dad. This was adventure.

Coleen was so happy she wanted to laugh. As she swung into the saddle on Spider's back she felt like she was in her element. The air was still brisk that early in the morning, and Spider pranced around, throwing her head and letting Coleen know she was ready to go.

Luke paused as he was about to mount young Keno, who was also excited and full of vinegar in the cool mountain air, to watch Coleen. Her eyes shone and there was a radiance about her face that seemed to reach out and grip his heart. She was happier than he'd ever seen her, and the feelings he was reluctantly experiencing whenever he was around her intensified. A knot formed in his stomach as troubled thoughts rushed into his mind. She was not of his religion. With her memory gone, there was no way of knowing who she was or who she might have loved in her past, *or even married.*

Angry at himself, he put his foot in the stirrup, grabbed the saddle horn, and swung onto Keno's back. The colt crow-hopped and pranced for a moment as Luke slipped his right foot into the stirrup and settled into the saddle.

Coleen didn't miss the change that came over Luke as he mounted his horse. Was it something she'd done she wondered. Or was it simply because he didn't know who she really was? Some of the euphoria left her, but she was still determined to have the best day of her life. Then, when it was over, life could take its course, and love, if it was ever to be, would simply have to come when it would.

Silly thought, yet it was already consuming her. There was nothing she could do to stop it. Nor did she want to stop it. She just hoped that sometime, somehow, Luke could feel the same.

He rode up beside her. "I kind of want to get a count," he said. "My cows will all have a brand on the right ribs. It's an *O*. And every cow should have a calf nearby. If you see one that doesn't, give me a shout."

He'd already explained to her how range permits worked. There were several ranchers' cattle in the same area. And they took turns checking the herds. Each rancher was naturally most interested in his own animals and how they were faring. But any dead cows or calves they came across would be inspected and the brand jotted down so the owner could be notified. Luke didn't expect to see a lot, if any. The range was usually free of lions that bothered the cows, and accidents were rare.

Coleen wanted to ride right beside Luke all day, but he'd already explained that they could get a better feel for how the herds were doing if they separated from time to time. They carried small walkie-talkies on their belts so if they drifted too far apart they could quickly locate one another. They rode together for about a mile, then Luke pointed to the left and said, "Why don't you go that way, and Monty and I'll veer to the right. Keep a close eye out, and if you see anything out of the ordinary, give me a call and I'll swing over."

None of this was ordinary to Coleen, so it would be tempting to call him a lot, but she pretty much knew what needed to be done, so she simply said, "Okay, Luke. You guys take care."

Coleen was quickly growing fond of the area. She spooked several head of deer, and simply sat on Spider's back and watched them bound away. The cattle looked at her with little interest as she passed through small bunches from time to time. She kept an accurate count of those with Luke's *O* on their sides. She didn't see any cows, either of his or any other brand, that didn't have a calf beside them. She was a little startled the first time she rode out of a stand of trees and came face to face with a huge bull. But he simply looked at her with an expression of pure boredom as she spurred Spider and hurried past.

A small herd of elk startled her a few minutes later, and she watched with growing fascination as they ran rapidly away from her. She could still hear them crashing through the timber long after they disappeared from her view. Coleen was delighted beyond words as she rode on. Several times she stopped to watch squirrels as they chattered and ran up and down the tall pine and fir trees.

After about an hour, she rode over a ridge and was surprised to see Luke standing beside Keno, a big grin on his face. "Been awhile," he observed with a drawl.

"Oh, Luke, I love it up here," she gushed. "I've seen deer and elk and squirrels and . . ."

"Any cows?" he asked, still grinning.

She laughed. "Of course. But you didn't warn me how big those bulls are. The first one I saw about scared me right out of the saddle."

"Pretty harmless critters," he said as he looped Keno's reins around a sturdy branch and walked over to where Spider and Coleen were. "Here, I'll help you down," he offered. She didn't need help, but that wasn't the point. She accepted his outstretched hand and slid to the ground. Her foot hit a stick and she stumbled, falling into Luke.

As naturally as if they had been together for years, he simply folded his arms around her and pulled her against him. Her heart began to race as she let her head fall against his shoulder. For several minutes they stood there, content to simply hold one another. Finally Luke said, "You okay?"

Coleen looked into his eyes and said, "I've never been so happy in my life, and my foot's fine."

Luke stepped back, and with a mischievous glint in his eyes said, "You certainly look good."

"Where's Monty?" Coleen asked suddenly.

"Oh, he's just over there," Luke said, pointing to his right. "There's a small lake there. He likes to throw rocks in it. He's fine, but I guess we better check on him anyway." The lake was just a few yards away, hidden from the ridge by a heavy stand of timber.

When they led their horses into view, Monty looked up from his perch on a large rock near the water and shouted, "Hi, I just seen a fish jump."

"*Saw* a fish jump," his father corrected.

"Yeah, I did," he agreed, bringing a smile to Coleen's face.

"We better get mounted up, son," Luke told him. "We've got a lot more country to cover."

They had lunch a few hours later beside a gurgling, clear stream that meandered slowly through the center of a meadow. They tied the horses to some small trees near the edge of the clearing and let them graze the rich grass as they ate their own lunch. Coleen sat between Luke and Monty as they ate. She helped Monty unwrap his sandwich and then cut up an apple for him. She was growing very fond of the young boy, and was amazed at how polite he was. He thanked her for every little thing she did. *Luke must be a good father,* she thought.

Later, when Luke stretched out on the soft grass, she stretched out beside him. He reached over and took her hand, and they lay contentedly for several minutes as Monty played nearby. Luke felt like he could stay right there forever; he hadn't felt so at peace with the world since before Jamie's death. But once again, as they finally rose to their feet, his contentment was disturbed by the gnawing questions of Coleen's past life.

And Coleen was thinking, as she saw that worried look come into Luke's eyes, how she wished the past could simply forever remain a secret. She no longer even wanted to know. It couldn't possibly be as good as riding this forested rangeland with Luke and Monty Osborne.

The afternoon became very hot, and eventually a few clouds drifted over the towering mountains that rimmed the valley they rode in. By six o'clock the heat turned to cool and thunder began to roll in the distance. "Better peel out the slickers," Luke announced as he pulled Keno to a stop and dismounted. "The storms hit fast and hard up here and they're gone just as fast," he said as he began to unroll Monty's raincoat.

Coleen dismounted, and as she unrolled her raincoat, said, "I can't believe it's so cloudy. It's been clear all day. And it's been so hot."

"That's the way it is up here. And it's almost always hottest just before a storm comes in. Then it cools off, rains, clears up, and before long it's hot again," Luke explained.

Coleen was sure he knew what he was talking about, but she was still surprised at the fury of the storm when it hit, and at how quickly it passed over and the sun again began beating down upon them.

Twenty minutes later, as steam rose from the grass and drifted like fog through the trees, Luke announced that they needed to split up again for a little while and cover two small draws that ran parallel for a half mile or so. "There'll be quite a bunch of cows in both, or I miss my guess," Luke explained.

And there were a lot of cows, and several bore the distinct O of the Osborne ranch. Coleen rode slowly through the last bunch she'd encountered, counting and checking that each cow had a calf. Then she rode on. Around a strand of trees several hundred yards down the draw she reined her mount to a sudden stop. She was terrified at what she saw lying on the ground in front of her. She stifled a scream as she reached for the radio on her belt.

"Luke!" she cried, as she circled the horribly mutilated figure in the bloody grass. Then, before she could say anything else, she saw another.

The scream that did rip from the radio almost lacerated Luke's eardrum and curdled his blood. "Coleen," he shouted, but the screaming continued. "Monty, hold on son. We've got to ride hard," he shouted as panic surged through his chest. And he dug the spurs into Keno's side.

CHAPTER 10

Keno and Fox carried their riders quickly across the short ridge. Before Luke ever reached Coleen, he could hear her screams echoing through the canyon. He'd have ridden faster, but he didn't dare. Monty could get hurt. He looked back to make sure Monty was okay. Then he hurried on. The screaming stopped and he wondered what had happened. Then his concern for Coleen intensified when he met a riderless Spider running wildly toward them, its head held high and to the side in an instinctive attempt to keep the reins from under her feet.

The frightened horse followed Keno and Fox as Luke and his little boy raced on. As Luke entered a clearing, he spotted the bright blue of Coleen's blouse. She lay in a tangled heap on the ground. He left his horse's back in a leap before Keno had even stopped. Out of the corner of one eye, he checked to make sure Monty was still okay. The little boy had both hands on the saddle horn and his eyes were wide as silver dollars as Fox slid to a stop.

Luke was at Coleen's side like a flash, but as he dropped to his knees beside her, she stirred. After a moment, her eyes opened, and she said, "Luke, what happened?"

"You must have been thrown from your horse," he told her as she rose to her knees and he took her gently into his arms. "Are you all right?" he asked.

"I think so," she said. Then she remembered what had frightened her and she began to tremble. "Luke, there's something horribly dead over there," she told him, pointing back across the meadow.

Luke groaned to himself as he realized what it must be. But his first concern was for her, and he made no move to see what it was that had frightened her until he'd made sure she wasn't hurt. Relieved that there were no broken bones or any cuts, he helped her to her feet and then caught the two horses who had already begun to graze on the cow-cropped grass of the meadow.

He led the horses and walked beside Coleen as they started back across the clearing. Monty, still excited from the hurried ride, followed behind them on Fox. Coleen threw both arms around Luke when the first dead body came into sight. It was that of a young calf, and it was horribly mutilated, much as the other cattle Luke had recently inspected.

Luke immediately turned and grabbed Fox's reigns. "This way son," he said to Monty before the boy was in full view of the cattle. "I need you to stay away from here and guard the area while I do some police work. You keep a sharp eye out for anyone coming over here. We don't want them messing up a crime scene."

After Luke felt sure his son was safely out of view of the awful scene, he carefully examined the first body, then approached the calf's mother. Luke examined the hide and found an *O*. The cow was his. This horror someone had brought into the county had just taken on a personal urgency.

Luke said very little as he painstakingly examined the entire scene. With the grass it was difficult to find footprints, and when he did, they were again from a pair of sneakers, quite similar to the ones used before.

Coleen had seated herself in the grass some distance away and was holding Monty, who was becoming very tired. She'd tied the horses close by, but some distance from where Luke was working. He caught her eye as he crossed the meadow. Fear still lurked there, and he steered himself away from Keno and the saddlebag that held a small camera he always carried. Photos could wait a little while.

"Hey, it'll be all right," he said as he reached Coleen and dropped beside her. He tousled Monty's hair and then slid an arm around Coleen and pulled her close. She let her head drop onto his shoulder. "It's just another incident like I've seen several of lately," he told her.

"But there were two this time, and both the cow and calf were yours, weren't they?" she asked.

"Yes, I'm afraid so, but they could have belonged to any of the ranchers who run cattle up here," he told her.

"It's horrible, Luke," she said. Then pulling in closer, she added, "I'm sorry I screamed. It frightened me so bad. I just lost my head."

"It's all right," he said soothingly. "By the way, do you have any idea what happened to your walkie-talkie?"

"Oh, I forgot. I'm sorry. It must be somewhere in between those dead cattle and where I was thrown from the horse." She paused and a sheepish look came over her. "I can't believe I fell off."

Luke gave her a squeeze. "I don't think you were paying much attention to your riding. And I can't say I blame you. Are you sure you're all right, Coleen? You did take a hard fall."

"I'm okay," she said. "I think I'll have a few sore spots tomorrow, but I'm not hurt," she said, looking up at him with affection she simply couldn't hide.

Luke grinned. "I was kind of hoping, since you lost your memory from falling off a horse, that this would restore it for you."

The look that remark caused on Coleen's face shocked Luke. "Did I say something wrong?" he asked. "I was only teasing."

She struggled free of his arm, scooted Monty off her lap, and stood up. Luke followed her, and gently turned her to face him. "I'm sorry," he said.

Coleen shook her head. "Don't be. It's just me. I've been so happy today, at least until this," she said, pointing across the meadow at the massacred cattle. "I enjoy being with you and Monty. And Luke, I'm so afraid . . ."

When she failed to go on, Luke asked her gently, "Afraid of what, Coleen?"

She looked away, not wanting to see the expression on his face when she said what was on her mind, but she decided it needed to be said. "I'm afraid of what I might remember. I don't think I want to remember," she said honestly. She struggled free of him again, and before he could respond to the revelation she'd just made, she added, "I'll go see if I can find the radio." Then she turned to the sleepy five-year-old at her side. "Do you want to help me, Monty?"

"Yeah, I wanna help," the little fellow said eagerly as he grabbed Coleen's hand.

Luke took her by the shoulder and once again turned her gently toward him as Monty clung to her. "Coleen, I'm sorry I said that.

You're the best thing that's happened to Monty and me since Jamie was killed. Please, forgive me. I like who you are and what you are."

Coleen felt a tremor in her heart. She was feeling things for this man that would probably shock him. She couldn't say them, so she simply gave him a quick, spontaneous kiss on the cheek, and said, "Thank you, Luke."

As she and Monty started across the meadow, Luke felt guilty. He did like who Coleen was, more than he should have ever allowed. He did like the kind of person he saw in her, but he still wanted desperately to know who she'd been. And without her knowing it, he intended to keep searching for her past. He had to know; the feelings in his heart were leading him in a direction he could never go if she had a husband out there that she didn't remember.

Monty found the radio as he and Coleen were searching. Luke took all the pictures he had film for, and then they left the desecrated meadow. Both Luke and Coleen felt a strange blend of emotions as they rode back to the waiting truck and horse trailer—from revulsion and fear, to peace and hope.

* * *

Bianca Turner heard the fire trucks, sirens wailing, as they tore through town. She turned on her police scanner, curious as to where the trucks were heading. Her blood froze when she heard the dispatcher say, "Luke Osborne's place. It's a big one, that's all we know."

She was out the door and into her car before she even had time to think rationally about what she was doing. She couldn't help fight a fire, she'd only be in the way. If Luke was even home, he was probably so stressed that the last thing he would need would be her poking around. But she went anyway, joining the procession of trucks headed toward Utahn.

She had scarcely topped Blue Bench when she saw the sky filled with dark smoke. It was billowing and surging upward in massive clouds. Tears stung her eyes and she silently prayed that Luke and Monty were both safe.

At the lane to his ranch, she felt a weight in her chest that threatened to smother her. She couldn't see into his yard, for the smoke and flames shot a hundred feet into the air. An explosion rocked her car, and a flaming missile was launched into the air and flew hundreds of yards toward the river before crashing back to earth and exploding into a sheet of fire that shot three or four hundred feet in every direction. She recalled the five-hundred-gallon diesel tank that Luke kept full of fuel near his barn; she was certain that it had been the source of the missile and explosion.

Sickened, she cried uncontrollably as she rolled her car to a stop in the smoke-filled yard. She got out and looked frantically for Luke's truck, but it was nowhere to be seen. She ran toward the house where one fire truck was already shooting water. To her surprise the house was not on fire, and it appeared that they were only spraying it in an attempt to keep it from igniting under the intense heat of the nearby flames. It took her a moment to figure out that it was Luke's stackyard, with hundreds of tons of baled hay stacked for use in the coming winter, that was burning. She actually sighed in relief. Then it occurred to her that the barn was fully engulfed in flames as well as the nearby outbuildings.

Total helplessness washed over her, and she sank to the ground near Luke's white picket fence and sobbed.

* * *

A feeling of unrest, even fear, came over Luke as he was driving home that evening. He said nothing to Coleen, who was sitting close to him in the center of the seat. But something wasn't right, and he had no idea what it was. Yes, he was upset over the loss of a cow and calf, but that wasn't a disaster. Ranchers lost cattle all the time. It was something else, and he simply couldn't put a finger on it, but he coaxed a little more speed out of the truck.

Coleen could feel the tension that seemed to emanate from Luke. She rode in worried silence for several miles before she finally asked, "Is it the cattle, Luke?"

"What?" he asked, his own dark thoughts interrupted.

"You're all tense," she said. "Is it because of the cattle that were killed?"

He glanced over at her, and the look in his eyes answered her question. Something far worse than the loss of a cow and calf were reflected there. "Coleen," he said, "you might think I'm nuts, but I have the feeling that something far more serious has happened."

"How can you know that?"she asked.

"The Spirit," he answered, knowing as soon as he'd said it that she couldn't possibly understand.

"You mean, like God?" she asked. "God's trying to tell you something?"

"Yes, something like that," he answered, surprised at her comprehension. "Let me tell you sometime about the Holy Ghost," he said. "Then you'll understand more clearly."

Monty spoke up from beside Coleen. "Yeah, when I'm eight, I'll get the Holy Ghost too," he informed her with innocent but unshaken faith.

At that moment, a feeling came over Coleen that was new but pleasant. Somehow she believed them, and she wanted to know more. "Will you two teach me?" she asked.

Some of the gloom lifted from Luke's face and he said, "I'd love to, Coleen. The things I believe are truths. I'd like nothing more than to share them with you."

Luke felt good about the interest Coleen had just shown in the gospel, and he honestly looked forward to helping her come to gain her own understanding of the truths he held so dear. But the feeling also persisted that something was terribly wrong, and when he noticed the cloud of smoke that was building overhead, a more distinct impression came to him.

"Coleen," he said in a tone that made her stomach begin to roll, "I'm afraid there's a fire at my place."

She too had noticed the smoke, but she'd had no such thoughts. However, when he made his statement, she somehow knew that he was right, and his worry became hers as well.

As they began the gradual decent toward Duchesne from the northern end of Blue Bench, it was clear that the smoke was coming from Utahn. And not a word passed between them as they looked at each other, but each knew that something terrible was happening at Luke's ranch. Silently, he reached for his cell phone, surprised to see it was turned off. Then he remembered that he'd turned it off when they stopped to unload the horses that morning. There was no signal, and he'd known it would be useless to carry it with him. His mind had been so preoccupied with either his dead cows or the sweet companionship of Monty and Coleen, that he'd simply forgotten to turn it back on.

He dialed now, and the dispatcher confirmed his fears. When he'd finished talking to her, he slowly put the phone back and said, devastated, "It's my hay, barns, sheds . . . and my corrals. She said my house is okay . . ." He stumbled a little in explaining.

Coleen put an arm around his shoulders and felt him fight back the sobs of frustration that she knew were so close to coming. What she felt for this man was more than pity or concern over the loss he was experiencing. This was different; she felt the loss with him, and it tore at her heart with a pain like she never remembered feeling before. *It could only be love,* she thought.

Of course, her memory was short, but somehow, she didn't think she could ever have felt such a thing before, especially a feeling this intense. She truly had come to love Luke Osborne, and in her mind, his loss was her loss.

They were both silent for several minutes as each was deep in thought. Luke was thinking about the loss and wondering how he'd ever rebuild, and he was also remembering Rooster and his warning. Coleen was thinking about Luke, wondering how she could help him, as she wanted more than anything to not only comfort him, but help him rebuild. She wanted to be part of his life.

The prolonged silence increased the tension, and Coleen finally couldn't stand it anymore and she asked, "What could have started the fire, Luke?"

His answer surprised her, and revealed his thoughts of the past few minutes. "Victor Hampton," he said with conviction. "He's behind it."

* * *

Bianca was standing beside her car watching the smoldering remains of the fire when Luke's black truck and white horse trailer approached. What she saw as Luke drove past her and pulled the truck to a stop hurt her worse than the fire. Close beside Luke was Coleen.

With the help of one of the other deputies, from whom she'd extracted a promise that he'd say nothing to Luke, she had launched her own attempt to find out who Coleen Whitman really was. In the meantime, she had to do whatever she could to protect him from her. Bianca did not miss the familiarity Coleen was showing toward Luke as the two of them exited the truck and surveyed the smoldering remains of his haystack and barn.

Bianca was also smoldering as she watched Coleen bend down and pick Monty up. She resented the way the little boy threw his arms around her neck, as if seeking shelter from the horror that lay before them. And Coleen held his little head against her shoulder as if she were naturally the one to protect Monty from it.

Sheriff Robinson, black from smoke and soot, walked over to Luke. As the sheriff and Luke talked, an idea formed in Bianca's mind. When the two of them started toward where the barn had once stood, she noticed that Luke stopped and said something to Coleen, and that Coleen and Monty made no attempt to follow the men.

Bianca hurried to catch up with Luke and Sheriff Robinson and walked silently beside them as the sheriff said, "The state fire marshal's office is sending someone to look into this, Luke. We'll get to the bottom of it."

"I'll be doing some looking myself," Luke said with determination. "I'm certain that Victor is behind this."

"May well be," the sheriff agreed, "but be careful who else you say that to until we have some proof."

The two men stopped and were silent for a moment. "My big tractor was in the barn," Luke said after a little bit. "Tools, saddles . . ." He stopped as his voice broke.

Feeling an opening, Bianca spoke up. "Luke," she gushed sorrowfully, "I feel just terrible about this."

"Thanks, Bianca," he said, barely even looking at her.

"I'd like to help if I can," she added. "Maybe I could run Coleen home for you since she doesn't have a car. And I'd like to keep Monty tonight."

"Thanks, Bianca," he said, scarcely thinking of what she was saying as the enormity of the damage to his small ranching operation began to sink in.

Coleen had put Monty on the ground, and she was unloading the horses when Bianca approached. "Could you use some help?" she asked Coleen, trying to sound as sincere as she could.

"Thanks, I've almost got it, but I don't know where to put them now," Coleen said.

"Don't worry about it. Luke'll take care of them in a few minutes," she said slyly. "He asked me to gather a few things from the house for Monty and keep him tonight."

Bianca couldn't help but feel a touch of satisfaction at the disappointment that clouded her rival's face. "Oh, and he also asked me if I'd take you home. He said since it'll be dark soon and he needs to get some things done here, that it would sure help if I'd run you back to your apartment."

Despite the distrust and dislike she had for Coleen, Bianca couldn't help but feel just a little guilty when Coleen said, "Thank you," as sweetly and sincerely as could be, despite the keen disappointment that the woman clearly felt. "I'll help you find some clothes for Monty."

Bianca didn't know how to refuse her help, so the two women, with Monty between them, approached the house.

* * *

Victor Hampton straightened up as he pulled away from the powerful spotting scope he'd been looking through intermittently for the past hour. He was at the top of the hill nearly two miles from the destroyed ranch yard, and he was smiling with satisfaction. He'd just watched two women and a little boy get in a car and drive away from the ranch. "Well Sharps, that ought to keep Luke busy for a while," he said. "And there ain't no way he can even prove it's us. Clean job, if I do say so myself."

"I'd say," Sharps agreed. "But I still think . . ."

"It don't matter what you think," Victor reminded him. "We're doing this thing my way. And we're not through yet. I don't want Luke Osborne to have either the time or the interest to poke his nose into my affairs again."

He took the spotting scope off the tripod. "I'll put this in the case. You fold up the tripod," Victor ordered. "Then let's get back. We got things to do."

"It'll be dark soon," Sharps said. "Do we still have time?"

"We have time, and dark suits me just fine. Don't want to be seen now, do we?"

"Course not, boss. That'd be disaster," Sharps agreed, not particularly anxious for the next assignment Victor had cooked up. It seemed to him like it would be easier just to get rid of Luke, not mess with his life. But Vic was the boss, and when they got to cooking meth again, they'd both be making big money. So Sharps simply did as he was told. In a year or two he could retire to a beach house somewhere and just take it easy.

* * *

It was dark by the time Luke realized he hadn't done anything with the horses they'd ridden that day. But he wasn't worried, Coleen had probably taken them to the pasture. His insurance agent had come, and he felt a lot better about things after that. Most of his loss was covered, and even though it would be inconvenient for a while, he at least wouldn't lose his ranch—the ranch his father and mother had poured their whole lives into.

He wondered why his folks hadn't come out. Maybe they hadn't heard about the fire yet, although that seemed extremely unlikely. But they weren't here, so he decided he'd go break the news to them himself when he took Coleen home. The sheriff, who was still there, met him at the trailer where Luke was surprised to see that the horses had been unloaded but still stood tied to the trailer. He looked around for Coleen.

"Who you looking for, Luke?" Sheriff Robinson said.

"Coleen. I thought she'd have the horses turned loose. I wonder what happened to her."

The sheriff chuckled. "You've had a lot on your mind, I guess. You sent her back to town."

"I did?" Luke asked in surprise.

"Yeah, but I wondered if you even knew Bianca was talking to you when she asked if it was okay to give Coleen a ride to town and if she could keep Monty tonight," Sheriff Robinson said.

"Why would I send Monty with Bianca? He has a right to be here," Luke said. As he spoke he vaguely recalled Bianca speaking to him, but his mind had been on the loss of his tractor and barn and hay. He had no idea what he'd said to her.

"Well, what's done is done," Luke muttered, clearly annoyed. Already he was missing Coleen and Monty. "I guess I'll take care of my horses and run to town. I've got to let the folks know what's happened. Then I think I'll just swing by Bianca's and pick up Monty." He couldn't keep the bitterness from his voice as he spoke.

The sheriff simply nodded. "Bianca's only trying to help, Luke," he said in defense of his secretary.

"I suppose, but in case you haven't noticed, she's getting a little pushy lately," Luke said with more anger than he'd intended.

"Luke, face it," the sheriff said. "The girl likes you. And she wouldn't be such a bad catch. You can't go on grieving forever."

Luke decided not to pursue this conversation any further with his boss. "Thanks, Sheriff," he said. "I suppose you're right."

"Here, let me help you with the horses," the sheriff offered.

They were on their way back after turning the horses into the pasture when Luke remembered the earlier horrors of the day. "Oh! Sheriff," he said, "this isn't the only thing that's happened. We found a cow and calf today."

The sheriff turned to him with concern. "Mutilated?" he asked.

"Terribly," Luke answered.

"Where? Who's were they?"

"On the range where I have my permits. And they were both mine."

"But they could have been anyone's," the sheriff reflected.

"Yes, that's true. I doubt if the kids, or whoever's doing this stuff, have any idea whose animals they're killing. But I sure need to figure out who's behind it," Luke said.

The sheriff agreed. "You work on that. The fire marshal and a couple of the other deputies will look into the fire."

"Vic's behind it," Luke reminded him.

"Maybe, but remember, Luke, don't go making any accusations until we find proof."

Both men knew that would not be very likely. But neither spoke it. Luke knew what he had to do. He had to find Rooster and talk with him. He'd know something.

Twenty minutes later Luke pulled up to his parents' house. He found them sitting peacefully in front of the TV. "Didn't anyone call?" he asked after shocking them with what had happened to the ranch they both loved.

"Nope, fact is, phone hasn't rung all day," Luke's father said.

"That's strange," Luke mused as he walked over and picked up the receiver. "Guess it's not so strange, your phone's dead."

Just then a prickle ran up his spine as he wondered why it was dead. Victor Hampton again came to mind and Luke admitted to himself that the prickle was the beginning of fear. Not for himself, but for those he loved.

CHAPTER 11

Bianca was surprised but pleased to see Luke at the door. "Hi, Luke, come in," she said pleasantly. "I'm so sorry about what happened. It's horrible."

"Thanks," he said. "Where's Monty?"

"On my bed. I think he's about asleep."

Luke didn't want to seem rude, but he also didn't want Monty staying the night there. "I'm sorry," he said, "but I wasn't thinking when I let you take Monty. I appreciate it, actually, because I don't know what he would have done earlier, but I really don't want to be alone the rest of the night."

But as he thought about it, he did know what Monty would have done while he was worrying about the fire and checking his animals and all the other things he'd done before darkness set in. He would have been with Coleen, and Coleen would have been there to give Luke support when he needed it. Bianca was interfering, and he didn't like it. But he still had to be polite, since she was a friend and co-worker.

"I'll get Monty," Bianca said. "I just thought—"

"Thanks, Bianca," he said, cutting her off. "You've been a help." *Unwelcome help.*

After he'd left with his son, Liz came out of the kitchen, frowning. "Rude, wasn't he? First he asks you to take his son for the night, then he comes and takes him back."

Bianca hadn't been exactly candid with Liz when she'd shown up at the apartment with Monty. And she saw no reason to correct it now. So she simply said, "I guess he's under a lot of stress. Who wouldn't be?"

Liz agreed, but then she said, "He sounded almost angry. Was he?"

Bianca had thought the same thing, but she wasn't about to admit it. "No. Like I say, it hasn't been an easy day for him."

"What about Coleen Whitman? What was she doing today?"

Liz knew how Bianca really felt, and she knew how to get the truth out of her roommate. "With him, and for his sake I've got to get her out of his life. She'll only cause him trouble and he has enough without her creating more."

"So what are you going to do about it?" Liz asked.

Bianca thought for a minute, then she decided to let Liz in on what she and Deputy Roper where doing. "Steve Roper and I are going to see if we can find out who Coleen really is. He thinks Dane Bering will help."

"That eternally single, overbearing guy from Roosevelt who calls himself a private investigator?" Liz asked sarcastically.

"Yes," Bianca reluctantly confirmed. "Steve says Dane has a thing for me, and if I work it right, he'll take the case for next to nothing."

"Does he know what he's doing?" Liz asked doubtfully. "I mean, is he any good at this private investigation stuff?"

"Actually, Steve thinks he's okay. Anyway, we're hoping he'll give it a try."

"What will Luke think?" Liz asked.

"I don't plan to tell Luke," Bianca said. "It's going to be between me and Steve Roper and Dane. When we find out who the woman is and what she wants from Luke, then he'll be glad we found out for him. I just know there's something there. Luke is in danger, and I'll do anything I can to help him."

Bianca was sincere, and Liz knew it. The two friends both felt that Coleen wasn't good for Luke or Monty, and that Luke needed help, even if he didn't know it. Liz asked, "So when are you going to talk to Dane?"

"Tomorrow. I've already asked for the afternoon off. I'll meet Steve in Roosevelt, and he'll try to have Dane with him. We'll just see how it goes from there," she said. Bianca cared for Luke, and she would do whatever it took to protect him *and* to win him over. This was just the beginning. It never once occurred to her that Coleen might really be a nice person, even if her real identity was established. Bianca just preferred to think she wasn't.

* * *

Luke was steaming as he drove toward his home. He knew what Bianca was up to and he didn't like it. She was determined to *protect* him from Coleen, but she didn't know Coleen. Yes, he worried about her past, but his worry was not over what kind of person she'd been. He figured she'd been a good person, like she was now. What he worried about was if she'd left a family somewhere, particularly a husband. He had to know, especially since she was showing an interest in the Church, and he was developing feelings that would be very wrong if she had someone else in her life, someone she'd forgotten through no fault of her own. He'd gone nearly three miles before he decided he had to talk to Coleen tonight. There was a light on in her apartment when he arrived, but he wondered if she was just getting ready to go to bed. He knocked anyway. All he wanted to do was apologize to her and explain what had happened with Bianca. He didn't even need to go in. Anyway, Monty was asleep on the seat of the truck, and he would never leave him alone there for long.

He knocked a second time and waited. He was about to turn away when the door opened. Coleen smiled broadly when she saw him. She was wrapped in a robe, and her hair was wet. "Come in, Luke," she invited warmly.

"I can't," he said as he admired her fresh, clean face. "Monty's asleep in the truck."

"Monty? I thought you sent him to Bianca's," she said, clearly puzzled.

"No, not really. And that's why I came by. I have to apologize."

"You don't have to do any such thing," Coleen insisted. "Why don't you get him and bring him in for a few minutes. He can lie on my bed if he's too sound asleep."

She wanted just to have a few more minutes with Luke before this beautiful, and dreadful, day ended. "Oh, I better not," he said. "I just wanted to explain . . ."

"Please, Luke, just for a few minutes," she implored, reaching out and taking hold of his hand.

"Okay," he relented. "I'll get him."

Coleen followed Luke out to the truck and waited as he picked Monty up. She walked beside them as Luke carried him back to the apartment. By the time Luke had entered, Monty was mostly awake, and he brightened when he saw Coleen. "Hi," he mumbled.

She leaned over and impulsively kissed his forehead. "Hi, Monty. Want some popcorn and hot chocolate?"

He did, and so did his father. They relaxed and Luke explained what Bianca had done. "I was out of it, I guess. I would have preferred that you watch him for me," he told Coleen. Then he explained to her that as bad as the fire was, insurance would cover most of it. But he also shared his concern about Victor Hampton. "For some reason he's out to get me. I've simply got to get him first. And that'll be hard because the sheriff insists that I need to concentrate my time on the cow cases. Believe me, I'm as worried as he is about them, especially since they got to me personally. But what Vic can do is of far more concern, and I'm not sure anyone else in the department will be able to make a case against Vic. I need to be on the arson case myself."

Coleen listened intently, worrying more and more as he talked. Finally, when he'd finished, she covered his hand with hers and looked intently into his eyes. Then she said in a trembling voice, "Luke, you be awfully careful. He's a dangerous man." She didn't know what else to say. She'd have liked to tell him he shouldn't work the case at all, that the mutilation cases were the ones he should concentrate on, just like the sheriff wanted. But somehow she knew that he was right. No one else had the motivation he did to catch Victor and put him behind bars where he belonged. To think of the danger he'd be in, *was* in, was almost more than she could bear. It never occurred to her that she and Monty could also be in danger.

It was nearly midnight before Luke and Monty left. They were both exhausted; it had been a long and tiring day. And tomorrow Luke would have to immerse himself in his work—he had to stop the killing of cattle in order to keep the sheriff off his back, and at the same time find a way to prove that Victor Hampton had either started the fire or ordered it done.

Luke's parents showed up shortly after daylight. Luke was still tired and Monty was sleeping. They'd come both to watch Monty so

Luke could get to work, and to see for themselves the devastation that had occurred.

Luke's father walked slowly around the burned-out farmyard, the one he'd built and given his life to. Luke was saddened at the heartbreak he could read on his father's aged face. And he was more resolved than ever to bring Victor to justice.

He left his dad and began a thorough search of the surrounding area. He didn't know what he'd find, if anything, but for over an hour he scoured the ground.

And he got lucky. Two sets of footprints came up from the river. He even traced where two people had walked down the river for over a mile, staying as close to the trees that grew along the bank as possible. They had clearly not wanted to be seen. Then they'd made their way to the ranch yard by following an old ditch that was lined with trees much of the way. They had even crawled on their bellies in places. He studied their tracks intently. He took pictures, made measurements, and returned to the house, more convinced than ever that Victor Hampton had tried to burn him out.

Luke's mother had breakfast fixed by the time he got back. "You didn't need to do that," he protested, but was grateful she had. He'd worked up an appetite and didn't have the time to cook for himself since he had so much work to do.

The first thing he did, after a short, nine o'clock meeting with the sheriff, was visit the library in Roosevelt where he did more extensive research on satanic cults. Then, armed with several photocopied pages, he drove back to the old barn near Myton. He was bothered by what he'd learned. Something just wasn't adding up. He studied the site very carefully, noting how items were placed and photographing everything that might be important.

Then he sat in his truck and studied the pages he'd copied. An idea began to form in Luke's mind. The more he read and thought, the more convinced he became that he could solve these cases. In fact, when he finally drove back to Duchesne that afternoon, he'd developed a theory. He needed to do just one more thing to prove to himself that his theory was right. If it was, he knew what needed to be done next.

But Luke hadn't reached Duchesne before he got another call to inspect a dead cow. Fruitland again; but this time he had a feeling it was not the work of a mountain lion. He almost welcomed the trip out there because it gave him still another chance to prove his theory correct.

* * *

A meeting at the sheriff's Roosevelt office was too risky. Luke might find out, and Bianca didn't want that. So Steve arranged for Bianca to come to his house near Neola. When she got there, Dane and Steve were waiting. Dane really had let himself go, Bianca thought. He was practically bald, overweight, and didn't pay much attention to whether his clothes fit well or were even tucked in completely. She was definitely not attracted to Dane. But from the way Dane looked at her, she knew that Steve had been right. As distasteful as it was to her, a little flirting might just go a long way with Dane Bering.

Steve's wife was at work and the kids were with friends, so Steve invited them all inside. Steve had told Dane a little about what Bianca wanted, but he let her explain in detail. "It's very important that we establish her true identity," she told the investigator. What she didn't tell him was why it was important to her. The last thing she wanted Dane to know about was her interest in Luke. So she mentioned a few random reasons to throw him off the trail.

For an hour Bianca and Steve discussed what they knew about Coleen. And they gave Dane a copy of the poster that Luke had originally prepared. It was the picture of Coleen on it that was important. They discussed everything Bianca and Steve had heard from Luke and others about what Coleen had done since her accident. "If there really ever was an accident," Bianca said skeptically.

"That'll be easy to check out," Dane told her with a leering smile.

They also told him all about the woman who was wanted for kidnapping who looked so much like her. "Probably a twin," Bianca said.

"Ah, another good place to dig," Dane suggested as he scribbled on his notepad, feeling a bit pompous as he sensed Bianca's reliance on him.

Finally, when all they knew was in the hands of the large private investigator the discussion came around to the thing Bianca dreaded. "Now about my fees," Dane began.

Bianca did have some money saved, and she'd received an inheritance of several thousand dollars when her grandfather died. But she was prepared to spend as much of it as it took to discredit Coleen Whitman.

"Of course, expenses come first," Dane said. "I'll keep an accurate account of everything I spend. I'll need, from the looks of it, about two thousand dollars up front."

Bianca took out her checkbook and began to write. Steve had warned her, and she'd transferred several thousand dollars from her savings before leaving Duchesne. As she handed the check to Dane, she asked, "How much are your fees?"

Dane again smiled a little too suggestively. "Probably more than you can afford," he said, "but for you, I've got a special rate."

He paused and she forced a smile for him. Dane made Bianca extremely uncomfortable, but she also wanted to save as much money as she could. "Tell you what, if you'll meet me whenever I'm in town so we can discuss my progress on the case over dinner, I'll do it for fifty a day on top of the expenses we've already discussed." He said it with what Bianca was sure he thought to be a charming smile. And she swallowed her indignation at whatever he was thinking.

She also had no idea how many dinners that would be, and she was quite certain she'd be buying, but, she thought somewhat sarcastically, if she could rid the town of the imposter and win the love of Luke Osborne, it would all be worth it. She nodded her head firmly, though she didn't feel as good about it as her actions indicated.

"Good, I'll start in the morning," Dane promised. "And the first dinner will be . . ." he looked at his watch, "at about five at the Frontier."

Bianca could just see the rumors starting to fly, but she already knew from Steve that Dane's usual rate was two hundred a day. She was getting a bargain. If only Luke didn't figure out what was going on.

Dane smiled at her again, and her skin crawled, but she was committed now.

* * *

Luke knew that the Fruitland farmer was getting perturbed at him. The fellow even remarked that it seemed like he didn't take the case very seriously. Luke had smiled several times as he examined the tracks left by the perpetrators and as he determined the parts of the cow that were missing. But he was not about to share his theory with this fellow.

"Well, any idea why this was done?" the farmer asked.

Luke nodded. "There have been several, and I think I'm getting a clear picture of what's going on."

"Who done it?" he was asked doggedly.

"That I'm not sure of," Luke hedged. "But I have an idea."

"Care to share it?" the farmer hissed through clenched teeth.

"Wouldn't be wise until I'm ready to make an arrest," Luke told him.

"You don't really expect me to believe you have any idea who did this?" the man scoffed. "You don't give a hoot about my cow. You don't give a hoot about anybody's cows. How could anybody smile when he sees something like this?"

Luke was getting a little angry himself. "Listen, mister, I smiled because I think I know who's doing this, and because he left some telltale signs here. I smiled because I'm going to get the rotten guy who killed your cow. And I sure enough care. They got two of my animals, a cow and a calf."

That took the fight out of the farmer, and Luke finished, "I'll let you know more when I can. Until then, rest assured that I'm doing everything in my power to solve these cases."

It was after five before he got back to Duchesne, and the sheriff had left the office. Luke wasn't sure he was ready to tell him what he'd learned anyway. So he stopped by his folks' place and picked up Monty. "Want to eat out?" he asked the boy.

"Yeah," Monty said excitedly. "I want a Subway sandwich."

"Subway it is," Luke agreed, and they headed for the east end of town. As Luke ordered a twelve-inch meatball, he realized he hadn't stopped for lunch that day. He hungrily devoured his entire sandwich and half of Monty's. By six they were back in the patrol car and heading home, his hunger appeased.

When Luke's cell phone rang, the very man he was wanting desperately to speak to was on the other end. He had planned to call Rooster first thing the next day. "Hey man, you better meet me tonight. I've got something you'll want to know. And it'll cost you."

"Better be good, Rooster," Luke said, knowing from the sound of the informant's voice that it probably was.

"Same place as Sunday," he was told. "Make it seven, in your black truck."

"I'll be there," Luke said.

"Don't be late or . . ." The connection was suddenly cut off. What was Rooster up to?

Luke brooded for a minute before he decided to run Monty back to his parents' house. But when he remembered that Coleen should be off by now, he headed to her apartment instead. When she came to the door, her face glowing at the sight of her two favorite people, Luke said, "I've had something come up. Would you mind watching Monty for a little while?"

"You know I'd love to, Luke," she said. "What have you got to do?"

"Meet an informant," he said. "I've got to run home and grab my truck, so I haven't much time."

For some reason that information made her stomach tighten. But she acted cheerful. "Hey, how about if we ride to the house with you? I'll bet Monty and I could do some cleaning or something while you're gone."

"You don't have to do that—" he began.

"I know, but I'd like to," she broke in. "Anyway, I was thinking that when you got home you might talk to me about the Spirit, or as Monty said, the Holy Ghost. You promised you know." Luke liked the idea more than he cared to say. Coleen's presence in his house seemed very . . . right, he decided. Especially if they could talk about the gospel. But even as he loaded them in his patrol car, he felt the warning voice of the Spirit, and he knew that this might not be such a pleasant night after all. But he said nothing, and after dropping them off and getting his truck, he was soon on his way to meet Rooster, trying to shake off the feelings he was getting—the warning voice. He convinced himself that he just needed to be extra careful, very watchful, and he'd be okay. Meeting with Rooster was crucial to his building a case, and he wasn't about to stop now.

When Luke got close to the spot he'd arranged to meet Rooster, the feelings he had were so strong that he pulled off the road. He wondered if he was driving into another ambush. Rooster had always been as good as his word with Luke, but he was also a small-time crook, and Luke knew his information and loyalties came with a price. What if someone else had offered him a better deal than Luke? And there *was* the sudden mid-sentence end to Rooster's phone call.

The thought made Luke cringe. It also made him even more cautious and he took extra care to protect himself. He parked the truck well off the road in an old farmyard. Then he walked up a dry, abandoned ditch, one of many in the area since the advent of wheel-line irrigation systems. It made suitable cover and he made good time. He arrived near the rendezvous right on time. He watched for Rooster and for anyone else who might be lurking. His skin crawled and the hair stood up on the back of his neck.

Something simply didn't feel right here. He fingered the handheld radio on his belt, wondering if he should turn it on and call for backup. But that seemed pointless since there was no sign of anyone in the area.

Luke moved silently around the grove of trees where Rooster had hidden prior to their meeting Sunday. He used the ditch as cover, but he stopped frequently, cupping his hand over his ear in an effort to hear better. But only crisp silence filled the area. He dropped to his knees, crawled out of the ditch on his belly, and entered the grove of cottonwood trees.

After crawling several yards, he raised himself to his knees and spotted Rooster, or at least he assumed it was Rooster. The person was tied tightly, his head between his knees and lying on his side. All Luke could see was the back of his head, and as he studied the still form, he became alarmed. Rooster was not one to sit still. He was a nervous, fidgety sort of guy. If alive and conscious, he'd be fighting the ropes. Luke took a minute to calm himself, and then he began to carefully and slowly work his way around the area. Something, more than the still form that lay among the trees and bushes, was wrong. Luke felt a growing awareness of danger and he began a slow, painstaking retreat.

A dog growled and Luke stopped and pulled his pistol. He watched and listened carefully. The dog came into view only a hundred feet or so away. Its growl grew deeper, and Luke knew it was not a friendly animal. He wondered if he should simply make his presence known and let the dog attack, if that was what it was going to do, then he could shoot it. But a strong impression came to Luke and he felt he should continue to back away. He didn't want to have to shoot the dog anyway. Maybe it would leave in a little while and he could enter the trees after he'd gotten reinforcements and see what was the matter with Rooster.

The dog continued to advance and Luke backed toward the ditch, keeping about a hundred feet between them. The dog was near where poor Rooster lay, and its attention turned briefly that way, but it seemed to sense that Rooster was no danger to it, and it again advanced on Luke. Suddenly, it vanished in a cloud of smoke and dirt as a powerful explosion rocked the ground. Luke covered his head as dirt and rocks rained down on him. He thanked God for the warning voice of the Spirit and for the dog. Its life had been traded for his. Someone had set a trap, and Luke had been the intended victim.

He stayed still, letting the dust settle, but anxious to get to Rooster, fearing his informant was dead, but concerned that if he did still happen to be alive any wasted time could be fatal for the man. Luke was very careful, praying that there were no more bombs set for him. He felt like the safest way to approach was right across the area where the bomb had already exploded. He did that, and reached the shrapnel-riddled form in the center of the grove of trees.

Relief washed over Luke as he discovered that it had not been Rooster at all, just a carefully prepared dummy. What he wondered now was who had placed the dummy there and set the trap for Luke. It simply wasn't Rooster's style, so it had to be someone else, and Luke was almost certain he knew who that someone else might be.

If Luke was right, Victor had gotten to Rooster and either killed him or turned him against Luke. If Rooster was working for Victor now, Luke knew that he'd have to be extremely cautious. On the other hand, if he wasn't working for Victor, then chances were that Rooster was either badly hurt or dead.

Luke had to find out, and he reached for his radio.

CHAPTER 12

Luke couldn't get Rooster off his mind as he waited for backup to come. In a strange sort of way he'd come to like the guy, and prayed that he wasn't dead. But Luke was also concerned that Victor Hampton might be getting more violent since he'd teamed up with the man Rooster said was Sharps Thomsen. It was also likely that he was using more methamphetamine. It was a terrible drug, and it also made users extremely violent. If it was Victor who was responsible for the trap that had been so carefully prepared, then Luke's life was in serious danger. If it wasn't Victor, his life was still in danger, as someone had intended to kill him. That someone had known that he was meeting Rooster.

And Rooster is probably dead, Luke thought.

Sheriff Robinson responded personally when he was informed of Luke's call for assistance. He also had three deputies head that way. Luke was glad to see the four men arrive.

"Anybody hurt?" was the first thing the sheriff asked Luke.

"Not here there isn't, but I'm not sure that my informant, who was supposed to meet me here, isn't either badly hurt or dead. This was clearly a setup," Luke told him.

The sheriff began to rummage around and then he stopped and said, "This have to do with the mutilated cattle, Luke? I really don't want you working any other cases until you have that one wrapped up."

"I don't know what it was about," Luke told him. "I got a call. Fellow wanted me to meet him here. Said he had some information I needed. So I came."

"Okay, Luke," the sheriff said, clearly not convinced that Luke wasn't investigating something else. "I don't suppose you have any theories about who might be responsible for this? It was another attempt to do you under you know."

Luke shrugged but said nothing.

"You think it was Hampton, don't you?" the sheriff asked.

"Could be, I suppose," Luke said. "Or could be I'm making somebody nervous with all my poking around over the cattle business."

"Could be," the sheriff agreed, clearly not convinced of the latter theory. "Whoever it is, you be careful."

"I sure will," Luke said, trying to sound cheerful.

The sheriff scratched his head. "Luke, I don't know what's going on here, but I'm wondering if it wouldn't be better if you took a few days off. Some of the other guys can follow up on the cattle cases."

Luke didn't like where this was going at all. Nor did he like the way the other men were listening to his conversation with the sheriff. He really needed to talk to the sheriff in private. He could let him know what he'd learned today, that would convince the sheriff to let him keep working. He was getting close, and no one else would likely follow up on the evidence he'd found the way he would. It wasn't conclusive enough, unless you *felt it*, and Luke could feel it. He had to convince the sheriff.

He had an idea. "So do you want me off the case now?" he asked.

"Yes, I believe it would be best."

"Fine, then I better head back," he said, turning and walking away. But after just a few steps he turned back. "Sheriff, there's something in my truck you may want to see. Mind giving me a lift to where I parked it so I can show you?"

"Sure, Luke," he said. Then, turning to the other men, he barked some orders and told them he'd be back in a little bit.

The sheriff's little bit turned into nearly an hour, for what Luke had to tell him and show him grabbed his attention. Luke hadn't intended to share his theory of who was doing the mutilations and why, but now he felt he had no choice. He went over the evidence he'd collected and the things he'd learned from his study at the library. As he hoped, the sheriff also began to feel it. But his concern for Luke's safety was even greater.

"Luke, I'm afraid you may be on the right track. But this is just too dangerous for—"

"Sheriff, you've got to let me finish. You know as well as I do that if I don't follow this thing through, we just might lose it altogether," Luke argued.

Sheriff Robinson was still reluctant, but he also knew that Luke had the best chance of making an arrest, or arrests, and he finally gave in.

"Thanks, Sheriff," Luke said. "But don't let the other guys know what I'm doing. I've got to make this thing stick."

"All right, Luke, but you keep me informed. In fact, I want a call every time you head into anything that could be dangerous. I'll be the judge of whether to let you keep following this thing alone, and I'll also be the judge of when it's time for you to pull back. Got it?"

"Yes, sir."

"So what will you be doing next?" the sheriff asked.

"Looking for my informant," Luke answered. "He had something important to tell me, important enough he might have died for it. But if he is still alive, I want and need to get that information."

* * *

Coleen was getting more worried by the minute. Luke should have been back by now. It had been several hours. She'd fixed something for Monty and her to eat and she'd cleaned and straightened the house. She kept looking at her watch. *What could be keeping him?*

Cold dread crept over her. What if something had happened to him? She wondered if she should call the sheriff. She was sure Luke hadn't said anything to any of the other officers. No one would even know he was in trouble . . . *if* he was in trouble.

She paced for a few more minutes, then she tried reading to Monty, but her heart wasn't in it. Finally, she picked up the phone book, looked up Sheriff Robinson's number and dialed. "Is Sheriff Robinson at home?" she asked when the sheriff's wife answered.

"No, he got called out," she said. "But I expect he'll be back anytime. Could I take a message?"

"No, that's okay," Coleen said.

"Could I tell him who's calling?" she insisted.

"No, I don't think so," Coleen said and hung up.

The sheriff had been called out. Maybe Luke had called him. She began to be hopeful, and she even cheered up enough to finally read Monty a story. But after another hour, as darkness began to settle in on the Osborne ranch, Coleen again began to pace. She jumped when the phone rang.

She let it ring three times, wondering what someone would think if she answered Luke's phone. She didn't want any rumors to start. But on the fourth ring she finally threw caution to the wind and picked up the receiver. "Hello," she said.

"Who is this?"

Coleen almost hung up. She knew Bianca's voice. But she swallowed hard then said, "It's Coleen. I'm watching Luke's little boy for a while."

"I see. Well, I'll get with him later," Bianca said, her voice as cold as ice. And before Coleen could say anything else, the line went dead.

Coleen felt herself tremble. That woman didn't like her, and she got the strongest feeling that Bianca would do almost anything to keep her away from Luke. The phone rang again, and this time she let it ring. Finally it quit, and she got to her feet, shaking badly. What kind of rumors would that woman start? Would she cause Luke trouble? Maybe she should just leave again. It seemed like she was always creating problems for Luke.

But leaving was not an appealing idea. Luke and Monty had become the most important people in the world, and she wanted to learn about his church. Coleen squared her shoulders and let determination settle over her. When the phone rang again, she picked it up on the first ring. If it was that woman again, she'd . . .

But it wasn't, and welcome relief washed over her. She had to fight back the tears at hearing Luke's voice. "Luke, I've been so worried," she said. "Are you on your way home? I've fed Monty. But it's almost his bedtime and—"

Luke broke in. "Coleen, who were you on the phone with? I've tried to call twice. The first time it was busy, and just a couple of minutes ago, no one answered."

"I'm sorry, Luke. I hope I didn't cause you any trouble. I didn't know if I should answer the phone. But I did and it was Bianca."

"That woman!" Luke thundered. Then he chuckled. "What did she say when you answered?" he asked.

"Not much, but she didn't sound very happy. She said she'd get hold of you later and hung up. I didn't answer the next time because I was afraid it might be her again."

"You picked up right away this time," Luke observed.

"I decided not to let her worry me, but I hope I didn't cause you any—"

"You didn't," he interrupted, still amused that Bianca would call and get Coleen instead of him. "Anyway, I've got something I've got to follow up on. I wonder what Bianca will think of what I'm about to ask you to do for me." He chuckled, then said, "Would you mind putting Monty to bed and staying with him for the night? I know it's an unfair imposition, but I'll try to get back in time to get you home so you can get ready for work."

"Luke, are you all right?" she asked once again as worry began to press on her.

"I'm fine," he said, pleased at the concern in her voice. "But I'm probably going to be all night. You can use the spare bedroom. I'm sure you can find something to sleep in. Just feel free to rummage around. You will stay with Monty, won't you?"

"Of course I will, Luke, but I'm worried about you."

"I'm fine," he said, wondering how she'd react if she knew how close he'd come to being blown into a million little pieces. Again, he was grateful to the dog for its unwitting sacrifice and to the Lord for the clear warning he'd provided despite Luke's stubbornness. "Thank you, now I've got to run," he told her as cheerfully as he could muster. He really needed to get to work, and he'd just pulled up outside a bar he needed to check out.

"Luke," Coleen began.

"Yes, what is it?" he asked, getting a little impatient.

"I miss you," she said, and he was ashamed at his impatience and warm all over at the same time.

"I miss *you*," he returned, and was surprised at how strong that feeling was. He really had to guard his emotions more closely.

* * *

Luke found Rooster. The gangly informant came crawling home just before sunup, and Luke was waiting for him. It had taken him until just after midnight to find someone in one of the bars in the east end of the county who could tell Luke where Rooster lived. Then, when he'd been unsuccessful in finding anyone who knew anything about the man's whereabouts, he finally—in sheer desperation—located the run-down house outside of town and simply waited. He parked where his truck couldn't be easily seen from Rooster's house.

Luke fought the drowsiness that came over him as he waited. He was more tired than he'd been in a long time. The strain of the past couple days was taking its toll and he needed rest. He finally got out of his truck and walked around for a few minutes, letting the cool night air wake him up. Then he waited in some bushes beside Rooster's house.

He really didn't expect the man to come home. So he was surprised when he heard footsteps in the distance. Somebody was coming, and that somebody was moving very slowly, like he was hurt. There was just enough light from the approaching dawn that Luke, to his relief, recognized Rooster. He waited until his informant had opened the door and started to step inside before he came out of his hiding place and spoke.

Rooster nearly fainted when Luke said, "Glad to see you're alive, my man."

After he recovered from his fright, Rooster let out a stream of obscenities that made Luke discreetly cover his ears. "What are you doing here, man?" Rooster finally asked.

"You wanted to meet me," Luke said evenly. "Let's step inside."

"No, you better beat it, man," Rooster said. "Are you trying to get me killed?"

"Just the question I was about to ask you," Luke said firmly as he pushed Rooster ahead of him into as filthy a dwelling as Luke had ever been in.

Luke shut the door, then felt for and found a light switch and flipped it on. "Hey, keep that off," Rooster snapped as he reached past Luke and pitched the room into darkness again.

But he didn't turn the light off so fast that Luke couldn't see that Rooster had been severely beaten. "Looks like you've had a rough time of it," Luke said.

"I'm lucky to be alive, and if you don't get out of here, I won't be for long," Rooster growled. "You're bad luck, man. Now beat it."

"I'm lucky to be alive too, Rooster, but no thanks to you," Luke countered angrily. "I'm not leaving until I get some answers."

Rooster argued a little longer, but finally seeing that Luke meant business, he said, "You've got some folks mighty upset, Luke."

"Who?" Luke asked.

"You know who."

"Victor Hampton?" Luke asked quietly.

Rooster simply nodded, as if not saying Victor's name might make his revelation less dangerous to him.

"Who else?" Luke pressed.

Rooster hesitated, and Luke poked a finger in his face. "You better say, and you better do it now," he said sternly, his voice carrying more of a warning than his words.

It was dark enough that it was hard to read Rooster's face, but when he finally said, "Sharps Thomsen," there was no mistaking the fear in his voice.

"There's more you intended to tell me," Luke said. "I already know how those two feel about me. They sent bullets after me, remember?"

"That's not all they done," Rooster said after another long and tense pause.

"Spit it out, Rooster," Luke said. "Tell me everything you know."

Rooster was clearly afraid, and from the way he'd been beaten, Luke didn't blame him. But he also knew he had to learn whatever it was Rooster had meant to tell him. *If* he meant to tell him anything. Rooster might well be in Vic's employ. Whether it was of his own free will or not didn't matter. Luke had to remember that Rooster might be part of his enemy's forces now. But despite that thought, he pressed on. "Everything, Rooster."

"I gotta sit down, man," Rooster said.

"Then sit. I noticed you were busted up some. Vic and Sharps do it to you?"

"I didn't say that. Don't ask no more."

"Sit down," Luke said, "and then I'll sure enough ask more. I'm not leaving until I get some answers."

"And if I don't give you none?" Rooster asked defiantly as he slumped onto his sofa. "I gotta have money, you know. You ain't forked none over yet."

"And I don't intend to," Luke said angrily.

"Then I ain't saying no more," Rooster said firmly.

"Okay, have it your way. Guess we'll be going now," he said, reaching for Rooster's arm in the faint light of the room.

Rooster jerked it away. "Hey, you get out of here. I ain't going nowhere with you."

"I'm afraid you are," Luke said as he again grabbed the skinny arm. This time he brought Rooster roughly to his feet. "I'm taking you to jail."

"What for?" Rooster asked defiantly. "You can't jail me for not giving you information you won't pay for."

"True," Luke agreed. "But I can arrest you for attempted murder."

"Hey!" Rooster shouted. "You're talking crazy now, man!"

"Am I really?" Luke said as he jerked Rooster toward the door. "You called me. You set up a meeting. You named the place and time, and I nearly got blown to bits. Seems you're the most likely suspect."

"Okay, okay, I'll talk," Rooster whined.

"That's better," Luke said. "You can sit again, but there'll be no more nonsense. You better start talking."

Rooster more than talked. He sang. And he whined. And he bawled.

Luke learned what he already suspected, and his stomach began to churn. He knew who started the fire. He knew who set the bomb. He even knew who was killing the cows. After listening for close to a half hour, only inserting a question here and there, he finally said, "Thanks, Rooster. Now I'll see what I can do about keeping you alive. Come on. You can't stay here, and you know it."

"Where you taking me?"

"Right now the safest place for you is jail, until I can make arrangements to get you out of town."

Surprisingly, Rooster didn't argue, and Luke delivered him to the jail as promised and then headed for his ranch. As Luke pulled into his yard, Coleen came out of the house. And when he shut off his engine and climbed out of the Ram, she ran to him. To his amazement, she threw her arms around his neck. "I've been so worried, Luke. I was afraid you wouldn't come back." She was almost crying.

"I'm here and I'm fine," he said as he held her tightly for longer than he thought prudent. After all, there was still so much he didn't know about her. Until he did, even if she by some miracle accepted the gospel, he had to keep his feelings in check.

A very hard thing to do.

* * *

"You should've let me waste him," Sharps Thomsen complained when he and Victor Hampton discovered that Rooster was missing. They'd stopped by to pick him up a little before noon for his next assignment.

"We need him," Victor growled.

"Yeah, great, and what happens now?" Sharps asked. "My money says he's gone with Osborne. And if he has, he'll sing for all he's worth."

"Won't help him a bit," Victor said smugly. "He set the bomb, not us."

"But we made him do it," Sharps countered.

"Says who? Me and you, we don't know anything about it."

"But he'll tell him about the fire," Sharps went on.

"He wasn't there. He don't know a thing," Victor said. "Quit worrying. We'll find him, and when we do, we'll see to it that he has nothing more to say to anybody about us."

"Why we messing with Rooster?" Sharps asked suddenly. "Why don't we just find Osborne and end this thing. You ain't scaring him. Nothing we've done has turned his attention away from us. He's going to keep at it until he gets us. We gotta get rid of him once and for all or we'll never get back in business."

"Shut up!" Victor shouted. "We tried to kill him twice now, and he's still walking. I gotta quit listening to you."

Sharps wanted to say something about Victor's fear of the detective, but he knew better. So he simply said, "Let's get out of here."

"Yeah. We'll make things real hot for Luke Osborne," Victor threatened.

He didn't see Sharps roll his eyes, and it was well for Sharps that he didn't.

* * *

Three days passed without incident. Rooster was safely out of the way, and Luke began to put together his evidence on the cases involving the killing of the cattle. He went over everything he had, revisited every scene, and reviewed and compared his photographs. He thought about what Rooster had told him and wondered how he'd ever make an arrest stick. He needed more evidence.

In the office, Bianca was acting a little strange. Luke knew it might be because of her phone call to his place that Coleen answered, but somehow it seemed like it might be something else. He couldn't put his finger on it. He suspected that she was up to something, and he suspected it even more when he walked into the office after the latest attempt on his life and saw someone go into Bianca's office and shut the door. He wasn't sure who it was because he hadn't gotten a good look. He only knew that it was a deputy.

And he guessed, for the moment, he couldn't worry about it.

Meanwhile, behind the door to her office, Bianca was forging ahead with her plan to steal Luke back.

"What have you heard from Dane?" Steve Roper asked.

"Funny you should ask," Bianca said, smiling brightly. "He's working hard. He's been to Indiana, he's been to Colorado, he's been to New Mexico. He's convinced Coleen's the twin of the woman wanted for kidnapping in Indiana."

"We already figured that," Steve said. "Has he learned anything new?"

Her smile grew. "Not yet, but he soon will. That Detective Blume in Indiana has sent out pictures and posters of the twins. He said he'll help Dane in any way he can. The two of them have spent several hours going over the leads that are coming in from the wanted posters."

"And . . ." Steve pressed.

"A couple of them look pretty good. One guy called who says he knows the woman on the poster. He wouldn't talk on the phone. Detective Blume has arranged to meet him. He told Dane he could sit in on the interview. They'll be seeing him tomorrow."

"Sounds good. Hope things go well."

"They will," Bianca said. Then her smile faded. "But they better hurry. Can you believe that Coleen spent the night at Luke's a few days ago?"

Steve's jaw dropped. "He wasn't home," Bianca clarified quickly. "But she stayed and watched Monty while Luke was working. It was the night he almost got blown up. Luke's a great guy, but he's blind when it comes to that woman."

"He'll learn to see soon," Steve said confidently. "Dane's really a pretty good private detective."

"Maybe tomorrow," Bianca confirmed. "Dane's going to call me as soon as they've met with the man who called Detective Blume. The whole thing might be cleared up then."

* * *

Judd Aspen put the phone down and sighed with relief. Gil Stedman had just checked in with him. It seemed he had a meeting the next day in Indiana. He was about to learn where Carly Crockett had gone, and Gil knew what to do.

She had to be silenced—permanently—and Gil might not be the man for the job.

CHAPTER 13

There had been another cow killing reported, but Luke wasn't so concerned about that now. He would end it shortly; Luke knew the *who* of the cattle mutilations. What he didn't know was the *why*. It had nothing to do with satanic rituals, it was only made to look like it. His research had convinced him of that. The dead cows were nothing but an attempt to keep the department, and him in particular, busy.

But why?

He scratched his head as he thought about it. Then it hit him. It was so simple really. The fire at his place was not only done out of hatred, but for the very same purpose as the mutilations, and by the same men. And of course the attempts made on his life were also for the same purpose.

Luke had hampered Victor Hampton's illegal drug manufacturing operation. And if Luke was either dead or very busy on other investigations, it would give Victor what he wanted—the time to cook up some meth.

That was what Rooster had called him about! All that about how he'd made somebody very angry wasn't the reason Rooster had originally called him. It wasn't even because Luke's life was in danger. Rooster might like Luke in his own way, but he wouldn't put his own life on the line for Luke, unless he was worried about a future loss of income should Luke disappear. And that was it—the income! It was because Rooster had somehow learned that Victor was ready to start *cooking* again. And even poor old Rooster knew that Luke was busy on other stuff and would let Victor slip right by. That's why he'd said it would cost extra.

Rooster could care less about Victor's meth lab or Luke's saftey. But he needed money, he always needed money. That's what had made him a pretty decent informant.

But somehow Victor had discovered what Rooster was up to and things had changed.

Rooster was out of the way for now, but Luke had to talk to him again. He needed enough information to get a search warrant, and then he'd nail Vic and Sharps. And when he did, he'd be able to show motive for the attempted killings, the arson, and the cattle deaths. He'd put the man away for the rest of his natural life, and Sharps Thomsen with him. Luke left his desk and headed up the hallway to speak with the sheriff.

Bianca looked up as Luke stepped through Sheriff Robinson's door and closed it. She knew him well enough to know that something big was about to happen. It was written on his face. She wondered if he'd finally cracked the case involving the slaughtered cattle.

They were in there for quite a while, and when they finally came out, she heard Sheriff Robinson say to Luke, "You've done a good job, Luke. Drive carefully and good luck when you get there. I'll talk to you in the morning."

Luke must have cracked the case all right. And now he was going somewhere. She wondered where. She was tempted to ask him, but when he didn't even look her way as she came out the door of her office, she decided not to. There was time enough later to get him to pay attention to her. She should be hearing from Dane anytime. And when she did, it could only be good news.

* * *

It was a warm day in Indiana, and Dane Bering wasn't used to the humidity. He wasn't in very good shape, and the thick air made any exertion on his part even harder. He was mopping his brow as he left the street and entered the police department building. It only took him a minute to find Detective Blume's office. The two shook hands as Dane asked, "Is he here yet?"

"Haven't seen him," Howie answered, "but I'm sure he'll come."

Dane sat down heavily and Howie said, "I'll do most of the talking until I give you the signal, *if* I give it to you. Remember, he's here about my wanted poster, and we won't focus much on the gal out your way until I'm satisfied that we have all we can get from him about my case."

Dane had no choice but to agree, but he did have some questions he intended to get in. He was convinced that if the guy knew the woman on the poster, that he'd know Coleen. He mopped his brow again. It was even warm in Howie's air-conditioned office.

Howie stepped out, and when he came back in, he was accompanied by a dark-complexioned man. Dane smiled to himself. If Coleen knew this guy, she must be a bad apple, just like Bianca suspected. Granted, he was clean cut and dressed expensively, but his greased-back hair and uncultured expression belied his general high-class appearance. Dane stood and extended his hand as Detective Blume said, "Dane Bering is a private detective that is working with me. Dane, this is George Strong. He's the fellow that called about the poster."

Dane had a strong feeling that "George Strong" was not really the man's name, but at this point it didn't matter. Later he might need to look into the man's identity a little closer. The three men sat down and Howie held up a picture of the girl he wanted for kidnapping. "So, you think you know this woman?"

The man who called himself George nodded his head. "Yeah, I know her all right."

"What's her name?" Howie asked.

"I knew her as Kyla Crockett," George said.

"When did you last see her?"

"Oh, maybe five, six months ago. I don't recall exactly."

"Tell us how you know her."

George shifted somewhat nervously in his seat. Dane wondered how much of what this man said could be believed. "She was just a friend," George finally answered.

"A friend," Blume stated. "Girlfriend?"

Hesitation and shifting in his seat again made Dane suspect the man was making his story up as he went—he wasn't very good at this show he was putting on. Dane was already beginning to feel like he was wasting his time here. But when George finally spoke, he said, "Her sister worked with me."

Both Dane and Howie took interested notice of that statement. Dane wanted to throw in a question right then, but a sharp look from Howie kept him still. Howie asked, "What kind of work are you in?"

"Real estate," George said after only a slight pause.

"Where?" Howie fired at him.

"Uh, New Mexico," George responded.

Dane was getting even more interested, but Howie steered George back on to the woman he was looking for. "So tell me about this Kyla woman. Did she work with you too? How well did you know her? Did her sister talk a lot about her?"

George seemed to have trouble handling so many questions at once, so Howie had to walk him through them more slowly. In the end, they learned that Kyla had applied to work at the same office George and her sister did, but she had a serious drug problem and the boss there refused to hire her. That had made her sister Carly angry, so she quit. The boss felt bad about that because Carly was a decent worker. He'd take her back if they could locate her, but George, even though he'd heard from her sometime back, had declined to let the boss know he'd found her because he'd learned that she had a drug problem too. She'd just managed to keep it hidden from the boss. George doubted if Carly even suspected that *he* knew.

Howie wasn't getting much, Dane could see, but he still shook his head as Dane started to speak. Then Howie asked, "So this Kyla, do you have any idea where she's at now?"

The pause this time was longer than any before, and Dane again wondered if anything they'd been told was true. When George answered, he simply said, "Last time I heard she was in New York."

"And who did you hear that from?" Howie asked quickly. Howie now doubted if "George" even knew what kind of persona he meant to put on.

"Carly. She said her sister had figured that with her good looks and all she could probably land a job in a big city. She's a looker you know," George added.

"Has Kyla ever been in Indiana that you know of?" Howie asked.

"Seems like Carly said something about it one day when Kyla came to see her sister at work. It was just before she'd applied," he said. "You know, I haven't heard from Carly for a while, and I'm not sure how to get hold of her. If I knew where she was at right now, I'm sure she'd know how to find Kyla."

Howie finally glanced at Dane and nodded. "Twin sister?" Dane asked.

"Identical."

"Do you know their birth date?" Dane asked. He was thinking that if nothing else, driver's license checks, records checks, and so on could be done nationwide with a birthday. Howie nodded with approval.

This time there was no hesitation. "That I remember clearly. Kyla's is March first and Carly's is March second."

The two detectives looked at each other. Dane said, "Those are different days."

George grinned. "That's right. Kyla was born just before midnight, Carly just after."

"The year?" Dane pressed.

"I'm not sure. I think they're about twenty-four or twenty-five. That's the best I can do."

That was good enough. If George was telling the truth, surely Dane could find out a whole lot more about her in fairly short order. But he thought it was still worth it to ask a few more things. "When did you last talk to Carly?"

"Let's see," George said, and then he hesitated again. It was as though he were trying to do some complicated computing in his head. "Four or five months," he finally stammered.

"That's quite a while ago," Howie broke in.

"Yeah, I know."

"Where was she then?" Dane asked.

George thought for longer than was necessary, and Dane had the sinking feeling they were being fed a line. All he'd gained had been lost, he feared. But again, George finally came up with an answer. "Colorado," he said.

Dane felt like he was riding a bucking horse. One minute he was about to get thrown, the next he was firmly in the saddle. *Colorado* put him firmly in the saddle. He already knew that was where Coleen claimed to have been just before coming to Utah. He'd been unable to confirm that, but when he coupled that with the fact that her accident had been in New Mexico, the very state George said they'd worked together, there had to be some substantial truth to what George was telling them.

George surprised them with the next question. "Where did you say you were from?" he asked Dane.

"I'm a private detective in Roosevelt, Utah," he said.

"Not familiar with the place," George said. Then he stood up. "Sorry I couldn't be of more help. But I've got to go now."

"What's the hurry?" Howie asked. "I've still got a few more questions. Like how can I get a hold of you again?"

But George was suddenly interested only in leaving, and since there was no legal basis to prevent it, Howie and Dane watched helplessly as he walked out of the room.

"That was one of the strangest interviews I've ever conducted," Howie said. "I think half of what he told us he was making up as he went along."

"I agree," Dane said thoughtfully. "But if by any chance the names and birthdays are correct, we might be able to find out a lot more from somebody who is more helpful. What I wonder is why he even wanted to talk to us. Was he looking for information rather than giving it?"

"That was my thought," Howie agreed. "I just wish we knew who he was. George Strong he is not, I'm certain of that."

The men talked for a few more minutes and decided how to proceed from there. Clearly, they would have to use a small range of birth years, but by trying the names and birthdays in various state driver's license bureaus, and maybe with the Social Security Administration, they'd soon know if there were twins by the names of Kyla and Carly Crockett. It was getting late, so they decided to begin the next morning.

Dane returned to his hotel and wondered if he had enough to bother Bianca with. He thought about it as he checked himself out in the mirror. His hair was thinning a little, and he could probably do with a few sit-ups, but with his straight teeth, charming smile, and eyes no woman could resist, he was still a catch if he did think so himself. He wanted to hear Bianca's voice, and he figured she'd probably want to hear his too, so he decided the lead he had was enough. It was past five o'clock in Utah, so he dialed her home number.

She answered on the first ring. "Hi, Bianca, it's me," he told her, enticingly.

"I've been hoping you'd call," she said.

Dane felt a little shiver in his spine. She was one sweet girl. He'd sure like to get something going with her; he was tired of being single.

"How did it go?" she asked quickly. "Did you learn who Coleen really is?"

Dane smiled to himself as he prepared to answer. It would have been a lot more fun to tell her in person so he could see the reaction on her pretty face. And as he considered that, he wondered why it was she was so interested in this Coleen woman anyway. Why did Bianca care who she really was, especially to spend hundreds, maybe thousands of dollars? That thought, for some reason, made him uncomfortable, and he was suddenly determined to find out as soon as he could.

"I think so," he said in answer to her query. "In fact, I'm almost positive."

That might have been a little too strong, but Dane could picture Bianca's face lighting up, and he wished she were with him right now.

"Good," she said, and he could feel the smile in her voice across the telephone lines. "So what's her name?"

"Carly Crockett," he said. "And her twin sister's name is Kyla. They might be into drugs pretty heavy." He wasn't at all sure why he divulged that information, since without concrete confirmation it was very premature. But he enjoyed her reaction.

Bianca squealed in delight, and Dane wanted to kiss her, she sounded so cute. "Oh, Dane, thank you," she gushed. "You don't know how happy this makes me."

Again he wondered why, but she was so sweet right now that he decided not to ask. Instead he explained how he would proceed from this point, finishing with, "When I get back, I should have some concrete information.

* * *

Gil Stedman, who was using the alias "George Strong" only long enough to get the information he was looking for, was examining a map of Utah. He had only to get to Roosevelt, Utah, find Carly, and get his work done. He grinned to himself as he found the location of the small town in eastern Utah.

The grin was not only about that though. He thought he'd handled the two detectives pretty well. They'd bought his story about a real-estate office in New Mexico without question, and they'd believed every word he'd said about the drugs. And he hadn't given them very much to go on. At least, it would take a few days before they could confirm the names he'd given them, and even longer to find other people who'd known them and could give more accurate information.

And by the time that was done, he'd be gone from Utah and one of the twins would have been relieved of her burdens. And then his boss would have to get off his back and he could go back to doing what he did best—working all sorts of illegal deals for Mr. Aspen and receiving a handsome salary for his work.

Gil booked a flight for Utah the next morning and headed for the bar in his hotel. He'd earned a few drinks.

* * *

Luke smiled at Coleen as they drove down Parley's Canyon. He'd talked her into accompanying him to Salt Lake for his visit with Rooster. He was in his own truck and using his own gas, so the sheriff couldn't object. Coleen could watch Monty, and maybe spend a couple of hours at a mall or take in a movie while he conducted his interview. He just hoped Rooster hadn't left town. That was his only worry, but it wasn't a big concern because Rooster had a healthy fear of Victor Hampton and Sharps Thomsen.

"This is about where I passed the bus," he said, recalling the anxious day he'd spent trying to keep her from leaving.

"I remember thinking the truck was just like yours," she said with a smile as she brushed a stray lock of her long blonde hair over her shoulder. "I never dreamed it might actually be you."

Luke reached over and took her hand. "Couldn't let you get away, could I?" He grinned. "You're okay, you know that?" And then that old nagging worry came back to pick at him. It made him very uncomfortable that there was even a possibility he felt such things for another man's wife. As soon as he had Victor and Sharps behind bars, he'd seriously look into finding out who she used to be. He had to know. He was getting much too fond of her not to.

That afternoon, on the way to the city, she'd asked him if he would teach her about his church. There was no doubting her sincerity, and he'd promised to do just that. Then he had proceeded to explain to her about the Holy Ghost and the feelings that came from that member of the Godhead. She'd seemed to accept every word he said, so he suggested that she see the missionaries.

"You mean you can't teach me?" she'd protested.

"I could, but they can do it better and in an organized fashion. We'll invite them to my house. I'll be there every minute," he promised, after explaining how the system for teaching people the gospel was set up in the Church. "And I'll answer your questions. If you'd like, I'll even read the Book of Mormon with you."

That had been more than satisfactory to her, and he looked forward to participating as she learned the gospel. But again, he felt a most uncomfortable twist in his gut. That *what if* just wouldn't go away.

While Luke went looking for Rooster, Monty and Coleen decided they'd spend some time in the mall. Monty was easily persuaded with the occasional promise of a treat. Luke lifted his little son up and hugged him. "I'll try not to be too long," he promised. Then he turned to Coleen. He just couldn't help himself—he kissed her briefly, held her tightly in his arms for a minute, then said, "Thanks for your help, Coleen. You're the best."

Then he went in search of Rooster. When the time he'd arranged to meet Coleen and Monty rolled around, Rooster had still failed to turn up. It seemed Rooster might not be in the city where he'd promised to stay after the sheriff had pulled strings and secured him a job there. Not finding Rooster as quickly as he'd hoped meant Luke would have to spring for a hotel room for Coleen. The county would pick up his tab, but not hers. He'd have to take up the search for his less-than-dependable informant the next day, and he was glad he'd asked Coleen to arrange for the next day off just in case they didn't get back that night.

After meeting Monty and Coleen, setting them up in a hotel, and eating dinner, Luke left once again in search of Rooster. Luke found him in a bar getting very drunk at about ten that night. He just hoped Rooster wasn't too drunk to remember what he'd originally planned to tell Luke.

A fifty-dollar bill and an hour of sobering-up time finally got from Rooster what Luke had expected and hoped to hear.

In an almost unintelligible slur, Rooster, his eyes red and breath smelling like a brewery, said, "Vic, he just wanted to get you busy and worrying enough about yourself that he could get some strong meth brewed up."

"And he caught you talking to me on the phone?" Luke guessed.

The look that Rooster gave Luke was all the answer he needed. And then on another hunch, he asked the quickly sobering drunk, "And *you* set the bomb that was supposed to kill me?"

Rooster began to cry and blubber. "He made me. Sharps held a gun on me. They were going to kill me if I didn't do just what they asked."

Luke pulled the cell phone from his hip and told Rooster to stay put while he walked to a corner a few feet away. He dialed Sheriff Robinson, told him what he'd learned, and explained that he was in his truck instead of his patrol car and that Monty and Coleen had accompanied him to Salt Lake. That now became a problem because Rooster had to be arrested and held as a material witness, if not as an accessory to attempted murder.

"That's okay, Luke," the sheriff said. "You can go back after them tomorrow. Bring Rooster here tonight. I want him in jail where we can keep track of him until we make our case against Vic and Sharps."

Luke waited to groan until he'd hung up. Then he dialed the hotel, promised to meet Coleen and Monty there the next morning, and then arrested Rooster and headed for Duchesne. He wished he could be with Coleen instead of Rooster, but he was also excited that he had enough now to put Victor away for life.

* * *

Victor had no way of knowing what Luke was doing. He was under the mistaken impression that Luke was worried, busy with a case he couldn't solve, and not thinking of him at all. So he was now smugly at work. The meth he was making at that very moment would bring him several thousand dollars.

CHAPTER 14

It was a very long night, and Luke was tired. The last thing he wanted was to fall asleep at the wheel and give Rooster a chance to run. The closer they got to Duchesne, the more nervous the man became. Luke tried to keep him talking, both to calm Rooster down and to keep himself awake, but eventually Rooster slumped in the seat and fell asleep.

The exhaustion became too great for Luke and he knew he had to pull over and walk around in the cool evening air to keep himself alert. He pulled off the road on a scenic area overlooking the Strawberry Reservoir. Of course, there was nothing scenic about it this dark night, but it got him off the highway. He checked Rooster, who seemed to be sleeping soundly now. His prisoner's handcuffed hands lay on his lap under the seatbelt. Luke couldn't help but marvel at how long and skinny those fingers were.

After assuring himself that Rooster was not likely to wake up in the next few minutes, Luke stepped out of the truck, stuck the keys in his pocket, and began to walk around the area. He rubbed his eyes, did a couple of jumping jacks, and gulped in some big breaths of the cool air.

After a couple of minutes he began to feel more alert and stepped back to the truck, opened the door, and discovered that Rooster was not in it! In what couldn't have been more than a couple of seconds, Luke analyzed his situation, heard a very soft crunching sound in the gravel behind him, and instinctively whirled away from the truck, dropping low as he did. He felt a blur of wind pass his cheek and then something struck his shoulder with a great deal of force.

The blow dropped him to his knees, but Luke continued to roll and came to his feet, his right arm numb, but with his adrenaline pumping. The light from inside his truck was all he needed to see by. Rooster, a large stick in his cuffed hands, was already swinging again. This time his blow missed completely, and Luke came up like a bear and drove his injured shoulder into the prisoner's belly with such force that he felt the man's breath leave in a gush.

Luke grabbed the stick with his left hand and tossed it aside, then delivered a blow to Rooster's jaw that tossed his long body back against the bed of Luke's truck. Rooster began to slump to the ground, but Luke, his right arm still numb from the blow to his shoulder, grabbed Rooster by the shirt with his left arm and raised him back up, slamming him once more against the truck. Then Luke held him there. Rooster was gasping, trying to draw air down his long windpipe.

Luke continued to hold him tightly while Rooster's breath returned, and feeling slowly crept back into Luke's right shoulder and arm. At length, Luke said, "That was a stupid thing to do, Rooster."

"I had to," Rooster crowed. "You don't understand. Sharps Thomsen will kill me. You can't take me back there."

"Nobody will be touching you where you're going, Rooster. I'll see to it now that you're charged with attempted murder for setting the bomb that was meant to kill me. I'm beginning to believe that it was your idea, not Vic's or Sharp's." He was thinking no such thing, but he was angry. However, he had a new respect for Rooster's own treachery and he wondered what kind of relationship Rooster might have had with Vic and Sharps.

"No, man, it wasn't my idea. They made me do it," Rooster blubbered. The fight was gone from him, and self-pity had taken over.

"We better get going. And I'm not forgetting what you just tried to do," Luke told him as he freed one bony wrist from the cuffs, spun Rooster around, and secured the cuffs behind his back.

Rooster moaned and complained all the way back to Duchesne that the cuffs were too tight and that he couldn't get comfortable in the seat. But Luke had no pity. He kept thinking about what Rooster might have done had the stick connected with the back of his head as intended. At the least, it would have been terribly embarrassing; he would undoubtedly have taken Luke's truck and left Luke stranded there. At the worst, Luke could have been killed with his own pistol.

Several times as he drove, very much awake now, Luke offered silent prayers of thanks to the Lord. He also scolded himself for being so careless. He wondered again just how involved Rooster had become with Victor and Sharps. But as he tried to talk to Rooster on the ride to Duchesne, the man simply refused to speak. So Luke decided to wait. More questioning could come later.

Sheriff Robinson and his chief deputy met Luke at the jail when he pulled into the sally port at about two in the morning. They'd already woken a judge up and had a search warrant partly prepared. Now all he needed was a little more information from Rooster, and a team of deputies would be called out. Victor Hampton would get a most unpleasant surprise.

But Rooster refused to give any information. He denied everything he'd told Luke in Salt Lake, then he clammed up and stubbornly refused to say another word. The sheriff was not impressed with Rooster's behavior, and told him that he needed to think hard about what would happen to him if he didn't give them the information they knew he had. But Rooster was mad or scared and he continued to say nothing. The judge went home without issuing the search warrant, as he felt he needed more than the little bit Rooster had told Luke in the bar in Salt Lake City, especially since he now denied it was true.

Sheriff Robinson and Luke escorted Rooster into the jail part of the complex and turned him over to the booking officer. "We're charging him with attempted murder," Sheriff Robinson told the officer. Then to Rooster he simply said, "We'll have formal charges drawn up in the morning and get you before a judge. You might think this is all fun and games, but you're about to learn differently."

Rooster's eyes got real big, but he still said nothing. Luke and the sheriff left him there to be booked and returned to the sheriff's office. "You better get some sleep," he told Luke, "and then go get Coleen and your boy. Take your patrol car. You don't need to be burning your own gas. We'll take care of things here. There's not much more we can do until Rooster decides to talk."

"In the meantime, Vic's over there brewing up drugs with dollar signs in his eyes," Luke growled.

"Don't worry, we'll take him down, Luke. Your case is good, and as soon as Rooster comes around, we'll have all we need to bring all kinds of charges against Vic and that partner of his. Now go home and get some rest. That's what you're going to do. Take the rest of the day off. You've done good work and deserve a little breather," the sheriff said with a tired smile.

Luke didn't go home at all. His patrol car was at the ranch, but he didn't care to take the time to go get it, so he simply got in his truck and started west toward Salt Lake. He was angry and uptight and wide awake. He'd driven clear to the Strawberry Valley before he finally became drowsy again. Then he pulled off the road in the very spot where Rooster had made his escape attempt, shut off his truck, lowered the back of his seat, and dozed.

Luke dreamt of Jamie, something he hadn't done for weeks. He awoke thinking of her, missing her, longing for her, and caught himself with tears in his eyes. She had been so real in the dream that he could still feel her gentle touch, smell her favorite perfume, and hear the music of her laughter. He guessed he'd always miss her. Their love had been so complete, and so sweet.

And her death had been so bitter.

New resolve salved the bitterness. Victor was going to go to prison. Luke would not, could not, fail—for Jamie's sake.

It was fully light. Luke glanced at his watch and was surprised to see that it was almost seven. He started the truck and pulled onto the road again, trying to keep the images of Jamie in his dream bright in his mind. But as he drove, and as he remembered that the Lord wanted a mother for Monty, the images faded, and by the time he pulled into the parking lot of the hotel shortly after eight, he was anticipating a sweet greeting from Coleen.

And that was exactly what he received. He tapped on the door, and when it opened her face lit up, her arms reached out, and they fell into a warm, wholesome embrace. Luke loved Jamie. He would always love Jamie. But he discovered as his lips pressed gently against the warm sweetness of Coleen's that there was still room for more love, for another love.

He drew back, startling Coleen. He couldn't love her! She might have a husband somewhere. He had to know. And he had to know soon.

"What's the matter, Luke?" Coleen said, the hurt in her brown eyes cutting at his heart.

"It's just been a long night," he said evasively. "And not a very good one. I'm sorry."

Coleen reached for him again, but he slipped aside and said, "How's my little guy been?"

"He's been great, Luke," Coleen said, fighting to keep the hurt from her voice. She was an intelligent woman and very perceptive. She knew what was bothering him because it had been bothering her too. She couldn't imagine anyone else in her life but Luke, and yet she knew the reality was that there could be, or at least could have been, someone else. And she was afraid that until she knew who she really was, as much as she didn't want to know, he could never love her. And oh, how she wanted his love. Her heart ached for him, and for herself.

Monty was in his father's arms, and Coleen had to fight back the urge to cry. She wished they could be a family. She wanted nothing more. She silently watched Luke, whose back was now to her, as he held his son, hugged and kissed him, and told him he loved him.

She loved them both. Surely she could never have felt such love for anyone else in her life. But the past was a dark secret, begging to be opened, and fear filled her mind.

When Luke finally turned back to her, he seemed himself again. "You have the day off, and I've already put in enough hours for one day. How about if the three of us have some breakfast and then visit the zoo?"

Monty squealed with delight, and Coleen smiled, a positive response. "But first, Luke, you need to sleep," she said, noting the exhaustion in his eyes. They seemed a darker blue this morning, as if the tiredness and the weight of his worries eclipsed their brightness.

"I slept for a while in the truck on the way back from Duchesne," he said.

She stepped close to him, touched a finger to his cheek just below his right eye, and said, "Your eyes tell me it was not nearly enough. Lie down on the bed and close them. Monty and I will go out and find something to eat and bring it back. Then we'll eat here together."

Luke found it hard to refuse as he was very tired. So he did as she asked and stretched out on the bed. Coleen threw a blanket over him, and on impulse, bent and lightly kissed his cheek, savoring for a brief moment the roughness of his day-old beard. Her heart throbbed with love as she straightened up and said, "Get some rest. Monty and I'll be back."

"Coleen," he said softly as she turned to leave.

"Yes?" She said in the form of a question, almost adding *dear,* but catching herself.

"Will you call my father and ask him to check my animals?"

"Of course," she said, and once again she stepped near the bed and bent to kiss his cheek.

* * *

A fog filled Gil's head as he boarded the plane for Salt Lake City. He'd drunk too much and too late, and had almost missed his flight this morning. Security was tight at the airport, and it took over an hour to clear it. By the time he reached his plane, they were making the last boarding call. He handed the attendant his ticket, boarded the plane, staggered to his seat, and almost fell into it.

The lady by the window looked at him with disgust as he blew stale breath into her face. But he didn't care what she thought of him. The only person whose approval he sought was Judd Aspen's, and not because he liked the man—he despised him—but because Judd provided him with a good living when he was in favor. And he would be there again when the assignment that was now leading him to Utah was over.

The lady next to him started to get up, asked him if she could get past, and waited politely for him to get out of his seat and let her step into the aisle. He sat there, his bloodshot eyes staring defiantly at her face. She finally attempted to squeeze her way past him, and he angrily reached up and shoved her back into her seat. "Stay put, lady," he said. "It's time for the plane to take off."

"I don't feel well," she said, fear in her eyes. "I need to get out."

Gil, still drunk from his long night in the hotel bar, swore at her and told her to stay. Then he lay his head back and closed his eyes.

When he opened them again, he realized he must have dozed off and was surprised to see an airport police officer standing over him. "Come with me, sir," he was ordered.

That made Gil mad, and he swore and said, "I've got a ticket and I need to get to Salt Lake. I'm going nowhere with you."

It was only when the officer reached for his arm that he realized there were two officers, and both of them were very large. Resistance was futile, but their presence still made him angry. "What did I do?" he asked as he slowly got to his feet and stumbled into the aisle.

"You're drunk," he was told. "And you've created a disturbance on this plane. We can't allow it to take off with you on board. Please, come with us."

Gil's anger got the best of him then, and he swung at the officer. That got him taken down in the aisle, handcuffed, and forcibly removed from the plane. Then, instead of spending the day finding and getting rid of Carly, he went to jail. His one phone call was to Judd Aspen, asking the boss for bail money. But Judd curtly told him he was on his own and hung up on him.

Gil was then booked, fingerprinted, and escorted to a cell. "You'll see a judge in the next day or two," he was told, and the cell door closed firmly behind him.

As he sank onto the hard, cold bunk, hatred and anger welled up within him. This was all Carly Crockett's fault, he told himself. He wouldn't be here forever, and when he got out, he knew right where to find her. She would suffer for the problems she'd caused him. Gil would make that girl pay before she died.

* * *

Coleen quietly opened the door to her hotel room and smiled when she saw that Luke was sleeping soundly. She put her finger to her lips and whispered to Monty, "Your dad's asleep. He's really tired. Let's not disturb him." She then led the little fellow back into the hallway and shut the door. "Let's go find a place to eat. We'll check on your father later," she told Monty.

"But when will Dad eat?" Monty objected as she led him back to the elevator.

"As soon as he wakes up. We'll check on him again."

"But he promised we could go to the zoo," Monty protested. "Let's go wake him up."

Coleen dropped to her knees and looked Monty in the eye. "We have to be checked out of the hotel by noon. I'll bet your dad will sleep until then. And we'll let him," she said firmly. "But after that, I promise I'll make sure he takes us to the zoo."

That was good enough for Monty, and he went willingly with Coleen. They left the hotel, walked up the street to a bus stop, and sat there, eating their breakfast. When they'd finished, they returned to the hotel, and Coleen peeked in on Luke. As she expected, he was still sleeping soundly. She wrote him a note telling him they'd be back before noon, and left it where he could find it if he woke up before they returned.

She and Monty then spent the rest of the morning on Temple Square, where she viewed several films in the Visitors' Center, obtained a copy of the Book of Mormon, spoke with a pair of sweet girls who wore name tags that identified them as missionaries for The Church of Jesus Christ of Latter-day Saints, and then stood for ten minutes in front of the huge statue of Jesus that stood impressively at the top of a long, circular ramp. The peace and love that came over her was almost overwhelming, and tears moistened her eyes.

"That's Jesus," Monty said as he held her hand and stared reverently at the likeness of the Savior.

She squeezed his hand but said nothing. He waited patiently with her until she finally said, "Let's go see the temple."

When they were near it, she again looked upward in awe. Something touched her soul, and she felt a longing to enter that beautiful structure. But she already knew from what she'd learned that morning in the films and from the two girls, that it was a sacred building and only worthy members of Luke's church were allowed inside.

Coleen was startled when she looked at her watch. They had to be checked out of the hotel in twenty minutes. She took Monty's hand and said, "Come on, Monty, we've got to hurry. Your dad will be wondering what's happened to us."

* * *

Luke had read Coleen's note and now he was pacing impatiently. He was hungry and ready to go. It was checkout time in just a few minutes. Tension began to fill him as he waited. He flipped the TV from channel to channel, finding nothing of interest. Finally, he simply plopped down on the bed and tried to rest again.

It was five minutes to twelve when the door opened. Luke was about to say something sharp to Coleen, but the look on her face cut him short. He couldn't quite define it, but he read in her eyes a peace he'd not seen before. She looked so serene as she smiled at him. "Sorry we're late, Luke. Monty and I have had a good morning. And you needed the sleep."

He couldn't argue with that, but he was rested now and anxious for some lunch. "We've been to Temple Square, Dad," Monty said as he jumped onto the bed beside his father. "And Coleen cried when she saw that big statue of Jesus."

A lump rose in Luke's throat as he got up off the bed and took another look at this woman who was becoming far too important in his life. She was literally glowing, and in her hand was a copy of the Book of Mormon. "How long were you there? On Temple Square, I mean," he asked.

"Over two hours," Coleen said, "and I loved every minute of it. But I have a lot of questions now."

"Great," Luke said. "After lunch and the zoo, we'll head for home, and I'll answer any questions you want to ask, if I can."

Luke kept asking himself why he was letting himself fall for her as they walked hand in hand through the zoo, laughing together at Monty's expressions of delight. Luke kept reminding himself that he may well be setting himself up for a fall and a lot of heartache when he finally discovered her past, but he knew he had to do it. She was showing every sign of wanting to learn about the Church and even join it, and that was great, but her past was a dark abyss that had to be illuminated. He had to know who she really was and who might be lurking in that mysterious past, who might shatter those dreams of a future with Coleen that he was trying so hard to suppress.

On the trip home, she did indeed ask a lot of questions, and Luke was amazed at them. She had learned so much in those few hours at Temple Square. He couldn't help but be impressed. He answered most of her questions. There were a couple that were so deep that he simply told her they'd talk about them later, which she was fine with.

By the time they drove into Duchesne, Luke was finding it hard to believe that there could be anything bad in Coleen's past. She just seemed so good. The word *love* was floating around in his head, almost making him dizzy.

CHAPTER 15

The term "hitting pay dirt" best described Dane Bering's day. And he was thinking how happy Bianca would be when he unloaded all the dirt he'd uncovered about one Carly Crockett and her wanted twin sister Kyla. He dialed her number quickly, unable to wipe the grin off his face.

"Where are you, Dane?" Bianca asked after taking the phone from her roommate.

"I'm in Lexington, Kentucky," he said. "And I have some interesting stuff to tell you."

When he didn't go on, Bianca prodded, "I'm listening."

"First, before I tell you what I've learned, I want to know something," Dane said.

Bianca didn't like the tone of his voice, but she asked, "What's that, Dane?"

"Why are you so fired up about getting dirt on Coleen? I mean, what's she done to you to make you so driven?"

Bianca had to bite her tongue to keep from snapping at Dane. It was really none of his business, and she wished she could tell him so. But since she couldn't, she did what she had to do; she answered as sweetly but evasively as possible. "I guess I've been working with cops too long," she began. "I'm getting to where I don't trust people like I used to. This woman has come into town with all her lies about not remembering who she is and she's taking people for a ride."

She's taking Luke for a ride. But there was no way she could tell Dane that.

"Seems like kind of a poor reason to be spending your own money on finding out who she is. There's something you're not telling me," Dane said as casually as he could.

Bianca felt trapped. She hated to lie, but maybe stretching the truth wouldn't hurt too much. After all, she was doing it for Luke and Monty.

"Yeah, you're right," she said, her mind racing for something to say. "She's been rude to me and my roommate. In fact, she's been downright nasty. I grew up in Duchesne, and I just know she's going to hurt somebody before she gets through with the people here. She's sweet to some and mean to others, like me and Liz. I just can't stand to see what she's doing."

Pretty lame, she knew. Dane knew it too, but he could see he was not going to get a straight answer from Bianca. Anyway, there were other ways. He'd find out what was going on in her pretty head. Meantime, he'd back off.

"I see," he said, trying to sound convinced. "Well, it seems you have good reason to be concerned. Like I told you before, her name is Carly Crockett. She and her twin sister Kyla were born in a little town in Kansas. They grew up on a ranch, but when they were about seventeen their parents were killed. It looked like they were pretty well set, but no one knew what terrible debts their father had generated. He gambled a lot, and everything he owned was mortgaged. The ranch and everything that went with it were taken away to satisfy the debts. Poor girls were left with nothing. They had no brothers or sisters or other close relatives that anyone knows about. I guess they were pretty much left alone. They both started waiting tables and rented a small apartment together."

Nothing Dane had said so far was bad, Bianca thought with a sinking heart. In fact, it sounded like a real life tragedy. Not the sort of thing she wanted Luke to hear. He had a soft heart to start with.

But Dane wasn't through. "It wasn't long before they were spending more money than anyone believed they could possibly be earning waiting tables, so people became suspicious of them. Well, before anyone could figure out where the money was coming from, they simply left town. They showed up in a small town in Kentucky, about ten miles from Lexington. They began to make friends with the wrong kind of people and always seemed to have plenty of money."

"Where was it coming from?" Bianca asked.

"Well, people don't seem to know for sure, but everyone I talked to said they were sure that both girls were pushing drugs."

"Ah," Bianca said, wanting and willing to believe that was exactly what they were doing.

Dane went on. "They both liked horses, and before long, they were working at a big ranch about ten miles or so out of Lexington. They exercised horses, cleaned stables, that kind of thing. But one day Kyla disappeared. So did one of the ranch's trucks, a horse trailer, and an expensive brood mare."

"She took them?" Bianca asked.

"Seemed that way. Carly claimed she didn't know where Kyla had gone, but nobody believed her except for one of the owner's sons. He took her side, but everybody said it was just because she was paying a lot of attention to him. And I do mean *a lot,*" Dane said with emphasis.

"Figures," Bianca said.

"Yeah, well, anyway, the truck and trailer eventually were located back in Kansas. They were being operated with stolen plates by a man who claimed he'd borrowed them. He never would say who he borrowed them from, but everyone knew it was Kyla Crockett. The horse disappeared. But that's not surprising. Horses are stolen and just disappear all the time here in this part of the country."

"What about Carly?" Bianca asked. "What did she do after that?"

"She worked at the ranch for a few more months, but eventually she and her boyfriend had a fight and she lost her job," Dane said.

"Where did she go?"

"She disappeared for a while. Folks think she and her sister were involved in some kind of scheme, probably drugs again. But both of them eventually were seen back in their hometown. But before the cops from Kentucky had learned where they were, they left again. And it was reported that the people who then owned the place they grew up on reported missing quite a bit of cash. Kyla wasn't seen again, at least not that I've been able to discover, until the kidnapping in Indiana. Of course, she's wanted there now, as you know. They think she might have taken the kids and sold them to some rich couple who wanted kids. That, along with the drugs, could explain why Kyla had so much money all the time.

"Anyway, Carly eventually came back to Kentucky. And she was driving a new pickup. She was looking for work exercising and caring for horses again, and despite the word that had gotten out about her, she got a job with a wealthy landowner by the name of Judd Aspen. He has a ton of horses."

Dane paused and Bianca asked, "Then what?"

"That's pretty much it, from what I've been able to learn. Some guy that also works for this Aspen fellow got sweet on her, as they say. Folks say they moved in together out on Aspen's ranch. That was where she was working the last anyone around here knew. She seems to have vanished again. People claim they haven't seen her for months. I tried to talk to Aspen, but he has armed guards around his place and no one gets in without an invitation. They say he has some of the best horses around and the security is to protect them. Kentucky has a lot of good horses and security isn't unknown, but Aspen's seems a bit heavy."

"What about the guy Carly was living with?" Bianca asked. "Where's he?"

"People don't know. He hasn't been around for a while either. People think they might be together somewhere, but—"

"We know that's not true," Bianca interrupted. "She must have got tired of him." *And was looking for a new boyfriend,* she thought bitterly. Well, it wasn't going to be Luke Osborne. She'd learned enough already to make sure of that. "What are you going to do now?" she asked Dane.

"Well, it's your money, but I think it would be a good idea to do a little more snooping around in New Mexico. It was near Santa Fe that she had the accident where she supposedly lost her memory," Dane reminded her.

"Go ahead, Dane," Bianca said. "But I don't suppose we need much more. I think you've done a great job already. We have enough to discredit her."

"Be careful, Bianca," Dane cautioned her. "There have never been any arrests on either Carly or Kyla. And most of what I've told you is just what people think, you know, about them pushing drugs and all. Until I give the okay, don't breathe a word of this."

"Yeah, okay," Bianca said, but she was convinced it was all true. The best of what she'd learned, and which would really knock Luke for a loop, was the way Coleen had lived with guys. That would really upset him and be the end of his friendship with Coleen, or Carly, as Bianca intended to let everyone know was her true name.

"I'll call you from New Mexico as soon as I've learned something there," Dane promised before hanging up. "And remember, don't say anything about this until I give the word."

"I won't," Bianca said. She was beside herself with glee.

Liz came in and asked, "So what did you learn?"

"Coleen Whitman is really Carly Crockett, and she's a drug pusher and very immoral. She's lived with two guys that Dane's been able to learn about so far. Who knows, there may be others. And her sister kidnaps children, probably to sell them, and I suspect she knows a whole lot about that, too," she said, not really considering Liz as someone covered by her promise not to give out the information until Dane thought it was okay.

"Wow!" Liz said.

"Yeah, I'll say," Bianca agreed with a grin. "But we can't say anything yet."

* * *

Dane made another phone call. It was to Lt. Peterson of the Duchesne County Sheriff's Department. He found Lt. Peterson at home, and quickly explained where he was and what he was doing.

"Who are you working for?" the lieutenant asked.

"I'd rather not say," Dane stated carefully, "but there is something I've got to know, and I think you can help me."

"I'd be glad to if I can," the lieutenant said. Lt. Peterson had respect at least for Dane's ability, if not always for his tactics. The two had helped one another a number of times, and knew each other pretty well.

"Good, what I need to know is what interest Bianca Turner has in discrediting Coleen Whitman," he said.

"Is that who hired you?" Lt. Peterson asked in pure amazement.

"You know I can't tell you who hired me," Dane said with a grin that the lieutenant couldn't possibly see over the phone.

"Okay, okay," Peterson said. "Yes, I'm quite sure I know, but I don't know if I should say."

"Come on, Lieutenant, it's important," Dane begged.

"I'm not sure you'll like what you hear," the lieutenant said perceptively. "But you asked. This young woman, Coleen Whitman as she calls herself, has become more than a little cozy with Luke Osborne. The bottom line is Bianca's jealous. She dated Luke a little and wants to a lot more. He was even showing some interest, but all that seems to have changed."

"Thanks," Dane said, the wind knocked right out of him. "I better cut and run now."

Everything was suddenly clear to Dane. It made perfect sense, but what worried him was that much of the information he'd reported to Bianca had been nothing more than local rumor. There was not one shred of evidence to support the allegations people had made against Carly, or Coleen as she was now known. Dane believed the drug pushing was true, as no other source for Coleen's money had ever been discovered. And it appeared that she had indeed lived with a couple of men, at least she'd had boyfriends, but again, no one that really knew it for a fact had talked to him.

If Bianca didn't do as he admonished her, and began to make those allegations and they couldn't be proven, he could be open for a big law suit and his license could well be jerked. And as much as Dane had been attracted to Bianca, he was suddenly afraid that she was a little immature to be throwing away her life savings just to get the attention of a man. If she was that selfish and immature, she would use the information, and it would probably be within the next day or two. He had to make sure she didn't say anything until he had irrefutable facts to give her.

He considered his options. Calling Bianca again would probably be less than useful if she was in fact jealous, and Dane knew the lieutenant would never have made such a statement if it weren't true. Maybe he should call Peterson back, explain what had happened, and see if he could short circuit Bianca before she said something to someone in a fit of jealousy. Or he could call the sheriff. Maybe *he* could make sure Bianca kept her mouth closed. After all, the sheriff held her job in his hands.

Not one of those options were at all palatable to Dane. If he called anyone but Bianca about what he'd learned, he would be risking client confidentiality, which he'd already done just a little. Although he hadn't actually told Peterson he was working for Bianca, he'd certainly given him all the information he needed to draw the correct conclusion.

Dane was in a bind. He found himself wishing he'd never seen Bianca in his life, let alone allowed himself to go to work for her. He didn't care if he ever saw her again. She had used him! Flirting with him and giving him false impressions so she could take advantage of him. That made him so angry he could spit in her face. All he wanted now was the money she owed him, and he was off the case. But none of that assured her silence, and he really did need facts to back up the rumors he'd so foolishly passed on.

Then he had a thought. It was risky, but maybe he could still save himself. He picked up the phone again and placed a pillowcase over it and practiced talking into it. What he had to do was make an anonymous call, his voice disguised. It just might work. He looked up a number in his daily planner and started to dial. Then he slammed the phone down, wondering if the party he was about to call had caller ID. That would give the number of his hotel, and if it ever got back to Bianca, she'd figure out what he'd done. He had to use a different phone.

Time was important, so he hurriedly packed his suitcase, checked out of the hotel, hailed a cab, and asked the driver to escort him to the airport. He wouldn't be coming back to Lexington unless he absolutely had to. He'd look for his hard evidence in New Mexico. It took over an hour to get a flight and get through security using one of several false sets of identification he kept for use in situations like this. An hour later he was in Cleveland, Ohio. He again caught a cab, rode to a nearby hotel, and checked into a room, all under a false name.

Dane took a handkerchief out of his pocket to help disguise his voice and punched in numbers on the phone that sat on the stand beside the bed.

* * *

Luke was tired. He'd returned to the ranch an hour ago after taking Coleen home and had spent the next hour moving his wheel-line sprinklers. Monty was tired and hungry, so Luke decided not to work with any of the horses as he'd planned, and went to the house to fix them both something to eat.

The phone was ringing when he came in. He quickly picked it up and said, "Hello," hoping it was Coleen calling. He simply couldn't get her off his mind. And the last thing he needed right now was a call to go on a case somewhere in the county.

Luke tensed when the caller spoke. "Detective Osborne?"

Luke knew a disguised voice when he heard one, and that spelled trouble. He felt like slamming the phone down, but was too professional for that, so he said, "This is Detective Osborne."

"Good, listen carefully; I won't repeat myself. There's something you should know."

"Who is this?" Luke asked, certain he wouldn't get a straight answer, but it seemed like a logical thing to ask.

"You don't need to know, but listen up good. You do know a lady who's calling herself Coleen Whitman, don't you?"

Luke sank into a chair. This could not possibly be good. "Yes, I know her," he answered as his stomach began to churn.

"Do you know who she really is?" the muffled voice asked.

"No," Luke said.

"She isn't really Coleen Whitman," the mystery voice said. "But you know that, don't you? Her real name is Carly Crockett. She has a twin sister whose name is Kyla. Are you getting this?"

"Yes," Luke said as his heart pounded and his palms began to sweat.

"Good, now write this down. Do you have a pen and paper?"

"Just a moment," he said as he hurriedly grabbed some writing materials.

His hand was shaking as he listened and wrote for the next minute or so. Finally, the voice said, "You better act fast on this information. Others are ahead of you and know who she is. All kinds of terrible things are being said—some true, some not. Contact the people I've listed, and do it in person. Catch a plane tonight. You need to be in Lexington by morning."

The caller hung up and Luke, his mind whirling, did the same. He looked over the information he'd written down. It included the birth dates, which strangely were a day apart, of Carly and Kyla Crockett. Then he'd listed the names of several people in and around Lexington who supposedly knew them and could shed some light on what they were like. Luke would go there, as he had to know whatever there was about Coleen that he could learn.

Not once did he question the fact that Coleen really was Carly. The twin bit was the clincher. And he already knew the terrible thing the sister called Kyla was being sought for. Luke was still trembling when he again reached for the phone.

"Dad, I'm hungry," Monty wailed from the doorway to the kitchen.

"Just a minute, buddy," he said. "I need to make some phone calls."

"But I'm hungry now, not after your phone calls," Monty said with a long face and a whining voice. As the boy spoke, Luke jotted down the number listed on his caller ID. He really would like to know who the caller was, if he could figure it out. But he would look into that later.

"In a minute," Luke said firmly. "Right now I need to make these calls."

The first call was to the sheriff. When he got his boss on the line, he said, "Sheriff, has anything happened with Rooster?"

"He hasn't budged," the sheriff said. "But he will."

"I hope," Luke said. "Do you need me for a couple of days? I could sure use some time off."

"Take it," the sheriff said. "You've done a lot. Go out of town if you like. Relax a little if you can."

"Thanks, I will," Luke said and hung up.

He would leave town, but he certainly faced no prospects of relaxation.

His next call was to his folks. "Can you keep Monty for a day or two?" he asked when his mother answered. "And do you think Dad can take care of the place? If he's not up to moving my wheel lines he can just shut them off."

"Of course we can take care of things, son," his mother said. "But where are you off to?"

"I can't say," he told her, "but I'll have my cell phone with me. Call if you need anything."

"Are you leaving early in the morning?" she asked.

"No, right now. It's an emergency. I just need to pack a few things and gather up what you'll need for Monty, then I'll bring him down. Oh, and Mom, he hasn't eaten."

"I'll get something cooking right now," she said.

"I love you, Mom," Luke said. "You're an angel."

The third call was to the Salt Lake International Airport. He booked the first flight he could possibly make that would end up in Lexington, and then he packed and headed out the door.

As Luke headed to the airport, Coleen had begun to feel restless and decided a walk in the warm night air would do her some good. She had gone several blocks, her mind in turmoil. She loved Luke Osborne, but she knew that unless she learned who she really was, there was no future with him. But how could she possibly do that, she wondered. She had no money to hire someone to do the looking for her, and she didn't even know how to begin. She'd tried already and failed.

Her thoughts became more troubled as she walked, ignoring the passing traffic, until she heard an engine whining behind her and looked around just in time to see Luke's black truck fly past. He was clearly in a hurry, and his face was set in a determined frown. Her heart jumped clear into her throat. Something else terrible was happening. She just knew it. How much more could one man stand?

Or one woman?

* * *

Another private investigator was making inquiries that very night. He'd just talked to a Detective Howie Blume. He was looking for information on the current whereabouts of one Carly Crockett, and he was quite sure he now knew where to find her. As he scratched at the false beard he wore, he made a phone call to his client. He was ready for more instructions.

CHAPTER 16

This was racehorse country. Luke loved the rolling green fields and white fences. Well-maintained stables and barns adorned the countryside. Horsemen and horsewomen came from this part of Kentucky. He'd personally observed Coleen's skills with horses, and in his heart he already knew the anonymous caller had sent him to the right place. All he had to do now was talk to the right people and he'd know things about Coleen that even she didn't know.

He'd studied the list of names and addresses the caller had given him until he nearly had it memorized. He looked now at the map he'd just bought and simply headed to the closest address. But before he got there, he changed his mind. He was a cop, and professional courtesy called for him to let the local authorities know who he was and what he was doing here. It didn't take long to find the closest sheriff's office.

He was referred to Captain Alfred Ormm who commanded a regional drug strike force. After Luke introduced himself and explained what he was looking for, the captain seemed surprised to see Luke. "My goodness, this Carly Crockett is getting a lot of attention all of a sudden," he said.

"What do you mean by that?" Luke asked, puzzled but liking how open and friendly the older man was.

"Well, I haven't met the others, but I know that two men have been inquiring about her as recently as yesterday. That's in addition to the inquiries that have come our way from Indiana, from a Detective Howie Blume."

"Kidnapping investigation," Luke said. "I know, I've seen the picture."

"Kyla Crockett. Detective Blume is convinced she's a kidnapper."

"I realize that. He thought it was the girl out my way, but it wasn't."

"So Howie told us. Anyway, these other guys, I don't know what they've learned, but the reports I'm getting from my men in the field are that both men have seemed very professional in their approach," the captain said. "But both were talking to the kind of people we tend to work with, you know, people we try to get information from."

"Two men, both professional," Luke mused. "Private investigators?" he asked.

"My thought exactly," the captain said.

Luke wondered about the call he'd received the previous evening. A call like that didn't seem like something a really good private detective would make, but the man had clearly learned some things about Carly and knew enough to call Luke. That was the real puzzler. Luke went on to tell the captain more about Coleen and how she'd shown up in Utah with her memory gone. He showed the man a picture.

"That's the girl, all right," the captain said. "Carly Crockett. She and Kyla look so much alike it's unreal. We've done some checking ourselves since there seems to be so much interest in her and her twin sister. It seems that all kinds of accusations have been made about the two being involved in drug trafficking, but if they were into it, they were good."

"Good?" Luke asked with a raised eyebrow.

"Good at getting away with it," the captain explained, "because they have never been arrested or even come up in any sting operations run by my strike force. In fact, in talking to officers in most of the departments in this part of the state, all anyone has ever got is rumor. Seems the girls always had plenty of money, more than the jobs they held could possibly account for."

That last fact alone bothered Luke, as it did any good investigator. Honest people could point to where their money came from. This didn't look good for the girl he'd been falling in love with. He wished he could stop all this right now and go back and let Coleen's past stay buried. Perhaps it was better left alone. But he knew he had to go on. He had to know what she'd been like.

"Let me throw out some names," Luke said. "The man who called me last night seemed to think these people could shed light on who Carly and Kyla were and what they were like."

The captain shook his head as Luke read each name until he came to the last one. "Judd Aspen," Luke read.

"Wow," the captain said. "The other names aren't significant. Some I know, some I don't. However I don't think any of them could tell you anything but local rumor and gossip. But that last name, Judd Aspen, he's a mystery."

"What do you mean by that?" Luke asked.

"Well, we've suspected him of pushing drugs, but we've never been able to make a case. He owns one of the finest farms around. He has some of the best horses in the area. He races, breeds, buys, sells them, and so forth."

"But what does owning and racing horses have to do with drugs?" Luke asked puzzled.

The captain leaned across his desk. "That's exactly what we'd like to know. His place is a veritable fortress. Armed guards, locked gates, even lookout towers," he said.

"Sounds like some rich man's paranoia to me," Luke observed.

"That's probably what he wants us to think," Captain Ormm agreed. "But part of the problem is that he hires thugs, some with records, others who look like they should have. Of course he also hires some right good trainers and horse people. Fact is, Carly Crockett worked for him. Which makes me wonder if she really was involved in dealing drugs."

Luke felt like he'd been punched in the gut. For a moment he couldn't find his voice. But he quickly controlled his emotions and asked, "How long did she work there, and what did she do?"

"Exercised horses, tended to the stables, that sort of thing as near as we know," the captain said. "She even rode as a jockey in a couple of races. Good rider, from what I heard. But here's what bothers me, Luke. She was seen around a lot with a guy by the name of Gil Stedman. He's in his early thirties and the ladies seem to like him until they get to know him well. He's dark and what women must think is handsome. But he goes through a lot of girl friends. He has a clean record from what we've been able to learn. But there's just something about him that bothers me and my men."

Luke was beginning to feel sick. Questions swirled around in his head. He had to have answers, and yet he felt like a traitor to the woman he was in love with.

"This stuff is bothering you, isn't it?" the perceptive captain asked.

"Yes, it is. She seems like such a decent girl," Luke said, fighting hard to maintain his composure. He didn't care to share with Alfred Ormm what his personal interest in Coleen was.

"There's more, and I guess you'll want to hear it," the captain said.

Luke really didn't want to hear anymore, at least his heart said he didn't. He was already dizzy with worry. But he knew there was no choice.

"My men seem to believe she was living with this Gil Stedman. Might have even been married to him. When she disappeared a few months back, so did he. At least, no one that's talking to my officers has seen him."

Hot bile rose in Luke's throat. He thought he might throw up. All his worst fears were suddenly coming to life.

"Are you okay?" Captain Ormm asked.

"Yeah. I don't feel real well, but I'm fine," Luke said shakily. "Please, go on. You're answering most of my questions."

"Good. Well, there is really just one more thing that occurs to me. Until these past couple of days it didn't mean anything, but I'll pass it on to you for whatever it's worth. I got a call one day, several months ago. It was in March as I remember. The caller was a young woman from the sound of her voice. She refused to identify herself, but she said she had some information she wanted me to have about drugs. She said she couldn't talk on the phone but she did arrange to meet me the next day. But she never came. And now that I think back, that was about the time that anyone can last recall seeing Carly Crockett."

"You mean Carly might have been wanting to tell you something?"

"Yes, exactly, if it was her that called me. But like I said, the girl never showed up," Alfred said, and his brow suddenly became creased as he lapsed into deep thought.

Luke said nothing, fighting with his emotions as he simply stared at the captain's face. Finally Captain Ormm spoke again. "If it was Carly Crockett that called me, then she must have had information about Judd Aspen."

Again he lapsed into thoughtful silence. "Tell me again about your girl's accident," he said a moment later.

His choice of words cut deep. *Your girl.* Indeed, she had almost been Luke's girl. That had all changed these past few minutes, but he tried to focus. "It was in New Mexico. She was riding a badly winded horse as fast as it would go along a highway. The horse fell and she was thrown or tried to jump free or something. Anyway, she was dragged when her foot got hung up in the stirrup. A couple of local cowboys stopped the horse and saved her life," Luke reported.

"Strange. Was she running from someone?"

"A man on a four-wheeler was in the area. He left when she fell. The authorities there were quite sure he was chasing her. They back-tracked, and several miles across the desert they found where all the tracks ended on another road. That was all. There was nothing there."

"Luke," the captain said, "what if it was Carly that called me? I know that may be a long stretch, but what if it was and what if she'd been about to give me information on Judd Aspen and company? Could they have figured out what she was doing? Could someone, say this boyfriend or husband or whatever he was, have gone after her?"

"Could be," Luke agreed, and then a terrible thought occurred to him. He voiced it aloud. "Could he still be after her?" He thought for a moment, then again spoke his thoughts as they came to him, as if bouncing them off the captain. "If other inquiries about her have been going on around here, people are looking for her. Her life could be in danger."

Captain Ormm nodded his agreement, but then he threw a wrench in Luke's line of thinking. "On the other hand, why would Gil Stedman be inquiring around here? He knew her better than anybody in the area."

"Then she might have other enemies," Luke said. Both men were thoughtful for a minute, then Luke asked, "Has anyone checked to see if she has any bank accounts in the area?"

"Not that I know of," the captain answered.

"Will it do me any good to speak with any of these people listed here?" he said, lifting his notes from last night's phone call from his lap.

"You could try, but all you'll get is rumor. These people probably didn't even know her. You need facts, Luke, not rumor."

"Thanks. If you don't mind, I'll do a little digging before I head back to Utah," Luke said.

"Feel free," Captain Ormm said as he rose from behind his desk and extended a hand to Luke. "Let me know if I can help, and let me know if you find something that might help my strike force."

"I will, and thanks for your help this morning."

"Good luck, young man," the captain said. "And I hope you find out she's good, not bad. It's become personal I suspect, hasn't it?"

Embarrassed, Luke simply nodded his head and left, knowing that he'd just made a good friend, one he could call on for help should the need arise. And also a man whom he could trust fully. Luke was grateful.

* * *

Gil Stedman stepped out of the jail into the bright sunshine and squinted. His bail had just been posted, and the man who posted it had only spoken to him for a second. "Aspen says he changed his mind. There are too many people poking around, asking questions about Carly. He's got a lot to lose if she starts talking. You get your job done, Gil, then let Mr. Aspen know that it is, and get lost. He doesn't ever want to see you again."

Gil was more enraged than he'd ever been. Judd Aspen had given him the sack, and it was all Carly Crockett's fault. She'd led him along all those months, then she'd knifed him in the back. And he'd searched for her for weeks, not even getting paid by Aspen for doing it. Someone would pay, and he couldn't wait to make it be her. He was on his way to Utah today. And he wouldn't come back here to answer to the charges that had been brought against him the last time he'd tried to fly out. They could just forfeit the bail—they could have Judd Aspen's money.

Roosevelt, Utah. He'd be there tonight. He'd find Carly tomorrow, and she'd learn what a mistake it had been to betray Gil Stedman.

* * *

"Did you send what I asked you to?" the client asked.

"She'll get it today," the PI answered. "What is it?"

"Never mind that, but Carly deserves it," the client assured. "And you'll personally follow up with a visit to Duchesne?"

"You're paying the bill. But I can't leave until tonight."

"That's okay. But no later. Make sure she received the package. Don't let anyone know who you are or what you're doing. Oh, and remember, use the name she's using now. What is it?"

"Coleen Whitman," the PI reminded the client.

"Yes, address the package to that name. And take care. I don't want anyone knowing who it's from."

"I'll be careful. They'll scarcely even know I've been in town."

"Report back soon," the client ordered.

"You've got it," the PI agreed.

* * *

It took further help from Captain Ormm, but Luke was finally able to learn what was in the account he found in a Lexington bank bearing the name of Carly Crockett. It had not been accessed since the last day of February when five hundred had been withdrawn by Carly. There was still about twenty thousand remaining.

Drug money? he wondered. Where else could that much cash have come from? He could see now why people said what they did.

Kyla Crockett had no accounts that were active, but she'd had one at the same bank as Carly. It also had contained large amounts of money in the past. The Crockett twins were definitely a mystery. And from all appearances they were not good girls. Not the kind of woman Luke had perceived Coleen Whitman to be. Not the kind of woman he wanted raising his and Jamie's son or being the mother of his future children. It was all over between the two of them, just like he had feared it would be. Oh, how he wished he'd never had to learn about her past.

Luke boarded a late flight to Salt Lake City. He'd learned all he could here, and although it was clear that Coleen Whitman, or rather Carly Crockett, was not the woman for him, he felt a pressing need to protect her. She had enemies, and no matter the secrets of her past, she didn't deserve to die. He was afraid that was exactly what some people intended for her.

He dug in his pocket after settling into his seat near the back of the plane. He pulled out a piece of paper and unfolded it. It was a photocopy of the signature card on file in Carly Crockett's bank. It had taken a court order to obtain it, but Captain Ormm had been able to pull it off. Luke was to let the captain know when he asked her to sign that name, Carly Crockett, if it matched the signature on the card. This would be the clincher on her identification. In his mind he didn't need it, but just to be absolutely positive, it wouldn't hurt.

* * *

A package had been delivered to Coleen Whitman at the café shortly after she came on duty at three that afternoon. She was busy and didn't have time to open it, but she had noted with interest that there was no return address of any kind. That bothered her. The package had been marked urgent and was delivered by Federal Express. Who would be sending her anything? And who would know to tell Federal Express that they could find her here?

She carried it home with her after work and laid it on her table where she stared at it with concern. It wasn't a large package. It was maybe six by three inches. It wasn't heavy. It really couldn't have much in it, whatever it was. But she didn't know anybody who might have sent it to her, at least anyone who would know where to find her. Rick and Joe in New Mexico didn't know exactly where she was. Old employers she had worked for between her accident in March and her arrival in Duchesne certainly didn't have any way of knowing where she was, as if any of them cared. Nobody she knew could have sent it to her.

Coleen fixed herself a late snack and ate it beside the package, worrying more as the minutes passed. She wished Luke were in town because he'd know what she should do. He'd tell her if it was okay to open it.

Then she had a thought, a very good thought. She picked up the package with suddenly eager hands. Luke, how she loved him. He was such a thoughtful man. He hadn't called to tell her where he'd gone, but he was thinking of her. He must have sent the package. There just wasn't any other logical explanation.

Eagerly she tore the Federal Express packaging loose. The box inside was taped. She cut the tape loose with a pair of scissors. She had only to lift off the lid of the box to see what Luke had sent. A necklace, perhaps? No, it was too large a box, too heavy for that. A book maybe? Perhaps, but an odd-shaped one. She savored the moment, thinking fondly of Luke. She wished he was there to see her open it. She wished she knew where he was. Then another thought came to her. Another good thought. He might have his cell phone with him. She knew the number. She could call and open it while he was on the phone. Then she could thank him as soon as she knew what he'd given her.

That idea appealed to her, and she picked up her phone and began to dial. To her utter delight, he answered. "Hello?" his beloved voice came over the line.

"Luke, I've missed you so much," she cried as he answered.

"Coleen," he said. "What are you doing calling me?"

He sounded stressed. He must be on a big case. "I'm sorry, Luke, is this a bad time?" she asked. "Are you working a big case?"

"The biggest I've ever worked," he said in a flat monotone.

"I'm sorry," she apologized again. "If I'm interrupting something, I can call back later," she suggested.

"No, I'm stressed big time, but I'll tell you all about it tomorrow. Right now all I'm doing is driving. I'm almost to Heber and planned to stop and get a sandwich there."

"I can't wait to see you," she said. "Is Monty with your folks?"

"He is," Luke said.

He sounded so different, so distant. Was he angry with her over something, she wondered. Or was he just tired and worried about all the problems he had to deal with, especially his burned-out ranch yard? She couldn't blame him for being tense and out of sorts, he'd been through so much.

Again, she eagerly anticipated what might be in the package. She was certain it was not her he was upset with. "Luke, I won't keep you long, but I just got the package you sent and I'm opening it right now."

"Package?" he asked, feeling fear in his heart, fear for her. "I didn't send a package, Coleen."

"Oh yes you did, Luke Osborne, and I can't wait to see what's in it. I'm lifting the lid off the box right now," she announced with laughter in her voice.

"Coleen, don't open it!" he shouted as she lifted off the lid.

CHAPTER 17

Luke's phone battery went dead at that critical moment. He didn't know if Coleen had heard him or not. Opening that package could be the worst thing she'd ever done. But he hadn't sent her a package, and if she thought he had, it had come from someone who either posed as him or wanted to remain unidentified. That was dangerous.

His mind went instantly to Victor Hampton. Then he remembered Captain Ormm telling him about Coleen's former boyfriend, or *husband,* the man he called Gil Stedman. He also remembered the call that had sent him racing to Kentucky in the middle of the night, and the men who were asking so many questions about Carly Crockett and her sister. The terrible possibilities seemed almost endless. As Luke's thoughts raced, he plugged his phone into his accessory power source and it started charging at once. He had to try to reach Coleen, or to reach dispatch. He had to know she was okay.

He prayed that the package did not contain some kind of bomb. The thought made him ill, as sick as had the knowledge he'd gained of Coleen's past. Maybe even more. He had firmly resolved that he would break off his relationship with her as soon as he could see her again, but that did not change the feelings he'd been experiencing. He was so torn, but the things he'd learned had eroded his trust, as he'd feared they would. He simply wouldn't take the chance, no matter how much he'd come to care for her.

He carefully avoided that other word. The one that had been messing with his head these past few days. The word that led to marriage and a future together, for there was no future together for him and Coleen Whitman, more widely known, he corrected himself, as Carly Crockett.

But that didn't mean he didn't care, because he did. Finally his phone was active and he dialed Coleen's number. He still thought of her as Coleen; Carly just didn't fit. The phone rang and rang and rang. Surely she was all right. Luke's eyes burned. He could scarcely bear the tension. He knew he should hang up and get help to her, although it might be too late. Just a couple of more rings then he'd call dispatch.

"Hello?"

Luke's heart stopped for a moment. He was almost certain it did. He had to gulp for air and pull to the side of the road. She was alive!

"Hello. Is anybody there?" her voice went on as Luke ground to a stop. "Please, is that you, Luke?"

"Coleen," he finally managed to say. "Are you all right?"

"Of course I'm all right, but this package, it couldn't have been from you, could it?"

"No, it's not from me. But, my word, Coleen, you scared me," he said.

"Actually, it's more like you scared me, Luke," she said. "Just as you shouted at me, the top came off the box."

"Thank goodness it wasn't a bomb," Luke said.

"Luke, are you going mad?" she asked. "Did you actually think it might be a bomb? Who would want to bomb me?"

"Oh, Coleen, I hope no one does, but I have enemies, and you . . . you . . . Oh, never mind right now. But someone could have tried to hurt me by hurting you."

Coleen's heart began to race. So he wasn't mad at her at all. If someone could hurt him by hurting her, then it could only mean that he cared. And yet, she still wondered about her past. He would have to know before he'd ever let his heart go. Maybe he'd know what else could be done to learn who she was. She made up her mind to ask him when she saw him again, but not now, not on the phone.

"What was in the package, Coleen?" Luke asked as he eased his truck back onto the road.

"Well, it's really weird. I couldn't believe my eyes when I saw it. I tried to tell you but your phone cut out," she said.

"Sorry about that," Luke said. "The battery went dead, but I have it plugged in now."

Luke paused, expecting Coleen to tell him more about the package. She said nothing, so finally he asked, "Well, are you going to tell me what's in the package or not?"

"I'd rather show you," she said. "I'm stunned. Can you come here as soon as you get back in Duchesne?"

Luke didn't want to face her. It would be so hard, but he had to do what he had to do, and he guessed it was better sooner than later. "Sure," he said. "I'll be there in just a little over an hour."

"Aren't you going to stop and eat in Heber?" Coleen asked.

"No, I don't think I feel like eating right now," he said, and he really didn't.

"Good, then I'll have something fixed when you get here," Coleen told him.

"You don't have to do that, Coleen," he said as he panicked. That would only make things harder for both of them, and he hated what he had to say to her as it was. "It's so late," he added lamely.

"But I want to," she said firmly. "I still can't believe you thought it might be a bomb. Why would you even think that? That's so unlikely."

"Not really, Coleen," he said. "I didn't tell you this, but the other day when I went to meet an informant, there was no one there. But someone had left a bomb, and it was set for me."

"Oh, Luke!" Coleen gasped. "That's terrible. I'm so glad you didn't get hurt. But what happened? How did you get away from it?"

"Somebody's poor dog set it off. It blew him into a million pieces, like it was intended to do to me."

"Luke, who did it? Do you know?" she asked frantically.

"Yes, I know," he said. "And that's why I was so afraid they might have sent one to you. Knowing me is dangerous, Coleen. Too dangerous."

"I can stand it," she said. She could stand anything for Luke Osborne. "Is that where you've been?" she asked in her next breath. "Have you been after the men who tried to do this to you?"

"We'll talk about it when I get there," he told her evasively. "I think my phone is going to lose its signal any moment now. I'm heading up Daniel's Canyon. I'll be there pretty soon."

"And I'll be anxiously waiting." She said it so sweetly that it pierced his already aching heart.

* * *

Gil Stedman had made good time. He'd arrived in Roosevelt early enough that night to start nosing around. He'd already talked to several people and shown them the picture of Carly he carried. But no one seemed to recognize her. So he began to ask about a private detective by the name of Dane Bering. He'd begun to wonder if he'd heard wrong and not come to the right place. But several people knew Dane. Then why didn't they know Carly, or at least recognize the photo of her, he wondered.

Finally giving up for the night, Gil got a room and then found a nearby bar. He felt he'd earned a drink. He'd just have to be careful not to drink too much. He took his beer to the back of the room and sat down where he nursed it as he thought grimly about how he was going to get even with Carly for all she'd done to him.

A pair came in and sat down near him. The bigger of the two men had a very deep voice, and even when he whispered it carried very well. He called the other man, who was older and smaller, "Vic." He couldn't make out what the one called Vic was saying. But he became quite interested when he heard the deep-voiced one say, "Best meth we've ever made." That was Gil's language. "But we've got to get some help getting it out of here. Rooster seems to have disappeared."

The other fellow said something, then the big fellow said, "Ain't heard nothing of Detective Osborne, anyway. I think we done scared him off. Heard today he was out of town. Don't know where, but I think he's chasing ghosts." The fellow laughed and Gil lost interest.

He finished his beer and went to the bar for another one. As the bartender handed it to him, he asked, "Tell me, who are the two guys sitting over there at the table next to mine?"

The bartender eyed Gil's attire and expensive watch, then shook his head. "You'll want to stay away from them two. That's Victor Hampton and Sharps Thomsen. Wherever they go, the law follows."

"You don't say," Gil responded. "Sounds like they're not my type." And with that he returned to his table, drank a little more beer, and worked up his nerve.

Finally, he slipped over to their table and said, "Mind if I join you fellows?"

"Rather you didn't," Victor said. "This is a private conversation."

"Just take a minute. Wondered if you two might recognize this face?" he said, and he produced his picture of Carly.

"Sit down," Victor said. "Why are you asking?"

"I have my reasons. Know her?" Gil asked.

"Seen her," Victor said.

"I need to talk to her," Gil lied. "Can you tell me where I might find her?"

"Probably, but I'm not sure I'd care to," Victor growled. "What's your interest in her anyway? She don't seem like your type," he added, pointing to the photo and Carly's western-style outfit and benign smile. The fellow he was talking to looked like he'd never been around a horse, and he also didn't have a face to match the upright-citizen look he sported.

Gil smiled. "Old girlfriend of mine," he said. "Haven't seen her for a while. Heard she was out this way and thought I'd look her up."

Vic looked at Sharps, who was slowly nodding his head. Then Victor said, "Her boyfriend, he's a cop. Sounds like she's sort of changed types, huh?" he said smugly.

"Cop?" Gil asked, both surprised and alarmed. She might have already spilled the beans on both him and Judd Aspen. If she had, Aspen would see that he died. And Aspen could do it. He was not easy to hide from. Gil had better get to Carly fast and make her talk. He could do that. He'd done it before to others.

Sharps spoke for the first time. "Don't like cops, mister?" he asked sarcastically, voicing what both he and Victor were thinking.

"Not so you'd notice it," Gil agreed.

"We don't either, especially Coleen's boyfriend, Detective Luke Osborne," Sharps said.

"Hey, not so loud, Sharps," Victor snapped. "Want the whole town to hear you, you idiot? Keep your voice down."

"Sure boss," Sharps said, much quieter this time.

"Coleen, you say?" Gil asked.

Vic turned back to him. "That's right. Wrong girl?"

"No, I don't think so, just wrong name. Her name is Carly Crockett. And if she's with a cop it means trouble."

"Did we say she was with a cop?" Victor asked.

"Well, not exactly."

"That's right, not with him, just dating him. But he's out of town right now we hear. Perhaps you'd like to see her tonight," Victor Hampton suggested shrewdly. He would love to hurt Luke again, and especially if he didn't have to do anything. Unless he read the man across the table wrong, he had a beef with the girl, and meant no good by her. He had to be sure, though, so he asked, "She do you some dirt?"

The look of pure loathing that crossed the man's dark face was all the answer he needed. But Gil gave him more. "She's poison," he said.

"Well, here's how you can find her," Victor said. And he went on to describe how to get to the Twin Rivers and then which apartment she was in. "But remember, you've never seen us," Victor added.

"Are you sure she's in Duchesne?" Gil asked. "I heard she was here in Roosevelt."

"You heard wrong. Get on over to Duchesne, you'll see that I'm right."

"Thanks, I owe you two," Gil said. "See you around."

* * *

She'd outdone herself and with only an hour to prepare. She wasn't a great cook, but she was passable. Coleen was laying dinner on the table when she heard a vehicle outside. She ran to the window and peeked out, her heart racing. It was Luke's truck. She hurried back and finished putting everything right where she wanted it before she heard his soft knock on the door.

She took a deep breath, then approached the door and slowly opened it. She just couldn't help herself when she saw Luke standing there, and she threw her arms around him and said, "Welcome back, Luke, from wherever you've been. I've missed you."

Luke didn't respond to her embrace and she pulled away, hurt and puzzled.

"Smells good, but you shouldn't have fixed me anything," he said.

"I wanted to. Come in," she offered, and held the door open for him.

Luke had never seemed so awkward. Coleen couldn't figure out what was going on. She must have terribly misread him on the phone. He was like a stranger tonight. He moved past her and stood holding his hat.

Coleen took it from him and laid it on the edge of her sofa. "It's all ready. Sit down," she invited. "I hope you like it."

Luke felt terrible. As he watched her treating him like a king, he felt like a thief in her home. He was a thief. He'd stolen her heart and now was about to destroy it, but what else could he do? She wasn't the person he'd grown so fond of. But he had to lighten up now as he could see she was hurting already. He didn't want to hurt her more, so he forced a smile, "Of course I'll like it," he said. "But are you going to make me wait to see what was in the infamous package until after dinner?"

"That was the plan," she said as lightly as she could. Her heart was breaking. No matter what had happened to him that had caused him to suddenly become so cold to her, it didn't change one thing—she loved him.

"If you say so then," he said and sat down.

"Oops, I forgot milk," she said after she had sat down across from him.

She left the room and he thought again about what he'd been thinking about for the past hour. He knew danger lurked, but he had to break it off with her tonight. She might be so angry she wouldn't let him watch out for her after he told her why the future simply couldn't include the two of them together.

When she came back in, she sat a quart of buttermilk in front of Luke and poured herself a glass of milk from the gallon she'd brought from her kitchen.

Buttermilk.

She didn't drink it, but she knew he did, and she'd bought this just for when he came. Why, oh why, couldn't her past remain lost? She was so good to him, so thoughtful. He smiled despite himself as he opened the buttermilk and filled his glass. "You don't miss a thing, do you?" he asked. "This is my favorite drink."

"I thought it must be. You always order it when you eat out," she said, her smile as close to the one he loved as it was likely to get tonight.

The meal went well. She asked where he'd been, and he said he'd been in Kentucky. There was absolutely no reaction. But then, he knew her memory really was gone. There wasn't a question about that. When she asked what he was doing there, he told her he was on a case. Then they talked about Monty, about the horses, and about his burned-out ranch.

"I'll get some rebuilding started soon," he said. "These insurance things take time. And I've been rather busy since the fire anyway."

"I still can't believe anyone would do that to you, Luke," she said. "That's so horrible."

"So are guns and bombs," he reminded her. "I'm not in a business where you're popular with the clients." He grinned. "Of course, I have to admit, I seem to have stirred them up a little too much."

"That's because you're a good detective," she said. "You don't believe in letting the bad guys go. Do you know who set the fire?"

He nodded.

"And what about the bomb?"

"Same ones," he said. "It's the men I had the shoot-out with."

"Have they been arrested?" she asked. "I can't stand to think that they're out there still. If they've done this much, you surely don't think they'll quit now, do you?"

"They're still out there, but I hope to get them in jail in the next few days. The sheriff and some of the other guys have been working on it while I've been in Kentucky. I'll learn in the morning where we are on the case," he told her.

"And what about the cattle thing?" she asked, shuddering. "Do you have any idea who's been doing that?"

"Same men," Luke revealed.

Coleen was very surprised. "But why, Luke?" she asked. "That doesn't make any sense to me at all. Didn't you say it was something to do with satanic rituals?"

"That's what I thought," he said, "but I was wrong. These guys I'm after simply wanted me to get too busy on other things so they could make their meth without having to worry about me looking over their shoulders. It worked pretty good, actually. I expect they've been cooking up dope like crazy while I've had all these other things to worry about."

"You're not the only cop, Luke," she said, clearly puzzled. "Why aren't some of the other deputies after them too?"

He explained that they were, but he'd worked longer on developing informants and simply had a better handle on what they were up to. "And besides that," he added, "I had greater motivation."

"Oh?" she said quizzically.

"Yes, the guy behind all this is the man that killed Jamie," he said bitterly. "And I intend to see him locked up for the rest of his life if it's the last thing I ever do."

"And he knows this," Coleen said calmly even as her heart ached almost unbearably for the man she'd come to love, but who clearly didn't seem now to love her in return.

"Be careful, Luke," she said when he said nothing more. "But I hope you get them."

Luke looked into her eyes. She seemed so sincere. What would she do when she found out that she may have been involved with drug dealing herself?

That's stupid! he thought.

She couldn't have been involved with drugs. *But why the money?* He knew who she was, but she didn't. So he could ask her questions all night, and she wouldn't be able to tell him. What a mixed up, terrible situation this was. Why? he berated himself, had he let his heart get enmeshed in it all?

"I'll clean up later," she said after they'd finished eating and he started to take his plate to the kitchen. "Let's go look in the package I got today."

He felt guilty. He wanted to help her, to be with her on some kind of neutral ground, and doing dishes was neutral ground. What he really wanted to do was put off the terrible thing he was about to do to her, to delay the revelation of the awful things he'd learned.

If they were true. How could he ever know that, short of her getting her memory back? He knew that wasn't likely to happen. Her kind of amnesia, according to what he'd read, rarely reversed itself.

"Luke, are you okay?" she asked, and he realized he'd been standing still halfway in the kitchen like some kind of dummy while his troubled thoughts controlled him.

He slowly turned and laid the plate back on the table. Then his eyes met hers. They were misted, but he'd seldom seen her tears flow. She was so strong it seemed. "Luke, something terrible has happened, hasn't it? Something in Kentucky."

"Yes, something terrible happened, Coleen. And no, I'm not all right," he said, and when she came close, he simply could not resist her as she took him in her arms and held him.

For several minutes they stood, holding each other for support. She shed no tears, but he bawled like a baby. At last, she pulled away from him and reached up, wiping the tears from his cheek with her fingers. "Luke, will you tell me about it?" she asked.

Choking on every word, he said, "I have, to, Coleen. And I've never hated anything so much in my life."

"Not even the guy who killed Jamie?" she asked.

"I don't hate him, Coleen," he said. "I just want justice done, that's all. But I did hate what happened to Jamie. And I guess I hate that as much as I hate this thing I've got to tell you."

"It's about me, isn't it?" Coleen asked.

"Yes, Coleen," he said, and again he choked up.

"It's okay, Luke," she assured him as a look of profound sadness filled her beautiful brown eyes, those eyes he'd come to . . . *yes, okay, love*, he admitted to himself. And that was why this all hurt so much. He loved more than just her eyes.

"I wish that was true, Coleen," he said.

"It is. It has to be," she responded. Then she got this look in her eyes he'd never seen before. It was one of determination, fierce determination. Or was it the revelation of a fighting spirit that lay beneath her soft and lovely exterior? "Whatever it is you have to tell me, there is something I must say first, Luke. And don't try to stop me, please."

"Okay," he said, wondering what she had on her mind.

"I love you, Luke Osborne," she said. "I love you more than I've ever loved anyone in my life. I know I can't remember the competition," she laughed. But Luke didn't laugh, and she continued somewhat awkwardly. "But as . . . as you say whatever it is you have to tell me, please remember this, Luke, nothing you do or say can ever change what I feel."

Luke was ashamed. He was also overwhelmed, and thrilled, but then heartbreak took over. He wanted to tell her that he loved her too, but he couldn't. Not when he had to tell her they had no future. It was such a contradiction. He hated it. But he also despised what she might have been.

Might have been.

Suddenly he could see just a glimmer of hope. What if all he'd learned wasn't true? What if people had assumed things and spread them as truths when they were far from it?

But what about the unexplained money? What about a sister wanted for the kidnapping of innocent children? What about boyfriends and/or husbands?

"Luke, you're doing it again. Come back, Luke. We can sort through things. Please give us that chance, Luke."

"I'm sorry," he said, snapping himself out of his trance. "I guess I'm messed up, aren't I? Okay, Coleen, let's start by having a look at that package you got today. Then we'll talk. I'll tell you what I've learned."

Coleen reached up and kissed him lightly on the lips. "Remember, Luke, I love you more than I've ever loved anyone."

"How can you say that?" he asked. "You said it yourself, you don't remember who you've loved."

"I don't know how I can say it Luke, except that I feel it in here," she said as she held her hands over her heart. "I just know it, that's all, Luke. Like when you tell me how you feel when we read that Book of Mormon, you just *know* it's true. That's how I feel it, Luke. It's real. I know it is. Here, the package is on this end table."

Coleen handed the package to Luke. The lid was back on the little box. "Take it off," she said with a tender smile. "It won't blow up."

Luke took the lid off as a knock came on the door.

CHAPTER 18

Luke and Coleen looked at their watches simultaneously. It was after eleven-thirty. Fear passed across Coleen's face. The terrible men who'd been trying to kill Luke might be here.

But Luke was thinking someone from her forgotten past had finally come to hurt her.

Coleen's fear took a tremendous leap when a small pistol suddenly appeared in Luke's hand and the box he'd just opened dropped to the floor, spilling hundreds of bills of varying denominations on the carpet.

"Open the door and step to the side as quickly as you can," Luke whispered fiercely. "I'll be in here." He pointed to the bedroom door that lay off to the side. Luke was experiencing those same things he'd felt just before the growling dog had lost its life to the bomb intended for Luke.

Not entirely out of sight, but with just his head jutting around the door enough that he could see Coleen and the front door, Luke nodded for her to open it. She did so, stepping back at the same time. A dark-complexioned man stood there. "Hello, Carly," he said with as evil a grin as Luke had ever seen. Coleen moved back and to the side. The man stepped in and faced her.

Luke watched, breathless, ready to act at a moment's notice. But first he had to be absolutely sure this was an enemy. Coleen looked puzzled and even a little relieved. "You've got the wrong apartment," she said. "I'm Coleen, not Carly."

"No, I've got the right place," he said as his hand reached inside the jacket he was wearing. "Victor told me the right apartment number."

How Victor Hampton could be mixed up in this was beyond Luke, for he was almost certain that the man now smiling wickedly at Coleen was none other than Gil Stedman—ex-boyfriend/husband! He was a perfect fit of the description Captain Ormm had given him. Luke braced himself, ready to step out and defend Coleen, even fire if it became necessary.

"Carly, baby," the man said, "don't try to make me believe you don't remember me. You should never have left me. I wanted you, Carly. And I know you wanted me. It was silly to tell me you didn't love me when you know you did. I was your only protection. I would have taken care of you. How could you turn on me like that? You were a silly girl to get all self-righteous about Aspen's drug pushing."

He paused and Coleen stared blankly at him. "And you know what?" he continued with a twisted smile. "I almost got you that day in New Mexico. If your horse hadn't fallen, I would have. It might have been something we could have still worked out." He reached out a hand and fingered a lock of her hair. Coleen felt ill and petrified at his touch. "But this time," he continued, "I've decided we just can't work it out." As he spoke, he let go of her hair and touched the door as if to shut it, the other hand staying inside his jacket.

"Gil Stedman," Luke said as he stepped from behind the bedroom door, and leveled his gun at the man with one hand, his badge displayed in the other. "You're under arrest."

The reaction was exactly what Luke expected. Gil's face gave away the fact that Luke had called him by the right name.

"Don't even think of pulling that gun," Luke said.

But Gil tried it anyway, and two shots rang out. Gil was spinning as the shots were fired. He fell face down on the floor and a moment later a second man, another stranger, rushed in. Luke's gun covered him, and the man slowly raised his hands, dangling his pistol from his trigger finger. "I'm on your side," he said as he let the pistol fall on the carpet.

Coleen stood rooted to the floor, her hands over her mouth. She hadn't screamed, nor did she now. She was in shock. Luke stepped over, picked up the other man's gun and handed it to Coleen. "Hold this," he said. She took the pistol gingerly, and stepped away from the bleeding man on the floor. The man looked truthful enough. He was just a little heavy, had very short brown hair, and a round face Luke felt he could trust. There was nothing imposing about him, and he wasn't much older or taller than Luke.

"You stand back while I check this man and keep those hands where I can see them," he said to the man. The stranger must have fired the other shot, as Gil's gun had never made it beyond the zipper of his jacket

Blood was seeping from the upper part of Gil's left thigh where it had been struck from behind. That would have been the other man's bullet. Luke turned Gil over, not at all sure where his bullet might have hit since Gil was moving when Luke fired.

Luke was relieved when he saw that all he'd done was creased Gil's scalp. It was enough to render Gil unconscious, but other than the profuse bleeding that Luke knew was typical of all scalp wounds, Luke could see that his bullet hadn't done much damage. He was more worried about the damage being done to Coleen's carpet than he was about the man bleeding on it.

"Is he dead?" Coleen asked.

"No, he'll recover, but when he does he'll be in prison," Luke said. "Coleen, can you call 911? We better get some help here. And tell them we'll need Sheriff Robinson for sure." Luke no longer feared the disarmed stranger.

She turned wordlessly toward the phone. Luke again leaned over the wounded gunman. The stranger also leaned over. "Can I help you?" he asked.

"The best thing you can do to help right now is to identify yourself," Luke said curtly. "And explain why you shot at this man."

"Jim Redd, private investigator," the stranger said with a smile. "And I did it to save Carly Crockett's life."

"And who is Carly Crockett?" Coleen asked as she completed her phone call.

"You are," Jim said.

She looked helplessly at Luke. "That's right," Luke said. "And this fellow," nodding toward the man on the floor, as both his hands were busy trying to stop the flow of blood from the intruder's scalp, "is Gil Stedman."

"Am I supposed to know him?" she asked.

Luke looked up helplessly. "Can't we talk about this later, Coleen?"

"Tell me now. Please, Luke."

"Okay, he's an old flame of yours. Very close flame," he said.

Coleen looked absolutely mortified. "Him!" she exclaimed. "But that can't be."

"It's true," Jim said.

"And who are you?" she asked Jim.

"I already told you who—" Jim began.

Coleen cut him off sharply. "I mean what are you doing here? How do you know me? Why are you shooting at people in my house?"

"Actually, I'll be in hot water with my client now. I was supposed to slip in and out of town without hardly being noticed. My job," he said sheepishly, "was to see if you got your package."

His eyes drifted, along with Luke's and Coleen's, to the money that was scattered on the floor at the far end of the living room. "It looks like you did," he concluded as a siren started wailing in the background.

"You sent that?" Coleen asked, pointing to the money.

"I'm guilty, but I promise, I had no idea what was in it. I wasn't supposed to know."

Drug money. Another ghost from her past, Luke thought with a sinking heart.

"Who did you send it from?" Coleen pressed. "Who are you working for?"

"You ask too many questions," Jim said with a grin. "And I'm not allowed to answer them. I really should be going now."

Luke looked up at him sharply. "You're joking. There's been a shooting in this house. You and I are the shooters. This man," he motioned to Gil, "came into this house to kill someone. You're also a witness to that."

Jim raised a hand as if in defense. "I know. I'm just not looking forward to telling my client what happened. I don't usually screw up like this. But I couldn't let Carly die, and I didn't know you were in here, Detective, or I would have never appeared. I could only see Gil and Carly."

At that moment Sheriff Robinson ran into the apartment, skidding to a stop at the sight of the man on the floor. Luke looked at him and said, "Sheriff Robinson, meet Gil Stedman, would-be murderer."

"What in the world has happened here?" The sheriff asked as his eyes took in the money as well as the blood.

An ambulance arrived and EMTs poured into the apartment. "Don't let him out of your sight," Luke said, waving once more at Gil Stedman. "Oh, I better take this," he said, leaning down and removing the gun that now lay beside Gil's hand.

Deputies arrived, and after a brief explanation from Luke and an introduction to Jim Redd, a full-scale investigation began. The money was carefully counted and, at Coleen's insistence, taken to be placed in the sheriff's safe. Jim Redd swore that it was legitimate, all twenty-five thousand dollars of it. But he stubbornly refused to identify his client, finally admitting that he'd never met the person who'd hired him, immediately dimming the legitimacy of the money that had come into Coleen's hands.

Luke stepped outside and spoke privately with Sheriff Robinson. Luke gave him a quick rundown of what he'd learned that day in Lexington. Then Luke told him exactly what had occurred that evening before the shooting. He even mentioned Gil referring to Victor. "Sheriff," Luke said, "I'm beginning to feel haunted by Victor Hampton. It seems like he can take everything good in my life and destroy it."

The sheriff put a fatherly hand on Luke's shoulder. "Luke," he said, "I promise we'll get Vic now. I think Rooster is about ready to talk again. In the morning, we'll use this as more leverage. And then there's Gil himself. We'll do all we can to make him talk. We'll find out what he has to do with Vic. Keep your chin up. You've done great work. You're one sharp detective, and I tell you, we'll get this all behind us and you'll feel better about the world."

"Thanks, Sheriff," Luke said. "I'll try to stay positive, except for one thing."

"What's that?" the sheriff asked.

"Coleen, or Carly, rather. I'm sick over what she used to be. It makes me feel terrible, but I can hardly bear to look at her now and think of how she used to live," he admitted.

"Luke, don't give up on her just yet. Everything may not be as it appears. Give her a chance. Help her find out more if you can. I'll give you whatever time you need. Take her back there, back to Kentucky and Kansas. With her there, talk to people. Maybe it won't all be so bad in the end."

"But the money, Sheriff. With this cash today, I know of forty-five thousand dollars that belongs to her that has no explanation. What else could it be but drug money?"

"I don't know, but I still think there might be an explanation," the sheriff said.

"And I don't know if I want to know it," Luke moaned. "The more I learn about *Carly* the worse it gets."

"Well, sleep on it tonight. After you're rested, you might see things differently. Follow your gut and your heart. They've both served you well in the past. Now, we need to wrap up here. Get some sleep tonight and get in touch tomorrow." He clapped a hand once more on Luke's shoulder and started toward Coleen's apartment.

"Sheriff," Luke stopped him.

Sheriff Robinson stopped and turned back. "What is it, Luke?"

"I don't even know what to call her," he said in despair.

"Coleen, Luke. You call her Coleen. That's the girl you're in love with. Give her a chance until you know where her heart is. And call her Coleen," he repeated.

Does my love for her really show that much? Luke wondered.

Back inside Luke couldn't take his eyes off Coleen as she quietly cleaned up the dishes. His talk with the sheriff had helped. He really should give her a chance, but he wasn't sure he could. He watched her as Gil was finally loaded onto a stretcher and hauled off to the hospital where he would remain under armed guard until he could be taken to jail. He watched her as the deputies quietly went about their business, documenting everything, photographing, diagraming blood splatters, and asking occasional questions of each other.

Coleen was quiet, withdrawn, and speaking to no one. When the sheriff suggested that she couldn't stay there that night as professional cleaning would be required to get the carpet acceptable, she simply said, "I'll stay in a motel. That's not new to me."

Luke wanted to go to her, to hold her tightly and comfort her, but he couldn't. So he just sat by the table, his head in his hands as the officers finished up and left. After they were gone, he walked over to her. "Coleen," he said, "let me help you get some things together and I'll find you a room."

She looked at him from her position in the kitchen doorway and said, "I'm sorry, Luke. I've brought nothing but misery into your life."

"Oh, no, Coleen," he disagreed, "there have been some really great times."

The way he said it sounded so final to her. "Luke, I really do love you. But I won't blame you if you don't want anything to do with me after this. What am I? Who am I?" she moaned, almost as if she were speaking only to herself.

"Coleen, we need to talk, and it can't wait," Luke said. "Let's get away from here, find you a room, and get this over with."

He sounded so cold. Coleen felt a chill come over her. Was this really the end of a love that had held so much hope for her? Had who she was destroyed who she had become? Why couldn't the past be ignored? Still she couldn't remember anything beyond March, and to her mind, it was better if that past remained forever lost. It was obviously not a good one, and she wanted only good now.

But it was too late. Her past had already been found and she must suffer the consequences, whatever those consequences were. She got up from the sofa and began to pack. She didn't need much. She'd lived with practically nothing for most of the few months in her memory. Luke tried to help, but even his presence brought little comfort.

Fifteen minutes later they were sitting in a motel room, looking at each other across a small table, and wondering where to begin. Finally, Luke said, "Maybe this isn't such a good idea. Maybe we should wait and talk in the morning."

"No Luke," Coleen said, "It's got to be now. Please, tell me what you've learned. Tell me what I still don't know."

"Well, Coleen," he began awkwardly, "I really don't know just how to start."

"Why are you calling me Coleen?" she asked. "Everyone seems to believe that my name is Carly. You better call me that now."

"No," Luke said, remembering the advice of the sheriff. "You're Coleen to me. You'll always be Coleen. It's Coleen that I've fallen in love with," he said, shocked at his own words. *Why did I say that?*

Because it was true, he told himself. Not being able to have a future with her because of her past didn't change how he felt.

"Luke, do you mean that?" she said, gazing at him through eyes so sad they tore at his heart strings.

"Yes, I mean it, but we must both be realistic here. Things may never work for you and me. Your past can't easily be ignored, even if we'd both like for it to be. But despite all that, I love you. It is possible to love what you've lost, you know. I lost Jamie, but my love for her hasn't dimmed over the years. The same may be true of my love for you," he said.

"And mine for you," she echoed. Then with a sigh of resolution she changed the subject, as it was really a pointless one. "Now, Luke, tell me why you went to Kentucky. Was it because you had to know? And how did you know to go there?"

So Luke began with the phone call from the man with the disguised voice. He told her every word of that conversation as he remembered it. She sat silently and listened. "So I knew I had to go there," he concluded.

"You believed him, didn't you?" she said. "You knew he was telling the truth. How?" she asked. "What made you so sure?"

He smiled weakly and said, "That's horse country, Coleen. And from that first day I met you, I knew that you knew as much about horses as me, maybe even more. But I wasn't positive, about the call, not totally."

"Now you are. Gil Whoever-He-Is was the clincher, wasn't he?"

"Almost," he said, just then remembering the bank signature card in his pocket.

"Luke, I shudder just thinking he was my boyfriend," she said.

Or your husband, Luke thought.

"What will it take to prove I'm really some woman named Carly Crockett?" she asked.

There was a small writing tablet on the table. Luke picked it up and said, "Write it, Coleen." He laid the paper in front of her and handed her his pen.

"Write what?" she asked.

"That name," he said.

She grinned weakly. "I know this seems crazy, but you'll have to spell it for me."

He did, and she wrote. He knew even as he drew the signature card from his pocket. "Here, you look," he said. "Is it the same?"

They both knew it was. She had written slowly, so it didn't look exactly the same, but it was definitely her handwriting. "Well, there's proof," she said. "I can't believe I'm not happy to know who I really am. Those first weeks, those months until I met you, I wanted nothing more than to know who I was."

Luke reached across the table and took both her hands in his. "Are you ready to hear the rest of what I learned?"

Coleen took a deep breath, looked Luke squarely in the eye, and said, "Yes."

Luke then told Coleen everything he'd learned, emphasizing that most was totally unsubstantiated. He even told her of the rumor that she'd married Gil. "That can be found out," she said. "And if it's true, I'll divorce him."

"It may not be true," he said, fearing however that it was. Later, when he mentioned that some young woman had called Captain Ormm and set an appointment with him to give him some information on drugs, she winced painfully. "It could have been you," he said. "And that may be why Gil's after you."

"I hope there was at least a little bit of good in me," she said sadly. Then later, she interrupted Luke's narrative once more to say, "I want to find Kyla. She can't be a kidnapper. She just can't be."

When he'd finished, she laid her head down on the table for a minute or two. Luke waited, never moving his eyes from the top of her head. When she sat up again and brushed her hair back from her eyes, he saw determination there. "Luke, I'm going back there, back to Kansas and back to Kentucky. I want to talk to those people who knew me. I want to know what I was like."

Luke nodded his head in approval. "That sounds like a good idea, but it could be dangerous," he said.

"Will you come with me? Will you help me, Luke?" she pled. "I'll be okay if you're there."

"I will, Coleen, on one condition."

"Name it," she said bravely.

"That there be no expectations over what we'll do about us. I don't know that I can ever live with your past, and you've got to understand that," he said, knowing he was hurting her, but wanting to be completely honest at the same time.

"I'll have no choice but to live with it, Luke. My past is part of me, even if I don't remember it. But you certainly shouldn't have to. I do have one more favor to ask though, and this is for *me*, not for *us*. If I decide to join the Church, will you baptize me? The missionaries have asked me to decide how committed I want to be."

"I will," he promised. "As long as there are no strings."

"Even if I have to go to jail for something I did, will you baptize me when I get out?" she asked.

Luke realized then that she'd thought this out. In the apartment while the officers were working and she was doing dishes, she had been thinking and planning. He admired her courage, and he loved her all the more. But he still wasn't sure it would ever be enough for a long-term, eternal commitment.

"I better go now," Luke said, drawing his hands gently from hers. "I'll see you tomorrow."

After he'd left her motel room, Coleen did something she'd only done a few times, and all of those in the past few days. She dropped to her knees and called on her Heavenly Father.

CHAPTER 19

Luke didn't get much sleep that night. He was exhausted, but his mind wouldn't shut down; his thoughts jumped from one subject to another. He'd rarely had to shoot at anyone, and it bothered him that he'd had to lately; he loved Coleen and it seemed unlikely that he would ever have her; he missed Monty, and if it hadn't been that he'd have disturbed his elderly parents, he'd have gone after him right in the middle of the night.

Luke was up shortly after daybreak, and the first thing he did after taking a shower was jump in the Ram and head to town to get Monty. Together, the two of them got the wheel lines going again, worked with the colts for an hour, and fixed a late breakfast. He cherished every moment with his son. He loved the little guy far more than life itself. He'd do anything for Monty, Luke realized.

He'd even sacrifice his own desires so as not to risk Monty's development later—like not marrying a woman who had a terrible past, even though he loved her.

After breakfast, Luke saddled Keno and Fox and he and Monty went for a ride, just the two of them, the way it had been for the past several years. They enjoyed it, and Luke would have ridden all day, except that he had to get into the office as there was work to do. When it came time to take Monty to his grandparents, the little fellow surprised Luke with, "Can't I go to Coleen's?"

"No, Monty, I'm afraid not. We won't be spending a lot of time with Coleen now," he said sadly.

"But I want to," Monty begged. "She's fun!" he finished indignantly.

Luke's heart ached, but he was firm. "She's had a change in her life, Monty," Luke said, "and it means you and I will be kind of doing things the way we used to."

Monty sulked all the way to his grandparents' house. And as Luke walked him to the door, he said, "Dad, I want a mom now. I want Coleen."

"I don't know if that will happen," Luke said lamely.

"Why don't you like Coleen, Dad?" Monty asked.

"Monty, I like Coleen a lot, but our lives just aren't the same."

"But she likes horses," Monty argued.

Luke hugged Monty and said, "We'll talk about it later, son. Now you be good for Grandma and Grandpa."

Luke walked into the office a few minutes later to find the place buzzing about the previous night's events. Bianca ran to Luke and threw her arms around him. "I'm so glad you weren't hurt," she said impulsively.

Luke was polite, but he didn't appreciate the show of affection. "I was never really in much danger," he said. "It was Coleen that was at risk."

"Oh, I heard about her," Bianca gushed. "Isn't it just awful? Her own boyfriend coming to kill her. I'm sorry, Luke, that she's not what she seemed."

"I'm sorry too, Bianca," Luke said, but his was a much different kind of sorry than hers.

"What's she going to do now?" she went on. "Is she going back to Kentucky?"

It was all Luke could do to be civil, so he said, "I really don't know. That'll be for her to decide."

"Well, she sure would be uncomfortable staying here. People will be talking so much it'll make her life miserable."

"Maybe people shouldn't talk so much," Luke said, barely hanging on to his patience. "Maybe they should reach out and help."

"Yes, you're so right, Luke," Bianca said. "Maybe they will, but what if she has to go to jail somewhere? She'd never come back here if that happened, would she?"

"I'm sure she wouldn't," he agreed as he tried to slip away from her.

But Bianca wasn't to be slipped away from. "How's Monty doing?" she asked. "The fire must have upset him terribly."

"It upset both of us," Luke said. "But worse things have happened to us."

Jamie had been killed. And now Coleen was probably lost to them. What was a fire when compared to those kind of heartaches?

Sheriff Robinson observed Luke's plight and called him from down the hallway. "Luke, I need to see you if you have a minute."

"Excuse me, Bianca, I guess the sheriff's going to put me to work," he said. And a moment later he thanked the sheriff. "You saved me," he said with a laugh.

"So I noticed," the sheriff said. "I have good news for you. Rooster taped a statement today. The county attorney gave me an information for attempted murder," he said, referring to the legal document that would put Rooster behind bars. "After it was served on Rooster and he'd had a chance to read the charges, he decided he wanted to bargain."

"What did he tell you?" Luke asked.

"He's been working for Vic off and on for years," Sheriff Robinson said. "They've never got along, but Rooster would carry stuff for him from Roosevelt to Salt Lake to sell it from time to time. He also admits setting the bomb for you after Vic caught him on the phone talking to you. But he'll testify that Sharps and Vic made it and that they forced him to set it."

"Does he get immunity?" Luke asked.

"That's the deal, but I think he's solid now. Oh, and he knew all about the cows. He helped them set up the old barn near Myton. He'll also testify about the fire, although all he knows is what he heard them say. That one's weak."

"What about a lab?" Luke asked next. "Have they been cooking meth again?"

"They have. It's exactly like you said earlier, Luke. They were only trying to keep us distracted and busy. Actually, they wanted you busy. And it worked to a point, but thanks to your persistence, it's all folded on them now. We'll have a search warrant and arrest warrants within the hour for Sharps and Victor. Do you want to come?"

"I wouldn't miss it," Luke said.

"And while we're over there, maybe the two of us could have a visit with Gil Stedman at the hospital."

"I wouldn't miss that either."

* * *

Dane called just after the officers left to arrest Victor and Sharps. "You're slow, Dane," Bianca told him. "Luke went back there himself. He found everything you did, only he did it in just one day. And get this, Luke had a shoot-out last night with an old boyfriend of Coleen's."

"Gil Stedman?" Dane asked. "He may be her husband," he told her. Dane wasn't nearly as surprised about Luke's discoveries as Bianca thought he'd be. She'd never believe it, but if it weren't for him, Gil would probably have gotten to Coleen. He was glad he'd called Luke and glad Gil was out of the picture now.

"Did you know he might come after her?" Bianca asked.

"It made sense," he agreed. Dane was already in Salt Lake and would be on the way back to Roosevelt shortly. But what he wanted now was to stop in Duchesne that evening and collect his fees. He'd had all he wanted of the foxy but deceitful Bianca Turner.

"Looks like Coleen will be leaving now," Bianca announced, "so I won't be needing your help anymore. Not that you did much good. I should have known Luke would get the job done himself."

"I did the best I could," Dane said angrily, tempted to tell her Luke would have done nothing if he hadn't tipped him off. But if word got around that he sometimes crossed his own clients, he'd be out of business.

"I'll be back in Duchesne in a couple of hours. I'll meet you for lunch and we can settle your account."

"How much do I owe you?" Bianca asked, thinking that for what little good he did, she shouldn't owe him another dime.

"Looks like about another twenty-five hundred dollars," Dane said.

"Twenty-five hundred!" Bianca shouted into the phone. "There's no way I owe you that much. Maybe five hundred."

Dane was mad. He'd worked hard, spent the time, and chalked up the expenses just like she'd asked him to, and he had no intention of letting her off the hook for less than she owed. He'd given her a cut rate in the first place, and he told her so. "So have me a check when I get back. I'll meet you at whatever café you name."

"I won't meet you anywhere. You didn't even get the job done. I'll send you a check for a thousand dollars in the mail. And that's all you're getting."

"Then I'll see you in small claims court. We had a deal," he said.

Bianca was stunned. If it went to small claims, everyone in the department would know she'd hired Dane, and that included Luke. She was so angry she could claw Dane's eyes out, but Bianca had to pay. She agreed to mail him a check and slammed the phone down.

* * *

Luke covered the back door to the outbuilding where Rooster had told the sheriff Victor 's lab was set up. There were enough officers on the place to make a coordinated assault on all of Victor's buildings at once. Both his truck and one that was registered to Sharps were parked in the yard. The likelihood of success was high. The officers crashed through all the doors on the place at the same time.

Luke kicked open the door and for the second time in as many days, looked down the barrel of his pistol at a suspect. Victor was turning as Luke dove in, and when he saw the gun pointing at his belly, he reached under the counter where he was standing.

"Give me a reason," Luke said calmly, and the drug dealer had a quick change of heart. His hands flew into the air and his face turned pasty white. "This is the end of the line, Vic," Luke said as he pulled Victor's pistol from under the counter and tossed it to Deputy John Samuelson.

A shot rang out at that moment from the direction of the house, and Luke knew that whoever had run into Sharps Thomsen hadn't had it so easy. He silently prayed that no one was hurt, then he did something he'd waited four years to do—snapped a pair of handcuffs onto the wrists of the man who'd killed his wife, and recited the Miranda warning rights in clear even tones.

After shoving Victor outside, Luke was relieved to see all the men who'd been assigned to the house come out with Thomsen. No one was injured, and again Luke offered a silent prayer, this one of gratitude. It turned out that Sharps had fired, but he'd been stumbling back as he did and the bullet went into the ceiling.

Victor had a fully operational meth lab set up, and a substantial amount of finished product was on the counter where he'd been packaging when Luke came in. For the first time in four long years, Luke felt like justice was finally being served. Court battles lay ahead, but his case was solid. Victor would go to jail, probably for the rest of his life.

Sheriff Robinson had a big smile on his face when he approached Luke a couple hours after they'd begun the bust. "You did okay, Luke. Thanks."

Luke smiled and said, "It's been a pleasure."

The radios on both men's belts suddenly came to life. "Mike One," the dispatcher said, "we just got a call from the hospital. The prisoner there has escaped and we have an officer down! Roosevelt officers are responding."

"Steve Roper," the sheriff said in alarm. "Luke, come with me, the rest of you finish up here." Both men were on the run when they reached their cars.

"Sheriff, Coleen—" Luke began.

"Go get her, Luke," the sheriff interrupted as he read Luke's concern in his face.

Luke had never driven so hard and fast in his five years with the department as he did that afternoon. He prayed as hard as he'd ever prayed as well, and he called the café where Coleen was supposed to be at work.

"She didn't come in today," he was informed. "She called and asked for the day off. We had plenty of help, so we gave it to her."

"Thanks," Luke said and he next rang the number of the motel where he'd left her early that morning.

Coleen wasn't in. He called the deputy that was covering the city and told him what was happening and to look for both her and Gil. Then he dialed her apartment phone. Again there was no answer. He pushed harder on the gas and his car responded. It only took him a few minutes to reach Highway 40, and when he was westbound, he pushed his car to over a hundred miles per hour.

He put his phone down and concentrated totally on his driving. Fifteen minutes later he rolled into Duchesne. His first stop was at the Twin Rivers Apartments. Carpet cleaners were busy at work there, but they hadn't seen Coleen.

The deputy on duty in town met Luke as he was hurrying back to his car. "Haven't seen her since you called," he reported almost lazily.

"She can't be far," Luke said. "She doesn't even have a car."

"Well, actually," he said, pausing between each word, "I think she does now. Saw her driving an old pickup recently. Think she'd just bought it." The pace at which the man was reporting was driving Luke crazy.

"What was it?" Luke asked frantically.

"Can't 'member," he said with his slow, lazy drawl.

"I don't suppose you'd have any idea where she bought it?" Luke asked impatiently.

The deputy shrugged. "Here in town, I suppose. Other than that, no."

Luke grabbed his cell phone and quickly checked with local dealerships. Once he knew which one had sold Coleen the truck, he drove there, and after getting a description he called dispatch and broadcasted it. He didn't really believe she'd leave town, but he wasn't sure. He drove rapidly all around Duchesne, looking for her or her truck, and his alarm grew after failing to spot it. He really became frightened when he heard from Sheriff Robinson that Gil had an accomplice. "He didn't get out of here alone," the sheriff said. "Steve Roper was knocked cold and a nurse was tied up in the room. He may have been gone for as long as fifteen minutes before it was discovered."

Luke was afraid that he was too late. They might have already gotten to Coleen. He was absolutely beside himself and felt terribly helpless as he didn't know what to do or where to go. Then suddenly, and with a calm assurance, he remembered something he'd told Coleen several days ago. He'd told her she was welcome to borrow one of his horses anytime she wanted.

She'd never taken advantage of his offer, but she'd never had a vehicle until today either. He followed what he felt sure was the Spirit and sped to his ranch. The old pickup Coleen had bought didn't look like much, but Luke had never been so happy to see an old truck as when he laid eyes on hers. He bailed out of his car and made a beeline for the horse trailer. The door to the tack room was slightly ajar, and when he looked in, Jamie's saddle was gone.

Luke dropped to his knees right there beside his trailer and threw a prayer of thanks heavenward. Then he grabbed a bridle and ran for the horse pasture. In minutes he had Keno saddled, and he rode out the gate and onto the hill, Spider's fresh tracks leading the way.

Once he was at the top of the hill, he spurred Keno, and they raced toward the cedar trees in the distance. Coleen must have been riding for quite a while, because Luke didn't spot her until he was almost four miles from his house. She must have seen him about the same time as he saw her, for she kicked her heels into Spider's side and came racing back toward Luke.

Her face was radiant and her eyes were shining when Coleen slid Spider to a stop beside Luke and Keno. "Am I in trouble for stealing a horse?" she asked, smiling and patting Spider's neck affectionately.

"Of course not," Luke said. "I told you before that you were welcome to ride anytime you felt like it."

"Thanks, Luke," she said gratefully. "I was afraid after last night that I wouldn't be allowed to, but I took the chance. Spider and I have had the best afternoon. I just needed to get away."

"And it's good you did," Luke said.

Coleen's smile faded at the concern she saw in Luke's eyes. "What's happened, Luke?" she asked.

"Gil Stedman escaped. Someone got him out of the secure room at the hospital," he told her.

"Oh!" she gasped as fear drove the radiance from her face. "What am I going to do now?"

Luke had an answer ready for her. "You're going with me to Kentucky," he announced. "I'll see that Gil doesn't bother you again."

"Luke, are you sure?" she asked. "I thought you needed a few days to try to wrap up your case with Vic, or is that who broke Gil out?"

"Gil did have help, but we don't know who it was. It definitely wasn't Victor. He and Sharps are in jail. We arrested them this afternoon."

That brought her a little relief. "Can you keep them there?" she asked.

"Bond's ten million apiece. They'll stay put. We can leave tonight if you want to," he said. "I'll need to be back within a week or so for the preliminary hearings, but by then I hope Gil's back in custody."

* * *

"Mom, can you keep Monty for a few more days?" Luke asked as he entered the house carrying a small suitcase with Monty's clothes all packed. He was in a hurry, and Coleen was waiting in the truck out front.

"Sure, you know we'd love to," she said. "But I hope you get through with whatever it is you're doing soon, because I think he's having a hard time with you being gone so much."

"I hope this will be it for a while," Luke said. "Let me just give him a hug and I'll be on my way."

"Oh, he isn't back yet," she said.

"Isn't back from where?" Luke asked, his concern rising.

"Did you forget that you asked Bianca to pick him up after work, Luke? Why, you're getting as forgetful as your father and me," she said with a smile.

"Bianca!" Luke thundered as his mother's eyes flew wide open. "I didn't tell her she could take him. She didn't even ask!"

"I—I'm sorry,' son. His mother said, suddenly flustered. Bianca's—well, she's such a nice girl, and I was sure she said—" his mother began.

"That's okay, Mom," he cut in. "It's not your fault. And it can't hurt anything. When I get back from this trip I'll talk to her about making sure she clears it with me."

Luke was muttering when he got in the truck and Coleen asked what the matter was. "Oh, it's nothing," he said. "They just let Monty go with someone without checking with me first."

"Everybody loves Monty," Coleen said. "I'm sure he's fine." Coleen suspected who it might be, but she figured Bianca would take care of the little boy. Then her heart went out to the other woman as she thought about how she would feel if she lost Luke. She wished somehow that things could work out for all of them.

* * *

Bianca gave Monty another piece of candy and said, "You're such a sweet boy, Monty. Maybe someday I can be your mom. Would you like that?"

"I want Coleen to be my mom. Dad really likes her," Monty said innocently. He placed no stock at all in what his dad had told him earlier that day. Monty was very young, but he was also smart, and he knew his father really liked Coleen.

"Oh, Monty," Bianca said in alarm. "That would be terrible. Coleen is not a good person. She's done some terrible things and might have to go to jail."

"Coleen's good," Monty said angrily.

"Actually, Monty," she said, ignoring his assessment of the woman she despised, "she might already have a husband. She can't marry your dad."

Monty's eyes misted up and Bianca took him tenderly in her arms. "It's okay, Monty. I'll take care of you. Coleen doesn't love you nearly as much as I do." Even as she said it a twinge of guilt began to plague her.

CHAPTER 20

"What are you still doing in Utah?" Jim's client asked impatiently.

"Well, actually, things turned a little ugly last night," Jim Redd reported.

"Ugly?" his client asked. "Carly did get the package, didn't she?"

"She did, but—"

"Then why are you sticking around there?" the client interrupted. "I told you I didn't want anyone knowing you had any connection with Carly."

"Sorry, I guess I screwed up, but I had no choice," Jim defended himself. "Gil Stedman showed up, and—"

"Gil Stedman!" the client thundered. "You should have shot him!"

"I did, and so did Coleen's cop friend, but we didn't do a very good job of it and the guy escaped from the hospital today. Another of Aspen's men must have come," Redd said.

"I should just fire you, Jim Redd," the client growled. "But I can't right now, because you have more work to do, and you better get it right. Now, explain everything that happened."

Jim did just that, and concluded with, "I can promise you one thing, she has no memory at all of her life as Carly Crockett. She has a severe case of amnesia."

The client was silent for a moment and then said, "She's not faking it?"

"Absolutely not," Jim said.

"All right, but that's a most puzzling thing," the client said. "Where is the package now?"

"The sheriff has it, all twenty-five thousand dollars," Jim said with a sly grin on his face. "And it wasn't my fault that I found out what you were sending her, but as you can imagine, there were a lot of questions about where it came from."

"You remained silent?" the client asked.

"Of course, but what could I have told them anyway?" Redd asked.

"Nothing that would tie that money to me. At least I did one thing right; I didn't tell you who I am. So where's the girl now?"

"The last I saw of her, she was in the black truck of the detective she was with last night. That was just a few minutes ago."

"And Gil Stedman is around. You better make sure nothing happens to that girl." Jim could tell the client was angry, but none of this was his fault. He'd done what any good PI would have done in his place.

"I'll see if I can locate her. But then what do you want me to do?" Jim asked.

"Don't let that man get near her," his client said. "And let me know what she's doing. I've got to think a little. This amnesia thing will make matters quite difficult. I'll decide what to have you do about her later, if anything. Meantime, protect her." The line went dead, and Jim looked at his phone for a moment as if it could help him. It wasn't easy working for someone you didn't know and didn't fully trust. Finally, he clipped the phone onto his belt and started up the rental car.

He drove to the motel and checked the room Carly was at the night before. It was unoccupied. Then he went to the manager's office and was told that she'd checked out a little earlier. Next, he drove across the Duchesne River and checked the apartments where she lived. No one was at her apartment. A call to Sheriff Robinson got him nothing. The sheriff clearly didn't trust him.

Even though he was frustrated, he hadn't wasted his time that day. He'd learned all he could about Luke Osborne, and one of the things that stood out was that the sheriff's secretary was sweet on him—and jealous of Carly, or Coleen Whitman as she now called herself. Another phone call got him Bianca's address, and minutes later some information he could report to his client.

"I don't know where Luke is," Bianca Turner told him after inviting Jim in and inspecting his credentials. "I just took Luke's little boy back to his grandparents' house, and they told me he'd asked them to keep him for a few days, that Luke was going out of town."

"Did they have any idea where he was going?" Redd asked.

"I don't think so. Why do you want to know?"

"Was he going alone?" Redd was asking the questions, not answering them.

"I don't know that it's any of your business, but he probably did," Bianca answered.

Jim Redd didn't think so. He'd seen Carly Crockett with Luke not long before he'd called his client. But he didn't think he'd share that information with Bianca. He thanked her and gave her a card. "Call me at that number," he told her, "if you find out anything about where he's gone. It's important that I get in touch with him."

Bianca took the card and said she would, but Jim had an idea she wouldn't. She seemed awfully protective of Luke Osborne.

Another call to his employer sent the harried PI hurrying toward Salt Lake and the airport. "You better find out where they went young man," Jim's client said. "And let me know what they're up to."

* * *

Luke was cautious as he entered the airport, carrying both their suitcases. The long wait frustrated him; it gave Gil and his accomplice time Luke didn't want to give them. He doubted they'd have figured out he was taking Coleen to the airport, but he also knew anything was possible. He breathed a little easier an hour later after he and Coleen had passed the security area, but he also felt naked without his pistol. He'd checked it, and would get it back when they landed in Lexington, but in the meantime he could only hope none of Coleen's enemies could get past security with one.

They found the gate their flight would be departing from, then found a restaurant and ate. When they came out a half hour later, Coleen said, "I need to slip into the ladies' room. I'll just be a moment," she added. "We still have a few minutes before we need to board our plane."

As she went in, Luke did a double take as a man disappeared into the men's restroom nearby. He'd only seen him from the back, but something about him seemed familiar and Luke was uneasy as he waited for Coleen. He had the impulse to follow the man into the restroom and get a better look at him, but he couldn't leave and risk Coleen coming out before he did.

Luke had worked hard to convince himself that he and Coleen had no future together, but her safety weighed heavily on him, and seeing her so often, he couldn't avoid the feelings that overtook him. No matter what she'd been before he met her, he'd developed very strong emotions toward the woman she was now. Was that what mattered, he wondered. Was she really a different person? Did anyone deserve another chance like that—could she be trusted?

As Luke thought, he waited impatiently for Coleen to come out. He also watched the men who were coming out of the men's restroom. Every one he looked at was a stranger, except one man that walked away from him, heading down the concourse in the direction of their departure gate. It was the man's gait that seemed familiar, but not his face. Nonetheless, Luke was nervous, and when Coleen finally came out, he took her hand protectively and walked toward their gate, determined to keep her right with him.

Their flight was called and they waited as the first-class passengers boarded. Luke looked at their seat assignments when the next group was called; they'd have to wait a little longer. He looked about nervously, and then spotted that same man again. He was boarding their flight!

"Luke, what's the matter?" Coleen asked. "You're acting weird."

He looked at her and felt a stab in his chest when he saw the fear in her eyes. "Sorry," he said. "I'm just nervous I guess."

"No, you're watching for someone," she said firmly. "Who are you watching for, Gil Stedman?"

"I guess," he answered hesitantly. *Or anyone else who might be suspicious.*

Luke spotted the man when he and Coleen approached their seats. He was a half dozen rows behind them and had his head ducked, reading a magazine from the pocket of the seat in front of him. He still didn't appear to be anyone Luke should know, but he felt a chill in his spine anyway. He stared at the man for a minute before finally helping Coleen slide into her seat next to the window. Then he looked back again and caught the man looking right at him. He ducked his head almost instantly, but not before Luke concluded that he'd looked into those eyes before.

But where or when? He couldn't seem to associate those eyes with the dark hair and goatee.

He hated to sit down, turning his back to the man, but he had no choice. And when he did turn to sit, Coleen was watching him, the fear in her eyes more evident than before. He took her hand, squeezed gently, and forced a smile. "You look tired," he said. "Maybe you can sleep while we fly. It'll be early morning before we land in Lexington."

Coleen could read Luke like a book. "But you won't be sleeping, will you?" she asked. "There's someone on this plane that you're worried about. Why don't you point him out and then we can both keep an eye on him," she suggested.

Luke didn't answer as her words triggered a memory. Just now, as she so accurately read his mind, it reminded him of his wife. Jamie could always tell what was on Luke's mind. It had been uncanny the way she could read his emotions, his facial expressions, and his body language when he thought he wasn't giving off any clues. The memory brought bitter tears to his eyes, and he was embarrassed that Coleen was watching him. He closed his eyes to fight the emotions. At times he missed Jamie so much the pain was almost more than he could bear. But these past few weeks it had been better since Coleen had begun to fill the emptiness in his heart.

But what hurt the most was the knowledge that Coleen had begun to fill that place, that he loved her, but was losing her too.

He felt her hand touch his, and a shiver went up his arm and clear to his heart.

"Luke, what's the matter?" she asked tenderly.

But the *matter* was something he couldn't talk to her about. In fact, the emotions that rolled over him were so strong, so painful, that he couldn't speak at all.

"Here," Coleen said, as her free hand shoved a clean white handkerchief into his, "use this."

Luke was ashamed; he hadn't intended to let his emotions get to him like this. "When you want to talk about it, I'll listen, Luke," she said in a whisper. "And I really do wish you'd show me who it is that you're so worried about."

That reminder helped him to snap out of his brief emotional break-down, and Luke was finally able to speak. "I'm sorry," he said. "I guess the pressure's too much for me. Maybe I shouldn't be a cop at all."

"This has nothing to do with your being a cop, this has to do with you and me." The accuracy of her words stunned him for a moment. Why did she have to be so . . . right? She seemed so right for him.

But again he thought of how much he loved his son and how unfair it would be to ever give Monty a mother who couldn't be everything Jamie would have been had she lived. Not like Jamie in every way; that was unrealistic. But as good as Jamie, as close to the Lord as Jamie, and as devoted as Jamie.

As hard as it was, Luke avoided looking back at the familiar stranger until their flight was airborne and his emotions were totally under control again. Then he peeked back and caught the man's eyes a second time.

He definitely knew those eyes, even if he didn't recognize the face. And when he was again looking forward, Coleen said, "If you'd point him out to me, maybe I'd recognize him, Luke."

"Six rows back. Aisle seat. Black mustache and goatee. Black hair, somewhat frizzy," he said. "There aren't many people behind us, but don't be long looking." He paused, caught her eye, and then added, "I'm sure neither of us know him, he just reminds me of someone."

Coleen twisted in her seat, moved back and forth slightly, and then gasped and turned around. "His eyes?" Luke asked.

"No, he's looking down and talking on the air phone, but he was scratching his head with his right hand. He's left-handed, just like . . ." She paused, scrunched her eyebrows thoughtfully, then smiled in relief. "Jim Redd," she said. "Remember? He kept scratching his head last night. But it can't be him, he was clean shaven."

But Luke knew she was right. It was Jim Redd's gait and Jim Redd's eyes that he'd seen. But what was he doing on this same flight?

"Disguised?" Coleen asked as her hand grasped Luke's again, tightly this time, as she was suddenly frightened. "Why is he following us, Luke?"

"I don't know, but I intend to find out," he answered as he started to rise.

Coleen's grip on his hand tightened. "Be careful, Luke," she whispered.

He sat back down, looked her right in the eye, and said, "If he meant you harm, he would never have done what he did last night. You don't need to be afraid of Jim Redd."

Or does she? he wondered.

"Be careful anyway," she said.

She was right. He couldn't be too careful. "I will, Coleen, and don't you move," he said as he again rose to his feet.

* * *

Jim Redd had thought himself the master of disguise, but he was certain that Luke Osborne had recognized him. He'd grabbed the phone from the back of the seat in front of him and dialed as soon as Luke turned back around. When it was answered, he said, "I'm on the plane with them, and I thought I was sufficiently disguised. The detective with Carly is too smart I guess. I'm sure he has me pegged. What do you want me to do?"

The client didn't answer for a moment. Jim looked up, startled to see Luke staring down at him with eyes that were hard and determined.

"Well, what do you think?" he said into the phone as nonchalantly as he could, trying to ignore Luke.

"It's time you and I met," the client said. "Bring them to me."

"Where?" he asked.

Jim thought he had fast reflexes, but he never even saw Luke's hand move. The phone just sort of vanished and appeared at Luke's ear.

"Call me from Lexington when you land. I'll tell you where to take them then. But Mr. Redd, I warn you, don't let them slip away," Luke heard the voice from the other end saying.

Jim did all he could do under the circumstances. He grinned at Luke. But Luke didn't grin back. He spoke into the air phone to a startled client.

"If you want to meet Coleen, or Carly, as others seem to know her, then you can arrange it through me," Luke said in a voice that signaled how serious he was. "And you'll meet where I say and with me there, is that clear?"

"Who are you? Where's Jim Redd?" the firm, commanding voice of an elderly woman asked as Luke dodged Jim's grasping left hand. Jim had decided that grinning wasn't all he could do.

"My name is Detective Luke Osborne. And nobody is getting near Coleen unless I say so. Who are you, and what do you want?"

"Mr. Osborne," the client said with a sigh, "I gather from your voice that you care about Carly?"

"I don't know Carly, but I certainly care for Coleen Whitman," he said boldly. "And I'll do anything in my power to protect her."

Jim Redd's eyes were popping, and he quit trying to retrieve his phone. He looked forward, and saw that the girl Luke called Coleen was standing in the aisle and watching with wide, frightened eyes. He smiled, gave her the okay signal and winked at her, and she smiled back. A smile he thought explained a lot about why Osborne had admitted what he had about the girl.

"Mr. Osborne, I also love that girl, and I too will do anything in my power for her. Call me from a pay phone in Lexington when you land, and we'll discuss a meeting. And I want Mr. Redd there. He assured me he was as good as private investigators come; I have a little lecture for him planned. In fact, if you don't mind, I'd like to talk to him briefly now," she said.

"You better be straight with me," Luke warned. But somehow he felt that Coleen had nothing to fear from the old woman on the phone, and he handed it back to Jim as Coleen slipped her arm through his.

Jim spoke into the phone as he peeled his mustache off. "I'm sorry, Carly's friend is rather demanding," he said to the client.

"And so am I. I told him to call me from a pay phone when you land. I want to meet the three of you. But you need to take great care. As you have already learned, Carly has dangerous enemies."

"Who was it on the phone?" Coleen asked Luke.

"Someone from your past who loves you," Luke said.

"I was beginning to think there wasn't anyone in my past who loves me," she said sadly. "Are you sure this isn't some trick?"

"I'm not sure of anything, but I think she's genuine. I guess we'll find out though. She wants to meet us," Luke said.

"She?" Carly asked.

"Yes, an older lady," Luke answered as he and Coleen returned to their seats.

* * *

When the plane had landed, Jim Redd turned on his cell phone and checked his voice mail out of habit. Before he even got out of his seat, he returned the only call he'd received.

Bianca answered, and as soon as Jim had identified himself, she said, "Jim, something terrible has happened."

CHAPTER 21

Jim Redd wasn't sure that he should tell Bianca that he knew where Luke was, but he signaled to Luke, who was just getting a bag from the overhead storage, that he might be interested in the phone call. Luke and Coleen waited while Jim worked his way forward and crowded in beside them. Jim was listening intently on his phone, but Luke was surprised when he said, "I've located Luke. I think you better tell him yourself." Then to Luke, he said, "Bianca."

Luke gave Coleen a puzzled look, then took the phone from the PI. "Bianca?" he said. "What's going on?"

"Where are you, Luke?" she demanded.

"I'm out of town on a case," he said.

"How far out of town?" she asked.

"I guess it would be more accurate to say that I'm out of state," he told her after a moment of thought.

"The sheriff didn't mention that you'd gone anywhere, Luke."

"There are lots of things the sheriff doesn't tell you, Bianca," he said, trying to keep the anger from his voice. "What do you want, anyway?"

"You need to come home right now," she said. "Your father's had a heart attack and is in the hospital."

Luke groaned and Coleen watched as his face drained and his shoulders slumped. "How bad is it?" Luke asked as he turned on his own phone and discovered that his mother had been trying to reach him.

"Well, it must not be too serious, because your mother took him over to the hospital herself."

"Why did she do that?" Luke wondered aloud. "That's thirty miles. Anything could happen in thirty miles. Why didn't she call an ambulance?"

"There's something else you need to know," Bianca said. "The man you shot, Coleen's husband, he went to your parents' house asking about you. There was another man with him and he looked as rotten as Gil."

"We don't know that he's . . ." Luke stopped. Coleen didn't need to hear him talk about a supposed husband of hers. "What did he say to them?" he asked instead.

"It wasn't what they said, but how. He frightened them both. And he also asked about Coleen."

"What did they tell him?" Luke asked as the worry grew.

"Nothing. They said they didn't have any idea what you were doing or where you were at. Then your mother said that Monty came into the room, and when the men asked about him, she really became frightened. They left right after that, and your mother noticed that your dad wasn't looking so good. That's when they realized he was having a heart attack."

Luke felt helpless being so far away. And there was no way he could get back there for a while. "Is my mother at the hospital with him?" Luke asked.

"Yes, and so's Monty. I told her I'd come get Monty because I think she'll need to stay with your dad for a while."

Luke didn't like that idea. But he knew there was nothing else he could do right now, so he simply said, "Thanks, if you don't mind."

"I love the little guy, Luke. I'll protect him and take care of him. You know that," Bianca said.

"Yes, I know that," Luke agreed. "And I appreciate what you're doing."

"I won't let those men find him again, I promise. I'll do whatever I have to do to keep Monty safe."

"Thanks," Luke said again.

"I've already talked to the sheriff," Bianca added, "and he said I could have some time off."

"Good," Luke said, wishing he had another alternative for his son. He didn't want the boy to start wanting Bianca for his mother. Then he thought of his sister in Orem. He'd call her. She'd love to take Monty out there for a few days if need be. And it would be an adventure for Monty as well. "Bianca, I'll make arrangements for my sister to take him later."

"Oh, no, Luke. That won't be necessary," she protested.

Luke let it drop. He'd just call his sister and that would be that. In the meantime, he needed to find out how his father was, and he was also concerned about what Gil Stedman was up to. "Has anyone caught up with Gil yet?" Luke asked Bianca, intentionally avoiding contact with Coleen's eyes.

"No, and that has the whole department worried. The sheriff called a lot of the guys out to search for them, but so far they've had no luck," she said.

"Okay. Thanks, Bianca. I better go now and call my mother."

"Luke," Bianca said again before he could cut her off. "Are you going to Kentucky?"

"I'm on a case," he said, evading her question.

Then her voice hardened. "Coleen's with you, isn't she? Luke, can't you see what she is?"

Luke cut the connection, so angry he could feel his face beginning to burn.

"What's happened?" Coleen asked as soon as Luke had given the phone back to Jim Redd.

"My father had a heart attack. He's in the hospital," he said.

"And Gil Stedman had something to do with it?" she asked.

"He came by asking about me and you."

Coleen looked stricken. "You need to go back at once," she said. "Your poor mother and your son."

Luke looked at Jim and said, "Thanks for the use of your phone. We'll call your client as soon as we get in the terminal." Then he took Coleen by the hand and helped her into the aisle. He used his own cell phone to call his mother at the hospital in Roosevelt as he and Coleen slowly made their way toward the exit.

"It's not serious Luke," his mother assured him. "They're only going to keep him overnight. Then I can take him home, but he has to rest. I'm not sure what to do about Monty, though."

"I've taken care of that," he said. "Bianca is coming over to get him."

"But I thought you didn't want him going with her," she said.

"It'll be okay. Sometimes we can't have what we want," he said, thinking how much he wanted Coleen to have a different past, to simply be the girl he'd fallen in love with. But that was one of those things he wanted and couldn't have. "I'll call Carol and see if she'll come get him for a few days, if you don't need for me to come back, that is," he finished.

"No, you take care of your work," she said. "But I'm worried about the ranch. The water can't go long and it's about time to cut hay again, isn't it?"

Luke was also worried about those things and told her that he'd arranged for one of the neighbor's teenage sons to move the wheel lines. "The hay will just have to wait."

"Luke," his mother said, and her voice had suddenly taken on a worried tone. "Who's this Gil Stedman and the man with him? Do you know them?"

He told her that he knew Gil and that he was sure they'd be gone from Duchesne by now. "Don't worry about them," he said. "You just take care of Dad."

Coleen felt horrible. She was keeping Luke from his family. "Luke," she said, "let's go back. We can come out here later."

"No, Coleen. We can't risk it. I know what I told Mom, but I'm not at all sure that Gil and his friend aren't still around Duchesne. And he won't take any chances on messing up another time. He's really angry with you."

Luke called his sister's home, but she was already on her way to Roosevelt, to be with their parents. Luke relayed a message through his brother-in-law that they get Monty from Bianca.

That taken care of, Luke tried to relax, but he couldn't as he found himself wondering where Gil was and what he would do next.

* * *

Bianca's heart was pounding fiercely. She had just stepped out the door to find Gil Stedman limping from the darkness. "We need to talk," he'd said.

She was almost certain who he was, and when a second dangerous-looking man joined him and showed her the barrel of a pistol, she almost fainted. "Inside, lady," the second man added.

Bianca did as she was told, and Liz's eyes popped wide open with fright when they came in, the gun inches from Bianca's stomach. Gil wasted no time. "Where's Luke taken her to?" he demanded.

"Who? What are you talking about?" Bianca stammered.

"Don't mess with me, lady," Gil said, his dark eyes narrow and full of hatred. "Just tell me where they are."

Bianca had never been so frightened in her life. "I don't know for sure," she said. "They left."

"And where were they going?" the second man asked.

Bianca knew she shouldn't say anything, but what choice did she have? Luke and Coleen, if they were together, were far away, but she and Liz were right here—where these men could kill them! And yet she stalled. "Why do you want to know?" she asked, her voice trembling with fright. "What is Coleen to you?"

"Her name's Carly," he said.

"Is she your wife or something?" Bianca asked.

She was so frightened that she failed to notice the look that passed between the two men. But Gil said, "Yes, she's my wife, and he has no right to take her away. Where are they?"

So Coleen really is married to Gil Stedman, Bianca thought. Luke shouldn't be with her, if he was, and she was almost certain Gil had spoken the truth.

But she didn't want to tell them where Luke was, not that she knew for sure.

Gil tried again. Looking at his partner, he said, "Luke's boy will tell us."

That upset Bianca so badly that she made a desperate decision. "They're headed for Kentucky," she said. "But Luke didn't do anything."

"He shot me," Gil said with anger flashing in his eyes. "Isn't that enough reason for me to go after him?"

"It's her you want, not him," she said.

"Actually, I suppose that's right. And since you told me where they're going, I promise I won't hurt your boyfriend," Gil said smugly. Then he added, "Kentucky, huh? That's where Carly and I live. Well, I guess we better get going."

But the other man said, "Not so fast, Gil. What's to keep these two from calling the cops?" He waved his gun at them, and Bianca again thought she'd faint. Liz didn't think anything; she did faint.

"Turn around and put your hands behind your back," Gil's partner ordered Bianca. She did as she was told and didn't even realize what he was doing until something came down hard on her head. She felt a sharp pain and slumped to the ground, unconscious.

Liz was the first to regain consciousness. She screamed when she saw Bianca lying on the floor, her head bleeding. She ran to the phone and called 911, then she wet a cloth in cold water and pressed it gently to Bianca's scalp. By the time Bianca came to, the EMTs and Deputy Steve Roper had arrived.

"What happened to you, Bianca?" Steve asked as she blinked and looked around.

"Gil Stedman was here," Bianca answered, her eyes filling up with tears of relief.

He touched his own sore, stitched head and said, "And he wasn't alone, was he?"

She shook her head, and Steve asked several more questions while Bianca's scalp wound was being bandaged. Then one of the EMTs said, "We better get you to the hospital. That's going to take quite a few stitches."

"I'll drive over," she said stubbornly. "I'm supposed to pick up Monty, Luke's little boy, from his grandmother at the hospital."

Steve said, "You're in no shape to drive. Believe me, I know. It was several hours before I felt good enough to go out and help look for those guys. And the sheriff says I should still probably go home. How about if I take you over, get you stitched, and bring you and Monty back instead?"

Bianca gratefully accepted. Monty would be safer if they were with a deputy.

* * *

"Call him," Judd Aspen's man said to Gil. "Carly's your problem, and Judd isn't happy that you haven't fixed the problem."

So Gil called, not that he really had a choice. "You finished the job yet?" Judd Aspen asked.

"Well, not yet, but—" Gil began.

"Where is she?" Aspen demanded.

"She's, well, she and her cop friend are on their way to Lexington," he stuttered.

"Then I'll take care of her myself. But you get on back here, Gil. I'll settle with you later."

* * *

The first call Luke made after they were in the terminal was to the local sheriff's office. They told Luke they'd have Captain Alfred Ormm call him back as soon as they could locate him. Luke paced nervously. He wanted to get on the phone with Jim Redd's elderly client, but he didn't want to miss the call from Captain Ormm. But it turned out the wait wasn't long. The captain called back within five minutes.

Luke briefed him on what had occurred and why he'd returned to Lexington so soon. "Stay put, Luke," he was told. "I'll come out there right now. It'll take me twenty or thirty minutes, but we need to talk. Meantime, you three be alert."

"Oh, Gil isn't a danger right now," Luke said. "He's a long ways away."

"But Judd Aspen and his men aren't," the captain cautioned. "And even though Gil might want to do this himself, Aspen will simply want your girl out of the way. And the fellow with Gil has probably already contacted Aspen."

Coleen shook her head in dismay as Luke told them what the captain had just said. "I wonder what I did to make such bad enemies."

Luke entertained the same thought. Then he turned to Jim. "As soon as I make the call to your client, we'd better get our bags and then wait somewhere where we aren't so conspicuous until the captain comes."

"I'll get the bags, you two stand over there and watch for anyone suspicious," Jim volunteered.

Luke didn't argue, as he was afraid for Coleen. But nobody suspicious appeared, and Jim came back in a few minutes carrying their bags. "Now I'll keep an eye out while you call my client," Jim volunteered.

"First I want my pistol," Luke said.

"And mine," Jim agreed.

It took several more minutes, but once they were armed, Jim and Luke felt more confident, and Luke made his call.

"Are you young people safe?" the elderly lady said as soon as Luke had identified himself. "I'm worried sick about my Carly."

Her Carly. Who is this lady anyway? Luke wondered.

"We're fine, but we can't hang around this airport long," Luke said, trying to let the client know that he didn't want to be on the phone much longer.

"Good, you be very careful and you take care of her," Luke was instructed. "Now, here's what you are to do," the client began.

But Luke stopped her. "Why don't I make the arrangements for a meeting place? Just tell me where you are and—"

It was the client's turn to interrupt. "Mr. Osborne, I'm confined to a wheelchair. I can't go just anywhere anytime I want. I'm sorry, but you need to come here. However, you must be very cautious in doing so. It would be tragic if you were followed to my home. People's lives are in danger."

Luke wanted to trust the old lady, but how could he be sure it wasn't a trick, that she wasn't really one of Coleen's seemingly endless stream of enemies. He said so to the lady, but she became emotional at the very suggestion. "You must get my Carly here, Mr. Osborne. Please, you must trust me," she pled.

"And you must trust me," he said.

"I trust you. I've already checked on you, young man. I've talked to your Sheriff Robinson in Utah. He says you're the best."

"Then tell me where you are," Luke pressed.

"I can't do that yet," she said. "But I can tell you this much. I'm in another state."

Luke was feeling desperate. He was staying on the phone much too long. "Please, ma'am," he said, "tell me where to go then."

"That's better," she said. "I can see that my Carly has used better judgment this time. You sound like such a good young man." Then she gave him some directions to a small town in Ohio, and said, "When you get there, call me again."

"Okay," Luke said.

"And the three of you stay together. I don't want my Carly without protection," the old lady said. Luke was almost certain she was crying when she put down the phone.

"See anyone suspicious?" he asked Jim and Coleen.

"Nothing, but that doesn't mean we're not being watched, that someone isn't just biding their time."

Coleen shivered with fright, and Luke took her protectively by the arm. "I told the captain we'd wait for him in that little café," he said, pointing a short distance up the concourse. "He should be here before long." They carried their luggage to a back corner of the small dining area and sat with all three of them facing the open front of the café.

When the captain came in just a couple of minutes later, he announced that he wasn't alone. "I brought the troops," he said, swinging his arm in an arc, indicating at least a dozen officers who had fanned out both in the café and up and down the concourse. All were plainclothes but extremely attentive.

"We've infiltrated Judd Aspen's organization since you were here the other day," the captain said. "What we've learned is disturbing. His is a big operation and we're sure it involves drugs, but what we don't know is how they're being transported. At any rate, one thing we're sure of is that he wants you," he said, looking straight at Coleen, "because you apparently discovered some things that would have allowed us to break his organization wide open."

"If I could remember I'd tell you, but it's no use now," she said sadly. "I can't remember anything. I don't even remember having ever lived in this area."

"But your sister might know," the captain said, "if we could locate her."

"But she's wanted for kidnapping!" Coleen cried. "She doesn't want to be found."

Ormm looked thoughtful for a moment, and Luke thought he was about to say something more about the other twin, but then he simply sighed in frustration—at a loss for what to do. "We would have liked to question Gil Stedman," he said.

"If he shows up here, there's a warrant," Luke said. "And if he figures out that we came here, he'll follow."

"He'll come, and we'll—"

The captain didn't get a chance to finish his sentence as a scuffle suddenly broke out just outside the front of the café, in the concourse. "Aspen's men! Get down!" he ordered, and Luke dragged Coleen to the floor.

Jim Redd stood for a moment before he too dropped and said, "Let's move it. There must be several of Aspen's men out there." Luke and Jim both had their guns out.

Luke glanced to his left and spotted a door leading to the kitchen area of the café. He pointed and said, "That way, Coleen, and crawl fast."

The luggage was forgotten in their haste as they made it through the door. Shots rang out and wood splintered overhead. People were screaming, running, and crawling. In the kitchen, as they continued to move, Luke hovered over Coleen, sheltering her with his body.

Suddenly Captain Ormm appeared, carrying their bags. He dropped them and breathlessly said, "Go out that way," pointing farther back. "Call me at this number when you're clear of here," he said in rushed tones as he shoved a business card into Luke's hands. "I think we've got most of the men that Aspen sent here to look for you, but you can never be sure. Go now! A couple of my men will follow you until you're safely away from here," he added as he headed out the door again.

Ten minutes later they were in a taxi. "Where to?" the driver asked.

Jim and Luke looked at each other. "Bus station?" Jim Redd asked.

"Good as anything," Luke answered and instructed the driver. A half hour later they were on a bus bound for Ohio. Coleen scarcely said a word, but she clung to Luke like she would never let go, and in her heart she prayed that she would never have to.

CHAPTER 22

Liz was groggy but awake when Bianca came in. Steve had dropped Bianca off moments before and said he'd stay until she was safely in the apartment. She waved at him from the door and he left. Liz staggered into the living room and said, "Do you know what time it is?"

"After three," she answered. "I've got to pack some things, then run down to the Osborne's and get Monty's little suitcase. They told me where they keep a key hidden."

Liz wasn't so sleepy that she didn't realize what Bianca was saying was crazy. "You can wait a few hours to get Monty's things. And why would you need to pack? You're not going anywhere, are you?"

Bianca faced her and said, "That's exactly what I'm doing, because I'm not taking any more chances. I'm getting Monty out of town tonight. I promised Luke I'd protect him, and I'm not sure I can do that if I don't take him somewhere."

"Bianca, are you crazy?" Liz asked. "Luke didn't tell you to take him anywhere, did he?"

"No, but that was before those men came in here and frightened the two of us. Leaving town is the smart thing to do. It's what he'd do. All I'm doing is keeping his little boy—I hope someday *my little boy*—safe."

"Where are you going?" Liz asked.

"I better not say," Bianca answered.

"'Better not say!' Bianca, I'm your best friend! I'd never tell a soul! You know that," Liz protested.

"Liz, be sensible. What if Gil came back, and that other guy, the one who likes to split people's heads open? Do you really think they couldn't get it out of you if you knew where I'd taken him?" Bianca asked.

"Well, I'd hope that—" Liz began.

"They could, Liz, and you know it. Monty and I are leaving."

"Bianca, you're scaring me. I don't think I want to be here alone. I'm coming with you. Your head must be hurting terribly, and I could drive."

"That's a great idea, Liz. Hurry, let's get packed and get on our way."

* * *

Renting a car in Columbus, Ohio was risky, Luke thought, until Jim Redd produced a false ID. "We can use this name," he suggested, "if you'll promise not to turn me in for having this card."

"Get it done," Luke said. The PI's fake ID was the least of his worries. After traveling for several hours on the bus, and having slept only fitfully, all three were tired and in need of a good meal. Luke suggested they find a motel, get cleaned up and rested before eating, then call the client.

Coleen was getting increasingly anxious. If the woman they called "the client" really was someone who loved her, what would she be like? What could she tell Coleen about her past? Could she tell of good things about her that might temper the bad things Luke had learned? She hoped so and she began praying such would be the case.

While Coleen showered, Luke called Captain Ormm, who explained that they had arrested six of Judd Aspen's men, one of whom was wounded in the gun battle in the airport. "But not one will say a word. They're loyal to Aspen. He's got some kind of hold over them, and I suppose it's money."

"Are your officers all right?" Luke asked, concerned that anyone might have been hurt.

"One was shot, but he'll be okay. Is there anything I can do for you, Detective?"

Luke hesitated a moment, then said, "I've got to know if Coleen has ever been married, and specifically if she's married to Gil Stedman," he said.

"I'll see what I can find out. Keep in touch."

Rested, filled, and ready to go a few hours later, Luke called Jim's client. "Are you young people still okay?" she asked immediately.

"We're fine."

"Nobody's bothered you since we spoke last?" she asked.

"Well, I can't say that," Luke said.

"What happened?" she asked. But then, before Luke could answer, she said, "Never mind that now. We'll meet and you can tell me then. Where are you now?"

"Columbus," Luke said.

"Excellent, and you weren't followed?"

"No, I don't think so. We came here by bus."

"Excellent," she said again. "You will need a car now."

"We've got one," Luke said.

"Good, now listen carefully. There's a little town called Galena that's about twenty miles or so outside of Columbus. It's at the north end of the Hoover Reservoir. You'll need a map, for it's tiny and the road to get there is rather roundabout. Call me when you get there."

It was after six when they pulled into Galena. It really was small. It made Duchesne look like a metropolis, Luke thought. He pulled off the road, found the only phone booth in town, and again called the elderly woman. He couldn't understand her opposition to his using a cell phone, but he supposed she was just old fashioned.

She gave him detailed directions that would bring them to a large dairy farm. "The old house, the big one, is mine," she said. "And make sure you aren't being followed."

Luke was feeling reasonably safe now. But he'd also felt safe in Duchesne and had nearly lost his life there more than once in recent weeks. So they were cautious, and when they pulled into the prosperous yard of the large dairy and spotted the huge old house that stood beyond a smaller, newer one, he believed they hadn't been followed.

Coleen was tense, more tense than Luke had ever seen her. "It'll be all right," Luke said, putting his arm around her protectively. "The woman says she loves you."

"But I don't know her. I don't know this place."

He pulled her close and smiled at her. "Somehow, despite all the bad things we've heard about you, I think we're about to learn something good," he said.

"Or is that just what you hope?" she said in as close to a bitter voice as he'd ever heard from her. And he knew she was right, and he felt guilty since he was grasping at straws. But again, he thought of Monty and knew that his little son deserved only the best for a new mother. And that's what Monty would get, or he would do without.

Jim Redd tapped Luke on the shoulder. "I'll hold back a little here. You never know. I'm probably just jumpy, but I feel like we're being watched."

Luke shivered. He felt Coleen tremble and he pulled her even closer, feeling vulnerable himself and wanting badly to keep any more bad things from happening to her. Jim pulled his gun and slipped behind a large oak that spread its sprawling limbs over the fence and yard that encircled the big house. Luke opened the gate, removed the arm that encircled Coleen's waist, and let her proceed ahead of him. He reached inside his belt and pulled his pistol. Then, his eyes swinging rapidly over the yard, the house, the orchard beyond, then back to the house, Luke pressed Coleen's back gently, nudging her forward.

She started walking up the long sidewalk. It wound past a brightly colored flower garden, beneath a vine-covered trellis, past a small fountain, and up a short flight of steps to a large open porch. When they finally reached the door, she again looked at the man she loved, with fear and trepidation etched into her pretty features.

Luke smiled the best he could, looked back down the walk at where Jim Redd still watched from beneath the giant oak, then touched his finger to the doorbell. He could hear chimes inside, but nothing else. For a long time they waited, then finally, the door creaked slightly and began to move.

Instinctively, Luke slid to the side of the door and held his pistol beside his leg, ready to raise it and fire if the need should arise. Jim Redd, at that moment, left the protection of the tree and ran swiftly across the lawn to the side of the porch, he too with his gun ready.

The door moved slowly, and then Luke found himself staring into the wide, dark brown eyes of an old gray-haired lady in a motorized wheelchair. She smiled and said, "You boys can put the guns away now. You're safe in my home." Then her eyes moved to gaze at Coleen, who was simply staring back at her. Tears filled the old woman's eyes, spilled over, and ran down the rugged, weathered cheeks.

"My darling Carly," she said. "Have you a hug and kiss for your Aunt Amelia?" Coleen did not move but simply continued to stare. "Carly, it's me, Aunt Amelia," she said as her voice began to choke up.

"I'm sorry, but I don't know you, ma'am," Coleen said politely.

"Then what the young man here said is true? You have forgotten?" She wiped her eyes with a perfectly ironed white handkerchief and then said, "Well, maybe in some ways it is truly a blessing, my dear, for your memories were not all so pleasant. But where are my manners? Please, come in, all of you."

They followed Amelia into a large sitting room where she invited them to make themselves comfortable. "There, that's better. Now let me introduce myself. I'm Carly's aunt. My name is Amelia Crockett. Carly's father was my baby brother, younger than me by twenty-five years."

Coleen was grateful when Luke took over and said, "And I'm Luke Osborne. My friend here is your very own private investigator, Jim Redd. And this," he said, touching Coleen's knee, "is Coleen Whitman."

The old lady smiled. "What a very pretty name, but it doesn't suit you," she said. "Carly Crockett is who you are."

"I prefer Coleen," she said. "Do you mind?"

"Not at all," her aunt said, though added stubbornly, "but it really doesn't fit."

Luke decided that the best way to proceed at this point was to simply lay aside small talk and find out if Coleen really was this woman's niece. Then, if she was, learn what those bad memories the aunt had mentioned were all about. He feared there was far more than he'd heard already. "Ms. Crockett," he began, "would you mind producing some kind of proof that Coleen is your niece?"

"I wouldn't mind at all," she said, her eyes now beginning to twinkle. "You're not one to hedge, or beat about the bush as they say." She turned and poked a slender, bony finger at Jim Redd. "You, Mr. Redd, are still in my employ."

"Yes, ma'am," he said quickly. "What can I do for you?"

Her hand moved slowly but steadily until that same finger was pointing at a large roll-top desk that sat in a tidy corner on the far side of the room. "In that desk is a photo album. Do you think you could manage to get it for me and bring it all the way across this room without spilling the contents—unlike how you spilled the beans when I sent you to Utah?"

Jim grinned at the old woman as her eyes were laughing. "I think I can manage," he said as he moved to follow her instructions.

"Very good, young man," she said as he handed her the album. She turned to Coleen. "Come closer so we can all see," she said.

"Yes, Ms. Crockett," Coleen said stiffly.

"Aunt Amelia to you," she said with feigned crossness. "If I must call you Coleen, then you must call me Aunt Amelia."

"Aunt Amelia," Coleen said softly and more at ease. She liked the fit of it on her tongue.

Amelia opened the book. The first picture was of a young man in the uniform of the United States Army during World War II days. The older woman gazed fondly at it for a moment, than said, as she turned the book so they could see it, "This was the young man I fell in love with so many, many years ago. You can't possibly know how it hurt when he never came home to me, but I've kept the promise I made to love him forever."

"I'm sorry," Coleen said.

Amelia smiled sadly and turned the next page of the book. There smiling at them was a young woman dressed in the fashion of the forties. Her hair was fixed in the style of that day, but her face could have been Coleen's!

The old woman smiled as she saw the shock of recognition in both their faces. "That's your old aunt in her better days," she said. "But there is more."

She leafed through several pages, and then she opened a picture to them that brought a gasp from Coleen. There Coleen stood, her arm around Amelia. And on the other side of Amelia in the picture was another girl who looked exactly like Coleen, except that her hair was a different color and there was a small mole beneath her right eye. The twin sister wanted for kidnapping looked like a really nice girl.

"Proof enough, my dears?" Amelia asked.

Coleen's eyes were glued to the photograph. "When was it taken?"she asked, as it looked amazingly recent.

"This past February," Ms. Crockett said. "One month before I lost all contact with you. Three weeks before your sister left for New York."

Following the kidnapping in Indiana? Luke wondered. But he was beginning to doubt it. Kyla looked in that picture as innocent and sweet as Coleen.

"Mr. Redd," Amelia said suddenly.

"Yes, ma'am?" he responded.

"There is a wall safe behind that picture," she said pointing. "It's unlocked but closed. Inside there is a large green envelope. Would you bring it to me please?"

When he handed it to her she opened it and removed a sheet of paper. "If you need more proof, Luke, here's the certificate the hospital prepared the day the twins were born. Perhaps you'd like to compare that little footprint there with hers now?" she asked. "You'll find they are the same except in size."

"Ms. Crockett," Luke said, "I'm convinced. Are you, Coleen?"

Coleen nodded, her eyes glistening. "Tell us about me, about my family," she said.

For the next hour, they listened as the kind woman explained about her baby brother and how he'd always been irresponsible. He'd been given a farm in Kansas by their father. But he squandered his money gambling, mortgaged the farm, and eventually died along with his wife. "You girls were left with nothing," Amelia said.

They hadn't known their aunt was even alive since their father had once asked her for money, and when she refused, he angrily cut off any family contact. At that time Carly and Kyla were about twelve, and she had not been allowed to see them, to speak to them, or to even write. He'd told them she was dead. Amelia didn't realize that they were alone until several months after the death of their parents. Then she looked them up and found them living alone in poverty, supporting themselves by working in a café.

From that time on, she'd given them money, properly noted it, seen that taxes were paid and everything was legal. They had been grateful for the help but had preferred to live on their own rather than be completely supported. It was this money that had started the rumors that haunted them. But it was clean money, part of what they were to inherit as Amelia's only surviving relatives.

Amelia explained that they came to see her often, and even stayed with her for as much as a few months at a time. Both girls loved horses, and both ended up working on horse farms in Kentucky. And both were accused of running with bad crowds. "Which you did at times," Amelia said to Coleen. "I warned you both that bad company would create a bad reputation, but you were like me when I was younger—stubborn. You had to make your own mistakes. But the worst was when both of you began to work for that man named Judd Aspen."

"Not a good man," Luke said.

"He's a scoundrel," the woman said. "And the heartache that has come to me these past months is because of him. Your sister, my dear, is wanted for kidnapping, which I'm convinced she didn't commit. She had to go into hiding. You simply vanished, and I feared you were dead until Mr. Redd here found that you were in Utah living under a different name."

"Where is Kyla?" Luke asked.

"I can't say," Amelia said firmly. "For though I like you very much, and approve of your association with Carly . . . Coleen," she corrected herself, "you're still a cop with a duty to fulfill, and until someone can help me prove Kyla's innocence, her location will remain a secret."

Luke nodded, but he wondered if Kyla was really innocent or if it was just the hopes of a sweet old woman who couldn't bear to think that such a thing was possible.

It grew late, and finally Amelia said, "I plan for all of you to stay here tonight. There's food in the kitchen. You may prepare whatever you like, and I'll show you your rooms in a little while."

* * *

Luke called his parent's home late that evening and asked if his sister Carol had taken Monty to Provo yet, or if she was staying the night in Duchesne. "Oh, no," his mother moaned. "Not again."

"What, Mom? Where is Monty?"

"Didn't you tell Bianca to take him out of town where he'd be safe?" she asked.

Luke took a deep, slow breath to cool his anger. He'd wanted to talk to Monty. He missed him terribly, but Bianca had promised to keep Monty safe. Apparently that was what she was doing. As he thought back on the conversation he'd had with her before he got off the airplane in Lexington, he realized that he hadn't insisted that she turn Monty over to Carol. And after talking briefly with his mother, what he'd learned about what happened to Bianca and Liz at the hands of Gil and his new cohort made it logical for her to leave.

"Luke, I'm sorry," his mother said.

"No, Mom, it's okay. No one knows where Gil Stedman is. Bianca did the right thing this time. We won't have to worry about him hurting Monty this way. She'll see to that," he said with sudden conviction as his anger toward Bianca melted away. For once Luke was actually grateful to Bianca for what she was doing.

* * *

There was a terrible car wreck later that night in Indian Canyon, several miles south of Duchesne. The car went over the edge near the top of the canyon and burned. The lone occupant was unidentifiable, but a wallet was found partway down the steep embankment. The driver's license inside bore the name of Gil Stedman.

CHAPTER 23

It wasn't until the following morning that Amelia asked them to tell her what had happened at the airport in Lexington. They told her and she seemed to turn even more pale than she naturally was. "Oh, you poor kids," she lamented. "What can be done to stop that man?"

That was just the opening Luke was waiting for. "There is one person who probably has the knowledge that can help the strike force bring him down," Luke said shrewdly.

He watched as the elderly lady's eyes filled with the realization: she had to choose to protect one niece over the other. Slowly she said, "So Kyla is the only one?"

"The only one," Luke said. "Coleen was going to talk to Captain Ormm, commander of the strike force, but somehow Judd Aspen found out, and that was why Coleen was chased clear to New Mexico. That's why she had her accident and lost her memory. And that's why Gil Stedman is so intent on destroying her. I think Coleen told Kyla what she knew, and I think you know that too."

The old woman slumped in her chair. "Those two didn't keep secrets from each other. They were as close as two sisters could be. Oh, Luke, isn't there any other way they can accomplish it?" Amelia asked.

"There might be, but it will take a lot of time and risk more lives," Luke said.

"Please, Aunt Amelia." Coleen pled. "Will you help us? Will you talk to Kyla, to my . . . my sister?"

The old lady's eyes filled with tears, but finally she said, "Yes, I'll talk to your sister. But it must be her decision. I'll not force her, nor will I send you to her, Luke. She must decide."

Luke nodded his head. He could ask for no more, nor would he. He glanced at Coleen, but she was looking studiously at her hands which were folded in her lap. "Do you agree, Coleen?" he asked.

She didn't answer; her mind seemed to be miles away. Luke watched her closely, as did Amelia and Jim. Finally, she lifted her head and said, "I should talk to her too."

Luke opened his mouth to object, but Coleen didn't give him time to speak before she said, "I mean it, Luke. You've got to let me go with my aunt and talk to her."

"Maybe I could accompany them?" Jim suggested.

Then Amelia spoke. "None of you understand. We cannot leave here. She must come to us. I can't leave this house without risking damage to my heart, which is already in very poor shape."

"Then call her and have her come here," Coleen said. "But it must be soon. Will you do it, Aunt Amelia?"

The old lady looked at Luke for a moment, then back at Coleen. "You've picked a fine man, my dear, but he is sworn to uphold the law. There's a warrant for your sister and the only way I can allow Kyla to come here is if Luke leaves and goes back to Utah. I simply can't stand the thought of you two bringing danger to Kyla, even though you may not remember your feelings for her."

Luke didn't like where this was heading. He was not about to leave Coleen until her enemies were in custody. Once they were, he'd leave her forever if he had to. But he had to know she was safe.

Amelia was watching him. "She'll be safe with me, Luke," she said. He shook his head. "I can't."

Coleen took hold of his hand, "Please, Luke, it might be the only way. Jim will be here."

"I can't," he said again.

Luke felt a slight draft on his back, as if a door had opened behind him. And a voice, soft, sweet, almost familiar, said, "He can stay."

Amelia was facing the voice behind Luke's back. Her eyes grew wide and she said, "My dear girl, what have you done?"

Luke and Coleen both came to their feet and spun around. There, standing in the open doorway, stood a young woman. But for the dark hair and the mole beneath her right eye, she could have been Coleen. It was bizarre how similar their faces were, for with black hair and the same olive-toned skin Coleen had, Kyla almost looked Hispanic—a very different appearance from her blond twin. The two girls gazed at each other for a full minute. The rest of the world might have ceased to exist for all they knew. "Carly." Kyla said her sister's name softly. "I've missed you so much."

Coleen said nothing, as she didn't know this mirrorlike reflection before her, but she was visibly moved nonetheless. And when Kyla began to walk toward her, Coleen held out her arms, and the two fell into an emotional embrace. When Coleen finally pulled back and looked at her sister in amazement, Kyla said, "I thought I'd lost you forever. It's so good to see you."

Amelia appeared stricken. She bowed her head, brushed back a thin strand of gray hair from her face, and wept. "My child, my child," she moaned. "What have you done?"

Kyla, without so much as a glance at Luke, and only a cursory one at Jim, stepped beside the wheelchair, leaned down, and kissed the old woman's head. "I love you, Aunt Amelia," she said. "But this is my sister. And Luke is right, I can help them stop Mr. Aspen. I made Carly a promise, and I'm going to keep it."

"It could cost you your life, my dear," a sobbing Amelia said.

"And it could save my sister's," Kyla said firmly. "I've sat in there listening to every word you've all said, last night and this morning, and I simply couldn't sit there any longer." She finally looked at Luke. "Hi. I'm Kyla Crockett. And for what it's worth, I don't abduct children. I could never hurt anyone, especially a child."

She stopped, her eyes never leaving Luke's face. She looked so much like her sister, but looking into her eyes there was a difference. He could never mistake the one for the other. "I hope that's true," he answered feeling very weak.

"It's true," she said. "I won't say I've never done anything wrong, because I have. So has Carly, or Coleen, as you all seem to think she should be called now. But when she learned what Mr. Aspen was doing we made a pact. We agreed that neither of us would ever again do the kinds of things we had done as long as we lived."

Luke couldn't help himself. "What kind of things?" he asked.

"Things I'm ashamed of," she said. "Things it's better that Coleen never be told. She's the lucky one, forgetting it all, and I hope she never remembers. Things I will never tell you, because she's changed, Luke. She changed before she ever left here and was in that accident and lost her memory. Don't make her learn about things she hated about herself."

Luke was touched by what Kyla had said, but he wasn't satisfied. "Criminal things?" he asked. "Actions that could land you both in jail? Say, perhaps, something like stealing money from the man who bought your father's farm?"

If Amelia could have gotten out of her wheelchair, she probably would have, and Luke might have felt her wrath. But she couldn't, although she certainly spoke her mind. "That was but one of the nasty rumors that started when I gave them money. They went back to their old farm, and they spoke to the man who'd bought it when it was auctioned off. I warned them that he wasn't an honest man. He was one of those their dad had become indebted to. He'd wanted the farm for years and finally found a way to get it."

"All we wanted was to see if he'd sell us some antique furniture that had been our mother's," Kyla said. "It was supposed to have been ours in the first place. It was in our father's will, but the man who bought the farm kept it, said it was part of what he'd bought. We offered him a lot of money. He wanted more, so we offered him more. We had nothing that had belonged to our mother, and we wanted something. When he saw that we had money, he said we couldn't possibly have come by it legally. He accused us of selling drugs, like others had, but we hadn't. He accused us of worse things, things we would never do. We told him the money was legally ours, but he said it couldn't have been and threatened to call the police."

Amelia took up the narrative again. "That was my fault. You see, I didn't want anyone knowing that it was my money, or rather money I'd given to them. I was afraid that man would seek my money if he knew I was related to the twins' father, as he still believed m brother was indebted to him—despite that he got the girls' farm. It was money that would be theirs when I died anyway, for they're my only heirs, and I intended only they get it. They'd promised never to tell where they got it. That was why they couldn't tell him where the money came from. But he chased them off. Then, out of meanness, he called the police and told them they had stolen his money. That's the kind of man he is."

Once again, Kyla spoke. "The police talked to us. They accused us, but he couldn't prove he'd ever had any money that we could have stolen, and they finally let us go. But he kept the rumors alive. People in our hometown believe we're thieves to this day."

Luke drew a deep breath and slowly exhaled. The long narrative was convincing, but it had not answered his question. Once again he asked, "Kyla, did you do things that you could go to jail for?"

She looked away from him. He stared at the side of her face until she finally looked back. "We did what others talked us into doing. We were ashamed, and we didn't hurt anyone but ourselves. Now, please, that's all I'll say."

Luke reluctantly let it drop, but there was something else he had to know. "Did Coleen marry Gil Stedman?" he asked.

"That terrible man!?" Kyla said it so harshly that her face turned red. "She despised him. She hated him. But . . . but . . ." She couldn't go on, and she seemed suddenly very weary.

Luke thought he recognized that look, had seen it before in his line of work. Sometimes criminals did want to start over, did want to change, but the past was a heavy burden, and some just couldn't overcome it.

"Luke," Coleen said, and when he turned to her she was close to tears. "Please, let it drop."

"But it's important," he said harshly, bringing pain to her eyes. He had to ignore her hurt and press on. "Is she married to Gil Stedman?" he asked Kyla again.

"No," Kyla said firmly. "He was a persistent man, but she despised him and so did I. She's lucky she doesn't remember him. Now, can't we leave it at that?"

Luke wanted to ask for a clarification. He wanted to know if they ever *had* been married, and if so, why they had gotten a divorce. But it was clear that Kyla didn't want to talk about Gil, so he decided to let the matter drop. There was probably no point in pursuing it anyway, as Monty needed a mother who was as good as Jamie—not perfect, as even Jamie wasn't that—but someone as good as she'd been. And it didn't appear that person could be Coleen.

But he loved her still, secrets or not. And this decision would only bring him pain, but he was familiar with pain. He'd lived with it daily for over four years. He could handle it, he told himself. He caught

Coleen's eye. She was suffering. He'd made her suffer and he hated himself for it, but he had to let go.

He's lost to me, Coleen was thinking. And something inside of her felt like it was going to burst and destroy her. But she willed herself to go on.

"Now, let's talk about you again," Luke said, turning to Kyla, all cop now. "Will you talk to Captain Ormm?"

"Yes," Kyla said firmly.

"And about the kidnapping—" Luke began.

But Kyla cut him off. "Yes, I was in Indiana, and I was even at that daycare center, but all I did was apply for a job. Then I left. The next thing I knew, I was wanted for stealing two little children. I'd never even met them. I didn't do it—I swear I didn't. And I can't figure out who would want to accuse me. I didn't do anything to anyone who worked there."

Luke believed her, and from the look in everyone else's eyes, he could tell that he wasn't alone.

"But Howie Blume said he could prove it," Luke countered.

There was a warrant outstanding, and Luke should see that it was served. But when he opened his mouth to tell Kyla that he was going to have to turn her in to the authorities, the words he was thinking didn't come out.

What he did say surprised even him, but he felt suddenly compelled and he knew it was from the Spirit. "I guess we'll just have to prove you didn't. Will you help me, Jim?" he asked, turning to the investigator who had silently watched the interplay about him.

Jim turned to Amelia, but before he'd even opened his mouth, she said, "You're still on my payroll, young man."

"Then I'm in," he said.

Luke turned to Coleen again, "And you'll have to help too," he said. "Because I still can't leave you. I feel responsible for you."

Coleen forced a smile. "But you aren't, Luke. And I know what our future holds. So just go save my sister," she added a bit sarcastically.

Luke was so focused on Coleen and the pain she was feeling, that he didn't even notice when Amelia nodded her head toward the door and quietly led everyone else in a little procession from the room. But

Coleen saw them go as Luke reached for her hands and took them in his own. He wished she'd cry, scream, jerk her hands away and slap his face, do something. But all she did was gaze into his eyes.

When he finally looked away from her the room was empty. "They gave us some privacy," Coleen said. "So we can talk for a minute, and we need to. Thank you, Luke, for not arresting Kyla. I love you, but I can tell I'll never be Jamie. I will be a member of the Church someday, but for me, not for you. Even though I know very little about it, I know that it's true. And I'll act on that knowledge. I'll also try to live a good life, the kind of life Jesus talks about in the Book of Mormon. I'll live far better than whatever it is that Kyla wants left buried. But I can see that I'll never be good enough for you, so let's agree right now that whatever we had is over. Then we can get on with ending this nightmare that Kyla and I are both in. Agreed?"

"I love you, Coleen," Luke said. He hesitated. There was a nagging doubt in his mind. He did love this woman, but finally he mumbled, "Agreed."

He dropped her hands. They didn't kiss, they didn't embrace, they especially did not smile despite the closure. There was just nothing to smile about.

* * *

Captain Ormm put the phone down and frowned. "Luke Osborne?" his second-in-command asked.

"Yes, that was Luke," he said thoughtfully. "But something was different about him. He didn't even think to ask me about what we'd learned about the marriage question he asked me to look into, whether Gil Stedman and Carly Crockett were married or not. Maybe he doesn't really want to know."

"Maybe not," the lieutenant agreed.

"But I guess I won't worry about it. Luke said he and the PI he's working with are following a lead. They'll give us Judd Aspen and his whole organization, but it might take a little time."

The lieutenant asked, "Do you believe him?"

"As a matter of fact, I do. That young man is driven. He doesn't strike me as the kind who would easily give up," the captain said. "I'd like to recruit him if I could, but I don't think his boss would appreciate that, and I wouldn't blame him." Captain Ormm frowned at the phone. "Something he said just now has me thinking." He was thoughtful for a moment more. Then he went on. "Luke said he had a hunch we might find it interesting if we were to look into what else Aspen might be hauling in his trailers besides horses. That was all, but I think we better get hold of our man inside Aspen's outfit. Maybe we should have him start watching the trailers. Who knows, maybe Luke's hunch is right."

* * *

Sheriff Robinson put the phone down and called his chief deputy into the office, telling him of the call he'd just received from Detective Luke Osborne. "He's going to need a few more days off. He's out to disprove Howie Blume's case against Kyla Crockett, Coleen's sister. But he only told me that so I'd know why he wouldn't be home for a few days. What he really called about was Bianca. She's apparently taken Monty out of town to keep him safe."

"Is he angry?" the chief deputy asked. "I'd think he'd be grateful."

"Actually, he's relieved that Monty's out of town," Sheriff Robinson said. "Luke explained to me that this Judd Aspen runs a huge dope ring. He could send men anywhere. Luke would just feel better knowing that Monty is hidden out with Bianca until Judd and his gang are rounded up. He asked me to contact him if Bianca comes back to town."

CHAPTER 24

Detective Blume looked up from his desk as Luke leaned across and extended his hand. "I'm Detective Luke Osborne," he said.

Blume rose and accepted the offered hand, but his eyes went past Luke to the young woman who stood behind him. Luke noticed and said, "Coleen Whitman, alias Carly Crockett. Coleen, this is Detective Blume, the man who's after Kyla." Luke then introduced Jim Redd as a private investigator who had been hired by an anonymous client to look into the matter of Kyla Crockett.

"I'm here," Luke told him honestly, "as a private citizen. I'm simply working with Mr. Redd on behalf of Coleen, who is suffering from what the experts tell us may be a permanent case of amnesia."

"I see," Howie said. "I'm not sure why you've come to me in that case. I'm quite certain that Miss Crockett is the person who committed the crime, and I have an eyewitness who will prove it."

Luke immediately noted the discrepancy from his earlier phone conversations with Howie. "Just one witness?" he asked. "I thought I understood you to say there were several."

Howie was suddenly uncomfortable and sat down again behind his desk. "Well, actually, I think I told you that there were several persons who could identify her," Howie said evasively.

"But only one who can tie her to the crime?" Luke asked as he helped himself to a chair and signaled for Coleen and Jim to do the same.

"That's right, but a good one," the detective said. He sounded quite defensive.

Luke observed him for a moment and wondered if he had much of a case at all, or if he was simply trying to make a name for himself with a high-profile crime. "All we're asking of you are the facts you've gathered," Luke told him. "You know, what the witness, or *witnesses* saw, who the missing children are, that sort of thing."

Howie analyzed the set of Luke's jaw and quickly determined that he could either share the information now or be ordered to do it later, as Luke appeared to be the kind of man who'd go clear to the top if it took that to get what he wanted. Howie took the easy way out. "All right, if that's all you need, let me get the file and we'll talk."

An hour later, after looking at the file in some detail, Luke simply thanked Howie and led his little group from his office. Outside he turned to Jim and said, "They have nothing except a vague description the mother offered; someone who 'looked' like Kyla drove off with the kids in a car it would be hard to ever identify."

"We need to talk to that mother," Jim said, stating the obvious.

They found her working in a bar that evening. They had to wait until after her shift ended for an interview. She was very hesitant to tell them anything, especially after learning that Coleen was the sister of the person she'd accused of kidnapping. Luke quickly formed the opinion that the woman was not a fit mother, and he asked the question that had been bothering him ever since he'd read the file that morning. "Where is the father of your children?" he asked.

"I don't know," she said.

"Have you tried to contact him?"

"I have no desire to see him," she said flippantly. "He left me alone to raise two little kids by myself. I hate him."

"But he does know about the fact that they're missing?" Luke asked.

"I don't know. I would assume he's seen the news or the wanted posters," she said.

"But if he has, he's made no effort to contact you or the local police?" Luke pressed, very much convinced at this point that this woman was not telling the truth.

"Not that I know of," she said. "But I think I've talked to you enough. There's nothing more I can tell you."

"But there is," Luke said firmly. "Tell us when you saw the woman you described put the children in the car and drive off."

Reluctantly, she complied, but Luke and Jim both noted big differences in the facts she was now stating and those she'd given to

Detective Blume. The description of the car was more vague, and the time was slightly off. Most glaring though was the description of the woman she'd accused of taking them. "A blonde that looked just like her," she said pointing at Coleen.

The picture Detective Blume was using showed Kyla with black hair, which is what the other witnesses had said. And Kyla herself confirmed that, for she'd dyed her hair about the time she left Kentucky.

Luke pressed on. "Are you certain that the description you just gave us is accurate?" As he spoke, it was not without a degree of satisfaction that he was thinking of the little tape recorder in Jim Redd's jacket pocket.

The lady indicated that she was certain, but then she said she thought maybe she shouldn't say any more. "That's fine," Luke said, coming to the conclusion that he should go out on a limb with her at this point. "Actually, you could clear up just one more matter for us. You have taken a lie-detector test, haven't you?" he asked, knowing full well she hadn't even been asked to.

"No, and I don't need to," she said rather hastily.

Luke looked at the others, putting on a puzzled face for the sake of the mother. "That's strange. I guess we'll have to see the local police again and get that arranged. That's a most unfortunate oversight."

The look of anguish and fright that crossed the woman's face removed any doubt in Luke's mind—Kyla Crockett was not guilty of *anything* involving this woman's children. "We'll be in touch soon, and in the meantime, if you think of anything you can tell us, call us at one of these numbers." He then handed her a paper containing the numbers of both his and Jim's phones.

Coleen was amazed at the ease with which Luke conducted himself. She was impressed by everything she learned of him. She so wished things could be different for the two of them. But she couldn't worry about that now. She needed to concentrate on helping Luke and Jim find the evidence to prove this woman was lying about her newly found twin sister—and why.

"Can you really make her take a lie-detector test?" Coleen asked Luke after the interview was over and the woman had left.

He smiled and shook his head. "I'm afraid that was a bluff, just to get her thinking. The next time we talk to her she may have a much different story, and that should be all we need to force Howie to take a more objective look at this case."

The next day they planned their next moves, making a list of tasks that needed to be done, then they split up. Jim Redd took part of the list, Luke and Coleen the rest. That evening they sat in a restaurant and analyzed what they'd learned. It was substantial.

The parents of the missing children were divorced about three years before. The mother had later been charged and convicted of neglect and the children were removed from the home. At that time the father could not be found despite a fairly extensive effort. After a year's probation and counseling, the children had been returned to their mother's custody. A few months later, the father showed up with an attorney and asked the court that custody be given to him. A study ordered by the court found him an unfit parent, and the change in custody was denied. One month later the children were reported missing. The father had again vanished and couldn't be located for questioning.

The third day in Indiana brought Luke and Coleen back into Detective Blume's office. When he was presented with their findings, he agreed to officially question the mother again. In the meantime, having essentially been given a blank check by his wealthy client, Jim Redd was calling on a network of private investigators in several states.

By evening, Howie Blume expressed to Luke and Coleen his concern over his witness's changed story. A visit with the prosecutor did not bring a dismissal of the charges as Luke had hoped. However, an agreement was reached that if Kyla would turn herself in, they would ask the judge to release her on her own recognizance while further investigation was conducted.

The next morning to Luke's amazement and delight, when Coleen and the sister she couldn't remember embraced, real tears trickled down Coleen's cheeks. And the depth of affection and trust that Kyla felt for Coleen was evident when she agreed to accompany them, along with a good lawyer, back to Indiana that afternoon. Kyla wasn't out of the woods yet, but with Jim Redd and his network of detectives now working with Detective Howie Blume, she had hope that the truth would soon come out.

The next day, from back in Ohio, Luke called Captain Ormm. "Have you done any good?" the captain asked Luke.

"Yes sir, we've found Kyla Crockett," he said.

"I guessed you had," the captain said with a chuckle. "She was the source of your hunch about Aspen and his horse trailers, wasn't she?"

"Yes, sir," Luke admitted. "But I didn't dare let you know we'd found her until reasonable doubt was created with Detective Blume in Indiana. I'm convinced now that there's no way they can convict Kyla of anything there, but while she waits, at least she's not in jail or having to hide from the law, only from Judd Aspen and his men."

"If she'll talk to me, I think we can soon have Aspen and his people in custody," the captain said confidently.

"She's ready. How soon can you be in Columbus?" Luke asked.

"Two hours by department jet," he was told.

"I'll meet you at the airport," Luke said.

What the captain didn't say, was that based upon Luke's hunch of several days ago, evidence was already being collected and warrants for the arrest of Judd Aspen and several of his men were pending. The captain didn't need a lot more information from Kyla, but he wanted to talk to Luke face to face, so he flew up to Columbus.

* * *

Bianca felt that enough time had passed that Luke should be home, or at least on his way there. Monty had been so good, but he was missing his father. That was another reason Bianca figured the little unplanned vacation needed to end. She couldn't wait to see Luke. She'd called the sheriff earlier and learned that Luke was relieved that she was keeping Monty safe. She couldn't wait to receive his thanks in person. She was confident that the three of them would be a family yet.

* * *

Captain Ormm clapped Luke on the back when he met him at the airport. "You have a job waiting for you here anytime you'd like one," the captain said. "And I mean that. You do good work."

"Thanks," Luke said, "but I have a good job already, and I have a ranch to run back home. But it's nice of you to offer."

"If circumstances should change, my offer stands," the captain said. "Now, let's go have a talk with Kyla Crockett."

The interview went well, and Captain Ormm and the detective he'd brought with him assured both Coleen and Kyla that the drug ring would be destroyed. The captain also promised to let them know as soon as the arrests had been made. "In cases like this," he said, "it's sort of like an earthen dam. Once a little water starts to find its way through, it's not long before the whole thing comes down. And the water is coming through already on this case. One of Aspen's men was arrested as we left to fly up here. When drugs were found in a secret compartment of the horse trailer he was pulling, he decided to talk. My lieutenant reported this to me just before we landed in Columbus."

Kyla, who still carried a burden of fear and stress, felt like it had once again become lighter. She hugged Coleen and said, "If you could remember what those men were like, you'd be as happy as I am. We're both lucky to be alive."

Coleen was grateful, and she frankly didn't care now if she never regained her memory. But despite the good news, her heart was heavy. Luke was leaving tonight from the airport after he'd taken the officers from Kentucky back to their plane. And she didn't know if she'd see him again.

"Why don't you two have a little talk before you leave," Amelia suggested, though it was really more of a command.

So Luke had a few minutes alone with the girl he'd come to love and was now leaving. "You'll come to Duchesne again, won't you?" he asked.

"No, I don't think so," she told him. "I've already called and quit my job. And I called the manager of the apartments. He's going to box my things up and send them to me UPS. I hadn't accumulated much you know. Luke, I enjoyed my time in Duchesne, but . . ."

She couldn't go on. Luke looked at her stricken face helplessly. Was he doing the right thing? He wondered. She had found the gospel now, so she didn't need him for that anymore. And she would find happiness again with someone. He was sure of that. He just wished he could have been that someone, but she just came with too many unanswered questions, and for some reason that seemed to matter to him.

It was awkward being alone with her like this with nothing to say. At least, not anything meaningful. So he simply said, "It's been good, Coleen," cringing inside at the lame attempt.

"I might go by Carly now. It seems sort of different, but I suppose I'll get used to it," she said.

"Yes, I guess you will," he agreed. "We learn to adapt when things change in our lives . . ." he was at a loss, and felt worse with everything he said.

"Luke, I'll never forget you. I sure hope that somehow you can eventually adapt to your loss. I'm so sorry about Jamie, and I know it still hurts," she said.

It did still hurt, and it was that sweet memory of her and the good life she'd lived that had caused him to turn away from his love for Coleen. He had to admit to himself that he'd done exactly that. He was still trying to bring Jamie back for himself as well as for Monty. He knew that couldn't be done, but he simply couldn't move on. He'd come close with Coleen, and maybe someday he could with someone else—but not now, not yet.

"I'll make do," he said at last. "It still hurts, but I'll get over it someday."

"At least you got Victor taken care of," Coleen said.

"Yes, I did," he agreed, but even that didn't really help as much as he'd always told himself it would. Perhaps nothing could ever fill the void in his life. "I better go now," he said. "The captain needs to get back."

"I understand," Coleen said. "I'll miss you, Luke. Thanks for helping me find out who I really am."

"You're welcome," he said. "And I'll miss you."

"Tell Monty hello for me, and tell him I love him," Coleen said.

"I'll do that," Luke promised. Then he simply turned to leave, placing his hand on the doorknob. But the thought of never seeing her again was almost more than he could stand. So, before he turned the nob, he said over his shoulder, "If you ever want to ride one of my horses, you know where to find them." Then he opened the door and left Coleen with nothing but a few memories, a lonely future, and what sounded like an invitation but probably wasn't.

Luke had a few minutes to wait before his red-eye flight left the airport. So he saw Captain Ormm to the twin engine Baron he'd flown up in. "Don't forget my offer, Luke," he said.

"Thanks, I'll remember that," Luke said, knowing he could never leave his little ranch in Utah.

The captain started across the tarmac to the Baron whose engines were already running. But he suddenly turned and walked back. "I almost forgot to tell you something," he said. "My men and I did some checking like you asked about Gil Stedman. Seems he's never been married. But he was engaged to Carly Crockett for a while. She broke the engagement when she learned what he was really like. She didn't want any part of him after that, and he threatened her. That must have been about the time she learned about the drugs and tried to contact me. Aspen's driver that we arrested told me that Gil would either get Carly back or kill her. Thought you'd like to know that."

Luke mumbled a thanks, then turned and walked away. Had he judged Coleen wrong, he wondered. Luke stopped, and for several minutes, he simply stood staring at the tarmac but seeing nothing, his mind numb with pain.

CHAPTER 25

Luke stopped at his parents' house as soon as he got into town. He'd called daily to keep track of his father's progress, which was more positive every day. Luke was happy to see him feeling well and moving around the house and yard again. He looked really good. He also knew that Bianca had called his mother to say she was on her way home with Monty. He'd hoped they'd be there by the time he got back, but he was disappointed.

"I've missed Monty," Luke told his mother. "I thought they'd be here. I've got to spend as much time as I can with him now."

"We've missed him too," his mother agreed. "But at least we know he's with someone else who cares about him. Bianca has his best interest at heart."

"I really am grateful to her," Luke agreed. "It was good knowing he was safe until I could get back to him."

"Bianca's a good girl, son. I'm in no way trying to tell you what to do, but you might consider giving the poor girl a chance. She's certainly pretty, she cares a lot about you, *and* she's active in the Church. You've been single for a long time now; Monty needs a loving mother."

Luke couldn't get angry with his mother. She meant well and she could be right. So he said honestly, "I'll think about it, Mom."

"You really will?" she pressed hopefully.

"Yes, I really will," he promised. "Now, I'd better get out to the ranch. Call me if Bianca brings Monty here. I'll come right to town and get him if she does."

Luke pulled into his yard and got out of the truck. Looking around he sighed. It felt good to be home, even if he was alone. He pulled his suitcase from the backseat of the truck and started toward the house. But at the front door he stopped, sat his suitcase down, and looked toward the burnt disaster that used to be his barn, stackyard, corrals, and outbuildings. He had to start rebuilding as soon as the insurance adjuster finished his work. He changed his focus to the hay fields. The alfalfa was turning purple. It would soon be in full bloom. It should have been cut several days ago. He needed to get right after that. Then he looked toward the horse pasture. He ached to saddle up Keno or Spider and just go for a long ride.

Glancing at his watch, he knew there was plenty of time. Perhaps he'd just do that, catch one of the horses and spend an hour or two in the saddle. Keno and Spider both needed work, especially Spider.

There was a painful twist in his gut as he thought about riding Spider. He'd almost come to think of her as Coleen's horse. But Coleen wasn't here now and would never ride Spider again. The thought hurt, but Luke forced it aside and headed down the walk. Within ten minutes, Spider was carrying Luke onto the hill, and when he touched his spurs to her side, loosened the reins, and leaned slightly forward, she exploded into a rapid gallop.

Luke tapped her lightly again, and she stretched her long neck out and produced a burst of speed that brought a smile to his face. Spider was fast. No, she was *exceptionally* fast. He'd never attempted to coax all the speed he could out of her, so he didn't really have a feel for what kind of speed she had. The blood of a horse named Dash for Cash flowed in her veins, as well as that of other quality racing lines, though that didn't always mean a horse would be fast. But when he'd watched the big bay filly run in the field with the other horses, she'd always seemed to be in the lead. And the way her body seemed to flow with graceful precision and power had been an indicator of the speed she might have.

Wind whipped Luke's face as he and Spider raced swiftly along the dirt road, heading for the cedar trees that lay ahead. Once again, he touched her ever so lightly with his spurs, and he immediately felt the response of her powerful muscles as she strained for and gained more speed. It was hard to know just how fast she was going, but Luke felt a thrill course through his body as he began to envision Spider becoming a champion racehorse as her predecessor had been.

He could almost see the headlines with her name, Rainy Day Spider, typed in bold letters, declaring her the winner of race after race. Was this all she had, he wondered, or did she have still more speed? Again, leaning even farther forward, Luke called out to her, "Go, Spider. Run for all you're worth. You can do better."

As he coaxed her he could feel a slight increase in speed. Luke didn't think he'd ever ridden a horse as fast as this one. The little extra speed she was now responding with was what might well be that little bit that marked the difference between a champion and an "also ran." He was thrilled with the prospect of what this horse could do, what she could become.

Reluctantly, he applied gentle pressure to the reins, as he knew that it could do her harm to run too far at this incredible speed. But she failed to respond. Spider wanted to run. She wanted to show Luke what she could do. Spider had the heart of a champion. Luke could feel it in every stride. He pulled harder on the reins, and finally she responded and began to slow down. Soon she was at a slow, easy lope, and after a few moments he brought her to a walk.

Luke patted her neck, crooning and speaking praises to her. "You're something else, Spider. How about if we prepare you for some races? You'll be a winner. I just know you will. What you need now is a racing saddle and someone smaller and lighter to ride you, like . . ."

Luke choked up. He'd about said, "Like Coleen." The euphoria he'd been feeling vanished. Depression set in, and Luke turned Spider back toward the ranch.

* * *

Gil Stedman prowled restlessly about the house, reflecting on the past few days. It hadn't been easy getting here from Indian Canyon. He'd walked many miles. But he'd lived in comfort since breaking into Luke's house. He'd peeked out the window whenever he heard something, but every time it was just a young man on a four-wheeler, doing some field maintenance work, Gil assumed. No one else seemed interested in the place, and that had been just fine with Gil. But now the waiting was practically over, and he just wanted to finish the job.

There'd been plenty of food in the house. And even though he had to keep the lights off at night, there was a room in the basement without windows where he'd taken the TV and watched it there without worrying about being discovered.

Best of all, there were plenty of guns and ammunition in the house he was borrowing. He had planned for hours how he would use them when Luke and Carly came back.

Gil smiled to himself, remembering the last call from Judd Aspen and what he'd said about Carly. The boss had reported that Carly had gotten away and several of his men were arrested. Then he'd asked to speak to the other fellow, the one whose name Gil didn't even know, and who was definitely not his friend. Gil wasn't sure what Aspen told him, but Gil had a pretty good idea. And he simply hadn't been ready to die.

So the other man died in a fiery car crash an hour later. And Gil had left his own wallet several feet from the fire, where it would be found relatively undamaged. Now he was that other man, Carly would come back to Duchesne, and he would even the score.

Gil had been ready to confront the troublesome young detective when Osborne had suddenly left his suitcase on the porch and gone off to ride his horse. If Luke was back in Duchesne, then reason told him that Carly wasn't far off and he'd soon get her too.

Patience was not an attribute Gil had attempted to cultivate, and what little patience he had was long gone. These past few days had been long and had him on edge. Now, with Luke and Carly almost within his grasp, he was being forced to wait again. He wanted to end this thing and then sneak away and see if he could figure out a way to hurt his boss—now his enemy—Judd Aspen.

Gil parted the closed curtain of the living room window. But Luke still hadn't returned. He would though, and he'd come in the house, and when he did . . .

* * *

Bianca pulled off State Road 33 at the view area overlooking the vast Avintaquin country. The canyon below her was so far down it was almost dizzying, and the heavily forested mountains lay before her for miles. It was a beautiful sight, even a spectacular sight. She never tired of it. Liz and Monty stepped beside her. "When are we going to be home, Bianca?" Monty asked.

"Really soon now," she promised. "I just needed to get out and walk around for a minute. I was getting tired and I sure wouldn't want to drive if there was any chance of hurting my little guy, now would I?"

"I've been sleeping, Bianca," Liz said. "I'm wide awake now. Why don't you let me drive the rest of the way?"

"Thanks Liz, but I want to be driving when we take Monty back to his father. It just seems right. Anyway, I'm feeling fine now. Just let me walk around here for another minute or two and then we'll go."

Bianca took Monty by the hand and said, "Hey, I know, let's race, just like we did on the beach. I'll bet you can't outrun me up here in this thin air the way you did at Long Beach."

Monty's eyes lit up, and he said, "Race you to there," and he pointed to the other end of the turnout.

"Liz, you start us," Bianca said.

Monty leaned forward, his little hands on his knees, as Liz said, "Ready. Set. Go!"

Bianca hesitated as Monty burst away. Then she ran, staying just behind him. He looked back, and seeing her struggling to catch up, he grinned and ran for all he was worth, his little legs pumping furiously.

Laughing, Liz shouted, "You better hurry, Bianca. He's beating you."

Monty looked back again, grinning broadly. "I'm about to catch you," Bianca said from just one pace behind him. "I think I'm going to win this time."

But like a gallant racehorse, Monty found just a little bit more speed, and when he reached the appointed ending spot, Bianca was still a step behind him. "I won," he said between great gulps of the fresh mountain air. "You're so slow, Bianca."

"No, I'm fast, you're just faster," she said. Then she dropped to her knees and said, "Here, come get your prize, a big hug from the loser."

His eyes sparkling, Monty ran into her arms and accepted a hug so big it was almost overwhelming. And Bianca thought of how much she ached to hug the little boy's father like this and have him return it with the same enthusiasm Monty did.

"Luke doesn't know what he's missing," Liz said with a chuckle as she watched. "He better marry you, Bianca. Don't you think so, Monty?"

"What?" he asked as he stepped out of Bianca's embrace and looked up innocently at Liz.

"I said, don't you think your dad better marry Bianca and make her your mom?"

"Yeah," he agreed. "That'd be fun." But his little mind was thinking and remembering. He liked Bianca, but he still liked Coleen better.

"Tell your dad, will you?" Bianca asked. "'Cause I really love you and your dad." Monty didn't say anything more, and Bianca wondered what the boy was thinking.

As they started down the canyon, Bianca was thinking only of Luke Osborne. She couldn't wait to take Monty to him, to listen to Monty tell his dad how much fun they'd had on their trip. She yearned for the thanks Luke would give her, and maybe she'd even get a kiss as a reward for keeping his boy safe. It just had to work out for her with Luke. It just had to.

"Hey, Bianca, stop!" Liz said urgently. "It looks like a car's gone over the edge back there. I'll bet that's where Gil Stedman was killed. Remember what the sheriff said? Back up."

As Bianca applied the brakes she shuddered at the very thought of Gil. He was a terrible man. She couldn't even make herself feel bad that he'd died.

"There! Right there," Liz said.

Both young women jumped out of the car and peered over the edge. Far below was evidence of a fire. It was confined to a small area, but a badly charred one. Gil must have died a horrible death. She shuddered. At least she didn't have to worry about him anymore. And the man who had been with him that day in her house was certainly long gone. She sighed with relief at the evidence of Gil's death and turned back to her car.

* * *

The man who had *not* been in the accident peered from the curtains again. Finally, Luke rode past, and Gil grew tense. The time for reckoning was almost here. He started to turn away from the curtains again, then took a closer look. Gil was a criminal, a killer, and a drug dealer, but he was also an expert on horses. He knew a good one when he saw it, and the bay filly Luke was riding was a beauty. He admired the fine lines of her muscles as they rippled beneath her glistening hide. And he admired the way she was formed, the way she walked, the way she carried her head.

She was built for speed. And Gil added one more task to his agenda before he left Duchesne. He had to steal that horse. Gil even knew that her name was Rainy Day Spider. He'd had a lot of hours on his hands as he waited in Luke's house the past few days. There wasn't anything in this house that Gil hadn't inspected. That included, of course, Luke's file of horse papers. Gil wasn't ignorant when it came to big names in American quarter horse history. This filly came from some top lines, not the least of which was Dash for Cash. He'd not only take the horse, but he'd take the registration papers as well. He knew men who'd give him a fair price for a horse that was put together like Rainy Day Spider.

* * *

Luke was bothered by the soft tinkling sound he heard from one of Spider's back hooves. A shoe was coming loose. It should probably be tightened right then. He dismounted beside his horse trailer and removed the saddle and blanket, then rubbed her down. She was sweaty, and the rubdown felt good to her. She rubbed her nose against his shoulder affectionately. When he'd finished, he put a few oats in a feed bag and slipped it on over her halter. While she contentedly ate the oats, Luke checked her back feet.

As he'd suspected, one shoe was loose. He looked it over carefully, then set her foot down and stepped into the tack room of his horse trailer to grab a hammer and a couple of horseshoe nails.

With her foot securely held between his knees, his back bent to the task, Luke pulled a nail out and drove another in its place. Then he put Spider's foot down and looked toward the house. For the briefest moment, he thought he saw movement of the curtain in his living room window. *That's strange*, he thought. *Surely one of the cats hasn't gotten itself locked in the house for the entire time I've been gone. There'd be an awful mess to clean up.*

He bent again, replaced another nail, and felt a shiver go up his spine. It made no sense, but Luke felt like he was being watched, and he'd come to trust those feelings. He'd had the same feeling when he'd approached Amelia Crockett's house in Ohio. It wasn't until later that he'd learned that Kyla had watched them the whole time they were in the yard and walking up the walk. She'd been in a room upstairs and had peered through the crack of a curtain.

Luke put Spider's foot back down and looked again toward his living room window. There was no question, the curtain had moved again. He stared at it for three or four seconds after that, but no more movement occurred.

Except in Luke's stomach.

And in his mind. The impression came to him so strongly that he knew he had to act on it. Someone was in his house! And whoever it was knew every movement Luke was making.

Acting as normal as he could, he again entered his tack room and grabbed another tool. He also instinctively checked to see that his pistol was securely in the holster on the inside of his pants. As he again approached the filly he resisted the impulse to look toward his house. He patted Spider on the rump as he slid around behind her, and then he bent and again lifted her foot. Luke crimped the nails, inspected the shoe again, and picked up his hammer. He tapped each nail until he was satisfied the shoe was secure, then he put her foot back down. As he returned the tools to the trailer, he again did not turn his head toward his house, but he did turn his eyes.

Luke was certain that the curtains were parted just the tiniest bit. He removed the feedbag and led Spider back to the pasture. Luke didn't even pause beside the horse trailer when he returned from the pasture. Instead, he walked to the truck, climbed in, and drove up the lane. As he drove, he grabbed his cell phone and dialed. When nothing happened, he looked closely and discovered that he'd let the battery run dead. He plugged it into the charger, gave it a minute, then dialed Sheriff Robinson's home number.

He found the sheriff at home. "Luke, I've been trying to call for hours. Have you had your cell phone off?"

"No, but I let the battery run down," Luke admitted.

"I also tried your house several times. Of course, you didn't answer there either, but when I talked to your mother an hour ago, she said you were back and had gone home."

"I haven't been in the house. I took one of my horses for a run," Luke explained. "But what I was calling you about was the house. I might just be going crazy after all the close calls I've had, but I'd swear there's someone in there."

"Luke, don't go in!" the sheriff ordered, alarming Luke with the intensity in his voice. "I've been trying to reach you to tell you that we got results back from the lab today. The man who was burned in Indian Canyon was not Gil Stedman!"

"He's in the house!" Luke exclaimed.

"Exactly," the sheriff agreed. "Where are you now?"

"I'm headed up the road. I was going to hide my truck and then walk back down to the house and come in the back way. I can make it without being seen if I take my time and crawl some."

"Okay, but don't try to go in alone. I'll get some of the men together and we'll be there as fast as we can," the sheriff said. "Be careful, Luke."

* * *

"Luke asked us to give him a call if you got back tonight," Mrs. Osborne said after hugging Monty and sending him off to see his grandpa for a minute. "He's anxious to see Monty and said he'd come right after him."

"Oh, don't do that," Bianca objected. "I already dropped Liz off at the apartment so I could talk to Luke for a little while. I came here first because I thought he might be here, but since he's not, I'd really like to take Monty out to Luke's place myself."

Luke's mother thought that was a good idea. And she was even more positive about it when Monty came running back in a minute later and said, "Come on, Bianca, let's go find Dad."

What a fine wife she would be for Luke, and what a good mother for little Monty. "I think Luke would like that," Mrs. Osborne said.

"And that will give him a chance to thank you personally for being such a great help."

Bianca chatted with Luke's mother for a few minutes, then loaded Monty in the car and headed through town and out to Luke's place. Meanwhile, Luke was crawling through the only field that could expose him to sight from the house. When he heard a car coming down his lane, he thought, *It must be the sheriff.* But as he lifted his head and looked, Luke's heart stopped cold at what he saw. Bianca's car was just passing out of sight in front of the house. Monty was undoubtedly with her. Luke surged to his feet and began a desperate race to the house.

CHAPTER 26

Bianca wondered where Luke's truck was. She hadn't passed him as she'd driven up from town, and his mother had specifically said he'd gone home. "I don't think your dad's here right now, Monty," she said as she knocked on the door. "But I'm sure he'll be back soon because he left his suitcase sitting right here."

"Let's wait for him," Monty said. No one answered the door. Bianca tried the doorbell this time. "I know where the key is," Monty said. "I'll show you."

"Just a minute," she said as she reached for the doorknob. "It might be unlocked. Your dad probably unlocked it and then decided to go do something and just left his suitcase."

The door opened, and Bianca let Monty go in ahead of her when he said, "Come on, Bianca, I'm hungry."

"Maybe I can fix you something to eat," she began as she turned and shut the door. Monty gave out a sound which, if it had been louder, would have passed for a scream.

Bianca whirled and faced the leering grin of Gil Stedman, the very man she'd taken Monty all the way to California to avoid. He was standing in the doorway between Luke's living room and his kitchen, pointing a pistol at Monty. For only the briefest moment Bianca felt faint, but then a motherly instinct kicked in, and she was ready to fight.

"Thought I was dead, didn't you?" he chuckled. Then he shook his head. "You really shouldn't have come busting in here like this."

"Me!" she stammered indignantly, still stunned at seeing Gil alive. "You're the one who's trespassing. This is Monty's house," she said, pointing at the little boy. "He can come in here anytime he wants to. You get out of here this minute."

"And if I don't?" he asked.

Bianca didn't have an answer, but she instantly stepped forward, pushing Monty behind her back and facing Gil's deadly pistol before he could stop her.

Luke had reached the back door. He was certain his son and Bianca were inside. He prayed that he could get there in time to save their lives—Gil was a killer, and a desperate man.

The door was locked, but the key was in Luke's pocket. He pulled it out, slid it silently into the lock, and turned. He left it there as he began to open the door, praying that it wouldn't squeak. When it was open wide enough to get through he peered around it. Gil stood with his back to him, facing Bianca. He could see Monty's little feet behind her.

"Give me the boy," Gil said.

"You'll have to shoot me first," Bianca said bravely.

"I'll do that," Gil said in a tone that gave no room for doubt.

At that moment Bianca saw Luke as he was quietly making his way toward Gil, his off-duty Smith and Wesson .38 in one hand. With the other, he was touching his lips, indicating that she wasn't to do anything that would let Gil know he was there.

"Now!" Gil said. "Shove him to me."

Thinking fast, Bianca reached behind her and took hold of Monty's arm. She was just ready to shove him hard to one side when Monty saw Luke and screamed, "Dad!"

In unison, Gil whirled, Bianca dove to one side carrying Monty with her, and Luke said, "Drop it."

Gil Stedman hadn't quite got his gun around when he saw Luke, and he froze. He'd learned already that this cop would shoot when he said he would.

"I won't miss," Luke hissed. "Put it on the floor, Stedman."

Slowly and deliberately, Gil Stedman placed the gun on the floor and raised his hands into the air.

"Step toward me," Luke ordered. "All I want is one little excuse to blow you off the face of this earth." Then he called to Bianca, and she stepped into view.

"In my closet, on a hook just inside the door, is a set of hand-cuffs," he said.

She didn't need to be told a thing more. And a minute later, Gil Stedman was cuffed. He congratulated himself on still being alive, but he cursed as he realized he'd also just lost his freedom forever.

Sheriff Robinson came through the same door Luke had entered only a few short minutes earlier and said. "Looks like I was just a little late." Then he keyed the handheld radio that was strapped to his belt and spoke into the mike that was clipped to his collar. "Everything's secure in here. You can come on in."

The sheriff helped Gil to his feet as Luke stepped forward and called his son to him. His little boy ran into the kitchen and flew into his father's arm as tears streamed down his face. "I'm sorry I've been gone so much," Luke said as he hugged his boy and kissed his little face. "I love you so much, Monty."

When Luke finally looked up, Bianca was standing just a few feet away, tears streaming down her face. And Luke saw her with different eyes. He'd seen her literally offer her life for his son. He held out one arm while the other held his son, and she stepped into his embrace. "Thank you, Bianca," he said, and she got the kiss she'd hoped for.

* * *

"You're late," Liz kidded Bianca as she entered the apartment at about ten-thirty that night. "Where have you been?"

Bianca smiled and said, "Luke took Monty and me to dinner."

"Wow!" Liz exclaimed. "Did he kiss you?"

"Yes," Bianca answered, but it was then that Liz noticed there was no sparkle in her friend's eyes.

"Are you all right, Bianca?" Liz asked. "Did Luke tell you to get lost or something after dinner?"

"No, in fact he said we should do it again sometime."

"Then what in the world is eating you?"

Bianca drew a breath, exhaled, and wiped a tear from one eye. She held one hand up and created a space of about an eighth of an inch between her thumb and forefinger and said, "When you come that close to dying, Liz, the world takes on a whole new look."

Liz turned pale. "What happened?"

Bianca took her through the evening's events blow by blow. And when she'd finished her story, she told a totally shocked Liz, "Luke was real nice. He thanked me for watching out for Monty and told me how much he loved him. And as we were eating our dinner, he talked to me a lot, but I got this awful feeling that he not only doesn't love me, but that he never will. And the strange thing is, I realized that he and I simply would never be happy. We just don't match."

"Oh, Bianca, don't be silly," Liz said. "You were willing to give your life for his son."

Bianca waved a hand in the air in a self-depreciating manner. "Liz, are you in love with Luke Osborne?"

Liz looked shocked. "No, of course not."

"What if you'd been in my place tonight? What if I'd asked you to take Monty home, and it was you there with him; would you have risked your life for Monty?"

Liz sat for a moment before answering, but then she said, "What choice would I have?"

"Exactly," Bianca said. "What I did, I would have done regardless of my feelings for Luke. And having made the decision, and having been seconds away from death, I've begun to grow up I think."

"So you don't still want to marry Luke?"

"I didn't say that, but I don't think it's a choice I'll ever get to make, and I can live with it without hating whoever he does marry. I asked him about Coleen tonight. She was never married to Gil Stedman. And she wasn't a drug pusher, Liz," Bianca said sadly. "What I did to her and what I said to her was horrible. I was wrong. And I told Luke that."

"Is he going to marry her, Bianca?" Liz asked. "She isn't even a member of the Church."

"I don't know what he'll do. I don't think that Luke knows. One thing I do know, however, is that Luke will never marry anyone unless he can take her to the temple. He's that kind of guy."

Luke was also wondering what he was going to do with his life as he faced the same question from his son the next morning.

"Dad, are you going to marry Bianca?" Monty had asked him. "She wants to be my mom."

"What do you think I should do?" Luke asked, not really wanting to hear the answer. "Do you think I should marry her?"

"I guess," he said, "but I miss Coleen."

"Son," Luke began, "I know you'd like to have a mom, but it's got to be right for both of us. Bianca is a good person, and she's been really good to you. But I don't think she's right for me. And Coleen, well, she's gone now, Monty."

"Won't she ever come back?" he responded as a little tear trickled down his cheek.

"I don't know," Luke said honestly. "But probably not. Now, the sheriff says I can have a few days off to spend with you. I'll have to go to court one day next week, but other than that, you and I've got some hay to put up. Let's go get at it."

The next month saw Luke get his second crop of hay up, Victor Hampton and Sharps Thomsen bound over to the district court to stand trial on a host of serious felonies, Gil Stedman bound over on a number of serious charges as well, Judd Aspen's drug ring brought to its knees and then annihilated, and Carly Crockett baptized. Luke was either involved in or kept informed of each thing as it happened—but one. He had no knowledge of Carly's baptism.

Luke also got an interesting call from Jim Redd. He reported that Kyla Crockett had finally been cleared of the kidnapping charge. The missing children had been located with their father in Chicago. It turned out that he'd been sending small amounts of money to his ex-wife, who had agreed outside the court, and against the law, to let him take the children if he'd pay her. "I guess she really needed the money," Jim had said sarcastically.

Luke further learned that the couple had conspired to accuse someone of kidnapping the kids to divert the law's attention. Kyla had simply been at the wrong place at the wrong time and the children's mother had randomly picked her to take the blame. Both parents were now in jail and facing charges.

Jim didn't say anything about Coleen, nor did Luke ask.

Luke also spent many hours training his two colts. He even asked one of the top racehorse owners in the area to take a look at Spider. He was told that she had the makings of a great runner, and the fellow made an offer to Luke that nearly knocked his boots off. Luke considered it for several days, but something nagged at him to keep her, and he finally turned down the offer.

A contractor began to build Luke a new barn, and he was amazed at the minor cost for the building that was going up. It seemed to him that he was getting a building worth at least twenty-five or thirty thousand dollars more than it was costing him. He had no idea that a young lady from Ohio had secretly sent a large sum of money to the contractor on top of what he was getting from Luke's insurance settlement.

So, less stressed about rebuilding, Luke decided he and Monty needed a break. One Monday evening, shortly after work, Luke picked Monty up at his folks' place. "How would you like to spend two or three days in the mountains?" he asked his son. Of course the boy was excited. "Then tonight we'll start to get some things together. Let's stop by Al's Foodtown and buy what we'll need to eat while we're there, and when we get home, we'll start to organize things. Tomorrow night we'll shoe the horses and if I can get some things done at the sheriff's department that need to be finished up, then maybe by Thursday morning we can head up Fall Creek or to the Rock Lakes."

Early Thursday morning, Luke loaded Keno, Fox, and a pack-horse in the horse trailer. By shortly after daylight, they were leaving the trailhead at Rock Creek and starting their way around the reservoir. Luke was relaxed and happy, and he enjoyed the company of his son. But when they made camp that night beside a lush meadow about ten miles up the trail, Luke felt the familiar loneliness that so often came over him these days.

The next day the loneliness continued, threatening to ruin the trip for both him and Monty. He tried to keep a smile on his face whenever he was talking to Monty, but he couldn't fool his son. "What's the matter, Dad?" the little fellow asked. "Aren't you having fun?"

"Of course I am," Luke said. "That's what we bring the horses up here for, to have fun."

"I'm not having fun," Monty announced, bringing a stab of pain to Luke's heart.

"Oh, Monty, I'm sorry," he said. "I thought you loved to ride Fox up here. Just look around you, son. There isn't a more beautiful or rugged place on earth than right here."

As he spoke, he looked across the deep ravine at the sheer cliffs beyond. Water cascaded over the cliff in one place and fell in a silver ribbon straight down for hundreds of feet. The soothing sound of rapidly running water from the river far below them blended with the soft murmur of the wind in the trees. Ahead, the trail wound through dense forest filled with wildlife of all kinds: deer, elk, squirrels, even mountain goats. And overhead the blue sky was dotted with fluffy white clouds. A more beautiful and peaceful place than this didn't exist.

By the time Monty and Luke rode out of the timber and onto the broad expanse of high mountain meadows dotted with tiny streams and small stands of fir, they'd been on the trail for several hours and hadn't seen another human being all day. They rode their horses for half a mile across the lush grassy ground before pulling up on a bare ridge. Luke scanned the area below them and spotted a large buck grazing several hundred feet away. He reached into his saddlebags and pulled out his binoculars to let Monty watch the deer for a few minutes. Then they rode on.

That night they camped in some light timber beside a lake, at well over ten thousand feet elevation. Luke stretched a tarp for shelter as there was the feel of an impending storm in the air.

When the clouds came and blocked out the sun early that evening, it was a gentle rain that followed. Luke and Monty sat on their sleeping bags beneath the tarp and simply watched it fall. "Where does the rain come from?" Luke asked Monty, sensing an opportunity to teach his son.

"Heavenly Father makes it," Monty said. But before Luke could gather his thoughts together and explain to Monty how God made the rain, Monty said, "I think it's because Jesus is crying."

"Oh, Monty, why would Jesus cry tonight?" Luke asked. "We're together, and we're having a good time. There's nothing for Jesus to cry about tonight."

"He's crying because I'm sad," Monty said, his words once again piercing his father's heart.

Luke pulled his son close and said, "Why are you sad, Monty?"

And Luke reeled at the answer he got. "I miss Coleen, and she misses us."

Then Luke knew why he wasn't feeling the way he had at other times in these mountains. His son was right. He missed Coleen Whitman.

* * *

No one had called Coleen by that name since the night Luke had left for the airport. She was becoming used to being called Carly, but somehow, she wasn't ever sure she'd be comfortable with that name. She'd taken the necessary steps in court to make herself legally Carly Crockett again, and she'd been baptized by that name after finishing lessons with the missionaries who never even knew there was another name. But every day, many times a day, she thought of Luke Osborne and how she'd loved to hear him call her "Coleen." She'd thought he loved her, but her past had gotten in the road and their ways had parted.

She couldn't count the times she'd picked up the phone and almost dialed his number. But each time she put it down. She smiled to herself now, wondering if Luke had any idea why he was getting such a large barn. She'd sent Jim Redd to Duchesne in one of his expert disguises to deliver the money. He'd done so without anyone but the contractor knowing he'd been in Duchesne at all, and that contractor had been sworn to secrecy. She really couldn't explain even to herself why she'd done it. She knew it wasn't to repay him for what he'd done to help her find out who she was or for the good times and happiness he'd shown her. Nor was it a reward to Luke for introducing her to the Church; nothing could ever adequately pay for the blessings of the gospel in her life.

There was one possible reason that made some sense to her; she must have wanted him to have something of hers, something he'd appreciate without knowing it came from her. Maybe that was it, and maybe it was simply that she needed to feel some connection, however remote, to the man she'd loved and lost.

Several days later, Coleen came in with her arms full of groceries. As she put them away, her aunt came into the room in her wheelchair. She watched for a little while, then, when Coleen had finished, she said, "Come, sit down my dear."

Coleen had come to truly love this woman, as she had her twin sister. After these few weeks with them, she was finally beginning to feel like she really knew them. And she'd had many good talks with them as they told her of her past. But something about the old woman's face and tone of voice told her that this talk was going to be different.

She pulled a chair out from the table and sat down, facing her aunt's wheelchair. "Okay, I'm sitting," she said with a tone as solemn as that of her aunt's.

Amelia reached a bony, thin hand out and laid it on one of Coleen's. "My dear, you'll never know what it's done for this old woman's heart having you here with me these past few weeks. And it pains me to say what I am about to."

"If it hurts, then maybe it shouldn't be said," Coleen suggested tentatively.

"It hurts, but only in a selfish way," Amelia said. "I would like to have you girls here with me for the rest of my days, which I have a feeling may not be very many. But I've lived a long life, and . . ." She stopped and smiled. "I digress. I'm sorry. I want to talk about you, my dear girl. You're here with me, but your heart is with your cowboy. Go to him, Coleen. Please, go to him."

Coleen felt like her heart would burst, but she patiently said, "Aunt Amelia, you're right, I love him. But I can't just go to him. We agreed that we wouldn't see each other. My past will always haunt him, and I can't live with that. Neither can he."

The old woman's hand slowly patted Coleen's. "That's silly, dear girl. This church you just joined, I know a little about it. Does it not teach forgiveness?"

"It does. That's what Jesus taught," Coleen agreed.

"Then go to your Luke and ask him to forgive whatever it is in your past that bothers him," she said wisely. "And you be willing to do the same. There, I've said it. Think on my words. My years have given me some wisdom I hope."

An hour later, Kyla came into Coleen's room and said, "The mail was just delivered."

Coleen looked up. "I never get any mail."

Kyla grinned. "You did today. Aunt Amelia asked me to bring it up to you." She held out a plain white envelope. "It's postmarked Du-ches-ne," she slowly spelled out the word.

Coleen's heart leapt and she reached for the letter. She took it and read the return address and felt a burning disappointment. "It's from Bianca," she said.

"You never know what it might say," Kyla said. "Hurry, I'm curious."

Coleen's hand trembled so badly that Kyla took the letter back and opened it for her. Coleen was almost certain what it would say. Bianca was probably writing to rub her nose in her loss. She was probably writing to tell her that she was about to become Bianca Osborne. "Here, read it," Kyla said.

"I can't. If he's marrying her, I'll just die. I don't want to know that. You read it."

Kyla did as her sister asked, and Coleen watched her face as she read, so tense she thought she'd explode. Kyla smiled, she even chuckled, then she said, "Here, read it now. It's not so bad."

"Tell me what she said," Coleen requested. "I can't even hold the paper steady."

"Okay, but you'll want to read it later I'm sure," Kyla told her. "Bianca says she's sorry for the way she treated you. And she says she wishes you'd come back to Duchesne, because she'd like to get to know you. She said she had an experience that changed her life, made her grow up, and that she'd like to tell you about it in person. Finally, she says to tell you Luke is doing well but she thinks his heart is breaking and no one but you can ever mend it."

"Nice try, sister," Coleen said dryly. "Now tell me what it really said."

"That's it, Carly, I'm not kidding," Kyla said as a big grin spread across her face. "Oh, I almost forgot. There's another letter here," and she pulled it from the back pocket of her jeans. "It's from Duchesne too."

Coleen covered her face with her hands and tried to stop the shaking that had taken over her whole body. "Carly, I can't read this one," Kyla said firmly. "It's from *him*. Take it. You can tell me later what it says."

Carly took the letter in her hand, gripping it tightly so she wouldn't drop it. She walked to the window that overlooked the front yard and the huge old oak tree. She pulled up a chair, and finally found the courage to look at the envelope. It was addressed to Miss Carly Crockett. The return address simply said Luke.

She fought with her emotions and finally prevailed. When the trembling was almost gone, she opened the envelope and pulled out the two handwritten sheets it contained. "Dear Coleen," it began, and she struggled for a moment with her emotions again. Then she read on. Luke told her it seemed like ages since he'd seen her. And he said that Monty was doing fine but that he missed her a lot. That caused her to pause for a moment as she thought about Monty and how much he'd come to mean to her. Luke also told her that the barn was looking good and that he couldn't believe how much bang he was getting for his buck. He also informed her that most of the horses were coming along well. He mentioned that Victor, Sharps, and Gil were all facing trials in the very near future.

"But I'm concerned about one of my horses, Coleen," he'd written. "Spider is showing speed that could make her a good racehorse, maybe even great," he told her. "But I'm too big for her and I've never trained a racehorse. And when she's trained, I'll need a jockey."

The page ended, and she turned to the next one. It began, "If you're not too busy with other things, I'd like to offer you a job. Will you come and ride Spider for me?"

Coleen looked up from the page. She wanted to do that more than anything she could think of, but would that only lead to more hurt later? She feared that it would. She again looked at the sheet in her hand. "I would be honored if you'd say yes. Call me if you'd like the job, and I'll arrange to come get you."

Then he signed it with his first name. But under his signature was a post-script. "Coleen, I've been a fool. I miss you terribly. Please come."

Coleen thought about it for about ten seconds before her decision was made.

* * *

Well over a week had passed since Luke had mailed the letter to Coleen, and he hadn't heard a word. That afternoon was a Friday, and he left the office early. After picking up Monty, he drove slowly home. He wished she'd call or write or something. Anything would be better than simply not knowing. Then he wondered if she'd even gotten his letter. She could be anywhere now, picking up the pieces of her shattered life. She was probably somewhere that he couldn't even guess at. And if so, he'd never hear from her.

Luke was surprised to see a truck and horse trailer in his yard when he turned into the lane. He couldn't imagine whose it might be. He hadn't told anyone he'd sell them a horse. As he came closer, he noted that the truck had Kentucky plates, and then he really wondered what was going on. He pulled up and got out, helped Monty out, then looked around. He couldn't see anyone. He walked around to the far side of the trailer and his heart nearly stopped.

Coleen Whitman was sitting on the fender, smiling the smile that lit up his world. "Hi, Luke," she said easily as she came to her feet. "I got my truck and trailer back." She paused as he stared at her.

"Still need a trainer and jockey?" she asked.

EPILOGUE

Twenty-one months later

The crowd was cheering wildly as the slender blonde jockey rode her big bay filly down the homestretch. They were in second place, but running solidly. Spider had her own style, and Coleen liked it. At the last minute, Spider always gave it just a little more at the coaxing of her jockey, and she always finished first. She had yet to lose a race, and this was her fifteenth. Luke watched as his wife leaned lower and said whatever it was she always said to her horse. Then he felt the awe he always did as Spider suddenly gave a burst of speed and quickly overtook the lead horse, finishing a full length ahead.

He and Monty hurried down to the winner's ring where they stood proudly beside Coleen as she was handed the trophy. Then Coleen leaned down and kissed Monty on his head. "Way to go, Mom," he said proudly. Then she stood straight and stepped into Luke's waiting arms. Cameras flashed as the registered owner of Rainy Day Spider kissed the jockey he loved, and held her tightly for a full minute before releasing her to the congratulations she deserved.

Coleen had taken a talented horse and made it the greatest racing horse in the west. Spider was famous, and crowds had grown every time she raced. But this was to be her last race because Spider's jockey had just learned that she was to have a baby; Luke was not about to take any chances with the health of either his wife or his unborn child. And there was simply no way anyone else could ever be Spider's jockey.

Anyway, Luke had heard of a great horse that was standing at stud, and he and Coleen were both anxious to see what kind of speed a foal from Spider would have.

Rainy Day Spider had a great past already, and she would long be remembered in racing circles. Carly Crockett Osborne, better known simply as Coleen, had become a much respected jockey. She'd never recovered her memory, nor would she, but that didn't matter to her or Luke. They were making enough memories together to more than make up for those she had lost. Those didn't matter anyway. What did matter was the love for each other that they had found.

ABOUT THE AUTHOR

Clair M. Poulson spent many years in his native Duchesne County as a highway patrolman and deputy sheriff. He completed his law enforcement career with eight years as Duchesne County Sheriff. During that time he served on numerous boards and committees, including serving as president of the Utah Sheriff's Association and as a member of a national advisory board to the FBI.

For the past eleven years Clair has served as a Justice Court Judge in Duchesne County and currently represents the Justice Court Judges of the state as a member of Utah's Judicial Council.

Church service and family have always been priorities for Clair. He has served in a variety of stake and ward callings, and he and his wife, Ruth, an accomplished piano teacher, have five children and nine grandchildren. Clair also does a little farming, his main interest being horses. Both Clair and his wife currently help their oldest son run the grocery store in Duchesne.

Clair has always been an avid reader, but his interest in creating fiction began many years ago when he would tell bedtime stories to his small children. They would beg for just one more "make-up story" before going to sleep. *Lost and Found* is Clair's eighth published novel.